NOTHING TO GET NOSTALGIC ABOUT

NOTHING TO GET NOSTALGIC ABOUT

EDDIE BROPHY

atmosphere press

Published by Atmosphere Press

Cover design by Josep Lledó

Nothing To Get Nostalgic About
2020, Eddie Brophy

atmospherepress.com

For Dylan and Ryder.
The two of you have given me
Both the privilege of fatherhood,
And the courage to step into the darkness
And come out a survivor.
I love you.

I

BURNHAM COUNTY, MAINE. MARCH 21ST, 2018-

I do not think you ever outgrow your fears. Just the opposite. I think your fears develop right along with you. When age begins to diminish fear's power over you, it figures out a way to burrow itself deep into the recesses of your subconsciousness. Fear never takes the wheel, so to speak. It is never the driver, always the passenger, and navigating the course.

I never conquered my fear of the dark; that fear just simply evolved in the subtlest of ways. When I was four, the dark represented the total absence of bodily and emotional security. A vast abyss that masticated rather than devoured, beginning with the perversion of your sense of security and ending with the larceny of your sanity. At seven, the dark itself could no longer hurt me; rather, it corroborated with the nefarious individuals who used the dark to travel incognito and manipulate my naively developed trust of a once formidable foe.

At seventeen, the fear became more existential. Dark. Absence of light, absence of life, absence of love, loneliness. At thirty, the dark is now an amalgamation of every single one of those things. The dark represents a loss of security from its potential to corroborate with all these entities who harbor a desire to murder me and my family, the loss of a faith in humanity brought on by a sad and lonely man who started as a scared little boy.

That's how fear stays with you. I come from a school of thought that, no one knows you better than your fear does. How else does it manage to compete with feelings and senses that are far more, rewarding, should I say? Like, the first time you ever experienced the orgasm that followed a masturbatory act. Surely, that would be something that could dull the power of fear.

Then what happens if a seemingly innocuous discovery of one's own body at say, ten, or maybe twelve, goads you into destructive patterns of overindulgence. Your ability to appreciate the persuasive nature of a vice while still succumbing to it despite your best interests, perhaps that might be a bit fearful for you? The pursuit of an initial sensation to the point of complete and utter destruction, be it of one's own self or of trust—the trust of self, or the trust of loved ones. One sip. One sip and you'll lose your boy. One sip and you'll lose all of it.

However. One sip. And you'll stop seeing your father. He can't hurt you anymore. One sip. His voice will no longer resound from synapse to synapse until it tremors from your tear ducts and cascades down your pockmarked cheeks, down to your trembling nicotine-stained fingertips. One sip becomes two. Two reaches for a refill, and enough refills empty a bottle. The dark. The fear. The sobriety, the inability to reconcile with what emerges from the darkness to take you.

It'll masticate you rather than devour. And once it is done, it'll come for him. It'll rape him of his innocence and demoralize the integrity of his smile. It'll come back for you. If you're not accounted for when it returns, it'll settle for him. Little Dylan. You are not a survivor; you're simply delaying the inevitable. Make it easier for yourself; you still have a choice. You cannot protect him. You are simply too haunted. Let us take our bounty.

"Charlie!" His wife shouted.

"Monster-check! Come on!"

The frenzied mind of a tortured writer cried out all over a word document as a thirty-year-old man introspectively stared into an abyss in the form of damaged laptop screen hanging on by an actual thread of its innards. Charlie Harris carefully lowered the dilapidated screen down on the keyboard, his face moistened by the mere thought of challenging his gravest fear.

"Charlie!" She yelled.

"He's waiting for you!"

Charlie sat up from his leather desk chair and exited what appeared to be his office. As he closed the door behind him, he fiddled in his pockets for a few moments before pulling out a small key. Pleased with his discovery, he padlocked the door shut and briskly ran up an adjacent spiral staircase to his infant son's nursery.

Wobbling against the bars of a wooden crib was his towheaded, blue-eyed baby boy. The baby immediately squeaked and giggled at the sight of his father, who was giving him a toothy grin from behind the whiskers of his unkempt beard. He wrapped his arms around his son's tiny body and kissed him squarely on the crown of his head. He knelt to get directly at eye level with his baby.

"All aboard the Sandman Express!" He hollered.

"Choo-Choo! Chugga Chugga Chugga Chugga. Choo-Choo!"

"Alright, buddy." Charlie smiled.

"Got to sweep this place for monsters before I lay my favorite little guy down."

He then motioned to his son's closet door before knocking three times.

"What do you think buddy?" He asked.

“Any monsters in here?"

His son remained vigilant over his father in case a monster did emerge from the closet. Charlie nodded at Dylan, who mimicked his father endearingly. Charlie then pulled the doors wide up and announced,

"Nope! No monsters in here!"

Charlie then pointed under the crib.

"What do you think?" Charlie asked.

His son was now bobbing back and forth, squeaking and cooing. Charlie carefully kneeled down on the carpeted floor, scanning the nursery and admiring the commitment to infantile cheerfulness, save for the plush Beetlejuice mixed in with the rest of the conventional stuffed animals and the Freddy Krueger autograph resting on a shelf among other framed photos of dead grandparents and early milestones.

He then turned his attention to the skirt of the crib and started peeling it back carefully. He lifted his head up to address his son after he saw two orange eyes staring past the darkness at him. Seemingly transfixed, Charlie stared into what felt like a waking nightmare when a mouthful of rotten enamel smiled at him.

"No monsters under here. Daddy." Something hissed.

Charlie distanced himself from the crib in a feverish panic. His baby boy was still standing and now appearing alarmed by the sight of his fearful father.

"If he can't have you," the voice snarled,

"We'll settle for him. Chooooooo.... Chooooooooo"

It sang as a bloodied and festering arm began to stretch from underneath the crib toward the baby. The fingers attached to the mutilated hand danced up the bars like a spider.

"Dylan," he cried.

Dylan was in tears when Charlie lunged his body toward the arm to prevent it from harming his son, slamming his face into the bars and knocking himself out cold. Dylan's cries carried out of the room with deafening decibels of fear as Charlie was sprawled across the floor, as the carpet absorbed a pool of blood underneath his skull. His eyes were now squinting as if to focus on the lighting fixture above him, forcing himself to come to.

"Are you fucking drunk?" she shouted.

Charlie managed to finally see clearly, only to find his wife Lorraine attempting to soothe their startled baby while Charlie laid motionless beneath them.

"I can't fucking believe you would do this to us," she scolded.

"You promised!"

Charlie massaged the wound on his forehead, rubbing his thumb against the trickles of blood on his fingertips before stumbling to his feet to address his wife.

"You know what," she shouted.

"Get the fuck out. Get the fuck out of my house!"

It would not matter if he were sober; she would always think he was drunk. It reminded Charlie of when he as a teenager and everyone would accuse him of being on drugs. You run away from one small town out of fear of being stigmatized by your family, only to wind up in another small town to be stigmatized for what you look like. All teenagers go through a myriad of identities; Charlie was not the exception. He felt the most comfortable looking like a musician in the last era he remembered fondly. Namely, because it was before Rachel was dead and Janet went AWOL.

Unfortunately, you cannot walk out into the world without succumbing to the court of public opinion and the incessant need to label what you cannot understand. Charlie always feared being alienated because of the unpleasant details of his past, and then he entered high school. Now, he was the creepy, heroin-using Kurt Cobain kid. Charlie was never able to decide if it was a matter of not wanting to disappoint the status quo. After all, his honorary new title was not nearly as bad as the one he left Bear Hills with. Eventually, he wound up abusing the same substance he was often rumored to be abusing.

Long after he had cleaned up his act, his fleeting romance with drug abuse just seemed to follow him everywhere he went. It made him feel like a microcosm, but then he discovered a more socially acceptable vice in his twenties. Unfortunately, it's socially acceptable until the disease part kicks in, and then he became the creepy alcoholic Kurt Cobain kid. That is how it felt every time he sensed Lorraine's lack of faith or trust in him, scrutinizing his every move. He knew for his own kid, and for the sake of restoring that trust, that he needed to reach out to his sponsor.

Unfortunately, his sponsor must have failed to pay a phone bill or eight because his phone is disconnected. The only other place Charlie could think to find him was at a meeting, something that was not exactly Charlie's style.

The best thing to come out of it was a chance meeting with a former writing professor named James Conroy. When he struck up a conversation with the former academic, two things were given to him. A phone number, and an insistence to refer to the man as "Jimbo."

Charlie found it relatively strange for someone who had previously been such a highly revered teacher to adopt a nickname that made him more townie than scholar. Before long, he discovered that his new sponsor and his "drunken alter-ego," as he was referred to it, i.e. "Jimbo," had destroyed James Conroy, the man who once upon a time was one of the most revered professors at Southern Maine University. He'd taught a myriad of philosophy courses in addition to creative writing. He was also the president of the campus magazine where Charlie was first published. There were even rumors that he was on track for tenure. Then he lost his daughter to drug addiction, to opiates.

After that, he went on a path of self-destruction and destroyed his promising career, his marriage, and was well on his way to reaching the destination by destroying his liver. That did not seem to be the case when they first met in A.A., but afterwards, based on subsequent phone calls any time that marriage, parenthood, or his past made drinking feel like the only viable option for solace. The phone calls stopped, and apparently so did Jimbo's last refuge...the meetings at the church about a fifteen-minute walking distance from where Charlie and his family lived. Charlie was surprised not to find Jimbo holding court among the other men who seemed less melancholic when he regaled them with his sordid tales of his drunken antics.

One was a retired police lieutenant who frequently

answered the calls about Jimbo's public drunkenness and disturbing the peace. While Jimbo never explained how the officer he used to drive crazy became one of his closest confidants, Charlie chocked it up to it either being an A.A. thing, or maybe Jimbo had eventually endeared himself to the old timer.

Charlie's ass had barely reached the hard plastic of those chairs usually reserved for school children when the meeting's self-proclaimed elder statesman barked something from under his Bruins cap.

"You must not own a calendar," he grumbled

Charlie turned to see the curmudgeon still scrutinizing the person currently speaking.

"It's HER anniversary," he shrugged.

"If you're looking for your sponsor, I'm sorry to say you're looking in the wrong place"

Charlie quietly nodded and stood to his feet before tapping the man on his shoulder as a gesture of thank you.

"Congratulations on your award," the man praised

"Jimbo hasn't shut up about it since he found out."

As Charlie exited the basement of the church, he could not help but have a sense of humor about how many package stores were within a proximity of a place where people were trying to get clean. That was not Jimbo's M.O. though, he would not be the kind of guy to fall off the wagon and grab a six pack to take it back home without an audience. Charlie had walked for a few blocks when he spotted a few guys congregating outside the back door of a V.F.W. hall smoking butts and figured it had Jimbo written all over it.

The lighting was terrible; none of the televisions looked like they had been manufactured in the modern age, but sure enough, there was Jimbo, knocking back whiskey shooters, addressing the room...well, a couple of Vietnam vets and a few younger guys playing pool from the bar.

"I didn't know you were a vet," Charlie remarked,

Jimbo slowly sat up and out of his stupor and smiled as he grabbed Charlie by the back of his neck with his calloused hand and pulled him in for a hug. He then leaned in and whispered something in Charlie's ear,

"See the kid working the bar?" He pointed,

"Lifelong Yankees fan. I found that out after I overheard him talking shit about our Sox on the last packie run I made," he whispered

"Needless to say," he laughed, "Blackmail, and a room full of devoted Sox vets is an instant in!"

He then motioned for the bartender and winked,

"Two whiskey shooters and beer." He then turned to Charlie.

"Want anything?"

Charlie laughed,

"I'm two months sober," he insisted,

"Three whiskey shooters," Jimbo requested.

"Didn't you just say you came from a meeting?" Jimbo scoffed.

Jimbo received his drinks and handed one of the shooters over to Charlie,

"Only because I couldn't find my sponsor," Charlie laughed.

Jimbo clinked the two glasses against Charlie's and motioned to drink.

"Hi, my name's Jimbo," he laughed.

"I'm an alcoholic, and I approve of this uh, political

message."

The two men knocked their drinks back with conviction before exchanging a fit of laughter. Jimbo leaned into the bar and breathed through the dark nature of their meeting in a trailing laugh.

“Ah,” Jimbo echoed

“So, how are you doing Chucky? Big day tomorrow!”

Charlie reluctantly sighed before signaling to the bartender for another drink,

"She kicked you out again, didn't she?" He inquired.

Charlie nodded sadly.

"You saw him again," Jimbo pressed.

"Didn't you?"

Charlie began to sink in his chair while Jimbo ruefully pressed on about the specter haunting his friend.

"Does this have anything to do with tomorrow?" He asked.

“You get to walk across the stage of your alma mater, not just a guy who had all the odds stacked against him when he was a struggling student,” he started,

“and now you’re the guy who gets to come back as a hero who not only graduated, but as a literal figure of folklore. Here's Charlie Harris! Everyone!"

Jimbo stood to his feet while Charlie hid his face behind the palms of his hands. Jimbo was now holding up his beer and making a scene before motioning to his mortified friend.

"This here," he continued,

"Is Charlie Fucking Harris. As a published author of many fine tales of the macabre, you might otherwise know him as E-H Ramsey,"

Jimbo paused to let out a deplorable belch.

"However, as of tomorrow," He rambled,

"This man is finally going to own his birth rite and his rightful place in this pretentious little coastal town and not only reveal that he IS Charlie Harris but will do so with the prestigious Meredith Gunning Literary Award of Excellence."

Jimbo paused for a few moments to the sound of crickets.

"And also, there's money involved, and he'll buy us ALL a round of shots!"

The pool players placed their cues on the green, approached the bar smiling, and reaching for their drinks

"See," Jimbo assured Charlie.

"It's THAT easy."

Charlie gave Jimbo a grave stare before removing a pack of cigarettes from the breast pocket of his flannel and motioned that he was heading outside. Jimbo nodded while taking another swig of his beer. He then held up two fingers at the bartender, then turned them to motion for a cigarette break.

"Watch our beers!" He requested.

"I don't want any funny business out of you, mister!"

The bartender just shook his head and smiled at the two and gave Jimbo the finger, who was staring back with a toothy grin and a cigarette dangling from his teeth.

Charlie leaned against the brick exterior of the building, physically trying to fight off a shiver from a typically cold evening in Maine. Jimbo did his lamest attempt at moon walking before laying back on the brick exterior and groaning.

"Oh, come on," he pleaded,

"If you lose your sense of humor all you'll be left with

are actual thoughts. And who needs that, Chucky boy?"

Charlie just shook his head, took another drag and smiled some more.

"How do you always manage to stay so amused all the time?"

Jimbo removed another cigarette out of his pack and lit it with the one he was previously smoking.

"It's like I said, Chucky." He breathed.

"The day you stop laughing is the day you can't manage to do anything else but cry about this lottery called life. You know all about that; you were dealt a pretty shit hand. Unlike say...well, that guy right there."

Jimbo motioned to an older drunk outside of the club in a car, slumped over on the dashboard.

"This fear you still have?" He smiled,

"You may think it'll kill you. You may think it will ruin your marriage, or corrupt your child...but when we are done tonight? You will wake up probably sleeping in the parked car in your driveway waiting for her to cool off. She might still be mad. But she is not one to let you piss away this legacy you are trying to carve for yourself, so she'll let you back in and you'll shower and before long? You'll be addressing hundreds of people in a packed auditorium about why you never became one of these dope fiends here in good old' Burnham County. That is not to say you're taking advantage of her forgiveness. It's a learning curve. You need to learn how to battle your demons and she needs to learn how to let you. It's a tough compromise, but if you both think the family is worth it? Then you'll figure it out." He concluded.

Charlie tossed his cigarette to the ground.

"I always regretted never taking one of your

philosophy lectures, Professor," he gushed, "Why did you give it up?"

Jimbo appeared irritated, but also knew that this was the relationship he had with Charlie as both a friend and former student.

"Like you?" he sighed,

"Bereavement wasn't brief; it became a slow and tedious process. When my Linda died? That was it for me, man. I swear, Burnham County is where ALL of us sad pricks run to, thinking we can put a distance between ourselves and the pain. I was fortunate that I got through those years when you were a student. Maybe it was fate that we met? Maybe you are cursed? I just remember one minute I was teaching a lesson about Kafka and the next?

I delivered a drunken lecture on the virtues of indifference. My role as the town alcoholic bodes better for me now that people don't harbor a lot of expectations about my place in this life. Do you remember what you said to me the first time we acknowledged each other in A.A.?"

Charlie nodded.

"I told you," he started.

"That my gravest fear was no longer not feeling like I belonged to a family, or anything else. It was realizing when I did, that someday mortality would have the final word in how long I could appreciate it."

Jimbo smiled at him and poked his chest.

"I WAS a good-" he paused, "I was an EXCEPTIONAL father. I had to be. My dad was such a piece of shit. And how did the world reward my ability to conquer and break the cycle of abuse? It fed my Linda to a different kind of abuser. Heroin. I buried my fucking princess at fifteen years old, man. While Rain may never understand this irrational fear in your head about trying to kill yourself to save his life? I get it. There isn't a day that goes by where I didn't wish the needle went into my veins instead of hers. Is that how you got that, uh,"

he began pointing at the wound on Charlie's forehead. Charlie frowned.

"Monster check," he curtly answered.

Jimbo nodded like a man who had been there before.

"She's also pretty pissed that I stopped taking my meds." Charlie divulged.

Jimbo's eye bulged out of his head and he slapped Charlie hard against his chest.

"YOU TOOK YOURSELF OFF YOUR MEDS?!" Jimbo scolded.

"You can't do that, Chucky! Remember what happened to me when I did that?"

Charlie immediately started laughing.

"Yeah," he answered.

"You called me up because you were out of your mind driving all over the white mountains trying to find a toilet. Not just ANY toilet. THE toilet." He laughed.

"And do you remember what happened?" Jimbo begged.

"You shit your pants," Charlie giggled.

Jimbo's face became deathly serious.

"That's not funny," he asserted.

Charlie gave Jimbo a sincere stare.

"With those fucking doe eyes," Jimbo complained.

"I still can't believe you told Facebook," Charlie snickered. Jimbo tossed his arms in the air, "You threatened to tell Facebook first!" He argued.

"Like the sniveling little politician that you are, you were trying to blackmail me into getting back on my meds the same way you blackmailed that poor bastard who likes the Yanks?"

The two men stood laughing for several moments.

"How is the new book coming?" Jimbo asked.

Charlie took a few moments to smoke another cigarette,

"You know someone sent me those tapes." He answered.

"And you still don't know who?" Jimbo asked.

Charlie shook his head emphatically.

"I mean, they were in Donald's...her case worker's possession, initially," he started.

"But surely he had to turn them in, considering it was a criminal investigation." Jimbo took another drag of his cigarette, "Have you listened to them yet?" He asked.

Charlie shook his head again.

"I had to install a padlock on my office," he revealed.

"It's bad enough that I have to give up my pen name and subsequently my anonymity to beat all these tabloid websites to the punch. God forbid anyone find out what's on those tapes, what she said about everything that happened to us. The book is coming along, though. I was hoping I'd find you in attendance so you could hear me read the first couple of chapters I have finished for it."

Jimbo appeared maudlin and stymied by an invisible deterrent.

“You know I would," he assured,

"I just. I don't want to show my face on that campus any more than they'd want to see my face there. Any chance you'll be attending tomorrow night's meeting?" He asked.

Charlie nodded.

"A sign of good faith to Rain," he answered.

"I was sober for two months. God, what a fucking nightmare of a two months it was. It's weird; I felt like going stone cold sober would've erased all of the dark thoughts I was having, not exacerbate them." He pleaded.

"It's another component to the disease," Jimbo warned.

"That's why you can't take yourself off your meds. Why did you?"

"Rain wants another baby," Charlie lamented.

"Unfortunately, when you're on those meds, the first thing to go ISN'T the crippling depression. It's the ability to climax, followed by your sex drive." He sighed.

"She's starting to think that either I'm not attracted to her, or that I don't love her. Neither are the case. I just feel," he trailed...

"Like the more kids you have," Jimbo encouraged.

"The greater the chance I pass on this curse...just like he warned," Charlie mumbled.

"He TOLD you?"

Jimbo grabbed Charlie by the shoulders and tried to shake the gossamers away.

"He's DEAD Charlie. Unless you are suffering from the DTs or something man, I don't know how he could be saying ANYTHING to you," Jimbo joked.

Feeling like even Jimbo was starting to become dismissive, Charlie maneuvered his body away from Jimbo with an accelerated stride in his step. Jimbo now found himself talking to Charlie's back.

"Send me your chapters!" He shouted.

Charlie waved to him without turning back.

"Hey!" Jimbo called,

"Do you need me to call you an Uber?"

Charlie, without missing a step, simply answered,

"I walked here. I'm always walking in the dark."

Jimbo chuckled to himself before shaking the cold off his body.

"Poet to the very end."

He then stumbled his way back into the bar while chanting 'Yankees suck!' just to be a ball buster; surely that got him more free drinks as per his unspoken agreement with the bartender. Charlie drunkenly meandered the cobbled roads of the quaint town of Burnham County, entertaining morbid thoughts and wrestling with his legitimacy as a writer. As he passed by a local cemetery, he stopped and shed a tear at the thought of his own headstone. What would it read? He wondered to himself. Here lies a mediocre storyteller. A gin blossom with an affinity for suicidal ideation? The man who ruined his son's life?

As he bowed his head and wept quietly, a child's voice resonated in his ears.

"Come find me, Charlie."

Charlie's face revealed the dread of an otherwise unwanted memory.

"Come dig me up, Charlie!"

The sound of a past he continued fighting through was something he couldn't outrun, but Charlie did so anyway. The cold air got into his lungs as he breathed heavily, and with every spring, it felt as though they had turned into two cinder blocks weighing him down and crushing his chest.

When he made it to the intersection of Lochelt Ave and Barrett Rd, he paused long enough so the blood would stop rushing to his head. As he lifted the cumbersome weight of his head to face the icy fog permeating around him, he noticed a parade of dead friends following behind a necrotic old Indian that regarded him like a leper, despite their own respective festering sores and lacerated appendages. Survivor's guilt was as real to him now as it was when he was a young boy. If his head was a cemetery, his fear was exhuming all the ghosts from their final resting places.

Charlie told ghost stories to earn a buck, and it wasn't a bad living. The problem with it was feeling as if he owed a debt to the debt every time he did. Time seemed to always stop when Charlie thought about the past. Even though there was never anything to get nostalgic about. He walked up his driveway and juggled for the keys in his pocket. He approached a black Chevy Cobalt with two magnetic stickers, one that read "Support Halloween," and the other the logo of his favorite comedy "Ghostbusters." He struggled trying to unlock the driver's side door for several moments before falling into his driver's seat and lifting his frail body into a ball.

He assumed he'd surely freeze to death but snuggled himself in a pile of flannel shirts he pulled from his back seat. For as long as he could remember, he hated the idea of sleep. When you were asleep, you let your guard down. He learned this when he was five. Bad things always seemed to happen at night. Out of a rolodex of memories, he always seemed to pull the ones that fucked him up the worst. When he was five, he was awoken out of a sound sleep by his mother and sisters who were hysterical and rushing to get out of the apartment they shared with their father. His memory wasn't reliable enough to fill in the gaps of what came before the dark and the sun peaking in through the blinds of his mother's friends' condo.

How did he get there? He'd rather not think about it. Thinking was always the bane of his existence. It usually involved way more macabre than a Stephen King or H.P. Lovecraft novel. That immediately brought him to when his son was first born, and his wife, who was still recovering from a cesarean, pleaded with him to follow their baby who was being wheeled from their room into the NICU. He spent the entire night keeping vigilance over his son, wondering if this was his penance for what happened to his father.

That first night in the NICU he was alone. That much he can attest to. The second night, he remembered encouraging his wife to sleep in her room—to recover. During some point after he nodded off, he could remember watching as a group of teenage boys passed his delicate son around as if he were a totem to them. They were all flushed, wounded and soulless. Charlie had a knack for keeping the dead around, no matter how desperately they could've used the eternal rest. Charlie's grandfather would always tell his grandmother he'd sleep when he was dead. Clearly, these guys didn't get the memo.

Charlie was startled by a knock on his driver's side window. He awoke to see a small, blonde-haired child with this seemingly harmless smile on his face.

"Come on, Charrrrrrlie." The voice sang.

Charlie tried to sit up from his initial slump and fidgeted with the handle until his body was sprawled out from his seat and onto the concrete. As he laid in a moment of stupefaction, he heard the scraping of rubber soles against a grainy driveway, moving their way closer to his home. He could taste the warm saliva under his tongue, which was normally the precursor that regurgitation would soon follow. He managed to lift all one hundred and forty pounds of dead weight and stagger down the concrete steps toward the side glass door of his home. The little boy kept motioning for him to come closer.

When he managed to drag his soles and bones over to the glass door, the little boy was missing. He stared blankly at the glass door and into the orange Christmas lights he forgot to turn off before he departed at his wife's behest. When he reached for the handle, he looked up and came eye to eye with those ominous eyes. The salivating, disgusting, necrotic look of a ghost come back to life was cradling a human in its arms. Charlie didn't want to entertain the very reality of what his eyes were telling him.

"Dad," he cried.

The scrawny and bloodied man who fashioned a pair of Dickies slacks and a dark, bloodied, long sleeve sweater revealed a tiny infant in his arms while he heckled Charlie.

"You didn't kill me," he proclaimed.

"You released me."

Charlie's eyes grew more concerned for the little baby cradled in the calloused and bloody fingers of a ghastly sociopath.

"Choo. Choo." The man snarled.

He then lifted the child up by his ankles and slammed him face first into the glass in an explosion of blood and shattered brain matter. Charlie fell to his knees screaming.

"Charlie!" A voice echoed.

"Wake up!"

Charlie shook the gossamers and chill out of his bones to see his wife indignantly acting as a human alarm clock outside his window.

"You're going to be late!" His wife reiterated.

Hours later, Charlie found himself pacing around and chain smoking outside of the propped door to a campus auditorium. He couldn't forget the awful thoughts from that evening. Maybe Jimbo was right; he shouldn't have abruptly ended his intake of the meds he was prescribed to treat his manic depression. They made it difficult to perform sexually. A lot of stuff did. Intimacy issues aside, Charlie couldn't help entertaining the drunken truths that Jimbo laid on him the night before when they were at the bar.

He wanted a better life for his son. That's also why this invitation to address this auditorium full of readers and curious students was a big catalyst toward owning the past he could no longer outrun.

Of everything Charlie has published over what was becoming a modest career for him, he was only credited as Charlie Harris in that campus magazine. For his first and subsequent books, he'd written under a penname. There were a lot of reasons for this, namely so he wouldn't be buried under the cumbersome weight of the controversy his name started to carry after 1998. With this new book (which he would be revealing during this speaking engagement), he was finally ready to discard the penname and not only hold a hardcover with his legal birth name, but also one that detailed the events leading up to that harrowing year.

This was a revelation after many years of therapy

sessions in which he'd talked himself through pain that was both aware of itself and unrealized. The visions, along with the sounds of a predatory specter, managed to manifest around the time he sat behind his computer for the first time and worked his way through the "fear," once more. He also figured one of two things might come of it: he would either spend the next few months dedicated to a profoundly cathartic exercise or, he could potentially write the book that affords him the future that felt so elusive from the time he was cognizant of his curse. He extinguished his cigarette on the ground and walked through the doors into the backstage area of the auditorium, where he was greeted by several former professors and the dean of the university.

Despite his uneasiness and irritability with the touch of another human hand, he endured the encouraging pats on his back and the awkward hugs of educators and committee members who were tipped off to the monumental bomb he was about to detonate in front of the crowd. His agent stood quietly in the wings with her arms folded, hiding a smart phone with a kind of chokehold around it. The dean made his way out to the stage and behind the podium where he waxed rhapsodic about the prestige of the Meredith Gunning Literary Award of Excellence. Its namesake was one of the finest literary professors to ever educate behind the walls of the institution. Charlie had one class with her before she retired.

He had fond memories of a woman who not only challenged him creatively but also intellectually. It was she who inspired the poetry that Charlie first published. During a classroom discussion, the two jested over the detriment of idolatry. Charlie asserted his belief that while he believed Jesus Christ did in fact exist as a man, his reputation grew more mystical and even rock star-worthy following his martyrdom. He quipped, "Jesus Christ was essentially the Justin Bieber of his day." Meredith began to cry; she'd laughed so hard at his abrasive but observational wit.

She then encouraged him to put that line in one of his poems. Sure enough, he wrote "Charles Darwin's Deathbed." It was his commentary on the hypocrisy of humanity and the ramifications of deification. Aside from that first line (which was later edited in order to make it into the actual magazine after a polarizing argument ensued amongst the staff), the rest of the poem was inspired by a story a buddy of his told him about Charles Darwin allegedly discrediting his theory of evolution after confiding that he was actually a God-fearing man. The other inspiration was a quote from a magazine in which one of John Lennon's friends recalled the singer becoming incensed over his finances, to which the friend mused "Imagine no possessions; I wonder if you can."

John allegedly hissed "It's just a bloody song!" after he was mocked by his own lyric. It made Charlie think about how Catcher in the Rye factored into Lennon's eventual murder from a fan who felt he had become "too phony." That would more than likely be a speaking point during his speech. Not necessarily, THAT poem or even THAT anecdote, but the power words can have on readers. Enough so that J.D. Salinger became a total recluse following a few other notable attempted and successful murders which were inspired by one of literature's most enduring characters.

Since the birth of Dylan, Charlie obsessed over a fear that his words could be brandished like weapons against him. As the Dean spoke, Charlie began to wonder if he should even be here, and if burying the Ramsey penname was a good idea. What if he puts this book out and people start getting superstitious on him again? Maybe that's why he kept seeing this monster. Maybe it was a familiar that was leading a greater evil toward Charlie and his little boy. His agent couldn't help but notice the cautionary demeanor in her client, but before she could make her way over to comfort him, the dean was motioning off stage for Charlie's entrance.

"He is the author of three novels," the dean celebrated,

"Two of which became New York Times Best Sellers one of which has been optioned for a potential motion picture. His name is E.H. Ramsey, and while little is known about this talented young writer, I can share that his first publication was actually a collection of poems in an issue of our highly revered literary magazine "Northern Accents." However, the reason many of you sitting before us today may be completely unaware that one of horror's highly acclaimed new voices is not only a local, but that he attended this very campus, is because of his name.

E.H. Ramsey did not attend and graduate from Southern Maine University with his first publication under his belt, no. Charlie Harris did, the same man who adopted a moniker for reasons he will reveal in just a few moments."

“Today, it is my honor,” the dean continued.

“It is my privilege to introduce you to not just one of horror's greatest writers but also one of its greatest actual living survivors. Please join me in giving a warm hand to

Mr. Charlie Harris!" The crowd was much louder than Charlie expected. Maybe that's because the Dean was much more eloquent than Jimbo, and everyone in this auditorium were presumably sober.

Charlie and the dean shook hands before Charlie held himself up against the podium and stared out past the burning stage lights to see an endless sea of admirers or morbidly curious strangers. As the fanfare died down, Charlie was one with the silence that frequently haunted him in the middle of the night. He carefully leaned into the microphone.

"Fear," he spoke.

"I don't think you ever really outgrow fears..."

He tried his hardest not to stumble over his every word or succumb to the insecurity that everyone thought he was a massive fraud, or one of the worst writers to ever grace a page. While the topic of fear lingered on for a while, Charlie couldn't help but have his attention drawn to a few members in the audience. There was an older woman nonchalantly pantomiming jerking off with one hand while she mouthed "hack." The other was a young male who bore an uncanny resemblance to a brutish childhood bully from his past. He kept snarling "We're going to fucking kill you," quietly to Charlie.

As Charlie stood frozen before a massive audience, he couldn't help but wonder why Jimbo had freaked out so much about abruptly taking himself off his medication. Charlie had spent enough time trying to figure out what was real and what was potentially his mind playing tricks on him. It became exceptionally difficult when he was off his medication and heavily drinking. He squeezed his eyes shut as tightly as he could only to find an overly enthusiastic crowd clapping while he stood before them for what felt like an eternity. He eventually snapped out of it and nodded graciously to them.

For the next forty-five minutes, Charlie regaled the audience with anecdotes about his time as a student on campus and teased the synopsis of his new book, which would give readers a look inside the lunacy that overtook a family and a small town in the early 90s. While he admitted that the story was in its earliest draft, he had two potential names for it: "Turtle Rock and the Curse of the Bear Hills Blonde Boy," and "How to Destroy a Monster."

He was then joined on stage by a member of the English department who would act as a kind of moderator while Charlie sat and would be asked several questions by members of the audience and engage them in an open discussion about his life and career. The first question came from a young woman in her early twenties. She was fashioning flowers in her hair and wore a pair of Lisa Loeb eyeglasses. Her ensemble consisted of ripped denim jeans and converse sneakers. Her flannel shirt and faded tour shirt were no doubt thrift store purchases. In other words, every girl that Charlie had fawned over or written poems for when he was a young, single college student years ago.

Charlie had a type, even if he would never admit it. His wife constantly pointed it out to him whenever she would joke about her marrying someone who wasn't her type. Any time Charlie would insist he didn't have one, she would bring up ex-girlfriends of his she remembered from high school. That was the problem with reconnecting with someone you graduated with; his wife knew more about Charlie's awkward past than he probably did. Whenever Lorraine would assert her proof of Charlie's type, he would get these fleeting flashes of one of Rachel's friends.

She was a product of her time: alternative but feminine, confident in politics but vulnerable with sensuality. At least, that's how people would describe her. Charlie just knew her as the cute girl who treated him like he was a human. It was a problem Charlie walked into virtually every relationship with; if they were sweet and treated him like he deserved to be recognized? They must really love him. Turns out, people aren't as ready to love as much as they are to wind up getting sick of you and abandoning you.

Lorraine hadn't done that yet, despite having a habit of screaming and wanting him out of the house. It's hard when you lose someone to depression, only to wind up marrying someone with it. She didn't want to abandon Charlie; she was just trying to protect herself and their child from the inevitable—kick him out before he exits first.

That was the difference between his "type" and the woman he'd married. She was the real thing; she did love him, despite his best efforts to sabotage himself. The reason this woman in the audience had him transfixed was that she reminded him of one of the few memories he'd managed to salvage from childhood. It was a good one. She looked like someone or maybe something he missed. Maybe it was the feeling childhood affords you right before you grow up and become so jaded and eventually nihilistic.

Unfortunately, Charlie became so lost in his thoughts that he completely ignored her question.

"I'm sorry," he apologized,

"What did you ask? I completely spaced out. You look like a girl I wanted to date when I first came here."

The crowd was profoundly amused by his honesty.

"And what did she say when you asked her out?" The girl smiled.

The crowd immediately joined in with the juvenile chorus of OHs and catcalling.

"She wrote me a very sweet four-page rejection letter," he replied, "that I still have in a keepsake box somewhere after I revealed to her that one of my first poems ever published was written about her."

Charlie smiled as the crowd let out a chorus of 'Awes' as he pretended to wipe imaginary tears from his eyes. This is what made him a good storyteller; he was relatable.

"That wasn't your question, though," he laughed.

The young woman was now bubbly and swaying back and forth with her arms behind her back and hands clasped together.

"Your first book," she restarted. "For those of you who haven't read it, was about a man who is killed after his family crashed their car. He was then given two options when he transcended: he could go to heaven and wait to reunite with his wife and son, or he could be reincarnated. The catch? He would either wait an eternity for his wife and son to find him in heaven and potentially learn that his wife had fallen madly for someone else had and started over, and that his son was too young when he was alive and seemingly forgot any attachment he had to his father, OR, he could come back, but would lose all memory of his previous life, and more so, the memories of his wife and son.

So, my question for you is, I read that you, as Ramsey at the time, were inspired to tackle this after reading stories of people retaining memories of their deaths after being reincarnated before eventually losing them. What is one memory you would like to lose? And one that you couldn't bear the thought of losing?"

The girl bit the bottom of her lip and moved her eyeballs nervously as she continued swaying back and forth, awaiting his answer. Charlie smirked at the quirky young woman who packed a severe punch for being the first question of the session.

"Wow!" He shouted.

"Way to make it WAY harder for everyone else to ask questions."

A laughter trickled throughout the auditorium.

"What memory would I like to lose?" He wondered aloud as he tapped the microphone against his lip.

"That's difficult. I don't think it would shock any of you that most of my life would probably be better off forgotten."

The laughter rose at his remark.

"My wife and I," he began.

"We had a really difficult time from the point leading to our marriage and eventually the birth of our only son. The reason? Her mother committed suicide when she was younger. At the time? I was in the process of just realizing and accepting everything that had gone on in my early life which made me the proverbial train wreck I became during the writing of my first book. At the same time, the man who became my guardian was diagnosed with Stage 3 Esophageal Cancer and died months before our wedding. My drinking and her temper were VERY odd bedfellows during that time period, and we said and did a lot of things to each other I wish we could both take back. Then she found out she was pregnant...ironically on my birthday, and it was just not a fun time to be around each other. Which is sad. Because we both experienced a lot of death as kids and during those first years as a couple. So, this new life should have really brought us closer. Instead, it divided us more. We'd reconcile, fall apart, reconcile, then fall apart again. It just kind of stayed that course until neither of us had the energy to board that crazy train anymore. The one thing that sticks out is when she was pregnant and we both told the other that we weren't happy in this relationship anymore and we came THAT close to quitting. That is a memory that comes up every time we argue or disagree on something regarding the baby or just innocuous day to day things. It's that memory that continues popping up in the back of my head when those things happen, that make me wonder is this going to be THE fight."

On a more positive note?" He smiled to a crowd divided by morose faces and smiles.

"The memory I could not live without is the first night we brought our son home from the hospital after spending almost two weeks in the NICU with him. When we came to that realization that he was OURS, ALL OURS, and we would never have to go back to that god damn maternity unit ever again. My wife and I have, and continue, to go through a lot. However, that whole experience I feel may have shaved a good ten or twenty years off our lives." He finished.

The young woman revealed her top row of pearly whites after she bit down on her bottom lip and nervously answered,

"Thank you."

Charlie turned to take a drink of water when she

turned back to the microphone and flirtatiously said,

"I wouldn't have said no to you."

The crowd immediately rose from their seats as she walked back to her seat with her head over her shoulder making a kissy face at her favorite author. Charlie's eyes got big, and as he turned to his literary agent, she had a look on her face that told the story of where his career had the potential to go. Charlie and Autumn, his agent, could be clairvoyant like that. He immediately said with his eyes, 'No way.'

"Alright!" The moderator announced.

"We have time for two more questions."

Charlie tried to stretch his back as his fidgeted in his chair.

"You!" the moderator pointed.

An older woman approached the microphone with methodical steps. She was dressed like a wayward bohemian from her black shawl down to her Birkenstocks.

"Hey Chucky," she smiled warmly.

Charlie sat up with an ear to ear smile across his face as the woman coyly smiled back at him, to a standing ovation from the crowd.

"Ladies and Gentlemen," the moderator smiled,

"The namesake for tonight's award, Meredith Gunning!"

Charlie stood to his feet and applauded with the rest of the audience. After several moments of fanfare, Charlie finally sat back down and smiled at his former professor.

"I hope this isn't a bad surprise," she opined.

Charlie vehemently shook his head with tears in his eyes.

"So," she laughed. "My question for you.

"What did you put on that fateful mix-tape?"

The crowd immediately burst into laughter and catcalling as Meredith smiled at Charlie. He held the microphone up to his mouth when he noticed Jimbo cackling at his former colleague's question. The crowd was wild with anticipation for what such a tortured purveyor of the macabre would put on a CD to court a cute girl.

"Springsteen," Charlie began.

"The only song that mattered. I'm on Fire by Springsteen."

Meredith never lost the smile from her face.

"Shame on her," Meredith joked.

"Shame on her."

Meredith stepped away from the microphone and took her seat next to Jimbo, while the two whispered to each other and smiled.

"Last question!" The moderator called.

Charlie became distracted by hoping that his best friend had finally reconciled with the second love of his life and the only one he had left, his academic legacy. When he turned to face the next person behind the microphone, the color completely disappeared from his face as tears streamed down his cheeks like the saline broke the dam. The man behind the microphone this time was haggard, disgusting, and brooding with malice.

"Hey Chucky." He howled.

"I have a question for you. Ever hear a dead baby joke?!"

His snaggletooth was moist with venom and his orange, blood-shot eyes focused in on the grey of Charlie's. The man then held up his arm, which held the cadaver of Charlie's son. He smiled as his hand maneuvered his bloodied son's head around and retracted his mouth.

"Hey daddy!" The man teased.

"What do you call a man who can't perform sexually for a woman? I'll give you a hint. It's also what you call the bundle of sticks that start the fire that incinerate his corpse. Give up?! A FAGGOT!" The body screamed.

Charlie fell into a catatonic state and wondered if this might be the vision that would kill him.

"Charlie! CHARLIE!" The moderator repeated.

He then motioned to the black gentleman standing behind the microphone in a Black Lives Matter t-shirt with his hands placed in the pockets of his denim jeans.

"Sorry," Charlie apologized.

"Did I remind you of someone else you had a crush on when you went here?"

The awkward tension was immediately relieved by the hysterical laughter of the audience.

"She wasn't nearly as cute as you," Charlie retorted.

The man clapped his hands and whistled at Charlie.

"You credit a young black man for teaching you how to read when you were a youngster." He asserted.

"What did he read to you?"

Charlie immediately became nostalgic and smiled so big even the crowd fell in love with both men in that moment. Charlie finally stood to his feet and with conviction simply spoke,

"Batman Returns.

“It was one of those Golden books. I was such a little bastard to that poor kid. It was a program initiated at my school back at Pine Banks. The older kids, usually fourth and fifth graders, would have story time with the kindergarteners. He got stuck with me and he tried

EVERYTHING. From Seuss to Blume. Finally, my older friend realized that I only read novelizations based on popular films. He was so proud that he reached me because he knew how much I loved Batman. There's a Polaroid out there somewhere of when he finally got through to his reading buddy, and he just smiled so big knowing that he succeeded." Charlie finished.

"Do you remember his name?" The man asked.

Charlie stood for a few moments trying to rack his brain.

"Christopher..." he trailed,

"Christopher Carlisle," the man vehemently answered.

"I'm his junior. My parents separated early on in my life, but I remember THAT book because he used to read it to me too. He passed a few years back with a needle in his arm. When the family cleaned out his possessions, I was given THIS book,"

The man held it up.

"This was the book that he used to read to US. But, unlike you, I didn't learn how to read because of it. My mother had one of your books. Your second, I think. In the foreword, you told that story. She read it to me anytime I asked her to until I memorized every single word and could read it myself. I didn't know my dad until I read that. Your gift is pain. It's that head of yours that traps everything no matter how awful or trivial. You gave me that memory of my dad. When I was asked to speak at his service, I read that passage. I couldn't read what came after; the damn book was about lonely guys fucking robots."

The crowd laughed hysterically while Christopher tried to keep a straight face.

"Don't downplay your legacy, whether you're Ramsey or whether you're Charlie. And please don't be afraid of all your readers. Yes, you have no control over what we do with your words. Some of us need them. Some of us needed a father. I understand you're scared to death of being a dad as you, but as a dad. You're exceptional. I can already tell. As a writer? You brought me here with the only book you'd let my dad read to you. I'm hoping you'll sign it for me. Just, if you're fighting a monster, please, let us fight it with you. It doesn't belong to only you now, once you let it free. You're giving us the chance to face our own demons and monsters."

Christopher stepped away from the microphone and began to weep. Charlie immediately hopped off the stage and embraced the progeny of a mentor and his agent handed him a felt pen. When Christopher handed Charlie the book, he opened it to find that storied Polaroid scotch taped to the opening page.

"For your dad," Charlie whispered in Christopher's ear as he let go of the embrace and handed him his signature on the photo. Charlie then re-embraced Christopher while the moderator thanked everyone for attending and hyped the next guests who would be part of the prestigious alumni series. Hours later, Charlie found himself once again backstage and desperate for another cigarette. His agent was in tow, trying to gush over his successful speaking engagement. Eventually, she grew tired of trying to chase after the manic writer and stopped to remove her high heels and finally stabbed him in the back with one to get his attention.

"What a fantastic turn out!" She gushed "Do you think the crowd will be this lively for your book tour?"

Charlie let out a groan at the thought of having to repeat such an intensely personal evening every night with a room full of total strangers.

“Whether you like it or not hun, you have readers. And they're obsessed with the details of your work."

Charlie appeared restless by the revelation of his agent.

"When do we leave?" He asked.

"Wait," he answered as his attention was now turned to a phone call from his only living sister.

"Hello?" He spoke.

The voice on the other end of the receiver sounded profoundly disturbed.

"Charlie," she answered.

"They found Ricky's body washed up on the banks of Turtle Rock today. He's dead Charlie. That means we're the only two left. You need to come home."

Charlie stood despondently before his phone slipped right out of his clammy hand and cracked on the concrete below.

"I have to go home," he muttered back to himself.

His agent stared at him, not sure whether to get him a driver or console her client.

"Is everything alright?" She hesitantly asked him.

"No," Charlie defiantly answered.

When he eventually found himself in his little boy's room, he rocked by himself in the chair he and his wife were gifted at their baby shower. Lorraine eventually made her way through the door in her nurse scrubs, completely frazzled and wondering how her husband's speaking engagement went.

"Where's the baby?" She asked.

"He's downstairs with your parents," Charlie answered.

"Are you okay?" She begged.

He stood to his feet and approached her. He held her face in the palms of his hands and kissed her on the forehead.

"I have to go back," he answered.

"Rick is dead. I have to go to his funeral."

His wife looked horrified by the news.

"How long will you be gone for?" She asked.

Charlie reached for a backpack on the ground and tossed it over his shoulders. He fidgeted around with the straps until it felt comfortable against him.

"Did I ever tell you," he started.

"How my dad told me his first dead baby joke?"

Lorraine shook her head adamantly and disgustedly.

"When Rachel was sixteen," he started,

"Her answer to Destiny crying all the time was to feed her. Our uncle joked that this must've been the reason for the morbidly obese infant with the three chins. There was one night where Destiny almost drowned from being force fed TOO much formula. Rachel stood there as formula came out of Destiny's nostrils and ears; literally, it was like witnessing an Edema of formula killing this kid. Our father, being somewhat skilled in first aid, managed to keep her from dying. When my sister ran out of the room feeling like the worst teenage parent in the history of mistakes that could have been prevented, my father looked at me and asked me,

"Do you want to hear a dead baby joke?"

I was ten.

He then answered

"How do you kill a baby? Impregnate your sister."

Charlie just stared off for miles after he finished.

"What's in the bag?" Lorraine demanded.

Charlie turned his head over his shoulder.

"My book," he curtly responded.

Lorraine could see the hurt in her husband's eyes; the last few years of their marriage, all she could feel was anger. Not because her husband was tortured, but because she knew that no matter how good Charlie's wife could be, that hurt would always manage to find its way back in. Subsequently, her husband's pain unfairly but unintentionally tethered to the anger she still felt for losing her mother to depression. She did not agree with his decision to go back home and potentially knock on all the proverbial graves of his demons and ask them to come out and play; she knew that this might be the last chance he would get at trying to put the past behind him, behind them, so they could finally be a family with a future. As Charlie approached the door to catch an Uber and then a train, she grabbed his arm and pulled him in for the kind of hug they both lovingly referred to as a "never let me go" hug.

Lorraine realized in that moment, that she'd also married Charlie's past and all his trauma. Charlie could feel that by how tightly she held onto him to the point where he wasn't sure if she didn't want to let go because of her fear he might never return, or if she wanted him to remember what it was like to be loved knowing that he would be spending the next few days in a place that embodied the antithesis of that.

"I love you," she cried into his ear.

"That's why I'm coming home when this is over," he

answered.

They held each other for several minutes before he finally walked out the door and took an Uber to the train station. When he boarded the train and finally situated himself, he removed a recorder from his bag and a pair of headphones, which he placed in the proper input. He then placed the headphones over his ears and stared at a blank Word document. The innards of the cassette tape began to spin inside his player with a label across it that simply read "Harris, Rachel" He closed his eyes and adjusted his neck against the head rest of the train before falling into something of a rest and taking in what he was about to hear.

His fingers hovered over the keyboard of the laptop as the baritone voice of a man echoed throughout his ears. Immediately he began typing, thinking, and remembering. He opened his eyes to see an empty train cart. When he closed and opened them again, he saw the specter staring back at him from the first row of seats.

"Choo-Choo," the specter mocked.

Charlie sat and anticipated the hell he'd managed to get himself into. He thought to himself, 'I killed you once, I can kill you again.'

II

BEAR HILLS, MASSACHUSETTS. JUNE 13TH, 1998-

She never used to believe in destiny. Fate. Kismet. Whatever tongue you chose to describe a preordained vestibule of a quasi-future. It seemed irrational. Myopic. Frankly? A cheap and pathetic way to sully one's autonomy. She realized that she didn't have much life experience to surmise a certain amount of wisdom from, but she wanted to believe that she was able to come to an educated conclusion on revising her rationale upon the incidents that took place there.

"So, Ms. Harris," a baritone voice spoke,

"Is that to confirm that you now believe in fate?"

The erudite older gentleman seated across the table from an emaciated looking girl, hiding behind her greasy brown hair, furrowed his brow as he motioned his hand across his face to cut through the miasma of cigarette smoke she was exuding, awaiting a response.

"That's why I named my baby girl, Destiny," she stoically answered.

The man pursed his lips and bit the inside of his cheeks, which created two noticeable dimples as he motioned his head with a concentrated nod.

"The agreement still stands, no?" She asked.

The man nonchalantly played with his tie while staring

down at a stack of paperwork he pretended to read. Meanwhile, the woman across from him emphatically dressed him down with her impatient stare.

"Provided you tell us what we need to know." He curtly answered.

"I suppose-,"

Rachel held out the palm of her right hand before extinguishing her cigarette in it without emoting or releasing even a grimace of discomfort or pain.

"You know," the man started,

"Our people provided you with cigarettes, despite the pleas of this institution. And if you keep that up, I'm going to have to confiscate what would otherwise be considered contraband in someone else's case."

Rachel let out a breath, subtle enough not to be construed as laughter but condescending enough to discredit the man's attempt at authority.

"Forgive me," she quipped,

"I just have a difficult time trusting these verbal contracts everyone keeps trying to sign with their lip service rather than their firm laws and ethics. I may only be sixteen," she offered,

"But, I'm certainly not stupid. I'm sure all those records and psychological evaluations you keep thumbing through are evidence of that."

The man smiled almost nervously at the girl before removing several photographs from an envelope and sliding them across the table to her. As she reached her frail arm across to receive them, her almost translucent pigment revealed several festering blisters, no doubt from other cigarettes she used her flesh to extinguish. The moist palms of her hands left a trail as she maneuvered the photographs over to her side of the table before carefully turning them over and meticulously studying them as if to commit every fine detail to memory.

"She's a beautiful baby," he answered.

"She looks a lot like you."

Rachel's face remained covered by her hair, concealing the fact that she was now quite emotional and teary-eyed seeing this little person grow up outside of this place she was being kept.

"A deal is a deal," the man offered,

"But I'm not going to lie to you, Ms. Harris. Your testimony must be substantial, otherwise you're correct. A verbal contract is nothing more than mere lip service just to get you to talk to us so we can cross you off our list of people to talk to. And while you may not believe you owe myself or my department anything," he continued,

"You owe that little girl a chance to know who her birth mother is. It's called compromise. You're a parent; you will learn all about compromise the older she gets. Trust me."

The young woman folded the photos down onto her lap as she bowed her head down to the ground and nodded.

"Do you have children?" she murmured.

"Yes. Two." The man politely answered.

"Girls or boys?" She asked.

"Both, actually. An older boy, and a little girl." He continued.

"Here,"

the man retrieved a leather wallet from the back pocket of his slacks and removed two photographs of his children and slid them over to her. Rachel leaned over and once again, carefully flipped them over to study them.

"They're beautiful," she complimented.

"What are their names?" She asked.

"Richie and Maeve." He answered.

"You must be so proud," she smiled.

"I can hear in your voice how happy just talking about them makes you."

The man reached across the table as the young woman handed the photographs back to him.

"Thank you," he gushed.

"My wife and I, Well, we never thought we would be able to have any children of our own. So, I like to make a point of being grateful every single day that they are here. I'm not a deeply religious man, otherwise I might thank God."

"You still should," Rachel abruptly answered.

"Are you religious, Ms. Harris?" He asked.

"Very similar to my thoughts on fate," she answered.

"I'm the kind of person who makes deductions based on experience and evidence. It would simply be apathetic of me to deny the existence of something following the events that brought you here to me. Do you mind if I offer you some advice?" she asked.

"Advice?" The man laughed.

"Well, surely you can. I can't promise I'll stick to it. But, I'll at the very least humor it." He chuckled.

"It's important," she insisted.

The man crossed his left leg over his right and interlocked his fingers before resting his hands on his lap and gestured for her to continue.

"Your integrity and character," she started,

"While I certainly would appreciate to speak to a man

of virtue and decency, these things are not nearly as important for us, given the context of being merely passing acquaintances. As a woman though, I can't emphasize enough how detrimental having a daddy with no moral character or conviction can be. In fact, it's probably how I wound up in this place: this demoralizing purgatory of tedious routine and meritless existence. Being a good daddy should always take precedent over your job, your fallibilities, peccadilloes, and often even your own personal security." She sighed.

The man's demeanor began to change from cautiously distant to almost compassionate.

"You're a very bright young woman," he applauded.

"Even your verbiage is quite accelerated. You must be a writer." He insisted.

Rachel shook her head and let out an endearing but quiet chuckle.

"My brother," she began,

"He will be the writer in the family. I attribute a lot of that to his relationship with our mother. I knew from the time he could begin emoting and communicating his discoveries of the world, both serene and sordid, that he was an exceptionally gifted little guy. Maybe that's why, unlike a lot of my peers, I haven't graduated from cigarette burns to actual suicide attempts to escape the painful reality of my rightful imprisonment here." She mused.

"What did you want to be?" He asked.

"A social worker," she confirmed.

"My siblings and I were never treated like human beings; more like walking and talking mistakes that were ingesting our parents' very sustenance and excreting all their hopes and dreams into the very toilet bowls they now called their lives . Like my siblings, I learned very quickly that children are not regarded with the reverence or endearment, as many propagandist televangelists and pop singers swear we are. I learned that educators, peace officers, lawyers, doctors, nurses, well...they're just uniforms. They're not people. The people wearing those uniforms still harbor the same prejudices, apathy, and indifference as anyone going to work in a uniform who don't warrant a sort of indoctrinated belief in unquestioned righteousness. In my life up to this point, I had made a point to shelter myself in other miscreants and misanthropes who shared the same domestic horror stories as the next kid on the block." She finished.

"Wouldn't a social worker fit into that exact uniform?" The man asked.

Rachel smiled.

"I'm sorry," she apologized.

"This isn't the smile of someone who feels wounded by astute observations of blatant contradiction. I adhere to my statement about experience. I've never had good experiences with some of the occupations I mentioned, but the social worker assigned to my family was...well, she was a kind of revelation about good." She smiled.

The man folded his arms on the table and smiled back at the young woman.

"In my line of work?" he started.

"I'm elated to hear such a thing. Hun-I'm so sorry...I often get in trouble for referring to young women such as yourself with that word, but I find it difficult to separate how I speak to my children and how I speak with everyone else." He answered.

Rachel brushed the hair from her eyes and behind her

ears and slowly looked the man in his eyes as if to let her guard down.

"It's okay," she smiled.

"I've been called worse."

The man felt comfortable enough to chuckle.

"It won't happen again," he assured her.

"I'm not here to hurt you or manipulate this conversation to serve my own interests, be it professional or otherwise. Your little brother, who I believe you genuinely care a great deal for, is still missing. Now, until we had arranged to have our conversations, I might have been more cynical about its destination. While you committed a terrible crime, I want you to know that I am not accusing you of having any involvement in his disappearance. I also don't believe he's dead, which leads me to believe that if you did have any involvement, it wasn't malicious." He assured her.

The man stood up to remove his suit coat and placed it on the back of his chair very neatly before hiking up his slacks and bending over the table to reach out his hand to Rachel.

"I know you weren't very perceptive during our last interaction, but I want you to know that my name is Donald," he offered.

Rachel finally reached her hand out to Donald to shake it,

"I'm Rachel," she answered.

The man sat back down and reached his arm around the chair to retrieve a small recording device which he held up so she could see. Rachel nodded, and Donald placed it flat on the table and firmly pressed his index finger against the play and record buttons.

"Thank you," he began.

"I hate the informal nature of my job, Rachel. I appreciate the proper introduction to you, your life, and what is important to you."

Rachel paused for a few moments.

"Is everything okay?" He asked.

Rachel retrieved the photos of her baby daughter and placed them next to the recording device.

"Would you mind putting your kids' pictures next to the ones of Destiny?" She asked.

The man gave her a confused look before nodding and accommodating her request.

"Thank you," she began.

"I know this is your job, and your job is to solve mysteries and punish guilty parties. I am not trying to make anyone's life difficult, or their jobs harder. After all, the longer I keep you from getting what you need? The longer they wait for their daddy to come home to them." She lamented.

Donald smiled, "You're very considerate."

"Since I have accommodated your request, can I ask you for a favor?" He politely asked. Rachel nodded.

"I am not a smoker. I gave it up after my daughter was born."

He began fidgeting with the buttons on his right shirt cuff before rolling it up to his shoulder and revealing a cigarette patch on his arm.

"In fact, she's quite asthmatic," he revealed.

"Could I trouble you to limit your cigarette smoking a little?" He smiled.

Rachel reached into the left pocket of the gray hooded sweatshirt on the back of her chair to retrieve a soft pack of filtered cigarettes. She held them up to the man's face before crumpling them in her palm and tossing them into the trashcan to her right.

"You'll feel better about that when you're my age," he joked.

"More importantly, Destiny will appreciate your decision." He assured.

"Rachel," he started,

"If it's not too much trouble, I was wondering if you could take me back as far as you possibly can. At least, as far back as would be considered relevant to this interview. The nature of my inquires may become somewhat invasive simply by nature of what I do to connect all the dots. Will you please stop me, and let me know if my questions are becoming too difficult for you?" He asked.

Rachel nodded politely.

Donald then reached into the breast pocket of his dress shirt for a stick of gum, which he offered to Rachel. She smiled and reached back.

"I smoked for almost twenty years," he revealed.

"I've always been partial to wintergreen. I hope that's not a problem for you," he apologized.

She shook her head and folded the stick of gum in half and began chewing as politely as she could.

"Alright," he began, just before pulling his chair closer to the table and ransacking through a folder and doing his best to lean into the recording device.

"It is Saturday, June 13th, 1998," he started.

"I am sitting across from Rachel Michelle Harris. She is a psychiatric patient at Bear Hill Memorial in Bear Hill, Massachusetts. She is the second oldest of three children that were kin to Roger Michael and Dianne Lynn Harris, who are both deceased. The eldest Harris child is Janet Marie, who currently resides in Hawthorne, Massachusetts with her boyfriend William David Foster. The youngest, Charles Francis Harris, is eleven years of age and still considered a missing person at this date. While I would like to give my due diligence to this case, I would like to point out that I don't appreciate my colleagues naming this case the "Curse of the Turtle Rock Blonde Boy." Rachel is sixteen years of age, and as of December 22nd, 1997, she is the only recorded guardian of Destiny Marie Harris. Forgive the improper nature of this recording,"

"Rachel, sweetie. Would you like a glass of water?"

Rachel nodded and Donald excused himself to walk across the room to the bubbler to get her a drink.

When he returned to his seat, he handed her a paper cup and returned to his dictation.

"Rachel," he said,

"To the best of your ability, I would now like to ask you a series of questions regarding the incident that took place on Saturday May 30th of 1998."

Donald stared into Rachel's hazel eyes for several moments before she held a fist to her mouth and let out a gravelly cough. The milquetoast girl leaned into the recording device much to the amusement of Donald.

"It all started in the spring of 1994," she answered.

Donald retrieved a notepad from the leather bag next to his feet and a pen from his breast pocket and began taking notes as Rachel waxed rhapsodic about the case that brought her to Bear Hill Memorial.

"The first incident was Friday, April 15th, 1994." she started.

"If you don't mind," Donald interrupted,

"While you are exceptionally intellectual for your age, how could you possibly remember the exact date of the incident to follow?" He asked.

She shrugged.

"It was a week to the day after they found Kurt Cobain's body in Seattle." She curtly answered.

Donald looked as if he wanted to say something but just smiled, shook his head, and resumed his previous disposition.

"Is... Is that okay?" Rachel stammered.

Donald smiled at her and gestured for her to continue.

"This would probably sound more credible," she started,

"If Daniel Stern was recollecting this much like he did for Fred Savage during the Wonder Years," she joked.

Donald tried to hide his amusement but again nodded at her encouragingly to continue her testimony.

"But that wasn't the only suicide to create a discussion in my home in 1994," she continued.

"A neighboring family had just experienced such a tragedy just a few weeks before suicide became part of the MTV zeitgeist. This girl Janet and I played with had lost her grandfather to suicide in the basement of the family home. While many of us kids didn't particularly understand the nature of how he died, we knew that it was taboo, and otherwise something scary.

One night, me, Janet, and my mom were setting up the kitchen table before we ate our microwavable chicken potpies when we noticed the absence of our younger brother, Charlie. While the calendar promised a New England spring, the sky was a less than cheery kind of backdrop. Ominous and chilly would be the best way to describe it. Our mother sent my sister and I to find our little brother, who had a habit of quietly finding solace in various places inside and outside the home.

Our mother, in a panic, ran upstairs to our grandparent's apartment to search for him while my oldest sister simply retreated to the bedroom, we shared to watch MTV for more coverage of Kurt's death. When I went out the back door, there he was. My little brother, with his head of blonde hair pressed against the bulkhead that led into the Thomas' basement, quietly having a conversation to himself."

Rachel began choking on seemingly nothing, as if she was trying to catch her breath while looking as if she wanted to cry.

Donald abruptly stopped his note taking to acknowledge the obvious pain of a memory.

"Charlie! Charlie!" I'd yelled.

"What the hell are you doing goofball?" I'd teased.

Charlie was in this almost catatonic state when I found him. I began to wonder if our mom was still giving him his "vitamins." He was panicked and almost erratic. I finally found a tiny pebble, big enough to get his attention but not big enough to harm a hair on his body...he had enough hurt at this point from all the adults. I threw it at him, not expecting to feel like Roger Clemens tossing a no-hitter, right at the crown of his head.

OW! He'd shrieked.

He then turned to me.

"Sissy! Sissy! I can HEAR him!" He'd squealed.

My brother was, for lack of a better word, dramatic.

I always found it rather endearing, whereas Janet and

our parents found it profoundly cumbersome. I remember carefully walking up to him and wrapping my arms underneath the arches of his before maneuvering him onto my shoulders. Charlie was deathly afraid of heights and HATED whenever I did that. Out of fear, he would cover both of my eyes so tightly, trying to prevent falling onto the concrete that was the only semblance of a yard for the other kids in this tiny area of Pine Banks.

I used to tease,

"Charlie! Charlie! I can't see! I might...."

Then I would sort of pivot around and spin as if I might drop him. He would manage to fall into my arms, and I'd bite his nose and kiss him while he did his best to fight me off.

"I HATE IT WHEN YOU DO THAT, SISSY!"

He would always cry, I would apologize, and he would have a single tear in his eye which showed me that I had hurt him. I would squeeze him SO tightly and kiss his forehead over and over to assure him that I was just joking, and I would never, EVER let him get hurt.

"Charlie," I would scold.

"You're not supposed to be over here. If the Thomas family found you, they'd bitch you out to Grandma and Mom."

He started to cry out of guilt and I immediately took my oversized sleeve from this atrocious B.U.M. Equipment sweatshirt my mom bought me to soak up all the saline pouring out of his tear ducts.

"He was talking to me, Sissy!" he pleaded,

"Honest!"

I laughed and sort of wrestled with him."

“Who did he think was talking to him?” Donald piped

in.

“So then, I got a little creeped out and asked; looking back on it, I really wished I let it go.” She groaned

"Who Charlie, who?!"

He got quiet when I planted his feet on the ground and looked up at me with this super serious look.

"Gunnar, Sissy!" He shouted.

"Gunnar was talking to me!"

Gunnar, of course, was the elderly grandfather who hung himself in that very basement a few weeks ago. Charlie hated being discarded, humiliated, or ignored, and a lot of the time I felt like the only person who ever let him speak.

"What did he say to you?" I humored.

"Sissy," he shivered,

"Louie is going to try and hurt me again.”

“Louie is going to try and humiliate me in front of everyone again."

Louie was Gunnar's youngest grandson—a monster. In three of the six years that Charlie had been alive, Louie had stabbed my little brother in the rectum with a lead pencil, beat him up in the schoolyard for wearing a similar San Jose Sharks windbreaker, and despite what the parents say, even tried to rape my brother in that very basement. My sister and I were friendly with his older sister Peggy, namely out of pity. She was a morbidly obese girl who had no real friends. At the behest of our grandmother, we would play with Barbie dolls, make doll houses, or indulge her seemingly mongoloid-like nature, hoping it would prevent her brother from hurting ours. Our father had previously instructed our brother to bludgeon the weird-looking bastard with the biggest piece of tar rock he could find from the driveway the last time Louie had picked on him.

When he failed to do so, our father beat our brother mercilessly to "toughen him up". Charlie did not have an abusive bone in his body. While he was often fodder for Janet's warped sense of humor, she often told me, after downing a bottle of the neighborhood mother Doreen's finest vodka, that she unconditionally loved Charlie and couldn't wait for him to come into himself so he could finally rid the world of our psychopathic, Lifetime movie of the week bastard of a father (who had been downgraded to weekend dad around this time). Her breath was rancid with qualms, insecurities, and profound sadness, much like the breath that lingered on our two parents. I do not know why they wanted to pick Charlie as their proverbial emotional punching bag. Charlie could not do it.

He could not hurt anyone, namely because of how much he had been hurt as a little boy. I remember he accidentally stepped on a ladybug once, and he spent three hours sobbing in his room because our sister had taunted him about killing something that is supposed to be good luck.

"I knew it!" She would tease,

"Charlie, you're nothing more than a curse on this family."

“Wow,” Donald interrupted.

She even titled a creative writing assignment about our family, "Curse of the Blonde Boy." I think there was a lot of resentment after his birth, being that our mother was constantly doting on him and wrote her own lore about the journey to finally having her baby boy.

I assured him nothing was going to happen to him, but he was almost inconsolable. I also had my suspicions that somewhere under the bulkhead, Louie was cradling a fifth of his mother's finest Kentucky bourbon while doing creepy voices to convince my gullible brother it was his recently departed grandfather. Admittedly, I probably would have fell for it too, considering the week we were having. After our parents' divorce was finalized, my dad resorted to some repugnant levels of vindictiveness.

All week, perverts had been calling my mother at her desk job and at all hours of the night at home after our father scribbled "Diane Harris has no gag reflex and she swallows: trust me," followed by her work and home phone numbers all over payphones and bathroom stalls around town. Unfortunately, being the single mother of three kids meant that no phone calls could ever go unanswered.

God forbid the one time our emotionally frail mother tried to evade the constant abuse of total strangers for a day and found out the body of one of her kids was found in a ditch? She also used to be a big-time drinker and chain smoker when she was with my father. To be the more "grown-up" parent, she had completely given up both of her vices, hoping that it might inspire us to avoid similar detriments to our collective futures. Janet and I had both indulged in our fair share of deviances. Janet had already lost her virginity and was not a stranger to alcohol or marijuana. While I am not sure if it counted, she would always give me the resin leftover in her makeshift pipes and whatever was left of the bottle.

"That's a lot for two teenage girls to deal with," Donald noted.

"Did your mother ever address the topic of sex with the two of you?"

"I was too young to even think about sex. When sexuality even crossed my mind, it would confuse and upset me. That made Charlie the only truly pure life form in the house. As we all sat across from each other in our own respective trenches, gobbling up this slop disguised as a dinner which came out of a freezer at the supermarket across the street, the ringing of the telephone cut through us like the church bells during or after a funeral procession.

Despite the fact that our mother would get these really harassing phone calls at work, potentially jeopardizing her job and humiliating her even further (the divorce was the result of a drunken incident that occurred after a work-thrown pool party), there were times where Janet and I would be home from school to watch our little brother and the phone would ring incessantly. Even though our mother pleaded with us never to answer the phone when she was at work, Janet, wanting to know what she was hiding from us, answered one of the perverts' calls...that's actually what led to her virginity being taken from her. Even for a young teenage girl, she still had the voice and the sense of humor of a phone sex operator. Every night after Mom put the three of us to bed, she would unplug the phone from the wall and wake up to over a dozen messages on our answering machine. I would say maybe a small handful were local perverts while the rest were messages left from our father.

Once, Janet and I made a game out of how drunk he was based on the slow deterioration from a maudlin misfit who fucked up to a drunken monster who often times would threaten to burn the house down with all of us sleeping inside of it. After two or three of those alcohol induced admissions of his homicidal fantasies, my mother finally decided to scoop us up in the middle of the night in total blackness and take us to her girlfriend's house out of fear that one of these nights he might actually follow through with his empty threats. While Janet and I were more annoyed by living the life of your contemporary domestic abuse refugees, it weighed heavily on our little brother.

He'd be laying, thumb in his mouth, his blankie held tightly to his chest, while still wearing his size 13 1/2 Velcro Power Rangers sneakers due to the leg braces that were strapped to him to correct his curved duck feet, still whimpering and pining for the daddy that did this to us. Childhood is absolute fucking hell. You are brought into this world without any consent. If you're lucky, you're brought into it by people who love you so fucking much that your childlike gullibility toward human beings manages to survive the fallout of persistent apathy and morbid desires to harm a creature too dumb to know that acts of cruelty aren't provoked by unconditional love, but resentment. Us? We were brought into this world by two people who were SO fucked up by their own parents, they mistook their desperation to be loved as actual love."

"It sounds like you all dealt with it in very different ways," Donald asserted.

"Charlie just wanted love and affection. He deserved it. We ALL did. Charlie was different, though. Despite his buck teeth, duck feet, and clumsy Barney Fife demeanor, he was endearing and cute as all hell. He loved, and in exchange? He was bullied, beaten, sexually assaulted, and constantly reminded that one day he would grow up with a hostage for a mother and a sociopath for a father, and instead of having the intuitive gift that would motivate him to run, run away as fast and as far as he possibly could from it? He still had unconditional love in his heart for his parents.

That was when my sister and I realized he did not take after either of them. She eventually let anger consume her, and me? I allowed myself to be the victim. While we both tried to shelter him and love him, we were incapable because of what we were going through on our own. Sometimes, it was difficult to look at him and not want to hate him for being so far removed from our gene pool."

"Did your brother ever hear voices coming from your neighbor's bulkhead again?" Donald asked.

Rachel nodded.

"The next morning, Charlie went out to play. It often started with him sitting in the sandpit surrounding our grandmother's above ground pool, putting buckets on his head because he was "Shredder," or indulging in his latest obsession. The previous year's obsession was "Jurassic Park," and typically our brother's obsessions lasted until the next birthday. This one was shaping up to be Power Rangers themed. As contently as you could possibly imagine a child playing alone, he was feeding his T-Rex some melting pot of G.I. Joes, Star Wars figures, and Ninja Turtles. What happened next is purely conjecture among the adults. Meanwhile, not one person ever thought to humor the horrified and humiliated kid, who was having an existential meltdown despite the cacophony of adults and their rhetoric.

When my sister and I tried to console him at different

times later that evening, he recalled a voice: something desperate but also sympathetic (my words, not his. He said it sounded like wind was talking to him in Grandma's voice). It drew him in like the Millennium Falcon to the Death Star when it got stuck in its gravitational pull (his words).

Normally he is a skittish kid. Our sister once inadvertently scared him by stepping out of shrubbery in the front of our house. He literally ran up the driveway screaming "Stranger Danger!" in a fit of pathetic and hilarious fear. That was maybe one of the only times I ever saw Janet feel guilty about her reputation. She was famously temperamental (like our father) and cruel at times (because of our father), but without the incremental guilt he was famous for showing (we all had cable boxes and color televisions in our bedrooms). She walked up the driveway with a genuine smile and gleam in her eyes, reassuring our brother that he was not going to be kidnapped.

She then commended him on how fast he managed to run away (whilst in his leg braces, I should note) from potential harm if such a thing ever did confront him. It was difficult to decipher most of the experience; he was never able to recall the event without immediately sobbing and recoiling from it as if he were experiencing it all over again in a completely lucid state. When he climbed down the bulkhead, all he recalls is this ringing in his ears like he just heard a bomb go off,

Completely embraced in darkness with the thud of the bulkhead door slamming behind him still ringing in his ears. In a kind of disoriented and petrified state, he tripped over his own two feet and attempted climbing up the stairs in his concrete tattooed flesh only to realize that someone had barricaded him in from the outside. No one recalls hearing the muffled screams of a small child who tumbled into another man's coffin, like Alice through a hellish rabbit hole. The pain of his imagination did manage to reach a fever pitch; that was the moment everyone does recall. Like a death rattle just before the future deceased gasps their final breath, a sound of metal scratching against metal made fingernails on a chalkboard seem like 1980's soft-rock in comparison, followed by the crash of an aluminum shovel being catapulted across the driveway and the cowardly shriek and begs for clemency from a not so scary bully. That was when the scene converged on the bucktoothed and leg-braced little wimp pounding the very soul out of Louie's prepubescent little body.

As tiny splashes of blood rained from the now bruised and scabby knuckles of his almost seven-year-old hands, we realized that the prognostication of Louie's dead grandfather was not the product of Charlie's imagination. Louie was going to try to humiliate him. In retrospect, time just slowed down before ending in a screeching halt. In reality? The scuffle ended relatively quickly once the adults were on the scene. Louie looked worse than he really was.

Then again, if you ever saw a child with two black eyes and a broken nose following a merciless beating from a younger child, the almost religiously profound reactions of the adults needed no further interpretation. Suffice to say, cops were called, threats of lawsuits were made, and the weeks that followed were profoundly awkward and tense between the three households that shared this driveway-turned-concrete backyard. For whatever reason, my mother felt fit to call our father to explain the situation to him. If Louie's parents had followed through with legal action, our father would have undoubtedly been included. It probably did not help matters that Janet was a terrible bystander.

Louie's sister tried at one point to break the brawl up, but the mere thought of "Peggy's sausage fingers," all over our little brother resulted in Janet tackling her to the ground and taunting her about her weight. Admittedly, I made a futile attempt at smack talk. However, typically when something sounds funny or cool in my head, I can almost always realize that it is the absolute antithesis of funny, cool, or a human language in some cases. While Janet tossed around rumors about boys teasing about her "FUPA-Fat Upper Pussy Area," and "People catch diabetes just looking at her," the best I could do was..."Jenny Craig just called...um, you're late for class!" Even the parents shook their heads at that one. "In other words, you're fat!" I had squealed as my big sister and I walked a distraught Charlie back into the house. Charlie was weeks removed from having a birthday party to celebrate turning seven, as a big surprise my parents had hired this elderly couple to make an appearance as "Power Rangers".

"Did the upcoming party do anything to boost Charlie's morale at all?" Donald asked.

Rachel shook her head.

"That was the furthest thing from our minds as telephone calls from vindictive parents and local perverts still permeated throughout the household. Unbeknownst to us at the time, when our mother called our father, he requested Charlie to be put on the phone. Rather than try to reassure his only son that everything was alright, he kept pressing Charlie about details regarding the brutality he had just unleashed on another child. I guess he became an even more unsavory version of Don King, Joseph Jackson, and Johnny Cochran all rolled into one. He kept trying to goad our brother into continuing such brutish displays of defiance for bullies, while all Charlie could do was sniffle and lament over what a bad kid he had become. That was when my mother ripped the phone out of Charlie's hands and went off on our father about our brother being a compassionate and remorseful person, unlike the bastard whose DNA was coursing in his veins. I learned that threats of not attending Charlie's birthday party were made as our mother ripped the phone out of the wall and tossing it across the room before folding up in her own mental breakdown.

That night, Janet and I just laid awake, staring at the ceiling fan in our bedroom while K.D. Lang's "Constant Craving," lulled us into this anesthetized state from our alarm clock radio. For what felt like a tedious amount of time, we remained silent and let Ms. Lang belt out all the sorrows of pining for love. To this day, I still think that she was lamenting over the stigma of her sexual orientation, or maybe that's what I wanted her to be doing because I was doing that very thing while hearing her voice perform all the introspection that I couldn't bear to. Finally, Janet broke the silence by asking the most controversial question of all.

"What do you think he saw down there that scared him so much?"

The snores that echoed from her nasally throat and nostrils were affirmation that this was of course a rhetorical question. Unfortunately, that night I was haunted by the question. The sensation of the dream made me feel bound and gagged with my eye lids taped open while I watched my little brother's descent into this six-year hell that was his life."

"Did you ever find out?" Donald asked.

"I tried to imagine it," Rachel began.

"The innocuous looking basement appeared more like a catacomb or labyrinth of living nightmares. I imagined what must have thrived in the darkness while this poor kid crawled on all fours hoping that God would release him. Did he see clowns? Our father once gifted us these porcelain clowns we found during a hardware store trip. When Janet mentioned how funny it would be to scare Charlie with these clowns if he misbehaved or annoyed us, our dad immediately salivated, and he talked Janet into doing just that. We had been staying with him for the weekend and at the time our brother had developed this weird habit of spitting and not being able to swallow his food. He later confessed that one of the times we SHOULD have been watching him and snuck out to hang out with our friends leaving him with the television as his babysitter he saw a PSA that scared him. It was about the lead in old paint chips and how they could kill you.

I do not know how or why this manifested in his head, but ever since he watched that he started to believe that we were trying to feed him lead paint in everything he was fed. That was when our mother began giving him "vitamins"; they were supposed to help him make up for all the weight he was losing by spitting up his food or going into the bathroom and gagging himself with his toothbrush. The house used to smell rancid from all the chewed up and regurgitated food that was caked in our dad's carpets. Our brother was a sound sleeper, so after our father brought him to bed, he paid Janet to prop the porcelain clowns all over the room. About an hour and a half later, I almost jumped out of my skin when I heard his cries for help.

When I looked over at my sister and father, they high fived one another and giggled, (Janet later admitted that by corroborating in scaring him, she hoped it would take him off the list of physical beatings) about it before my dad stormed into the room and gave the "Crying is for pussies" speech. Then my thoughts went into even MORE morbid terrain. Did he see the body of an elderly man swinging from the rafters just in front of the washer and dryer as I was told they found Gunnar? Gunnar was in the early stages of Alzheimer's and he was also a widower. I guess the combination of losing his wife and then his mind drove him to hanging himself.

Knowing Louie, it wouldn't have surprised me if he took one of his mom's mannequins (she was a freelancing seamstress who allegedly did a lot of Cher and Madonna's wardrobes for their concerts) and hung it where they found his grandfather. Then something even worse than that crossed my mind. Did he see Mark?

Not literally: it was just another story Janet had concocted to shut him up. Sadly, I did have a hand in co-authoring and perpetuating this myth. Our grandmother had this above ground pool that read "The Tub" outside of it. My sister and I both took to the water immediately; having been born and raised on the West Coast, we were raised by the water. Our mother had also been an athletic swimmer in high school, so it was important to her that her kids know how to swim, unlike our father, who always had this fear of the water. To date, I still really do not know why.

When we moved to Massachusetts in the in-law apartment of our grandparents' house, we were elated to find that she had an above ground pool we'd get to take full advantage of once the warmer weather permitted us do to so. It must have been assembled over a slope in the ground or something because whenever my sister and I would submerge ourselves under the water to see who could hold their breath the longest, we couldn't help but notice this big hump right in the middle of the floor. Of course, we did not make much of it until one day when our father had picked the three of us to take us to his one-bedroom bachelor apartment he resided in after the divorce. Before he went to his place, he brought us to his work so he could run in and lock something up in the warehouse. As kids do, while we waited impatiently in the hot car (his AC was not working and none of us thought to crack open a window), we began annoying the hell out of each other.

Charlie had an affinity for getting very whiny when he was uncomfortable or reached his saturation point with both us girls. To shut him up, Janet began spinning this yarn about what our parents did to "bad kids" who whined too much. I guess it never crossed our minds that our father was exceptionally hard on him because he was a boy. In our dad's mind, boys who whined, shed tears, or complained were not "real men", and such behavior often warranted physical and verbal abuse. So, telling our little brother, who was five at the time, that our parents' zero tolerance policy on whining could turn deadly...well, he bought every word."

“What did she tell him?” Donald asked.

Rachel let out a long sigh.

“It was a pretty innocuous story. His name was Mark, and he was the son our parents had prior to Charlie. One day, his whining became so cumbersome to our parents that they decided to murder him in his sleep and bury him in our grandparents' backyard...right where the pool would later be built.”

“I don’t think innocuous would be the right word to describe that,” Donald chuckled.

Rachel shrugged.

“Like our father, Charlie had a profound aversion to water. My mother had surmised that it was due to seeing all four of the JAWS movies way younger than he probably should have, but Janet and I knew the truth. Our dad's work had invited all its employees to a barbecue at a popular water park a few years before. Charlie was too young to go on most of the water slides or in the whirlpool, but there was this circular canal where parents could sit on these inflatable rafts and just sort of let the motorized current navigate them in circles. My father (like Charlie) hated being humiliated, and our mother had teased that my dad's co-workers would eventually pick up on the fact that he was bone dry through most of the day and would probably ask questions.

Outside of the five of us, no one else knew about our father's fear of the water, aside from his own family, but they all lived on the other side of the country. He begrudgingly agreed to take our little brother with him on the raft. My sister and I were in the raft just behind them when we saw Charlie roll off and into the water. Being as young as he was and having no concept of swimming, he started to drown. Our father just...waded and kept going. If not for an overzealous mother who abandoned her own children to pull Charlie out, he would have died that day. Dad played it off like he did not even know Charlie had fallen off, but Janet and I watched him nonchalantly shrug it off like "Good, that's not the son I wanted anyway". Ever since then, it was difficult to get Charlie into the water, even with inflatable floaters around his tiny arms and a bubble strapped to his back.

There was one time he bravely decided to dive off the pool ladder (I think to impress people) and he just sank like a brick. However, it was because of this that he knew what bump at the bottom we were talking about. We told him that was Mark. Watching my little brother grow up and recoil in terror anytime our parents would take us to the beach or try to fake sick if a classmate gave him an invitation to a pool party made me feel like the most nefarious person on the planet. Charlie was like glue; everything just stuck to him. To date, he will find any and every excuse to avoid the water. Between a young, near-death experience and then convincing him that his toes had grazed the buried body of his imaginary older brother must have done a number on him. All I could picture was Charlie curled up in his famous fetal position at the foot of the basement stares and hearing this fake, dead older brother taunting him or berating him for being the only son to survive.

In that moment, I also wondered if the imaginary friend "Frankie" he always talked about offered any semblance of comfort for him down there. Frankie came around not long after he turned four. Ironically, this was also the age where Louie began picking on him and alienating him from the other kids in that tiny area. I guess Frankie was a defense mechanism or something that made him feel less alone. Our father HATED Frankie. While he never divulged the actual reason he was constantly taunting our brother over him, and demanding that he "grow up" and make "real friends" no matter how much of a freak he appeared, I couldn't venture a guess outside of imaginary friends probably existed in the same wheelhouse as boys don't whine or cry. It was heartbreaking when my mom led Charlie by the hand, out to my dad's car whenever the three of us were to spend the weekend and he would be forced to leave Frankie at home all alone.

Our mother assured us that she'd keep Frankie company, but despite her “I don't drink or smoke” phase, she never stayed home alone and often times would grab drinks at the bar of some local Chinese food place with a guy her parents kept trying to fix her up with. She felt that it was a fair compromise that Charlie could still have an imaginary friend if he never talked about it or played with him anywhere near our dad. I guess out of sight out of mind was not good enough. Following the bulkhead incident, the three of us were going to spend the weekend at our dad's. Friday nights were our nights to shower or bathe in the tub, as our mother knew damn well our father had no interest in cleaning us while in his custody. Janet, being the oldest, did not adhere to a strict schedule when it came to the shower, so typically I would go in for a bath followed by Charlie. It was one of the first times I had shut the door for my bath. A year prior, I had gone to a friend's house for a slumber party and the mother had allowed all the girls to watch a scary movie.

She rented "A Nightmare on Elm Street," and while all the other girls found endless joy in the horrific presence of this burn victim turned dream demon, I, on the other hand, was completely traumatized. Namely, when it came to scene where the girl, Nancy, was attacked by Freddy while taking a bath. It was so bad that I peed my pants and immediately called my mother to take me home. Not my finest moment, even worse when she realized that I could not bathe myself with the door shut for the better part of a year without protesting in a fit of tears and feet stomping. Despite her veto of all horror films following this incident, our father made a point to show us nothing but whenever we spent the weekends with him. For the first time in days, I had just allowed myself to soak in the serenity of hot water and bubbles while still occasionally entertaining the following thought, "Where did the bulkhead take him?"

Rather, "DID the bulkhead take him?" He really was not the same after that. Then I thought about the perverts calling the house, all the scary answering machine messages from Dad, just trauma after trauma after trauma amassing into this really unconquerable monument of fear that would constantly sully his youth and inability to reconcile with fear. When I finally managed to empty all these terrible thoughts from my head was when I heard that now infamous cry of vulnerability and anguish. Without putting thought into the mechanics of my next motions, I sprung out of the tub, soaking the linoleum floor, (which my mother HATED) which consequently turned it into something of an ice-skating ring. I wrapped a towel around myself and desperately attempted to lunge my body toward the door when I slipped and cracked my head over the doorknob, which completely knocked me out.

When I came to, Janet was standing over me, nursing what eventually turned into a gruesome gash just above my left eye with a cold compress while my grandparents reprimanded our mother.

"What happened?" I managed to speak.

"You fell trying to get out the tub," Janet explained.

"I cleaned up the blood before mom saw. It was all over the doorknob and floor."

I managed to sit up while she continued to press the compress against the contusion. "What was that scream?" I asked myself. Before Janet could speak, our grandmother burst through the door and motioned to me while our mother peaked her head in with an almost annoyed lack of concern.

"Diane!" Our grandmother sneered,

"What in god's name have you been doing to these poor kids?"

She wrestled Janet away and wrapped both of her hands around each side of my face and began scrutinizing the wound.

"She's fine, Grandma," Janet protested.

"She just slipped on some water. Nothing new for Rachel; you know she's a total klutz."

Janet's attempt to diffuse the tension in the bathroom was an effort in futility as our grandmother helped me up to my bare feet and walked me out of the bathroom and into the kitchen. Grandpa Dickie was down on his hands and knees trying to clean up another mess on the kitchen floor.

"Did my blood get out here too?" I asked.

Grandma just pursed her lips and rolled her eyes to the back of her head in a look of utter disdain at our mother.

"Where's Charlie?" I then cried.

As I was seated on one of the broken wooden kitchen chairs, our grandfather conscientiously stood to his feet and pulled up his slacks.

"Why don't you ask your mother?" He sneered.

I looked at her in bewilderment as my Grandmother started divulging what had taken place after I knocked myself out.

She had been trying to do the laundry of us three kids so we would have plenty of extra clothing for our planned visit with Dad that weekend when she accidentally knocked over a bottle of bleach all over the floor. Allegedly, Charlie had walked into the kitchen at that moment, hysterically crying and claiming that he watched as Frankie had taken his own life by taking the bleach off the washing machine and quaffing it like some toothsome beverage. At least, that was the story our mother sold to us. When she was unable to calm him down, she immediately called our father and blamed him for yet another episode in which Charlie became erratic and almost psychotic from his sordid imagination. Our father (who coincidentally) was just a few blocks away picking up his dry cleaning had come to Charlie's rescue and taken him one night earlier than he was supposed to. Charlie was now in my dad's custody for the rest of the night.

"What in the hell were you thinking, Dianne?" Grandpa Dickie cursed.

"That's it," he rolled up his sleeves and motioned for the door.

"I'm going to knock some sense into that evil mother

fucker."

As he began to stomp toward the door, he was stopped by both Grandma and Janet while our mother became a melodramatic time bomb attempting to explain that the stress of raising three kids alone in such a chaotic house with little to no constructive input from her parents was driving her insane. As our mother continued her screaming match with our grandparents, Janet snuck me out of the living room and back to our bedroom. As I sprawled out on my New Kids on the Block comforter, Janet's voice resounded in my head.

"I think mom did this on purpose," she lamented.

My eyes shifted in her direction, but I still too weak to sit up.

"Did what?" I asked.

Janet explained what she heard before our father came for Charlie.

"I was watching Parker Lewis Can't Lose," she detailed,

"When I heard mom calling for Charlie. She had mentioned something about the mess on the floor and how sorry she was. Charlie had left the room for a few minutes to get some coloring books out of his room when Mom informed him that Frankie must have gotten into the chemicals while she wasn't looking. SHE was the one who put those thoughts in his head. All I remember was walking into the kitchen to ask Charlie what was wrong when Mom reached for his "Vitamins" and told me to get the fuck out of the kitchen. Rachel, I have never seen Charlie SO worked up. This was WAY worse than the bulkhead incident.

It's like she was trying to exploit him, like she needed

him to behave so badly so she could get Dad's attention or something. I'm starting to think she's using us to get back at him," She finished.

Janet was always somewhat theatrical in her narration of certain events and innocuous details. But this time, she sounded more disturbed than she would have with something she'd cooked up as a means of teasing me or making me feel stupid.

"Rachel," she cried,

"I don't want to go back to dad. And I don't even want to think of what he's doing to Charlie right now without the two of us there to protect him."

The more I thought about it, the more I began entertaining the worst-case scenarios with those two. Our father ALWAYS hated Frankie. Maybe if Mom eliminated him, maybe that would be her way of getting him to accept Charlie, who was one of the main reasons why she separated from him. Really, the main reason was because of the parking garage incident a few years back after that company pool party."

"The garage incident," Donald interrupted.

"You've mentioned this before. Can you take me back just a little further? I don't believe the reason your parents divorced was ever explained to me."

Rachel nodded and took a few breaths before going back to a memory that she and her two siblings would probably never recover from.

"Our father was an aggressive drunk," she started.

"We had been at this party for maybe three, three and half hours or so. Dad took full advantage of the open bar. Before any of us knew it, he was easily a dozen or so beers half in the bag. Dad wasn't a casual drinker. When he drank? He was a pro, like drinking was his career. Our mother overheard him getting volatile with one of the bartenders who was trying to shut him off, and that's when she decided that we should leave so she could be spared of the kind of embarrassment that would warrant a pink slip.

She gathered us kids up and waited for the valet to pull around with the Hyundai. Our dad staggered into the car. You would think our mom would offer to drive, but at that point she was still very timid behind the wheel. She HATED driving. Regardless, with her precious cargo in the backseat, you would think she would've put up more of a fight. At first, our dad seemed completely in control of the situation. That was until we could see the headlights facing a car just in front of him which he nearly collided with. He stopped, rolled down his driver's side window and a string of profanities followed.

Once we finally made it out of the parking lot, it was only a ten-minute drive back to the apartment. For the first four or five minutes, it was just a tense and awkward silence. Then our mother started in about how much he had humiliated her and began attacking him for his drinking and abusive nature. All I really remember next was getting into the parking garage (barely) and seeing him slam her face into the passenger side window while we all screamed. I lunged forward and began tearing at his eyes before he threw me back jerked the car into park and began choking me. I do not remember much after, as I blacked out from the lack of oxygen to my brain. When I came to, I saw the headlights chasing Janet around the parking lot as if she were being hunted by that car from Stephen King's book *Christine*. He eventually crashed into two other cars before parking. Janet had somehow managed to find an alarm and this loud siren echoed off the concrete and metal. He exited the car and went right for her.

Our mother jumped out of the car before pleading with me to stay with Charlie. She managed to calm him down after he pounded on Janet a little. While his demeanor appeared calmer, his eyes told the story. Our mother motioned for Charlie and me to exit the vehicle and join them in the elevator back to our apartment. As we all snugly fit into this tiny elevator, our father abruptly grabbed our mother back the back of her ponytail and slammed her face into the emergency stop button in the elevator. Her nose was completely split open, and blood was just spraying everywhere. When the nightmare was finally over, our mother, who was caked in what looked like gallons of her own blood, locked us in the bedroom we shared and brought our drunk and lethargic father to bed. The next morning, while he was working, our mother collected us and some belongings and we left to go stay with our grandparents in their two-family home which we had occupied when we first came to New England from California.

Even though Charlie did not make much of a peep during the whole ordeal, Janet and I knew that it was only because he was afraid his father would strike him next. Charlie's earliest memory of his father was that of a man who tried to murder his two sisters and mother. That will probably ALWAYS be Charlie's first lucid memory of the man who helped bring all three of us into this world."

"What happened when you and your sister were reunited with Charlie the next day?" Donald asked.

Rachel paused for a few moments trying to figure out how to articulate Charlie's even more bizarre behavior following his sleepover with their dad.

"He just wasn't the same," She sighed.

"That's the best way I could describe it. He was...he was more withdrawn. Charlie had always been painfully shy. But this was different. He looked like one of those dogs or cats you would find at a pet store who had been treated badly that would either lash out or totally recoil into themselves. Charlie was the latter.

His spitting up also became worse. He just would not swallow. It was like he could not. Everything people tried to feed him from that point on, he just believed to be poison. Then we would notice these weird tics and behaviors. He was ALWAYS washing his hands. Like, excessively. Some days he would be in the bathroom upwards of like, twenty or thirty times to wash his hands. Sometimes, I would spy on him in tears, like he was desperately trying to scrub something filthy off himself and not being able to. I did not think much of it until the two incidents the followed. His birthday party, and the time I watched him bury Frankie in our backyard." She answered.

"What happened at his birthday party?" Donald asked.

"He was just SO distracted," she said.

"Despite his entire t-ball team showing up a couple hours after their last game of the season, he just didn't look like he could be bothered. Then, the Power Rangers showed up and made Charlie the spotlight of the event, something Charlie never had the chance to experience. All the kids were cheering his name, clapping for him, and just everyone made such a big deal about Charlie...that kid that used to play shortstop but chased butterflies in the outfield. Charlie, that awkward kid who once was asked to play first base and completely ruined a little girl's day after she hit a line drive to him and he yelled "I GOT IT!" only to divulge he was talking about the loose tooth he had been distracted by and not the ball he was supposed to catch, Charlie...the little, cute but loveable misfit who had waited for this moment for seven years....just couldn't enjoy it.

There was another point where our dad showed up, despite telling Charlie he wouldn't. Granted, he didn't show up for Charlie's last game (he admitted to the rest of us later that it was because Charlie sucked so badly) but here he was at his seventh birthday party with the Power Rangers, with his now infamous RCA state of the art video camera to capture the whole thing. Like that was supposed to make up for nearly murdering his sisters and mother in cold blood? After the Power Rangers left, Charlie was just sort of stoically staring out our back-screen door at something. I was coming downstairs from our grandparents' apartment with the cake when I noticed Charlie just nonchalantly staring off at Louie staring back at him. Louie was just standing across the driveway, kind of pathetically admiring the birthday party with his two black eyes and broken nose from the comfort of his side of the driveway. He and Charlie just continued staring at each other when our dad yelled from across the kitchen,

"Hey Moron! Are you going to blow out your stupid candles or not?"

Donald started to fidget in his seat and wet his lips with his tongue. He then motioned at Rachel and excused himself before stopping the recording device. He stood up and approached the barrel where she'd had tossed her cigarettes. He retrieved the crumbled back and started ironing one of them out. He then reached over and peeled the patch from his arm and tossed that in the barrel. As he screwed one of the filtered cigarettes between his lips, he looked at her before ironing one out for her and gesturing that it was okay. He then retrieved a Zippo lighter from his breast pocket and lit his just before leaning over and lighting hers. He snapped the top of the lighter back over the flame, placed it back into his breast pocket and slammed his fist down onto the aluminum table before taking a seat across from her again. As he seemed to relish every puff of smoke quietly to himself, he started off into space and with a glassy far off stare.

As he blew these impressive smoke rings from his lips, he then turned to Rachel with a profoundly sad face and asked,

"Did Charlie ever tell you what he saw? Did he ever tell you what happened that night alone with your dad?"

Rachel shook her head and he simply nodded at her as his eyes widened. While he never came right out and said it to her, she could tell that Donald had come to the same realization she did when she'd first seen Charlie staring out the window at Louie. Somehow, Louie, despite how remarkably fucked up he was and how envious he was of the party, still managed to get the better end of the deal when it came to family.

"You saw him BURY Frankie?" He asked.

Rachel didn't know why, but she immediately began to sing,

"I saw the sign, and it opened up my eyes. I saw the sign."

Donald gave her a puzzled look.

"Sorry," She apologized.

"I remember it being really late at night. Janet was snoring and to combat her snoring, I had my clock radio on. I remember that song playing as I became distracted by the sound of creaking floorboards and shuffling feet.

I carefully peeled myself out of my bed and followed the sound out to the kitchen where I saw this tiny silhouette of a person maneuver their almost pygmy frame out our screen door, methodically, so it wouldn't wake the rest of the house. I tried to mimic those exact mannerisms so I wouldn't startle who I assumed was Charlie sneaking into the backyard. I covertly found a good vantage point where I spotted him holding his green blankie as if a newborn had been wrapped in it. That's when I could hear digging and debris being arbitrarily tossed around. A few snaps of twigs followed before I snuck back into the house and into my bed. I could hear tiny feet shuffling follow not long after. The next morning, while everyone else was still sleeping, I snuck outside and through this hole in the chain link fence that Charlie swore to our mother NEVER to cross as it could potentially lead to the roadway not far off. That's when I saw a mound of dirt with a makeshift cross resting on top of it.

I immediately started digging when I saw a green piece of fabric with all this dirt piled on it. It was his blankie. I don't know what he was trying to secretly bury that night. Maybe it was Frankie, maybe it was blankie, or maybe-"

Donald perked up.

"His innocence," he interrupted.

She took a couple of seconds before nodding back.

"Yeah," she ecstatically replied.

"You thought the same thing?" She asked.

Donald gave this kind of slow nod, as if he were piecing this very convoluted jigsaw together mid-thought or conversation.

"I got a new life," he began to sing.

"You would hardly recognize me."

In that moment, Rachel started to tear up, and immediately he ran across his side of the table and embraced her in a bear hug while the two of them both cried out,

"I saw the sign and it opened up my eyes. I saw the sign."

In that moment, Rachel realized that maybe she and her siblings weren't crazy. Maybe she and Janet were right for being so fearful for Charlie that night alone with their dad. He was never the same.

Donald then sadly spoke

“And then the three of you moved to Bear Hills."

III

She could not help but think it was funny how their mother kept putting so much emphasis on starting over and getting far away from their past. Bear Hills (at least, geographically) could not have been more than a ten- or fifteen-minute drive from where she and the kids had previously lived. At the same time? Once they were all settled in, and it started to feel like a home, it felt like Pine Banks never existed; that could have had a lot to do with the fact that their parents abruptly stopped communicating with anyone and everyone.

"Really, once the last of the boxes was unpacked," Rachel started,

"It became just the five of us."

"Why do you think that was?" Donald asked.

Rachel wore a look of introspection on her face as she quietly began arranging sentences in her head to form an articulate response. However, it proved futile.

"Honestly," she struggled,

"There is a part of me that looks back in retrospect and thinks that maybe our mother really did treat the move as a reconciliation. It is not like it was the first one they'd had. When she started planning the cross-country trip back to New England with her parents over the phone, there was absolutely no future with him in it. And absolutely no talk of him joining us. In fact, when we hit the road, we even did so without him." She laughed.

"So, how did the four of you wind up getting here together?" Donald inquired.

"He followed us," Rachel replied.

"He borrowed a friend's car and literally from time the U-Haul backed out of the driveway until our first road stop, he had been tailing us."

Donald excused himself following a belly chuckle,

"I'm sorry," he laughed,

"I'm sorry," he repeated.

He took a minute to poise himself and become more professional for the sake of both Rachel and the recording device.

"You said, he borrowed a friend's car?" He asked.

Rachel nodded.

"What was he planning on doing if he actually tailed your mother and you girls ALL the way to New England?"

Donald looked completely dumbfounded by their father's irrational nature.

"That was how he was," Rachel quipped.

"That's what made him so terrifying to the three of us. There was a vacancy of soul that showed in his eyes when his rage, or his insanity, took him over. The only other time I had seen that was with Janet. Around the same time that we were leaving Pine Banks, Janet had been diagnosed with something called Bi-Polar Disorder. I really did not know much about it other than a lot of reporters and writers were claiming that Kurt Cobain must've had it. When I asked our mother what it was, she simply called it a "mood disorder," in which our sister could go from psychotically happy to profoundly erratic and violent on the drop of a dime. I started to feel briefly for my mom during this period. Here she was, a single woman who left her husband to help her kids get out of this abusive relationship only to wind up with a child who was simply picking up where our dad left off. It was strange, though. Janet only seemed to get to that point of scary and homicidal when she was taking the pills our mother distributed to her.

At the time I thought, wow maybe she needed a higher dosage or a different kind of medicine? It was called Prozac. Again, I only knew this because that was becoming a controversial drug at the time...well, according to the local news. I guess a lot of kids my sister's age were taking it, but for many of them it seemed to actually work."

Donald skimmed through his reports and adjusted himself before freezing in place, as if he wanted to invest a lot of time drafting and re-drafting his next question before he asked it.

"You said your brother was on vitamins," he began.

"What kind of vitamins did he take?"

Rachel took a few moments and motioned toward the pack of cigarettes Donald retrieved from the trash can. He motioned as if he was granting her permission and she removed another crumbled, filtered cigarette from the pack as Donald slid his Zippo light across the table to her. She flipped the top back and took three or four puffs. She then held the wick of the Zippo under her nose.

"Sorry," she grunted,

"I've just always really loved the smell of a Zippo once the flame goes out. Our dad used to use these and ONLY these when he was both a cigarette and cigar smoker."

She placed her cigarette in the pivot of the ashtray and

let out another cloud of smoke before answering the question.

"Flintstones vitamins," she began.

"Rather," she held her hand up as if to excuse herself,

"They were pills in a Flintstones vitamin container. They were little pills...like, the kind you would get from the drug store. One side was like this booger-green color, and the other was white. There were two things that I look back on and should have put more thought into: the first was why she was lying about or at least trying to conceal the fact that she was not giving him actual Flintstones vitamins. I know this, because if she had, they would've made him throw up." She asserted.

Donald appeared confused.

"Why would he throw up?" He asked.

"Charlie had the stomach bug when he was four," she started.

“Except, he didn't know it at the time. Like, he showed no signs of being sick until dinnertime. He absolutely LOVED Kraft Macaroni and Cheese. Our mother only made us things that could be microwaved or came out of a box, but that felt like a step up from our father, who dined on take-out exclusively. Charlie had about two bites of his Macaroni when he barfed all over the table.

After that? He did not touch Kraft Macaroni and Cheese until he was almost ten. He just associated it with a really bad experience, in this case: barfing. He was like that with a lot of things, but specifically foods. One time, my brother and I went with our mother to the grocery store while Janet was in a dance class. We were in the medicine aisle when Charlie spotted Fred Flintstone on the container's label. Immediately, he started in on how much he wanted them (because in his mind? They were candy) and for whatever reason both me and Charlie began badgering her about getting them for us. After being inundated with a barrage of "PLEASE-PLEASE-PLEASE-PLEASES" she acquiesced. Later that night? Charlie and I got into them and ate almost the entire container. We got SO sick; I swear we were puking worse than that kid in Stand by Me during the pie eating contest.

She used to roll his vitamins up in a piece of cheese and then feed them to him. So, I thought, okay, maybe he does not taste it? One night after she had gone to bed, I snuck out in the kitchen to steal one and wrap it in cheese to see if he REALLY couldn't taste it and instead of finding these vitamins shaped like the Flintstones, I found these pills."

Donald's eyes became so wide it looked as if he had just bore witness to something truly horrifying.

"Rachel," he answered,

"Prozac are green and white pills."

He then paused for a moment and went through his notes.

"How long was she feeding him these vitamins?"

Rachel's eyes moved rapidly as she tried to remember.

"Actually," she began,

"He stopped taking them right as we moved out. I didn't see him take another one until a couple of years after our sister was put in a 51/50 hold when she was sixteen."

Donald then perked up in his chair.

"Do you know what her pills looked like?" He asked.

Rachel nodded,

"Hers were white and blue," she answered.

"Your mother," he sighed,

"It sounds like your mother was giving Charlie your sister's Prozac and your sister a placebo." He lamented.

"Like, water pills?" Rachel asked.

Donald nodded indignantly.

He then made a couple of notes before speaking.

"When did he start taking those?" He asked.

"Hmm," Rachel spoke.

"It was actually right around the time we moved back in with our grandparents. Right before the divorce was when Janet started showing signs of outward aggression towards our mother and anyone who tried stop her from accosting her. I cannot remember specifically the day or even the time of the year. I just remember she came home with a white lunch bag that read "Thank you," which were the same bags our family pharmacist down the street used.

I remember she pulled out two of those orange pill containers with the label around it, and a bottle of Flintstones vitamins. Funny thing was, I never became suspicious over the two pill bottles, just the Flintstones vitamins."

Donald's look of concern became even more evident after his next question.

"Were you ever given a vitamin?" He asked.

"Other than my prenatal vitamin when I was pregnant?" She answered.

"No. Although she tried to put my sister and I on these diet pills once, after convincing us that we were both becoming morbidly overweight." She divulged.

Rachel could hear the ballpoint of his pen tearing into his note pad and bleeding through into the pages that followed. His scribbles became more emphatic, as if time were becoming less of a viable option for him as he wrote, so each letter or sentence had to be quick and precise.

"Can you give me a timeline," he began,

"Of when your brother took these vitamins, and when he didn't."

Rachel attempted to clear some phlegm from her throat, then pulled her hair behind her ears and spit into her empty water cup.

"I don't know how consistent she was." She divulged,

"I just know that she gave him those vitamins around the time when our father became the most violent towards us. I asked her about it once and she claimed that Charlie looked so emaciated from all the fighting and violence that if not for those, he might develop bone problems later in life." She finished.

Donald sighed even louder this time and continued with his notes.

"By the time I last saw him?" She continued,

"He hadn't taken vitamins in a long time. Why? What would have happened if she were giving him my sister's medicine? And giving her placebos?"

Donald cleared his throat and began moving his hands around wildly as he spoke.

"The long and short of it is," he continued motioning with his hands,

"If someone with a mental illness is not getting the appropriate dosage of the medicine their physician prescribes to them, it can have both long-and short-term ramifications, both on their physical and mental health. The same could be said about someone who is taking medicines specifically prescribed for someone with a mental illness. If they are perfectly healthy, and of a sound mind? It can cause their behavior to change." He answered.

"In other words," Rachel sassed,

"Not giving Janet her crazy pills were making her crazier. And giving Charlie her crazy pills when he wasn't crazy, basically made him crazy?" She asked.

Donald nodded,

"Precisely." He affirmed.

"So, what I need from you now is a possible motive that could explain the most important piece that is missing from this puzzle. Why? Do you think you could do that for me, sweetie?"

Rachel shrugged and fidgeted with the cigarette butt in the ashtray.

"I could try," she shyly responded.

"That is, if you trust the stories, I'll have to tell you to possibly find that answer."

Donald smiled and began nodding and waving his arms side to side.

"Anything, and I mean ANYTHING!" he emphasized,

"That you could possibly tell me to explain why she was doing this to your siblings?"

Rachel then held her pointer finger up at him.

“What would have happened," she began, "if....if she had replaced my ACTUAL prenatal pill with something else?" She demanded.

Donald folded his fingers together and slowly leaned into her with a grave glare.

"There's a good chance," he curtly responded,

"That you and your baby could have profound issues down the road. So, I need you to be as honest with me as you possibly can and do your absolute best to provide any knowledge regarding your mother's thought process that you think would be pertinent to this case. Do you think you can do that?" He questioned.

Rachel sat stoically for what felt like hours but, was probably more like five minutes.

"Sweetie?" Donald politely asked.

"RACHEL!" He then yelled.

Rachel's eyes were morose, and the color faded from her face when she asked Donald,

"Can I please use the restroom?"

IV

“Sir,” the officer began,

“Could you walk us through the events leading up to the young woman’s death?”

“When I realized the patient was unresponsive to my pleas to open the door,” Donald began

I ran to the nurse's station and began pounding the palms of my hands against the caged window. Several orderlies and I tailed one of the nurses as she desperately fidgeted with a ring of keys to unlock and open the bathroom door. I am not proud, but I may have raised my voice at her to hurry up! However, I think the panic in my voice was indicative of something profoundly disturbing awaiting us once the door was opened.

When the nurse opened the door, the patient was slumped over the toilet bowl with her left arm languid on the tiled floor with her tiny fingers wrapped around a broken piece of glass, while her right arm was lacerated several times.”

Donald paused,

He took a few moments to try and forget but the image wouldn’t go away. The freckles on her rosy Irish cheeks, her brunette roots cutting through the red hair dye that accentuated her fair skin. The tiny scab on the bridge of her nose that looked like a pimple she had either popped or clawed at, which divulged teenage insecurities. The porcelain sink which was painted red from her blood contained several shards of broken glass. It appears she had smashed the mirror above the sink, and just as she made quick work on her wrists, she had enough time to leave behind a little graffiti. "DESTINY" was painted in blood across the only part of the mirror that was not completely shattered or cracked.

Donald began putting so much emphasis on that word. Destiny. While that was the name, she had given her child he could not help but consider the irony of that word today. In the short amount of time that this poor young woman had spent on this planet, she was plagued by bouts of bulimia, anorexia, depression, sexual and physical assault, and the trauma of being a child giving birth to a child. Donald just sat quietly with his back turned to the now open door to the room he had been speaking with her in. He was hunched over with his face resting in his hands. Immediately he became overwhelmed with guilt. While it was imperative for Rachel not to know that they had found Charlie days earlier, he wished that he had told her.

“That was when we found the body. She used the glass from the mirror to lacerate her veins,” He curtly answered.

The two officers nodded at one another as they continued making notes.

“Thank you for your time, sir” One of the officers spoke.

Donald returned to the room where he and Rachel were speaking just an hour or so earlier. His attention was turned to the table where he found the three pictures resting against the recording device. His two little ones, and now this little baby who had just lost her mother. Donald reached for his wallet and placed all three photographs in it. He then reached for the recorder and realized that in all the chaos he had forgotten to hit the stop button.

When he made it to the door to exit, he paused and turned his body slightly to survey the room and take it any energy that perhaps she might have left behind in it. When he finally emerged from the facility after providing information to the local police officers and detectives who were on the scene, he could not help but notice the color of the sky as the sun subsided.

"Cotton candy clouds," he spoke.

He just smiled at the thought and continued toward his car. As he began placing all his stuff in the trunk, he noticed the woods directly across from the parking lot.

There was a small building with a sign regarding boat rentals and a rack that displayed several one-person paddle boats. He stared off, his eyes rapidly shifting from one corner of his mind to another and he started remembering bits and pieces of the conversation that turned profoundly tragic. Her voice still resounded in his head.

"That's where they first spotted the pipe people," he murmured.

The temptation to retrieve the flashlight and play Kolchak the Night Stalker and begin an investigation for the "pipe-people," was nearly impossible to fight off. Donald tended to get too into the wild imaginations of not only his own children, but the children he was trying to advocate for. As a social worker, you see some profoundly disturbing things, most of which stay with you until the day you die. At least, that is how his sister Lisa described the unfortunate realities of the occupation when she helped her struggling younger brother find what she believed to be his calling. Lisa was one of the department's star employees, so she knew that anyone she tried to get in with them would wind up on the payroll by sunrise.

Donald then went back to that word, "Destiny". He could not help but consider that perhaps, like his now deceased kid, that "experience" would force his ideologies and superstitions to evolve as well. After all, the person who inspired them both to become social workers was Lisa. He just stood in that parking lot staring into the woods as the cotton candy sky faded into a vast abyss. As he contorted his body into the driver's side, he caught a glimpse across the parking lot of Rachel's covered body being removed from the main entrance of the facility and placed into the back of an ambulance. The first time Donald had ever seen a dead body was not even in person; it was in an issue of *Rolling Stone* magazine after Kurt Cobain committed suicide in 1994.

Suffice to say, it made an impression on the then twenty-eight-year-old. There was something about an entire culture galvanized by a seemingly wayward latchkey kid's poetic integrity, who even in the spotlight still could not reconcile with who he was when he walked off the stage. While Donald did not have a profound affinity for Cobain's music, he could certainly relate to the seething animosity Cobain harbored toward the counterculture movement of the 1960s who eventually turned into a staggering number of burn outs or sycophantic corporate hypocrites. Donald's father fell into the former. A brilliant creative writing professor in his native Cypress, Massachusetts, Donald's father Stanley became infatuated with the likes of Timothy Leary, Albert Hoffman, and Terence McKenna, all men who indulged in psychonautics.

In other words? They were all heavy drug users who managed to author these prolific schools of thought based on their ability to sojourn into the deepest recesses of their minds. Unfortunately, Stanley never comes up in the search for the most prolific minds of the 1960s as he became too overly indulgent in the drug culture to the point where it made him vegetative by the time Donald was five and Lisa, seven. Donald grew up most of his adolescence watching his mother Debra go from a liberated advocate of the civil rights movement to that of an encumbered wet nurse working multiple jobs to keep food on the table. Donald subsequently resented his father's addictive curiosity to know the absolute truth due to its detrimental effects on both his life and the lives of his family.

He also resented the fact that he shared that same trait. When his father eventually passed, his mother wound up re-marrying the total antithesis of Stanley. Leonard: A Cypress police officer with an affinity for hard booze, and an Irish temperament that became the bane of Donald's existence. If losing a parent was tough, then feeling both vulnerable and subordinate to the iron fist of a quasi-father made Donald's life THAT much worse. Like Cobain, he retreated into drug use to self-medicate all the pangs of puberty and bereavement over the death of what could have been an otherwise Nick at Nite, black and white, picket fence life.

Fortunately, Lisa took the brunt of the attacks at the

hands of their illegitimate stepfather for the sake of saving her younger brother. It is probably safe to say that is what thickened her skin enough that it goaded her into the world of social work. Unlike Lisa, Donald still could not ignore his predisposition for going TOO far down the rabbit holes of the children he was sent to protect. While Donald never came home from work miserable about how he provided for his family, he had become increasingly irritable about his inability to change the cycles that many of these children (himself included) fell into over the course of time. This obsessive need to fix broken domestic systems often came at the cost of his own. Many nights, his wife and he would argue over his desire to invest in children that he did not foster.

As the ambulance exited the parking lot with Rachel as a cadaverous passenger, he realized the depth of her testimony. He began to feel like he owed it to her to entertain these stories about pipe people. Why? Because Donald was never satisfied with paying visits to homes where children were abused by junkie parents who should never have bred in the first place.

Especially when it came to Bear Hills. Donald swore to his wife almost every night he came home that this town HATED its children.

This case? It predated the Harris family. It even predated Donald's parents. There was something that did not quite add up about this hauntingly nostalgic New England suburb. It had a history: a history that Rachel herself had become very much aware of. He continued staring off in the distance at that boat house that Rachel was able to describe to a letter T, right down to the chipping paint of the boats themselves. Then he kept picturing a kitchen table with an empty seat, two small children becoming restless, and a wife with infidelity on her mind while his steak dinner started to feel below room temperature. He slammed the driver's side door shut and started the engine.

"There are monsters here," he said to himself.

"And it's not just the parents."

He then took the car out of park and made the trek back to his family. The ride home consisted of him blasting his cassette copy of "Cracked Rear View," by Hootie and the Blowfish to drown out of the haunting and defeatist thoughts. When the third track "Let Her Cry" came on, he turned the dial up and rolled all his windows down and let out a primal scream. His eyes were flooded with tears, and he dedicated the song to Rachel. "Destiny" would be vindicated. He did not know how or when, but he was determined to solve all the mysteries of a family who was doomed to succumb to the curse of the bottle, the blonde boy, and the flames of indignation. Not a particularly religious man, but in that moment, Darius Rucker's voice filled his shit box sedan like a sermon in a beautiful cathedral.

There was a profound feeling of disappointment as he finally pulled into his driveway, and parked his car. He sat and tried to spot a tableaux image of the family he and his wife, Stephanie, had created. All the lights were off, and his nostrils filled with the birthday candle smell of two tapers blown out with a hurricane wind of giving up on him. As he approached his walkway, he stared down at the concrete that had two different blocks with concrete hand and footprints with the names of his two children. He started to walk toward his front door with the same trepidation he would walk to the front doors of his clients. Once you open it up? There is no turning back.

That ugliness of passion adheres to the walls and floorboards. Donald had seen it firsthand during many murder/suicides, especially involving children. Crimes of passion, they would call it, where fathers and mothers would extract revenge for years of gaslighting and physical abuse but could not bring themselves to be buried without the kids. They would be exhumed from backyards, basements, and Donald had seen his fair share of tiny caskets being lowered to a deep six. When his key unlocked the door, he was welcomed into an abyss. Total blackness. The kind of blackness that adheres to bedtime routines, and a wearied parent who desperately needs to catch some shut eye despite the lack of involvement from her spouse. Donald quietly navigated his way through the darkness as he had many nights prior. His routine was as endearing as it was heart breaking.

He missed parent teacher conferences where his wife found out how much of a delight his children were to teach. The colored belts his son was awarded during Karate tournaments, and his daughter gracefully spinning across the stage as a petite ballerina during recitals he watched back on video. He wrote his apology notes on the heads of his wife and children in the form of quiet desperation. He would press his lips to their skin with conviction, hoping and wishing that maybe tomorrow he would wake up as someone else: someone who did not have this innate desire to save total strangers from themselves. He would then retreat to the kitchen to ransack the refrigerator from that evening's leftovers before investing himself in more work until his wife found him passed out in the basement and would reprimand him for not coming upstairs into their bedroom.

Much to his surprise, he found his now cold dinner sitting in a Tupperware container with a yellow post-it attached. The note read "We're talking tomorrow. DON'T even think of coming to bed with me." He read it with all the condescending vitriol that his wife was famous for when she lectured her absentee husband. He immediately became outraged by the indignation she felt toward a man she famously encouraged to pursue what she insisted (much like his sister) was his calling in life. When the reality of the job became more evident, that encouragement was replaced by demoralizing remarks about how she wanted a husband not a man-child or "Holden Caulfield". He walked over to the trash barrel next to the refrigerator and emptied the contents of the Tupperware before flinging the empty container into the steel sink and causing a big crash.

He picked up his bag and immediately retreated into the basement where he tried to walk softly. When he made it onto the carpeting of the basement floor, he turned the knob of his office door to unload everything he would need to continue his work that evening. He then shuffled over to the family room where a child was sleeping soundly on the pullout sofa. There, sprawled out all over several blankets and pillows, was Rachel's brother Charlie. Donald stood at the foot of the bed and scrutinized him quietly from a distance.

He made a point not to make his presence known as the child had sustained a great deal of trauma over the past couple of months between the death of his parents, and now his second sister. Unfortunately, Donald would have to be the one to deliver that news to the young boy at a more appropriate time. Preferably, when he was not wracked with concerns over being thrown out of the home he shared with his wife and two children. He walked back down the hallway to his office where he sat behind a large mahogany desk completely littered with notes, documents, and folders, no doubt regarding the Harris case. He sat back in his reclining leather desk chair and appeared in a state of introspection for a few moments. He then reached down and removed a glass and bottle of whiskey from one of the drawers.

The glass looked like it had been previously used, as there was still a brown stain at the very bottom and smudges from what looked like lips and fingertips all around it. It was also discreetly placed in a mock bottom. This is also where Donald hid his ashtray and pack of cigarettes. He engaged in a staring contest with the near empty bottle of alcohol as if he were trying to reason with himself that perhaps tonight would not be a good night to get inebriated. He rubbed his thumbs over the glass quietly for several moments before he became startled by a loud horn, which permeated from outside and through the open window into his office.

"Nine o'clock," he spoke.

"Fucking nine o'clock."

He stood back to his feet and popped the cork from wrapped his hand around the neck of the bottle as if he were strangling it and made himself a drink. He then paced around the room and tried to shake off the willies.

He approached a large corkboard in which several photographs and newspaper cut-outs were pinned. He scanned over all the seemingly arbitrary articles and character background checks, thinking that everything might somehow be connected. His eyes navigated from one end of the corkboard to the other until they stopped on a tiny article regarding a missing man whose remains had been unearthed in the woods across from the hospital Rachel was staying in. The article opened on a suspicious vehicle that had been sitting in the facilities parking lot for a prolonged period. Eventually, it warranted local police to perform a discreet sweep of the perimeter. It took them right to an area Rachel had explained in detail.

"That's where we found the pipe people," her voice resounded in his head.

He took another sip of his drink before scanning another snippet about a young boy whose body had been found in 1986 in the woods right next to where the Harris family had lived. The mother of the young child had moved to Bear Hills to evade her ex and the child's birth father. Following a short stint in a prison a few hours away from where she lived after being convicted of assault and battery charges against the woman (she later filed for a restraining order, which prevented the man from seeing his child), he was incarcerated for a ten-year stint, but only served six. He was released for good behavior and passing several psychiatric examinations which deemed him ready to re-enter the civilized world. The day of the young boy's disappearance and subsequent death, the man had tracked down the home of his ex with the help of a private investigator who even drove him to the location.

After several hours of stalking the outside of the woman's home, he eventually forced his way into the residence armed with a machete. Unbeknownst to our would-be assailant, the woman had attended several self-defense classes and even acquired a license to own a handgun. The details were sketchy, but when police arrived on the scene, the man had sustained several gunshot wounds, none of which were fatal, but enough to immobilize the man from doing something that Donald could not even fathom. During the attack, the young boy had seemingly wandered off into the woods near the woman's home. This is where the private investigator became a person of interest until he was eventually released and acquitted of charges of conspiracy.

When the private investigator realized that his client had intended to murder his ex in cold blood, he sped off in a panic. However, when the child entered the woods, it was suspected that he was thrown from a cliff where he sadly plummeted to his death. To date, the mother still believes that her ex had conspired with someone to murder both she and the little boy. Following the funeral services and subsequent burial, the young boy's body was exhumed from his grave and seemingly disappeared without a trace. The woman fell into a kind of catatonic state and her home was foreclosed on. Once authorities had arrived with the woman's landlord, who also worked out of a pediatric office right across the street, the woman became enraged and attempted to stab the landlord / pediatrician to death with a kitchen knife.

As she was escorted off the property and sent to the same hospital Rachel resided, she cried out,

"Don't take me away from my baby!"

Later, she divulged to authorities that the grounds-keeper of the cemetery where the body of her son had been buried, helped her remove her son's body from his grave and bury him somewhere on the property. Due to the woman's questionable mental health, no one felt the need to investigate these claims further. Then Rachel's family moved in not long after. Donald stood sipping from his glass and trying to connect all the dots from his earlier conversation with Rachel to all the seemingly damning evidence in front of him that there was a lot of merit to what the woman claimed. To date, the mystery of her son's death still baffles investigators.

Rachel claimed the house was haunted during their second session. She even provided Donald with her own research regarding the events leading to her parent's renting the home the following session. Donald returned to his desk where he retrieved the recording device from his bag. He appeared hesitant to sit back across from that young woman and listen to her story once more. On the notepad he had been scribbling in during her testimony, he listed several key points that stuck out to him, "pipe people" for example. They might have been just minor details or delusions from a young woman's mind, but something about these things sparked immediate cause for concern to him.

He sunk down into his seat and clicked play on the recorder.

V

By their fourth session, she recalled one of the first times being in Bear Hills with her siblings, father, and a few of his drinking friends. They had attended a carnival that was being held in the parking lot of the Zoo. Charlie's affinity for wandering off led him down a pathway and about fifteen minutes away from the Zoo's main entrance. This would have taken him exactly where the boat rental office was, across the street from the Hospital. In a panic, everyone split up and searched the Zoo grounds until eventually, Rachel recognized the size thirteen and a half shoe prints of his LA Gear light up sneakers pressed in the marsh and sand. After informing the others, they followed the footprints to an abandoned old Victorian home about a ten-minute walk from the house they would eventually move into.

Save for the roof, which had caved in, and some exterior damage that exposed a fully furnished bedroom with an extensive library of texts, the home appeared (according to Rachel) and several others who had seen it, in near mint and habitable condition. It was here that Charlie was found standing just outside the home's main entrance. When Rachel approached him, he was in a trance-like state. Something in that house had him completely transfixed. She explained that it was even like the birthday party incident with Louie. Before she had the opportunity to ask what he so enamored by, their father and his motley crew wrestled their way through some brush and stumbled over to them. Everyone stopped to marvel over this piece of New England history that was still standing. As the adults all teased one another over who was too "chicken shit" to actually go inside, Janet stomped her away over to the chain link fence that was acting as a deterrent from unwelcome visitors and began to shimmy her petite body through a tiny opening.

Her efforts of showing up the grownups were stymied when Rachel let out an alarmed scream. A few feet away were a group of industrial pipes stacked on top of one another, and Rachel claims to have seen two naked gentlemen copulating inside of one of them. When her father became belligerent and shamelessly homophobic, the two men became startled and ran off.

"They didn't have any clothes," she'd sheepishly commented.

While the attention had been turned to Rachel, who was now frozen in both fear and humiliation, another scream came from behind them. When the party turned, they watched Janet wrestle out of another naked man's bear hug.

"She was able to free herself, but none of us stopped this time. Every one of us just ran like hell out of those woods." Rachel recalled on the recording.

"That was my first experience at Bear Hills." She asserted.

Donald reached for his bottle to pour himself another drink while intently listening to the recording device. He started to mouth the words that he offered her on the tape.

"In 1986," he sighed,

"This VERY facility, well the town really, became the subject of an investigative news piece for a nationally syndicated television program. Namely, regarding how the town and this facility were treating homosexual men and women. You see, back in the 1960s and 1970s, homosexuality was regarded as a mental illness, no differently than anxiety or bi-polar depression. Up until this program had aired, patients who came from different religious backgrounds or intolerant families were still being admitted, treating homosexuality as a disease.

That meant that individuals with no prior history of mental illness were being subjected to electric shock therapy, lobotomies, and heavy doses of anti-psychotics to treat their sexual preference. The program also exposed the facilities treating those who suffered from mental retardation as those with debilitating mental illnesses. Suffice to say, anyone residing in this facility without a legitimate mental illness, not just the homosexuals and mentally handicapped but also individuals who were heavy drug users who'd simply fried their brains, were immediately released, regardless if they had family or anyone to take custody of them. The people who you believe you had seen and nearly attacked your sister could very well have been the individuals who were released without anywhere to go." He paused.

"How could they do that?!" Rachel shouted.

As Donald listened to the tape playback, he could remember seeing that program when he was a sophomore in college. He was enrolled in a sociology class whose professor was horrified by what she had seen. Even though he was enrolled in a New Hampshire college, the sleepy New England town of Bear Hills still fascinated these folks north of Boston, more so when the death of that little boy occurred later that summer. David and Mallory Greenwood—Mallory was the mother, and David was the boy.

He always seemed to forget their names, which seemed strange considering how impossible it was to forget that story. The same could even be said of all the clients Donald had worked with. Even though he could meticulously describe the fragrance of their home still lingering under his nostrils, mimic the sound of their doorbell, or even tell what brand of cigarettes the mother smoked or what alcoholic beverage the father over indulged in... he was always struggling to put names to faces.

"How did your parents wind up here?" His voice questioned from the recording device.

"We went to the homecoming parade for that figure skater," she recalled.

"Kerri Manahan. You know? The one who became more famous for getting jumped by a fellow competitor than her actual performance at the Olympic games." She joked.

Donald's laugh was identical to the laugh on the recording. Rachel's matter of fact demeanor was unwavering and commendable.

"It was this big deal," she continued.

"I mean, she had just hosted Saturday Night Live. There was a potential Wheaties cereal box in the works, and the Lifetime Movie of the Week about her harrowing attack was just around the corner," she sarcastically quipped.

"Frankly? I did not know anything about her as an athlete. My parents were as swept up into all the tabloid celebrity garbage as everyone else. Mom waxed rhapsodic about the president's peccadilloes while my dad made Michael Jackson jokes. They watched hard copy and Entertainment Tonight probably more than they watched their children.

To them? This was a headline they could touch. It was stupid how many thousands of people lined up and down main street for a five second look at this person they didn't know, or didn't think of fondly if they did, in her red, white, and blue windbreaker and curly hair held up in a... you guessed it, red, white, and blue scrunchie. After she drove by in that red Cadillac, my parents decided to walk around the neighborhoods just around the corner from where we were in this quasi-hero and celebrity drive by. We had wandered around for a little while when they saw that house with the FOR-RENT sign in the front yard. I do not remember the specifics of when they decided THAT house was the one; I do not even remember them attending an open house.

All I remember was my sister telling all her friends that we were moving to Bear Hills and treating it like she had just been drafted to battle in Vietnam or something. Like no one would ever see her again." She laughed.

"What about you?" Donald asked.

"Who did you say goodbye to?"

Donald remembered how melancholic her response was.

"I didn't have anyone. I did spend my last day at the Pine Banks Public Library. Sadly, that's probably the thing I miss the most." She lamented.

"I don't know why, but it's never been easy for me to make friends. I just get too self-conscious. I like, start to rehearse what I am going to say before I can even say it. So, when it finally comes out? It is even more evident that I'm this awkward wallflower.

When we lived in Pine Banks, I was the really neurotic uptight person who really only felt comfortable in the pages of a good book." She paused.

"What was it about books?" Donald interrupted,

"That gave you the kind of security you felt that you lacked in yourself?"

Her silence indicated a moment of introspection or even clarity when he heard it back on tape.

"Books," she began,

"Much like film, or music...two things my brother and sister loved very much. With books? There was never any prejudice. If you wanted to invest yourself in a book, it would not deny you that privilege based on how you looked or how much money your parents made. It was overzealous about you picking it up and dedicating both your imagination and your openness for wherever it would or could take you. I remember Janet once saying something similar about music, and it was evident with my brother and his relationship with monster movies.

We all wanted the veneration of being who we were without judgmental scrutiny and rejection from a peer. All three of these things were stories, and they were stories that wanted to and often NEEDED to be heard or seen by someone like us. Sometimes, I think that's how the three of us managed to survive Bear Hills at all." She said.

"Your first night," Donald began,

"Did you immediately look for the local library?" He

asked.

He remembered the smile on Rachel's face as she hinted that she would have entertained that notion had she been able.

"Our first unofficial night," she started,

"The three of us went with our mother to drop off a few boxes. She was meeting with the landlord about something and suggested that the three of us go out and familiarize ourselves with the neighborhood a little.

At first, none of us were very enthused by our mother's subtle way of telling us to take a hike. It was humid. Like, sticky and buggy. The kind of night where no matter where you go, you could never seem to escape our outrun those tiny flies that always swarmed around your face in these giant hoards, We sort of just stopped in this little intersection of neighborhoods when this group of teenage boys on bicycles spotted us a few blocks away and waved at us from a distance. Charlie and I were still swatting these bugs from our moist and sticky faces, unlike Janet, who immediately was poised to make an impression on these guys one way or another. There were six in total.

Four of them were on bikes and two were riding passenger on the pegs of their friends' bikes. This was new for me. There were so many things that happened over the course of our time at Bear Hills that seemed so bizarrely innovative. Like pegs. Not to be confused with Pogs. Even those were strange to me and incidentally, these guys loved those too. The ringleader was a fifteen-year-old named Ricky. I say it with such conviction because after he introduced the rest of his little gang, we'd always wonder why he was the only one with a real name." She laughed.

"Real name?" Donald wondered.

He then tried to imagine how the scenario unfolded.

"Hi, I'm Ricky." He said. "These guys? Well, this deadhead mop of hair...we call him Sideshow Todd."

Rachel mentioned that this was an obvious Simpsons' reference considering how profound the likeness was between Todd and Sideshow Bob. That is, if he smoked a lot of pot and wore tie-dye Grateful Dead t-shirts.

He then pointed to the mullet-haired kid in cutoff denim jeans and a tight Metallica shirt.

"This is Hesh."

Rachel remarked how much she admired his conviction to heavy metal, despite how unfashionable it was in a grunge and gangsta rap culture.

"Dimes," she recalled,

"Smitty, and Scotty."

"You could tell out of all of them," Rachel remarked,

“Scotty was going to be the one with the best sense of humor. He had these coke bottle-like spectacles that sort of replaced his whole face in a way that made him look like that artist, Crumb. Also, he was teased quite a bit. By pretty much everyone." She added.

"What did you make of them?" Donald smiled.

"Janet took the words right out of my mouth," she laughed.

"She immediately asked why they ALL had Sandlot names. Like those kids in the movie about baseball? When they had this moment of looking around awkwardly at each other, she just became SUPER bubbly and said YOU HAVE A SANDLOT! DON'T YOU?!" We were in this weird huddle kind of thing when out of nowhere these two other boys came racing by on their bikes just taunting the Sandlot dudes. Janet and I immediately snickered at each other thinking like...oh man, are they going to have this like, stare down shouting match and then face each other at the other team's dugout?

That was when we realized that life was not nearly as endearing as the movies. It turned unsettling and scary, fast. The two boys were named P.J. and Austin. You could tell by their ratty clothing that they were not from this neighborhood at all. They must have lived down the way in either the Bear Hills Motel (which doubled as a seedy underbelly for one-night stands, and as temporary shelters for battered children and women) or in the projects across town. One of them even pulled a switchblade out and kept taunting all of us in a stabbing motion. Janet was never one to exude fear and immediately started taunting him.

“Who invited the greaser?" Janet snickered

"Next time you want to intimidate someone, you show up with the Army, NOT the Salvation Army,"

mocking his friend's clothes which looked like something he stole out of a secondhand bin. The friend then sneered,

"Shut up, you bitch!"

That was when, we both swore we would not have believed it if we did not see it with our four eyes, little Charlie just leaped over the crowd and managed to tackle the kid who called Janet a bitch to the concrete. It was eerily reminiscent of when he pounded Louie. That was when the greaser kid went to go at him with a knife and Ricky knocked the shit out of him, causing him to drop his knife to nurse his bloody nose.

Ricky held the knife up to the kid, retracted the blade and handed it to Charlie.

"There's a reason you only hang out with that retard P.J." He mocked.

"Were you REALLY going to stab a little kid? You do not have any friends because no one fucking likes you OR him. Now get lost, or it'll be six against two!"

Once again, Charlie shocked both of us when he immediately asserted himself into the fight by yelling SEVEN! This caused the Sandlot dudes to laugh and immediately embrace Charlie. That was the first time ANYONE had ever done so.

"You heard him," Ricky corrected.

"Seven against two."

P.J. helped Austin back to his feet and they screwed away on their bikes as fast as they could while we all looked on triumphantly. Janet and I looked at Charlie in this, like, 'we were two proud mommies' sort of way while the rest of the guys slapped his hands and gave him kudos on the punches.

"So," Ricky started,

"Do you want to see our Sandlot or not?"

Not long after, Janet and I found ourselves on the pegs of Ricky and Sideshow Todd's bikes while Hesh piggybacked Dimes, and Smitty piggybacked our brother and Scotty just kind ran circles around all of us doing these Simpsons impressions.

They brought us to this place called G.G. Rock. When Janet asked why they called it that, this scrappy little Chihuahua came barreling out of nowhere and began nipping at our heels.

"Oh my god!" Janet laughed,

"You even have a dog that guards your little Sandlot!"

As we made our way up the main trail, I realized that

G.G. Rock was not far from our new house at all. In fact? It pretty much overlooked it.

“Hey Janet!"

I remembered excitedly yelling.

"How's this for a backyard?"

Janet and I smiled at each other, realizing that we no longer had to share a tiny concrete parking area with a ton of kids anymore. That was when Ricky started asking us where we were from and what we were doing in Bear Hills.

"Our parents are renting the house right over there," she pointed.

“As soon as the guys could see where we were moving in, I don't know...their demeanor went from friendly and goofy to guarded and protective.”

"You're going to live THERE?" Hesh asked.

"What's wrong with that?" Janet barked.

"Nothing aside from that place being the Amityville of Bear Hills." He quipped.

"Amityville?" I asked.

Janet let out this condescending chuckle at me.

"Sorry," she apologized.

"Even though my little sister is a total bookworm, she hasn't graduated from Judy Blume yet.”

She then turned to me and condescendingly took me to school.

“Rachel,” she groaned,

“It's a true story about a couple who moved into a haunted house back in the 70s."

She then turned to the boys as we kept making our way through the trail and up to the rocky surface.

"Are you telling us that our parents are renting a

haunted house?" She asked.

Ricky stopped dead in his tracks and turned to the rest of us.

"It's not just ANY haunted house," he ominously responded.

"It's a haunted house with a dead body still buried in it."

I could tell all of this was starting to distress Charlie, so I immediately stopped and knelt to reassure him that they were just hazing the new kids, and everything being discussed was purely imaginary.

"Janet," I warned,

"You know how HE gets. Maybe we should talk about something else."

Ricky acknowledged the tears welling up in Charlie's eyes and immediately changed the subject to Scotty's house being WAY creepier.

"What's creepy about his house?" Janet asked.

Twenty minutes later, we all found ourselves in this dilapidated Victorian a couple streets over from where we would be living. The screen attached to the door was hanging on by a thread, and the porch area just outside the front door had carpet that was covered in cigarette burns and these huge brown stains. Charlie became distracted by the arsenal of NERF guns cluttering the floor and under the benches.

I became distracted by the tall bookshelf that had a myriad of Stephen King novels, Elvis Presley biographies, and self-help guides. Scotty caught me being nosy when he asked,

"Since you've never read Amityville, I can safely assume you're not familiar with King?"

I shook my head.

"He's my mom's favorite," he continued just before pulling a copy of *Carrie* out of the stack.

"Here," he offered.

"To get you started on your journey away from Judy Blume."

I reluctantly accepted it.

"Won't she be mad?" I asked him.

He just laughed before maneuvering a few books around and revealing a bunch of half empty liquor bottles.

"THESE she'd notice if they went missing," he solemnly answered.

"Besides, you look like you and Carrie White might have a lot in common." He smiled.

I pressed the hardcover to my chest and felt something I had never felt before. No one had ever thought enough about me to gift me with a gesture. Janet made kissy faces at me while I turned beat red. As soon as Scotty unlocked his front door, the odious smell of Virginia slim ultra-light 100s sucker punched us all right in our faces. You could tell that he was embarrassed by the lingering aroma of another one of his barfly mother's one-night stands.

"So," Dimes began,

“This is what the inside of Joan Rivers' vagina smells like." He joked.

Scotty frowned as he started picking up the living room area, which was littered in empty bottles, blankets, pillows, condom wrappers, and empty cigarette packs.

"Dude," Ricky addressed,

"What's with the camera?"

We all turned to see Ricky pointing at a camcorder resting on a tripod, much to Scotty's chagrin. He grabbed one of the sheets off the couch and tossed it over it. Sideshow Todd quietly mouthed,

"Bow-Chicca-Wow-Wah," as we all snickered.

Janet began scanning the room, which aside from the mess of Scotty mom's debauched skin-a-max inspired Thursday night, was relatively normal. There was a Super Nintendo plugged into the television: well, the smaller working television resting on what was the bigger broken one.

There was a crate of video game cartridges, a small cabinet full of VHS tapes, some which had titles and some that appeared to be blank tapes, and a bunch of Nintendo Power or WWF magazines everywhere.

"I don't get it," Janet spoke.

"I thought this place was supposed to be creepy as hell. This looks like a combination of my little brother's room and our living room after our parents send us outside so they could do it."

Ricky then pointed to the dining room table where a Ouija board was sitting surrounded by offering candles. Scotty was running around cleaning up after his mother, so he tried to sneak a glimpse when he was out of the room. Charlie parked himself in front of the television and immediately fired up the Super Nintendo.

Normally, one of us would have scolded him for being so rude. Unfortunately, we thought this might be the only chance we would get to ask the guys about our new house. When we walked around the table, there were dozens of magazine clippings and pictures of Elvis Presley all around the Ouija board.

"Jeez," Janet snickered.

"This lady REALLY likes Elvis, huh?"

Ricky sighed.

"It's way weirder than that," he warned.

"There were a bunch of rumors going around amongst our parents that the reason Scotty doesn't have a dad is that her obsession totally scared the guy off. Another rumor is that he is the lovechild of a one night stand his mom had with an Elvis impersonator. She is SO weird. I feel bad for Scotty. She tries to present herself as this totally righteous Jesuit who drags the kids to church every Sunday and stuff, right? The only time this lady even sees a church is when she is sitting in the basement of one at A.A. meetings.

She is not even there to get better, though. She is there to prey on these totally, like, lonely dudes who she can fuck later that night. That is, since she developed a reputation around here as being that horny barfly who would put out for anyone who so much as passed by her. Scotty does his best to hide it, but I know she is mean to him. I'm sure she beats him, too." He lamented.

"How Christian of her," I remember scoffing.

Ricky laughed.

"Right? On top of that, she's hardcore into performing these séances with other Elvis fanatics that she meets at, like, swamp meets and yard sales where she goes to find all these creepy ass religious figurines and Elvis memorabilia." He revealed.

"Where's all the creepy religious stuff?" Janet asked.

Ricky motioned to us and the other guys and we started making our way up the staircase.

"Scotty!" He yelled.

Scotty then ran to the bottom of the staircase.

"Where are you taking them?"

Ricky then nodded in Charlie's direction.

"Keep him distracted. I wanted to show them some of that stuff of your mom's that you showed me." He answered.

Scotty looked as if he were about to protest, then looked to have a change of heart when Charlie asked if he wanted to play Mortal Kombat II with him.

"Whatever you're thinking of doing, just don't," he started.

"Put everything back the way you found it. Please."

Ricky gave him the thumbs up and we all galloped up the rest of the stairs.

When you made it to the top, there was this cool but gothic looking steel chandelier hanging from the ceiling. As you made your way around the banister, there were several vanities lined along the walls with these candelabras. The mess continued from the living room to the walkway, leading to the three bedrooms. Satin panties, pantyhose, and skirts were just strewn about arbitrarily. We quickly learned that the fifteen-year old was the only qualified housekeeper in the home, and while our parents taught us how to do our own laundry and pick up after ourselves, they never tasked us to endeavor cleaning our house from top to bottom. Well, that could mostly be since our parents never trusted us to do anything to their standards.

As we approached the end of the hall, there was a doorframe sans door. No one ever explained to us where the door was. We followed Ricky up the creaky wooden steps to one of the creepiest attics I can honestly say I have ever entered. Directly across from where we entered was this giant felt portrait of Elvis. Underneath it was all these taper candles that were nearly burnt down to their glass holders. There was a small radio with several stacks of Elvis cassette tapes. A photograph was rested on one of the stacks. It was a woman in her thirties with a cigarette hanging out of her mouth as she pawed at a REALLY portly looking Elvis impersonator.

Ricky caught me staring at the photo intently

"That's who we think might be Scotty's dad," he breathed.

I turned to find the others congregating around this chest.

Ricky motioned for me to follow as he approached it. When Todd opened it, there were stacks of witchcraft and spell books on one side and Salem witch trial and historical documents about Bear Hills on the other. He started ransacking through all the texts when he retrieved this old newspaper that was caked in dust. He handed it over to Janet and immediately she turned white. The article went into extensive detail about a little boy around Charlie's age named David who died in the woods next to where they would be moving in.

"Is this?" She gasped.

"Not where we were today," Ricky assured her.

"If you go a little bit deeper you come to a section called Turtle Rock. That is where he died. NO ONE can go there. There's a whole town ordinance regarding it." He answered.

"But the house," I interrupted.

"That was HIS house?!"

The rest of the boys nodded in unison.

"No one knows what happened to him," Ricky continued.

"Some people think it was an accident. Some people think it was a murder. And everyone else thinks it has to do with the curse of this town." He confided.

Janet looked as if she were about to ask him another question when we heard Scotty barreling back up the stairs.

"Shit," Dimes whispered.

"Scotty's mom must be home."

As Scotty panted his way to the top of the stairs, Ricky and the others ran for his bedroom and propped open his window and started shimming their way down the back of the house.

"Where's our-" I started,

Scotty directed us to the bedroom window. Charlie was waiting in the backyard of the other house holding onto a video game cartridge.

The two of us immediately followed the others out the window when we turned to look for Scotty, he had shut the bedroom door behind us and then the window before locking it. When we made it down to the ground, the boys motioned for us to hop over a fence and make our way into a neighbor's backyard.

"What's going on?" Janet asked everyone.

I immediately grabbed Charlie by the hand and all of us knelt in the bushes trying to peek up every so often to catch a glimpse of this woman. Without missing a beat, there was Scotty's mom exiting her car with a strange guy.

"Where's Scotty?" I asked.

Hesh sighed.

"He doesn't leave the house once his mom gets home," he said.

"There was an incident a few years ago. His mom met

this guy at a bar. When she took him home, they got into some drunken argument and the guy tried to slit her throat. If you ever see or meet her, she has this scar across it. She said it was from a surgery. Scotty witnessed the whole thing, though. The man took off before he realized Scotty was there; he basically left her for dead. So now Scotty sits up in his bedroom the whole time with a shotgun he stole from a hardware store.

You know, just in case." He finished.

Janet was baffled,

"She seems like such a shitty mom, though," she gasped.

"Why would he want to protect her?"

Hesh shrugged.

"Because, that's his mom," Ricky piped in.

"You may not like your parents. In fact, you may even hate them at times. But you don't actually want something bad to happen to them." He asserted.

That was when Janet and I exchanged a look like we were two of the most fucked up people in the whole world.

"Honestly," Janet started,

"I think the three of us would probably be better off."

The other guys looked at her like she was a sociopath.

"I know you don't know us," she continued,

"So, it'd be easy to think we're so fucked up for thinking that way. You know why we are moving here? Our little brother had a psychotic breakdown after our mother convinced him that his imaginary friend killed himself by drinking her bleach. Why? Because her ex-husband was running around town giving out her work and home number to attract perverts and weirdoes to call her night and day to harass her and scare us: one of those

Stockholm syndrome situations. Maybe if she gets back together with him, and we go back to be this happy family and move away from somewhere that we have this reputation, everything will go back to normal." She finished.

That was the only time I ever heard Janet piece together how fucked up our situation really was. She stood out from the shrubbery and made her way back to the street. I immediately followed with Charlie in tow. The others were not far behind.

"It just sucks!" She yelled.

"I already miss my Pine Banks friends. I do not know anyone here. I do not want to live with that guy. I do not know what he's going to do to me and my siblings if we're all under the same roof again. I mean, this is a guy who even tried to murder us in a parking lot. And these are our parents!"

Her voice reached a fever pitch of emotion and indignation.

The boys circled around us as I placed her head down on my shoulder and she wept quietly with my hand firmly wrapped around Charlie's.

He was just so innocent and so oblivious; he just kept looking up at us, then the boys like he was trying to survey the situation. Ricky was the first to approach us.

"You do know someone," he assured her.

"You know us. And clearly, we are not going to judge you. I mean, look at Scotty's situation."

He motioned back toward Scotty's house.

"My parents are religious fanatics," he continued.

"My older brother Jake is being brainwashed by the local pastor because he's gay and our parents keep sending him to this guy to "pray the gay away," or some shit. I mean, look at the rest of these guys."

He motioned at the others.

"Dimes got his name because his parents have been smoking pot with him since he was in the fourth grade. Hesh's mom is constantly threatening to abandon him to escape his abusive alcoholic father and Smitty is allergic to BEES!"

We all started laughing at his comment about Smitty's bee allergy.

"Thanks bro," Smitty smiled.

"Make me sound like the pussy of the group."

Ricky turned to him.

"When was the last time your parents re-filled your Epi-Pen?"

Smitty placed his hands in his pocket and shrugged before looking at the ground.

"Fuck, anytime we try to go out and play ball or just hang out at G.G. Rock, all of us take shifts babysitting him making sure he doesn't accidentally step on a hornet's nest and go all My Girl on us. And Todd? His father is a god damn police detective. He is about the only one out of this whole group is remotely normal.

He hangs out with us because we are the only ones who do not think that he is a fucking NARC because of who his father is. And, his dad is super cool. He is the only good dad on the whole damn block. So, trust me when I say, we get it." He assured us.

In that moment, I don't think Janet felt like she needed to act as tough as she always had before. Like, the whole crazy bitch routine need not apply to our new friends. They'd started walking us back to our new house, when our mom pulled up in our dad's rusted out Hyundai and tried to hurry us along so we could finish packing up what was left at Pine Banks. We all gave our goodbyes; then Janet turned to Ricky as she was getting out in the car,

"Bye Sandlot kid." He smiled

"Bye Haunted House girl."

And we drove off, leaving them behind, standing outside of our brand-new life.

"Who were those boys?" Mom asked.

Janet and I both had these really goofy and embarrassed looks on our faces.

"They were just some boys," I answered from the backseat.

"Ah," Mom answered,

as she stared at me from the rearview mirror.

"I hope they were nice boys," she teased.

"They were really cool," Charlie answered,

still holding the video cartridge Scotty gave to him.

"You liked them, Charlie?" Mom asked,

still staring from the rearview.

Charlie nodded enthusiastically.

"See..." Mom insisted.

"I told you this move wasn't going to be the end of the world. Maybe if we unpack early enough and your father says it'll be okay, we can invite them over to the new place for pizza?"

Charlie appeared more excited about that potential invitation than we did. Even though we had made these fast and awesome new friends, Janet and I were still wrestling with the reality that dad was going to be a permanent fixture in our lives again. Sure, we had lived with the two of our parents since the birthday party, but once we were officially residents of Bear Hills? That is when it would be real and there would be no turning back. Janet and I did not speak a word the rest of that ride about our soon to be old home. She just stared out the passenger side window pensively while I thumbed through the pages of this book Scotty gave me called *Carrie.*

Later that night, the three of us spent our last night in the one bedroom of Dad's bachelor pad while he and mom got drunk and passed out after packing all day. I gave Janet the bed we had previously been sharing and was content to sleep on the floor in a sleeping bag namely so I could read my book with one of Dad's flashlights. Charlie was sound asleep across the room on the other bed, cradling his blankie. Two things that really resonated with me regarding *Carrie* was that it centered around a teenage girl who was an abuse victim. Her mother was this often-vindictive purveyor of religious fear to keep her daughter in line and undoubtedly more ignorant about the world. Because of this, Carrie was the punch line for all her classmates that started torturing her with tampons when she had a nervous breakdown because she did not know what menstruation was.

It is fucked up to say it out loud now, but I could relate. My sister and I did not learn about menstruation or even sex until late elementary school when they started teaching sex education, much to the dismay of our town. Then there was Charlie. Poor Charlie. He was the only one who got "the talk," and a bizarre, half-assed one at best. After Louie tried to get him to touch his penis and allow him to touch Charlie's, our mother immediately freaked out, knowing that her ignorant little baby probably would have let Louie do anything he wanted to him if our

Grandmother wasn't outside to witness and intervene. The night before Easter of 1993, our brother sat in his tub while our mother started explaining how condoms and diaphragms worked.

"Rachel," I heard Janet whisper.

"Rachel, are you awake?"

The room was pitch black, so I pointed my flashlight up to her bed where I saw her leaning into me. I let out the tiniest of yelps, which caused Charlie to stir a little.

"Why are you staring at me?" I hissed.

"Are you scared about tomorrow?" She coyly asked.

"Scared about what?" I asked.

"The move?"

She rested her chin onto her folded hands.

"The move," she started,

"Dad and mom, the dead little boy, all of it."

I tried to reassure her that it was not so bad.

"Those sandlot dudes were pretty cool."

Janet had this little twinkle in her eye just before bringing up Ricky.

"He kind reminds me of a mix between River Phoenix," she compared,

"And Luke Perry."

Janet had been boy crazy for as long as I could remember. You could always tell which half of the bedroom belonged to her, and which one belonged to me, based on the walls. Janet would plaster her side in clippings from *Tiger Beat* magazines of guys she found hot. Me? If I found a page in a book I really liked, I would highlight certain lines and tape them next to my bed.

"Do you like *Carrie* so far?" Janet asked.

This was unusual because Janet NEVER asked me

about any of the books I read. She would always just tease me about having no social skills and being too much of a nerdy stereotype.

"I like it. A LOT." I answered.

"I never thought a book could scare me. you know? Like the way Freddy Krueger scares me."

I think Janet could tell I was about to ramble on and on, so she immediately curtailed the conversation and brought up Scotty.

"Maybe what you're really afraid of," she teased,

"is that little crush you have on the kid who gave it to you."

I wanted to dismiss this claim immediately. Not because I was shy or even embarrassed. I wanted to dismiss it because I just assumed I would know I was a heterosexual the moment a cute boy gave me a book the first time he met me.

Because I did not swoon right away, I knew it had nothing at all to do with him and everything to do with him not having the right parts. I spent that whole summer thinking about sexuality like I never would have before. Everyone got on my case about the hundred or so times I watched Beetlejuice. I was always really scared they would figure out why. It was because I had a big crush on Winona Ryder. Like, the kind of way my sister crushed on those *Tiger Beat* pin-ups.

I could feel it tingling inside of me, kind of. However, Janet was not reputable for being the most understanding person in the world. She was also famous for her loudmouth and constantly repeating people's secrets or extorting them later if they had something she needed. So, I did my best version of the virgin schoolgirl giggle and let

Janet come to her own conclusions about it.

"I KNEW IT!" She exclaimed.

"Yeah," I trailed.

"Too bad he's a sophomore, and I'm still in middle school."

Janet appeared offended by the comment.

"God!" she hissed,

"Don't you know anything, like at all?"

I stared at her blankly.

"Older guys LOVE younger girls." She explained.

"Especially the ones who are still virgins. It like, gets them off for some reason. Well, in the experience I have had with older guys. They are totally into it. We should take Mom up on her offer and try to have them over tomorrow. We can see if Dad will rent *Carrie*. There's no better way to get a guy to make a move on you than putting on a scary movie." She assured me.

"Wait," I spoke.

"They made a movie about this?"

The idea seemed so farfetched and frankly offensive.

"Oh my god," Janet opined.

"That book is like, WAY old. The book and the movie both came out when Mom and Dad were both still in high school." She yawned.

"It was surprisingly good. Scary, but not scary like Freddy Krueger scary. Good night."

I could hear her body turning on the sheets as she rolled over and immediately let out a snore that made the mattress tremor. As I returned to a sleepless night of finishing the abysmal fate of Carrie White, I closed the hardcover to two affirmations.

The first? I did not hate her; she was not an antagonist,

regardless of what she did. The second? She got off easy. When we moved tomorrow, she would not have to fake not being gay.

VI

BEAR HILLS, MASSACHUSETTS
AUGUST 31ST-OCTOBER 29TH-1994

The entire ride back to Bear Hills was excruciating for me. I had to start the seventh grade as Janet Harris' sister. Prior to puberty, she had never taken any remote interest in me, save for the numerous beatings I had sustained at the hands of her short temper when I became insufferable. In fact, I still have the imprint of a Cabbage Patch Doll nose in the back of my head. We got in an argument over who would get to play with it; suffice to say, after having your oldest sibling try to bludgeon you to death with said toy...you simply lose interest.

Suffice to say, I lost my will to fight with her about ANYTHING. That would mean that if I ever found myself around boys (even if I wasn't attracted to boys), I would have to humor the idea that I was a budding heterosexual pre-teen. Fortunately, I fancied myself to own a pretty decent poker face after enduring so many years of incendiary verbal spats with my mother. They almost always ended with the threat of "wait until you father gets home!" I never stopped hating the sound of his or any car pulling into the driveway because of this. However, this was supposed to be the Harris family 2.0.

There would be times following the reunion and

leading to the big move where our mother would pull us girls aside when our father went off to work or to do errands with Charlie and plead for us to behave and even if he did something that upset us to just let it go. While that might be considered profoundly unfair to do to any child, especially ones who spent so much of their young lives enduring unwarranted physical, verbal, and sexual abuse, I think another garage-type incident would kill her before it did us. The car ride wasn't longer than fifteen minutes, but the inundation of wearied memories and nightmarish scenarios started to cause my hands to tremor not too dissimilar from my youngest brother. His developed after an incident involving a gallon of milk.

He had been trying to pour himself a bowl of cereal like a "big boy," and the gallon was simply too heavy for him to lift. Naturally, it plummeted onto the kitchen floor and caused an absolute mess. Our father screamed so loud; Charlie had been seen by his pediatrician to see if our father had caused permanent hearing damage. When the doctor sent him home with "I was brave," stickers and a clean bill of health, everyone ignored how bad Charlie's hearing really was. Unless he was upstairs in our grandparent's apartment, he always ate his cereal dry after that, a habit our mother chocked up to her little baby just being quirky like his mother.

As we turned into the driveway of our new home, I couldn't help but notice Charlie's eyes beginning to twitch. A stark contrast to our sister, who was staring out the passenger side window and lip syncing along to a Mariah Carey cassette in her Walkman. Our father arrived just a few moments after we started taking the smaller boxes out of his trunk and placing them in their respective rooms.

He oversaw the heavier stuff. Moving wasn't something he was completely foreign to as it was also his occupation. Charlie was instructed by our mother to go play in the new backyard, which was the gentler version of our father telling him to, "Stay the hell out of everyone's way."

Naturally, he did as he was told and nonchalantly wandered around the yard in circles. Even though it was a patch of land (unlike what we had at Pine Banks), it would barely be considered an upgrade. Charlie wasn't as fussy as I was, and at my age I really had no business frolicking around in the grass anyway. Well, according to our father, who assigned Janet and I several tasks to aide our mother in, at the very least, making sure the boxes made their way into the correct rooms. After five and a half hours of heavy lifting and essentially playing a literal version of Tetris, this place started to look less like a storage locker and more like a home. We were afforded the luxury of a break as our father took his car to go fetch us all a pizza.

When we were helping our mother clean up the bathroom that was adjacent from the staircase leading up from our basement, Janet immediately started in on how she would decorate HER new room. She wasn't too pleased when our mother cut her off and informed her that once again, the two of us would be bunkmates, as the intention for this room was for Charlie to play and our parents to entertain guests. Without missing a beat, Janet sounded off on one of her many diatribes in which she made sharing a room with me sound like serving a life sentence in Alcatraz. Our mother immediately was on the defensive and began motioning her hands up in down as if she were trying to fan the proverbial flames burning inside her hothead of a daughter.

"Janet," she firmly asserted,

"You NEED to calm down. This is the arrangement for the time being. Your father is going to be exhausted and probably very grouchy when he finishes moving everything in here. I don't need you getting him worked up." She warned. Janet's eyes told the story that we ALL quietly narrated in our heads. A new town, a new home, but it was still going to be the same family. Janet's arms were resting by her legs and her hands began to ball into fists. While I'd like to give her the benefit of the doubt, I'm not actually sure which incensed her more: that fact that we were just going to live the same traumas and humiliations of our parent's shitty relationship somewhere else, or that she wasn't getting her way.

Our mother's attention was then turned to Charlie, who'd managed to step out of her view. As she exited out the door outside of our future "Family room," Janet immediately turned to me with a look that needed no formal introduction.

"Decorate it however you want," I immediately answered.

"Take up all the room you want. Just let me keep my small portion of book pages." I finished.

I turned my back to her and made my way up the stairs. I went into the kitchen to find my book when I spotted my mother introducing herself to a congregation of people from behind the fence.

They must've been other families who lived in the neighborhood. I grabbed *Carrie* and took a seat on the patio steps and decided to people watch for a few moments. The people in this neighborhood seemed much different from our previous neighbors. In Pine Banks, our neighbors consisted of overzealous Jehovah's Witnesses and the morbidly obese. There used to be jokes about Louie's family; they owned this little white Toyota station wagon. Our grandpa used to call it the "clown car"; he could never figure out how so much girth could emerge from such a tiny vehicle. Janet and I simply called it "The Fat mobile". No wonder everyone seemed to hate our fucked up little family.

This neighborhood was different. As I watched our mother awkwardly accept a cheesecake from our new neighbor "Fran", who looked like the last girl from a Lifetime Movie of the Week, we were all improperly introduced

"This is my youngest daughter, Rachel," I overheard her speak.

I simply held up a hand and pretended that I was too busy for anyone. Meanwhile, she spun yarns about Janet, Charlie, and our working-class father who would've been fired from his Pizza delivery job as he'd exceeded the thirty-minute limit. I closed my book and went back inside only to find Janet in our new bathroom desperately ransacking the medicine closet for band-aids. All ten of her fingers looked like they went through a paper shredder. Her blood left tiny little signatures from what was soon to be Charlie's bedroom to the bathroom a few feet away from it.

When our mother came back inside to freeze the cheesecake no one would eat, she found Janet teary eyed and all bloodied. She immediately tended to the wounds and asked how she got them. Janet couldn't lie, as the blood trail led directly into Charlie's new bedroom. When our mother entered, she found dozens of magazine cut-outs of Power Rangers arbitrarily scattered over the walls. In that moment, our mother felt vindicated from the fight they had earlier, and Janet's seemingly subordinate gesture made her realize that she was going to make our 2.0 family work. After the sun went down and our parents were separated by our little brother happily resting in between them, Janet excused both of us to work on our new room.

When our parents obliged this, Janet took me into Charlie's new bedroom: namely, into his closet, where a portrait of the Power Rangers was scotch taped over something that made Janet breathe too heavily. She carefully peeled the cut out from its spot and revealed something that looked like a treasure map that a little kid drew. It read "Dig me up, Charlie" and had X's from one point to another. Janet then removed a bottle of Flintstones vitamins from under her heavy sweatshirt.

"I think they're trying to make Charlie go crazy, on purpose," she cried.

She then unscrewed the top of the bottle and emptied the tiny pills into her hand.

"These aren't vitamins," she sobbed.

"Rachel," she begged.

"I heard Mom talking to our neighbor Fran today. I was still downstairs, but I walked out into the backyard and saw Fran and Mom talking. Fran was begging Mom NOT to live here. Telling her something about this not being somewhere to raise your kids and how no family ever makes it longer than four years without an incident. She won't let her kids NEAR this house. Rachel, what if Mom wants Charlie to go crazy? What if she wants ALL of us to go crazy?" Normally, I wouldn't have humored it...but I saw the map on Charlie's wall."

Janet placed the Power Rangers picture back over it.

"We can't let him get sucked up into this," she pleaded.

"The adults. They're trying to make us go crazy. I just don't know why." She sighed.

I didn't believe her. Because SHE was crazy. A few weeks later...was when I felt bad for not humoring her. Charlie was dead asleep; I didn't hear her creep out of our room and into his. She claimed the sounds of children's voices brought her there. There were bloody handprints ALL over his walls as he slept. I woke up to find her with a paint brush trying to paint over the bloody handprints I couldn't see. I don't know why, but I immediately woke our parents up, who found her right wrist slit open as she turned to them with bloody palms pleading,

"I can't make their handprints go away."

What I didn't see was that she had lacerated her left wrist. We had only lived in Bear Hills a month and it was all starting up again: the conspiracies of my mother trying to corrupt my little brother, Janet's frail mental health, our mother picking up drinking again the second the last box was unpacked. Janet's first year in high school would become tedious for her. The same neighbors who seemed to embrace us with open arms the day we moved in were all congregating outside much like that first day, many of whom were in their bathrobes or pajamas, rubbernecking while Janet was loaded into the back of an ambulance screaming about handprints of dead children appearing on our brother's walls.

"I was just trying to SAVE him!" She shrieked,

while they slammed the doors of the ambulance shut. Our father immediately went into crisis mode and jumped into his Hyundai screaming obscenities at our mother as she tried her best to console me while Charlie was still sleeping in the scene of the crime.

"Watch your brother!" She curtly insisted, before drunkenly shuffling into the passenger seat of our dad's car. They trailed the ambulance as it carried our sister away.

I stood there in our driveway holding myself while our neighbors scrutinized every movement I made. After several minutes of awkward staring, I finally screamed, "GO AWAY!" at them before running back into the house and checking on Charlie. Despite having his oldest sister slash her wrist and paint his walls with her bloody handprints, Charlie was completely undaunted and in a placid slumber. I kissed him on his forehead before crawling into his bed and cuddling up behind him. The tears streamed while I choked on the sobs of my own mental faculties coming into question. I didn't sleep well that night.

The lingering thought on my mind? Who is going to pack his lunch and walk him to school the next morning? Before I knew it, five a.m. flashed on the cable box clock in his room and I managed to slip out unnoticed. I walked through the kitchen and onto the outside patio to see the same grease slick on the concrete where my dad's car should have been. In a fog, I remember rummaging through cabinets to make a peanut butter and jelly sandwich on white bread for my picky little brother.

I made a point to make sure the jelly to peanut butter ratio was right. This was something I learned from Grandpa Dickie, who used to prep Charlie's lunches when we lived in Pine Banks. He would also make a point to provide him with some extra snacks in the event that the Jelly soaked through and made the bread too soggy or the peanut butter took on a different taste after sitting in a plastic lunch bag too long. Something about the condensation. When I say Charlie was picky? He hadn't reached the point in his education to not only say the word condensation, but also say it properly. When I say he was picky? Oh, he'd raise hell with our mom about the condensation that made the peanut butter taste "weird".

Charlie's lunch prep became an art form because of Grandpa Dickie—peanut butter and jelly with a side of Cape Cod potato chips and a superfluous amount of Twix cookie bars. Unfortunately, our parents didn't take into consideration how much of a creature of habit Charlie was and didn't stock up accordingly. I tried to overcompensate with a superfluous amount of Shark Bites and Dunk-a-Roos in the event he hated my sandwich. I remember taking the butter knife and making two smiley faces before I closed the sandwich together. If anyone deserved to be happy, it was Charlie.

He never complained. He never cried. He never whined. I know he really wanted to. Our father would have none of it. Charlie was hiding a lot of physical pain from our parents.

His stomach was as sensitive as his soul. He couldn't keep food down, something our parents thought nothing of. He also HATED the dark. So much evil took place in the dark, which is why I was grateful he didn't see his oldest sister try to kill herself in his room.

He learned how to do laundry because he was too afraid for his dad to find out his fear of the dark was causing excessive bed wetting at seven. I used to go do a load of clothes (yes, our parents taught ALL of us at an early age to be self-sufficient for lack of wanting to take care of us) and find pee-soaked sheets, sopping wet. I just pictured him in the middle of the night in his white briefs and tube socks crying while he tried to do laundry poorly and earnestly. That's a fact I don't ever want him to realize.

Janet and I took care of him more than he realized. We kept his secrets from our father, because while the beatings never happened like our beatings...we knew there were still beatings when he acted like a "wimp" or a "faggot" as our dad would say. I held his blue Power Rangers lunch box in my hands, just staring at it for a while. I couldn't wrap my head around the kind of adult who could use words like "queer" or "retard" to describe a seven-year-old child. My sister and I weren't called nearly as many names growing up as Charlie was; everything our father disliked about us was just beaten out of us. I placed the lunch box on the kitchen table and made my way into the living room to sit on the couch.

I found myself channel surfing for a few minutes before I realized what time it was. If the channels hadn't turned into color blocks with that obnoxious "Beeeeeeeeeeeeeeep" sound, then it was wall to wall infomercials. I curled up on the couch and tried my best to keep my eyes open so I wouldn't oversleep and forget to walk Charlie to school. I can't remember how long I was out; I just remember how I woke up. The sun hadn't come up yet, so the house was still pitch black.

When I opened my eyes, I could see the silhouette of a small child just standing over me. Not thinking twice, I immediately grabbed his little hand and walked him down the hall and into his bedroom. Strangely, the door to Charlie's room was still shut. I found that odd but wasn't awake enough for it to process. I didn't get the door open more than a few inches when I spotted Charlie still sleeping soundly in his bed.

The grip of the child's hand grew stronger as I turned to him and saw two yellow eyes staring up at me. He then let go of me and held up his bloody handprints and began laughing. That was when the door to Charlie's room opened all the way and the walls were completely covered in bloody handprints except for the wall that Charlie's headboard was pressed against. A giant red X appeared with an arrow pointing down at Charlie. The child's laughter became louder and louder and I immediately woke up screaming.

The sunlight was now cutting its way through all the windows in the house. I started to panic when I realized the cable box read 6:30. I stood to my feet and was about to shuffle my feet down the hall to wake up Charlie when I overheard the loud crunching of a ravenous seven-year-old shoveling cereal in his mouth. I turned to find him still in his pajamas at the kitchen table reading a box of Cap'n Crunch with the same diligence as our father reading the paper. "Charlie," I called. He remained transfixed by the cereal box. "CHARLIE!" I yelled again.

"Why were you screaming?"

He nonchalantly asked in between bites of cereal.

"Just a bad dream," I answered.

"When did you wake up?"

He just shrugged and kept eating.

"Well, hurry up. I have to get you ready for school." I explained.

"Where's Mom and Dad?" He asked.

"Where's Janet?"

I didn't know what to tell him. I had so many amazing options to choose from. Did I lead off with, Charlie your big sister tried to off herself in your room while you slept? Or, there's a malevolent spirit in the house that wants to kill all of us?

"They left already," I lied.

"They went out for breakfast before a meeting at Janet's school."

Charlie finally pulled his eyeballs off the cereal box and turned to me with those sad doe eyes.

"Why didn't they invite us?" He sighed.

I helped him off the chair and took his spoon and bowl over to the sink

"Come on," I insisted.

"Get dressed. I'm walking you to school this morning."

I could hear him abruptly stop in the middle of the hallway for some reason.

"Charlie," I called,

"I'm not kidding, you're going to make us late!"

I then turned my attention away from the dishes and made me way down the hallway where Charlie was staring at the hardwood floor.

"Sissy," he asked.

"Why are there blood spots leading into my bedroom?"

I immediately played dumb before trying to change the subject.

"Did you get a nosebleed in the middle of the night? I'll clean it up. Go get dressed!"

When he finally complied, I grabbed one of the cordless phones and tried my best phony mom impression as I called myself out of school. Unfortunately, I was no Cameron from Ferris Bueller's Day Off and just sounded like more nasally version of myself.

Somehow, it managed to do the trick. I looked like a combination of a ragamuffin and a crack head as I walked Charlie to school. Somehow my seven-year-old brother had a better handle on dressing himself than his teenage sister. I had my hands shoved into the pocket of a Chicago Bulls sweatshirt which was three sizes too big for me. I'd thrown my hair into a bun but completely neglected all the fly aways peeking out. I couldn't find my shoes, so I stole a pair of Janet's white Keds and stayed in the sweatpants I wore to bed.

"Where's your backpack?" Charlie asked.

"Oh," I answered, "I'm going to get my stuff when I go back home."

Charlie nodded to himself.

"Aren't you going to be late?" He asked.

I just shrugged and gave him a goofy little smile. The concern for my tardiness never left his face. When we made it ten minutes from our house to the elementary school he went to, I knelt and gave him the biggest hug I could possibly give anyone.

"If you don't see Dad after school," I cautioned.

"Don't get upset; chances are I'm going to be picking you up from school."

He smiled and nodded before freeing himself from my arms and running down the hill, through the playground and into a line with the rest of the kids from his class. When he appeared distracted enough, I decided to walk another five minutes up the street to the public library. I knew if Charlie saw me chances are, he would have worried about me, or God forbid even come after me to ask me about the intention of my whereabouts. He could be sweet like that. Then again, we were all sure he had O.C.D and anything outside of regular routine (even routines that weren't his own) would freak him out.

In the month and a half since we'd moved to Bear Hills, the only two places I ever went were school and home. Before Janet's "episode" she wasted no time exploring our little town and all the guys in it. Frankly, I don't think she ever wanted to go back home. I started noticing that a few years ago when she'd wind up hanging out with kids, I knew she really didn't care for. I used to think her friendships with people were shallow.

Typically, she would surround herself with people who had something she needed: trendy clothes she could borrow, access to parties with a myriad of hot guys or drugs, but more importantly...a reason not to go home. One day after school, I came home to find the phone sitting on the table with a voice coming out of the receiver and Janet sitting on couch with one hand in a bag of chips, and the other wielding the remote.

"Don't touch that!" She snarled.

"It's Patti Young. She's so fucking boring, and the sound of her voice drives me nuts."

I remember standing there baffled and before I could ask why she would hang out with someone she clearly didn't like, she blurted out,

"She lets me borrow her clothes though. Nice clothes. Like, 'mom and dad can't afford' nice."

"So," I started,

"You are friends with her because our parents are poor?"

Nothing made Janet more nuclear than anyone addressing our place in the economic food chain.

"WE'RE NOT POOR!" She screamed.

"OUR PARENTS MAKE REALLY GOOD MONEY! THEY JUST CHOSE TO DRINK ALL OF IT THAN SPEND IT ON US!"

The conversation abruptly ended with her slamming the remote down on the coffee table, pushing me out of her way and disappearing into our bedroom with the bag of chips and portable phone. I then turned my attention to the small television resting on top of our bigger television that broke just a few days after we moved in.

"I'm pretty sure the small T.V. on the broken big T.V. is the official seal for broke suburbanites all over America," I said to myself.

Using people to sustain her constant state of denial about our lives? That was Janet. Me?

"I'm the bookworm," I spoke as I stood by the front doors of the Bear Hills Public Library.

VII

Of all the times to visit the local library for the first time, and it had to be just as it was opening and on a school day. Sometimes it was hard to argue with Janet's logic that I was a bit of an airhead. I just did not want to entertain the thought of sitting all alone in our creepy house; even worse than my people skills was my ability to get myself worked up over nothing. I just did my best not to draw too much attention to myself.

I kept my head down and stared at the scuffs on Janet's white sneakers to avoid any eye contact with the librarians who would undoubtedly note that I was skipping school. For whatever reason at that age, I was convinced that ALL adults were in cahoots when it came to catching kids doing anything they were not supposed to. In my case? Skipping school. What if the librarian called the school? Would they send someone to come collect me?

The worst case? They send my parents after me. I stood in the first row of the adult section, trying to hide inside my sweatshirt while I succumbed to one of the most intense panic attacks I had ever endured. After fifteen minutes of freaking the fuck out, I finally decided to scan the rest of the shelves.

As trivial as its going to sound, the fact that there were no Judy Blume or Shel Silverstein titles to be found made me feel like a grown up. I casually walked by the K's and started thinking about how much I enjoyed *Carrie* and started browsing some of Stephen King's other titles. While I crouched down to get a better look at his other books, I could feel someone's eyes on the back of my neck. I stood up and turned to see a girl my age staring at me. Would the school send a student to get me if one of the librarians tipped them off?

I stared gravely into the girl's grey eyes.

"You're the girl who lives in the haunted house." She whispered.

I was immediately taken by surprise.

"So, the school didn't send you?"

The girl furrowed thin black eyebrows and made a face.

"I mean, Yeah. That's me." I corrected.

The girl held her hand out to me.

I couldn't help but notice the rings on her fingers. A pentagram was on her index followed by a skull, and a mood ring on her subsequent fingers.

"I love your mood ring," I gushed.

"Oh! I'm sorry. I'm distracted."

I shook the girl's hand.

"Nice to meet you Distracted, I'm Tasha." she joked.

I smiled back while Tasha made a voice trying to cue me to say my actual name.

"I mean, I WILL call you distracted until you tell me your real name." Tasha teased.

I hid my face with my hands.

"I'm sorry. I mean I'm Rachel," I finally answered.

Tasha motioned toward the Stephen King books.

"Are you a fan?" she wondered.

"Someone let me borrow a copy of *Carrie*" I answered.

"I REALLY liked that. So, I figured I'd check out some of his other work."

Tasha reached her hand into the shelf and pulled out one of the biggest books she had ever seen. The jacket on the thick hardcover showed what looked like green tendrils reaching out from beneath a manhole for a paper boat. With two big red letters reading simply "IT." Tasha was thumbing through the book with a look of admiration.

"Little kid gangbang scene aside," she joked,

"This is still one of my favorites by King. It took me months to finish, but it's totally worth it if you love to read."

She then handed it to me, and I flipped through the pages.

"*Carrie* was my first non-young adult novel," I admitted.

"I might have to work my way up to this one."

I then placed the book back on the shelf.

"Was that your first horror novel?" Tasha asked.

"My big sister claims that she doesn't like to read," I started,

"But when we were unpacking after moving in, I found a ton of those Fear Street books. I read a couple of those. They were okay."

Tasha reached for my hand and led me around, showing me some of her favorites.

"Are you familiar with the Hellraiser movies?" Tasha excitedly asked.

"Are those the movies with the guy with pins in his face?" I coyly answered.

"Yeah," Tasha assured.

"That's Pinhead. He's a cenobite. He exists in Lemarchand's box. The films were based on this novella written by Clive Barker.

It's this excessively brutal story about this pervert who has run out of ways to get off. The box is supposed to open a gateway to a world of unknown pleasures. My cousin gave me his copy, after I finished *The Amityville Horror*." She finished.

"My sister yelled at me for not knowing what that was. " I said.

Tasha stopped ransacking the shelves and turned to me.

"You've never heard of *The Amityville Horror*?" She groaned.

"Oh my god! How do you live in a haunted house and know nothing about the DeFeo murders? Or what happened when the Lutz family moved in?

It's one of the most famous true stories about haunted houses. I think, like...ever."

I stood with my arms folded, shrugging and trying to hide in my bulky sweatshirt.

"First things first," Tasha announced.

"Let's find you a copy of that. That way, you can tell me if anything like Amityville has happened in your house." She smiled.

While Tasha dragged me by the hand over to the A's, I quietly spoke up about the incident that took place the night before.

"My sister saw bloody handprints," I whispered.

"All over our brother's room. At first my parents and I thought it was the blood on her hands that she kept pressing against them.

Then this little boy who looked like my brother held my hand as I brought him back to bed, only to find my brother was already sound asleep in there. The handprints were all over the walls. And there was this X pointing down at my brother. When we first moved in, my sister found this map addressed to my brother in the closet. She tried to cover it up with one of his Power Rangers posters. She also told me that a bunch of our neighbors kept talking about this blonde boy who was either murdered or died accidentally in the woods next to the house.

Did anything happen at Amityville like that?" I asked.

"Why were your sisters hands all bloody?" Tasha worried.

"Is your little brother okay? Is he hurt?" I shook my head.

"I actually walked him to school before I came here." I answered.

"Is that why you're skipping school today?" Tasha asked.

I nodded.

"My parents," I started,

"They just left the two of us to take Janet to the hospital. She slashed her wrist. I don't know why.

I thought maybe to get attention, then when I saw the handprints, I started to think that maybe she didn't do it on her own." I sighed.

Tasha had a look of sadness come over her as she held my hand tighter and wiped away a single tear from my eye with her thumb.

"I'm taking a mental health day," Tasha admitted.

"My mom tried to kill herself last April. She started drinking a lot after my dad abandoned us. One night she had too much to drink and tried to poison herself in her station wagon. I was the one who found her. The police told me that if I had shown up about five minutes later, she would've died.

I've been staying with my grandparents ever since she was admitted at Bear Hill Memorial's Institution. It's been Hell. My grandparents are nice people, but they're religious fanatics. They think that depression is the tool of the devil. So, my mom grew up in this super oppressive household.

A couple of her friends took me for a night here and there and told me all these stories about how my mom has low self-esteem and how my grandpa would beat her with a belt when she was younger. Back then, they called it "tough love". To me? That's just straight up abuse. She met my dad at some murder bar outside of town called "The Silhouette", like this super dive shit hole where an Elvis impersonator would perform. I guess a lot of the women from around here used to go.

They thought it was REALLY Elvis. I guess fame has a weird tractor beam on lonely and abused women. Anyway, she met my dad and she just ran away with him so she could get away from the abuse and the torment. Come to find out, my dad was even worse than her father was. One night, they were both drunk and he beat her badly.

My mom immediately ran off with me and her friends went back and beat the living shit out of my dad. The next morning when we went back, both he and all his stuff were gone, and I haven't seen him since. What sucks even more about where I live now is that I'm sort of into girls. God, if my grandparents EVER found that out? I'd probably get shipped to one of those gay concentration camps you hear all about. The only reason I even walk around in baby-doll dresses and Mary Janes is because my favorite singer does.

Otherwise I'd probably be head to toe in ALL black. Fishnets, lipstick, the works. Like a S&M female Trent Reznor." She laughed.

She couldn't help but notice the dumbfounded look on my face.

"Do you know him?" She asked.

"Courtney Love? Nirvana?"

I shook my head.

"I know OF Kurt Cobain," I answered.

"Only because of how often they would talk about him on MTV after he died."

"What do you listen to, then?" She demanded.

"Um," I nervously began.

"The only two concerts I went to were New Kids on the Block in Maine. And Downtown Julie Brown made a Club MTV appearance at a mall on the South Shore where Black Box performed." I smiled.

Tasha felt terrible but she couldn't fight the fit of laughter that followed.

"Funny," she answered.

"You don't strike me as a teeny bopper."

I didn't know if I should be flattered or more insulted.

"Music is more my sister's thing," I started.

"When she started getting into grunge music and gangsta rap, she donated all of her old cassette singles and CDs to me. Pretty much everything in there was Club MTV or like, stuff you'd hear on 90210."

Tasha put her hands around her waist and started kicking her foot around while making noises with her mouth as if she was mulling something over.

"Do you like mix-tapes?" she then asked.

I smiled.

"My little brother sometimes makes me tapes. He got a Talk Boy for Christmas. You know that toy from *Home Alone 2*?

Anytime Janet would be mean to me or beat me up, he'd press the microphone of his Talk Boy against our mom's alarm clock radio and record certain songs on the radio he thought I would like. Sometimes he would even talk over them like a real DJ." I smiled.

Tasha pressed her hands against her chest and smiled.

"Your little brother sounds like a sweetie," she gushed.

"He gets bullied a lot," I sighed.

"He has buck teeth and duck feet. So, he pretty much never stood a chance with other kids. To make matters worse, our dad is hard on him. My sister and I both know he does things to him too. We just can't prove it because it's never when anyone is around.

But anytime he goes somewhere alone with our father, he always comes back more messed up. The last time our dad took him out, he came back constantly tugging at or holding his crotch. It usually follows something Charlie says or does that bugs our dad REAL bad. This happened after our dad was taking us to the mall for back to school clothes. Janet was talking about celebrities she thought were cute or hot. Charlie didn't know any better, Hell, I don't even think he knows that Michael Jackson is a man. Then again, who could blame him?

He just wanted to belong in the conversation and randomly blurted out that he thought Michael Jackson was cute. After we got home, our dad insisted that Charlie had to go run an "errand" with him. He's always doing really fucked up shit to our brother, but never like he does to us." I paused.

"What does he do to you and your sister?" Tasha asked.

"He beats the crap out of us a lot." I bluntly answered. "But, it's different with Charlie,

Sometimes I swear we're asking for it. Like something just comes over and we almost want to get him so worked up that he'll throw the first punch at us. We're not a family that hug and kiss. We never say 'I love you' to each other before we leave the house. So, getting hit is almost in some bizarre way like an expression of love. One summer, Janet and I even got competitive about it. We tried to see who could get hit the most and that's how we determined who his favorite daughter was.

She won." I announced.

Tasha just shook her head and folded her arms.

"I know," I answered.

"That's SO fucked up right? I don't even know you and I pretty much just told you that my sister and I are Daddy's girls who were asking for it and that I'm pretty sure my brother is being molested or at the very least humiliated sexually by him. The 90s though, am I right?" I joked.

"I think I have a book for you," Tasha answered.

She brought me over to the P's and immediately reached for Sylvia Plath's *The Bell Jar* Tasha handed me that in addition to Amityville.

"I think you'll relate to this a lot," she insisted.

"I know I did."

As I took the books from her, I noticed some healed gashes up Tasha's arms. The second Tasha realized that I had noticed her scars she immediately tried to hide her arms.

"So," Tasha interrupted, "I think that's all the time I have left for today's book club. I can assume I won't be seeing you hear tomorrow, young lady?" She teased.

I shook my head.

"Provided my father doesn't beat me within an inch of my life tonight," I joked.

"I'll be back at school. I never did ask. What grade are you in?"

Tasha smiled "Eighth, you?"

I sighed.

"Seventh."

Both girls exchanged earnest looks of affection for each other.

"Alright, Haunted House Girl," Tasha teased.

"I expect a full report by the end of the week."

I laughed,

"No problem Ms. Tasha."

As Tasha skipped away, my heart began to flutter. I realized that I was starting to get that same sensation I did for Wynona Ryder in Beetlejuice. This time, there was also something romantic about the feeling.

Unlike Janet, I never thought about sex or even kissing. When I did? I always romanticized it so much in my head that I knew it would never come to fruition like the Disney movie I pictured. I brought my books over to the front desk and began filling out the paperwork for a brand-new library card. When I was finished, I realized that I had at least five or six hours to kill before I had to go back and pick up Charlie. I resolved to stay at the library and try to finish one, if not both of my books.

I opened *The Bell Jar* first. I started it by nervously

checking the clock every five minutes or so. By the time I had finished it, I'd completely forgot what time was, and now it was one o'clock. I had another hour or so before I had to pick up Charlie. The next time I checked the clock, I had five minutes to get to the school. My brother would have a massive freak out if the first face he saw wasn't mine. As I ran down the stairs, I handed *the Bell Jar* to the librarian as a return and took Amityville with me.

I managed to sprint from the library to Charlie's school with just under a minute to spare. When I arrived, I contorted my petite body through the crowd of parents who were all congregating outside the side doors for their respective children to emerge. I was on the shorter side so I had to balance myself on a ledge to make sure Charlie could spot me. At dismissal, all the kids came barreling out the doors eager to jump into the arms of their parent or parents who were waiting to receive them. I started to get sad about the fact that Charlie had never and probably would never get picked up like the other kids did. When the tow-headed blue-eyed little brother made his way out from the doors, he was seemingly one of the last kids out.

I immediately began waving my arms around like a crazy person, not realizing that most of the parents had left and were buckling their kids into their SUVs or station wagons. Charlie looked distraught by the lack of enthusiasm from a parent but was elated to find that his sissy kept her word. He immediately started running for me with his Jurassic Park backpack shimmying behind his tiny body. He embraced me with a tackle to the ground and we laughed for several minutes before cleaning the grass stains off our pants and holding hands as we walked back home.

"Hey!" Charlie started,

"You still don't have your backpack."

There were times when I couldn't stand how precocious my little brother truly was.

"Why don't you have your backpack, Sissy?" He asked.

"And where did you get that book? I want to see."

He ripped the book out of my hands and began studying it as I ran my fingers through his shaggy blonde hair while we walked home together.

"What's an AMY-VILL Horror?" He naively asked.

I reached down for my book and pulled it away.

"What did you learn today?" I asked.

"There's going to be a Halloween dance," he started,

"At the Boys and Girls Club. But I don't know if I want to go or not." he answered.

"Well, why not?" I asked.

"Haven't you made any friends yet?" I inquired.

"A few," he timidly answered.

"But I can't take a boy to a dance sissy."

She understood his point but pressed him regardless.

"Well, why not?" I asked.

"It's okay for boys to go to dances together."

He looked up me almost annoyed that I didn't get what he meant.

"I'm supposed to go with a girl, Sissy," he hissed.

I smiled as we kept walking.

"Are there any girls that you like?" I asked.

He immediately became flush and noticeably quiet at that question.

"There is, isn't there!" I teased.

"Is it that girl across the street? Danielle?" I pressed.

"She's a bubble girl," he immediately answered.

"At least, that's what the other kids in the neighborhood told me."

I was morbidly curious as to what he meant.

"Bubble girl?" I asked him.

"Yeah, Sissy," he answered.

"Her mom doesn't let her out of the house unless it's in their own backyard. And she's not allowed to leave her bedroom unless her mom tells her to on the intercom."

I stopped mid step.

"Did you see this?" I asked.

Charlie nodded.

"When I went over there the other day," he answered.

"It was weird. Her mom called her down to the living room from an intercom. Then she was burning this stuff that smelled like Janet's sock drawer and was waving it all around the living room and me before she sprayed some stuff on the controllers of the Sega Genesis we were about to play. She wouldn't even let me in or let me leave unless I prayed with her. Sissy, I don't know any prayers!" He vented.

"She is cute," he continued.

"And she loves video games, and Power Rangers. But I don't think her mom would let her dance with me. I overheard her mom telling her dad that I was THAT boy from THAT house. They kept staring at me the whole time I was there. I didn't like it, Sissy." He sighed.

I was baffled by all the details of our bizarre neighbors across the street, and while I wanted to learn more, I also didn't want to find out that Janet was telling the truth and that this woman truly believed that evil things happened in the home we were going back to.

"So," I continued.

"Who is the lucky girl that Charlie Harris has such a HUGE crush on?"

Charlie hesitated for several moments before blurting out.

"Destiny."

I tried not to laugh at such an unusual name.

"Destiny? Huh? That's a pretty name." I humored.

"She's an Indian," he continued.

"Her grandfather even took us into his tipi at school. He taught us all about their heritage in Bear Hills. I don't think he liked me, though." He asserted.

"How could NO ONE like YOU, Charlie? You're a cutie!" I assured him.

"He knew that I was new here and asked me where I lived," he rambled.

"When I told him, he began speaking a really strange language and couldn't continue the rest of the tour. Destiny won't talk to me now. She says it has to do with my curse."

I was even more perturbed by all the things coming out of my little brother's mouth. Why are the adults of Bear Hills so fucking demented and hell bent on trying to make a kid feel so unhappy? I thought to myself.

When we made it to our house, our father's car still wasn't in the driveway. I started fishing in my sweatshirt pocket for my keys when the back door swung open revealing our mother angrily calling people she didn't know, trying to figure out the whereabouts of her two children.

"Where the fuck have you been?!" She demanded.

Charlie immediately snuck underneath us and ran for the comfort of his bedroom.

"Your father is AT the school as we speak probably wondering where the fuck his son is!" She continued.

"I just got off the phone with YOUR school," she ranted.

"They said that someone called you out! Did you skip school today?" She gnashed.

I wanted to make sure Charlie was securely in his room before squaring off with our mother.

"Where's Janet?" I hissed.

My mother's eyes became angrier.

"Don't you DARE try to change the subject" she spewed.

I then folded my arms and slammed my library book on the counter.

"NO! You're not doing this to me. WHERE THE FUCK IS JANET?!" I screamed.

My mother started to back down and motion her hands for me to calm down the same way she typically did to Janet.

"NO!" I retorted.

"You left the two of us ALL alone. ALL NIGHT. I had to get up and make his lunch. I had to distract him from noticing drops of Janet's blood all over the floor. Did I get a single phone call from either of you? NO. OUR sister tried to slit her wrists last night, and you couldn't even call me to not only tell me what to do with Charlie but to tell me whether she was alive?

Fuck you. You don't deserve us. And so help me God, if he comes in here like a fucking storm trooper threatening to hurt either of us? I'm throwing you in the middle and he can have a fucking field day with you. I'm done. God help you mom; if ANYONE ever found out how that man really treated his children? You'd be sitting in a prison next to him. Unless you have anything else to say to me about how my sister is doing?

Then you can shut your fucking mouth." I ended.

My mom was completely stoic. I was right. She didn't have a leg to stand on. I grabbed my book and stormed out of the kitchen and into my bedroom where I slammed the door. I wouldn't see my mother again for several hours. I just assumed that in that timeframe she was feeding our dad booze to keep him from raising a hand to someone or screaming at me.

A little after nine o'clock, Mom drunkenly stumbled through the door as I was finishing the last couple of pages of my book.

"Janet is in a facility," she drunkenly slurred.

"We don't know when she'll be back. They're adjusting her meds. She is bi-polar, after all."

She began to wobble and use the door as a crutch.

"So," she stated,

"Now you know. Goodnight."

My mother slumped down the door and hit her head against the frame before crawling back into her bedroom. I wanted to cry, but instead finished my book. A little after eleven, I snuck out of my room and checked in on Charlie who had been sleeping soundly with his blankie.

I then shuffled down the hall and back into the kitchen where I immediately opened the trash can to find a whole thirty pack of beer overflowing out of it. I then noticed Mom's pack of cigarettes just sitting on the counter and grabbed one from the pack and slipped that and the lighter under the sleeve of my pajama top. I then went back to my bedroom where I opened one of the windows and propped a piece of wood under it to keep from shutting itself. With every puff of the cigarette I felt a giant weight being lifted off my shoulders.

Janet would later tell me that the first few nights at Bear Hill Memorial were traumatizing. She even divulged that she narrowly survived a brutal rape attempt from one of the other patients. I went to school the next day hoping to find Tasha skipping through the halls in her baby doll dress and Mary Janes with the same heroic nonchalance she exuded the previous day at the library. Unfortunately, there was no sign of her anywhere. I once again spent my lunch period in the girls' bathroom, re-reading the Amityville Horror and trying to make connections between the Lutz family and ours.

It started to become a trend for me. Each day started with the hope that either Janet would come home, or Tasha would appear in the hallways. Each day ended with the same heartbreak and disappointment. The only regularity in my life was stealing Mom's cigarettes after her and Dad blacked out after a night of heavy drinking and making sure bloody handprints didn't re-appear in Charlie's bedroom. Things seemed relatively normal. That was, until Charlie started digging up the backyard.

When he started? It was because he spotted a tree root that he believed to resemble a fossil much like in his favorite movie *Jurassic Park*. So, he felt compelled to keep digging. Several holes later, he started excavating toys. My brother being the toy fanatic that he was? It encouraged him to keep going. Four toys later, and one Saturday our parents awoke to find half the neighborhood in our backyard digging with Charlie who was convinced he had found a secret toy store buried beneath our yard. That did not bother me or my parents.

My dad wanted to tear Charlie's hide for ruining their backyard, whereas I was more upset that he dug up the bottom of a gravestone right in the middle of it. I did not want to ask my parents how; I knew they'd just lie to my face. They sat on the patio and watched as my brother convinced all the kids that he thought either the bones of a Tyrannosaurs or underground Child World existed where they stood. Naturally, that goaded all the kids to show up with pails and tiny plastic shovels. Seven toys later, our father finally put an end to the archaeological excavation in his backyard.

Charlie never told them what he found. They chocked it up to a wildly imaginative kid who was digging for fools' gold. One day, I went to check on some laundry that was drying on the unfinished side of the basement on a laundry line when I spotted a single shelf where my dad kept all his tools. There were seven different toys displayed like trophies. After I spotted them, I immediately snuck into Charlie's closet where I spotted that map my sister found. Charlie had taken a Crayon to the X's he uncovered. There were only two left.

I shuttered to think what he might find by the time he made it to the final X. While I was in his closet, Charlie spoke to me.

"Those are HIS toys," he ominously revealed.

"Tommy told me that. After we found the Basketball player figurine, he told me that it belonged to the little boy who died here."

I turned to Charlie who was caked in dirt.

"I'm not looking for Dinosaur bones anymore.

I am looking for his. I think he wants me to." He

finished.

"Charlie," I warned,

"I think you should stop, now."

I picked the Power Rangers poster off the floor and taped it over the map and walked out before he could protest. Later that night, our father went ballistic on Charlie for destroying the backyard. Charlie had never been grounded in his life, but the mere threat of it happening from both of our parents ended the excavation for good. Fortunately, Charlie never dwelled over anything for exceptionally long and immediately moved on to ruining our mom's plastic cups by freezing his action figures in them.

I am not quite sure what the end game was here, save for his fascination with seeing things seemingly frozen in time. This hobby also went by the wayside once my mother had Charlie focus on what he wanted to be for Halloween. He became as obsessed with the upcoming holiday as I was becoming with finding Tasha. It had been weeks since we first met at the public library. I even started asking around, but no one seemed to have any idea who I was talking about.

I started to think that I might be going crazy and taken a page out of Charlie's book by inventing an imaginary friend. Then, the second Saturday of October I found myself in the non-fiction section when a familiar stare could be felt on the back of my neck.

"Plug it up! Plug it up!" Tasha chanted.

"From *Carrie*?" She nervously chuckled.

I tried not to be mean but somehow still managed to have a good amount of vitriol slip out when I asked,

"I thought you said you were in eighth grade! I've been

looking for you at school for weeks!"

She laughed like I should feel like an idiot but also like she had been caught in a white lie.

"I am." She divulged.

"But I never said I went to school."

My eyes squinted every time I felt someone was trying to be intentionally evasive.

"I'm home schooled." Tasha answered.

"Remember how I told you that my grandparents were overzealous religious nut jobs? Well, they're also responsible for my education as well.

The problem? They only teach what is in the Bible. There's no science, no poetry or a single philosophy. It's all the rhetoric of pompous white men who have revised that book more times than the text books you read. So, when I can? I rebel. It's just a little fucked up HOW I rebel." She revealed.

"Well, how do you rebel?" I cautiously asked.

"I fuck with their pills a lot," she shrugged.

"My grandpa has early onset dementia. There are days he still thinks he's in the war. My grandma is constantly bringing him to the VFW hall to meet up with his old war buddies. The problem is? Most of them are already dead. So, she drops my grandpa off all alone at this bar frequented by the children of ACTUAL veterans. Not the veterans themselves. Often, they let my grandpa pay their tabs. Sometimes, if he's lucky? They'll ask for a drink when he's of sound mind.

Why does she do this? Because she just wants a break from him. From the voices, the visions and the sights of a hell he can remember easier than our names. I've heard her wake up screaming a couple times when they're sleeping. He keeps this knife in his nightstand drawer, and a couple of times he's held it to her neck thinking that she's an enemy soldier.

Her version of therapy, I guess, is pushing her faith on me. I DO feel bad. Her faith is all she has. Unfortunately, her faith doesn't cater to the likes of me. In fact, most lessons involve how much God hates me because of who I am. One day? I just needed a break. So, I messed with her pills and his. Nothing deadly.

They just slept MUCH later than they should or were WAY less cognizant of what was going on than usual. That's when I started coming here. My uh, "Mental Health Days". I found solace in these books and in ideologies that were way more open minded than what was being pushed on me. I felt shitty about it, and then I met you. Someone who had a family just as, if not more, fucked up than my own." She paused.

I immediately gave her one of the most awkward hugs I had ever given another human being.

"Whaaaaat, are you doing?" Tasha laughed.

"Sorry," I whispered.

"I've never even hugged my mom. But my brother watches A LOT of *Full House* and this always seems to make everything better when they do it." I joked.

Tasha smiled bigger than she probably did most of her life.

"How is the family?" She asked.

I pulled away and walked over to one of the chairs near the elevator and curled up in my oversized hoodie.

"Janet finally came home today," I murmured.

"She's not the same AT ALL. They have her on all these medications and diagnosed her with PTSD, Manic

Depression and she's like..." I trailed.

"Jack Nicholson at the end of *One Flew Over the Cuckoo's Nest*," Tasha interrupted.

I was confused by the reference.

"You know what?" Tasha started.

"We're in dire need of hang outs outside of this library and some much-needed movie nights because this game is getting old."

We did our best to muffle our hysterical laughter.

"Charlie started digging up the backyard," I continued.

"Oh?" Tasha asked.

"Did he FIND anything?"

I quietly nodded as I tried to swallow the giant lump in my throat and bury my fears about my little brother.

"I almost didn't recognize you," I blurted out,

"Without your baby doll dress and Mary Janes. Overalls and Converse? That doesn't seem very Courtney Love of you," I smiled.

"That's another thing," Tasha admitted.

"I don't dress that way because of Courtney Love. Those are my grandmother's old Catholic School clothes from when she was my age. Weirdly enough, everything fit me like a glove. She makes me wear that stuff when she's teaching me. I recently convinced her to let me wear normal clothes when I threatened to wear a bonnet."

Both girls broke out laughing again.

"I was actually thinking of heading to the Boys and Girls Club tonight." She revealed.

"There's supposed to be this Halloween dance. Was thinking it might be fun to try and socialize since I don't really get the chance to, not going to a conventional school." She hinted.

"My little brother is going to that!" I excitedly announced.

"So... you're GOING then?" Tasha wondered. "

My mom volunteered me to take him," I groaned.

"I feel like it's setting him on a pretty bad incestuous track in life. Taking his big sister to a dance." I hissed.

"Can I be his date?" Tasha joked.

I started laughing but saw the look on Tasha's face.

"I'm serious," she earnestly asserted.

"I mean, you're WAY cute. But I think your brother might get a better rep if he shows up with someone who ISN'T related to him." She smiled.

"Alright," I spoke,

"Is it sad to admit that he's WAY cooler than me?" I jested.

"He wants to go as Kurt Cobain."

Tasha held her hand over her head and pretended to swoon.

"A weirdo after my own heart," she joked.

"Should I bring my bonnet?"

I lifted one eyebrow at her.

"Actually, I was kind of hoping you could leave that at home."

The two girls smiled at each other.

"Are you done lying to me?" I earnestly questioned.

Tasha nodded.

"I promise."

She then held her pinky out to me, and I reciprocated. We kissed our hands as we pinky swore to each other.

"But you have to tell ME a TRUTH," she insisted.

"Why are you in the non-fiction witchcraft section?"

I was uneasy.

I then removed a piece of notebook paper from my sweatshirt pocket.

"My brother promised to stop digging up the yard," I started.

"Then I found this."

I handed the paper to Tasha. It was a map of the woods next to the Harris home. One half read G.G. and the next half had a crayon drawing of a turtle on it.

"I tried SO hard to decode his scribbles," I revealed.

"But I don't know where he plans to start digging next." I finished.

"Rachel," Tasha gravely warned.

"THAT is Turtle Rock."

I shrugged.

"Yeah, and?"

Tasha immediately tore the paper in half and tossed it in a waste basket.

"You can't let your brother find Turtle Rock." She asserted.

"Why?" I asked,

"What is Turtle Rock?"

Tasha then brought me down to the basement of the library where the town archives were located. She pulled a heavily leather-bound scrapbook out from one of the cabinets and placed it on a table between us.

"It's time you learn," Tasha began,

"How fucked up this town REALLY is."

My concern for Charlie grew even more profound.

"Back when women were being persecuted for witchcraft," Tasha began,

"Bear Hills had recently been discovered by Christian zealots who were passengers on the Mayflower. The land had previously been occupied by an indigenous tribe of Native Americans. Bear Hills isn't just some cute name they decided to call the town. It's the town's given reservation name. These Puritans mercilessly slaughtered, raped and ostracized the small tribe off the land so they could claim it as their own. The only survivors were the tribe's chief and his only daughter. Her mother had been raped and murdered by band of rogue vigilantes who claimed she was a witch.

The chief was a practitioner, a kind of medicine man. He raised his daughter to succeed him if he might succumb like her mother. There was a rule in the tribe. Only members of the tribe could practice the kind of magic they did. No white man or woman was to ever learn of their abilities." She paused.

She then turned the page to a journal entry from one of the earliest colonizers of Bear Hills.

"She was as caring as she was naive," Tasha continued.

"His daughter, I mean."

“A pregnant Puritan woman was found in the woods not far from where the daughter and father lived. She was hemorrhaging, a sign of an Ectopic pregnancy. The daughter attempted to save the woman's life by utilizing the medicine her father practiced. She was found by other villagers and accused of killing the child with witchcraft. She was taken, raped and beaten. She was also imprisoned and was forced to stand trial before the tribunal of white men. Then? Shit just got fucking weird.

All the expecting women in the town started going through similar issues with their babies. Turns out the earliest precursor to gynecology back then was solely responsible for this. However, the head of medicine back then was one of the most prominent chairs of the town council. Rather than accuse him and risk a political backlash, they chocked it ALL up to witchcraft. To offer an olive branch with the tribe's chief, they would grant amnesty for the daughter if the father cleaned the town and chased out the evil spirits responsible for killing these unborn children.

The chief acquiesced and agreed to the conditions. However, while he was busy attempting to rid the town of evil spirits? His daughter was tried and subsequently hung without his knowledge. When he came for his daughter, the council smugly informed him of his daughter's death and chased him out. His revenge? An unorthodox display of how nefarious the magic he possessed could be if used for ALL the wrong reasons. He manipulated his powers and returned to the town in the form of a child. In a kind of Pied Piper of Hamelin scenario, he came for all the children and led them to their deaths off a cliff known to the tribe as Turtle Rock, somewhere previously utilized for sacred worship. The chief was eventually caught and sentenced to death by burning. His final words before he burned to death? If ANYONE were to cross onto that sacred ground, his spirit would be released into the town once more to collect all the children and unleash a deadly plague on any survivors. Even though the town ordinance states that Turtle Rock is a land never to be trespassed...there have been some who have tested that Chief's powers.

Many cases of stillbirths and suicides proved the curse was real. Then in 1986, the little boy who lived in your house? It's believed that he crossed onto Turtle Rock to elude his mom's attacker. Hence why he perished the way he did." She revealed.

"What about Charlie?" I pleaded.

"How does he fit into ALL of that? I mean, where did you even know to find that book? The bloody handprints? Janet? Charlie finding all of this kid's toys?"

Tasha closed the book and stared in my eyes.

"Maybe its Destiny." She bluntly surmised.

"The little girl my brother has a crush on?" I questioned.

"Wait," Tasha interrupted.

"Your little brother has a crush on a girl named Destiny?" She asked.

I folded up in the chair.

"When we were walking home," I began,

"He talked about this little Native American girl in his grade that he had a crush on. He got really upset, fearing that he made a really bad impression on her because her grandpa didn't seem to like him when he visited their school." I revealed.

"Wait. What was the grandfather's name?" Tasha begged.

"Chief Meacheech." I guessed.

"What tribe did he belong to?" Tasha pressured.

"Charlie isn't good with details." I argued.

"Something about a great turtle. A keeper of formidable darkness." I breathed.

Tasha opened the book back up and flipped to a page where it listed the lineage of Native Americans linked to the Shaman who cursed the town. She took her index finger and directed Rachel's eyes down the bloodline.

"See this?" She asked.

"This is where the bloodline stops in the text. A

progeny of a progeny. Meacheech." She educated.

"Your brother literally has a crush on a girl who is a blood relative to the man who cursed this town." She laughed.

I held my hands over my mouth and sobbed,

"Curse of the Blonde Boy."

Tasha looked at me pointedly

"What?"

I shook my head.

"My sister Janet was ALWAYS jealous of Charlie. In middle school, she wrote a short story for a creative writing class that she called The Curse of the Blonde Boy. Essentially it was about how my brother ruined our family." I sobbed.

Tasha leaned into me and brushed the back of her hand against my cheek.

"NOTHING will happen to Charlie." She assured.

"As long as he NEVER finds Turtle Rock. Which begs to ask, why were you browsing the witchcraft section?" She demanded.

I sat up defiantly

"Because I need to know more about the boy who lived in our house," I curtly answered.

"I think he's trying to get into Charlie's head and lead him to Turtle Rock to dig something up that we won't be able to bury again." I coyly admitted.

"How did you plan on reaching him?" Tasha asked.

"Our first night here," I started.

"We went to this kid Scotty's house. His mom had this Ouija board on her dining room table..." I trailed.

"Stop RIGHT there," Tasha warned.

"Haven't you EVER read the Exorcist? Wait, of

COURSE you haven't." Tasha teased.

"Rachel, you don't want to invite something like that into your life."

I then grabbed Tasha's fingers and held up the one with the pentagram ring.

"Really?" I taunted.

"I DON'T WANT to invite something like that into my life?" I hissed.

Tasha pulled her hand away, almost offended.

"Alright," she argued.

"So, I'm a phony. I wear symbols and outfits I don't understand to get under the skin of my grandparents for potentially not loving their grandchild because of something she can't help. Sue me." She protested.

"What about YOU?" She harassed.

"What about YOU? What are YOU hiding? You know what..."

Tasha stood up and began to walk away when I immediately yanked her back down and held her cheeks with both my hands and planted a kiss on her quivering lips. The aftertaste of cherry lip balm made me lick my bottom lip.

"I'm SO tired of the facade," I cried.

"Maybe its middle child syndrome, or maybe I just can't live another day not saying it out loud."

Tasha wrapped her hands around mine.

"I know," she admitted.

"Sometimes you think that all these things you repress might bottle up inside you and explode..."

Tasha immediately pulled herself away again.

"What?" I cried.

Tasha stood up then pulled me up to my feet.

"I know what you should be for tonight's dance!" She squealed.

After fifteen minutes of walking into the town's square side by side, Tasha snuck her arm through mine and pulled me close so she could rest her head on my shoulder. I felt uneasy at first, but my body soon became overwhelmed with excitement. The kind that should only be reserved for the first love of your life.

"How are you going to make my little brother look super cool to all his little friends?" I joked.

Tasha made an inquisitive face before staring up at me.

"Maybe I won't wear any underwear under my dress?" She joked.

"What could make a guy look cooler than some lesbian, bare-snatch action?" She laughed.

I gave her a look before reminding her,

"You know he's seven, right?"

Tasha pointed to a small secondhand shop.

"There!" She declared.

"This is where we can get my Courtney Love costume, and YOUR super-secret costume." She declared.

We ran inside the store with a mission. I started eyeing anything that resembled something the First Lady of Grunge would wear while Tasha went the more conservative prom dress route. We held our respectable finds up at each other.

"Wedding Dress?" Tasha asked.

"Prom Dress?" I retorted.

"It kind of looks like her dress from the Violet music video," I answered.

Tasha smiled as if the pupil had become the teacher.

"You're not a Club MTV girl anymore!?" She laughed.

"I'll ALWAYS be a Club MTV girl," I retorted.

"Wubba. Wubba. Wubba. But I like Hole. A LOT. What's with the prom dress?" I asked.

"CARRIE!" Tasha sneered.

She then held up a pair of heels and a bottle of fake blood.

"I've worn heels ONCE," I argued.

"And that was at my Confirmation, YEARS ago. I wasn't steady then and I doubt I'll be steady tonight," I assured.

We then made their way down another aisle where I jumped up and down and grabbed a tiara off the rack and placed it on the crown of Tasha's head.

"Perfect!" I assessed.

Tasha approached the counter where they sold the wigs and costume jewelry. Tasha removed a platinum blonde wig from one of the mannequin heads displayed next to a mirror. She bent down to get a look at her jet-black hair tucked underneath the golden locks of an enormous wig. I helped her adjust the tiara, so the locks of the wig didn't get tangled up in it or obscure it. We then went into the two empty dressing rooms to try on our nearly finalized ensembles.

When we emerged, I was doing my best impersonation of Sissy Spacek while Tasha found a chair to mount her leg up on as she began strumming an imaginary guitar and making lewd faces. We left the store with shopping bags and renewed confidence that neither of us had experience prior to eventually meeting the other. Tasha could be abrasive and insubordinate whereas I was more methodical and diplomatic. We were the perfect complement for each other.

We arrived at my home to find Charlie already fashioning one of my long-sleeved flannel shirts over a white t-shirt that still smelled like a fresh permanent marker. I gushed over how adorable my brother looked in the blonde wig and drawn on goatee. I then pulled one side of his flannel over to find CORPORATE DANCES STILL SUCK hand drawn on his white shirt. I turned to Tasha, who was immediately smitten with the young boy who was as adorably innocent as he was charmingly precocious.

"Charlie," I introduced.

"This is Tasha. She's going to be your date tonight."

Tasha and Charlie shook hands, but a look of sadness came over him.

"Sissy," he began,

"Does this mean you're not taking me?"

I wasted no time in reassuring my brother that I wasn't bailing on him.

"Of course, I'm taking you," I laughed.

"We just figured it might make Destiny a little more jealous if you showed up with another girl who WASN'T your sister."

Charlie nodded his head in understanding.

"That's brilliant, Sissy!"

We walked up the patio steps and into the back door of the house through the kitchen.

"Charlie?" I asked.

"Where are Mom and Dad?" Charlie sighed while he sat on the floor, putting a pair of converse sneakers on to complete his outfit.

"Dad found something in Janet's room," he began,

"Something about her not taking the right pills and hiding them in one of my Flintstone vitamins bottles. Him and Mom got in this big argument and next thing I knew, they were gone. I don't know if they were going to find Janet, or if they were going to meet up with the Doucette family like they usually do on Saturdays."

Once both shoes were on his feet, Charlie ran into the bathroom and started mugging in front of the mirror.

"He calls you 'Sissy'?" Tasha mouthed.

"That is the cutest thing ever."

I started to blush.

"So," she continued.

"Your sister really is nuts, huh?"

I put my index finger up to her lips and grabbed Tasha's wrist and ran with her toward the bedroom I shared with Janet. As we passed the bathroom, I spoke to Charlie.

"Charlie, we're going to take a little bit to get ready." I started,

"While you're waiting, why don't you go downstairs and watch T.V.?"

We exchanged smiles and I brought Tasha into the bedroom.

Rachel had stopped long enough to draw Donald's attention from his note taking.

"Rachel?" He waved a hand in front of her glazed eyes. Her face had lost its sarcastic good humor, and what was left was the face of a young girl, haunted and guilt ridden.

"This sounds like a better memory. Why this face?"

The self-deprecating smirk returned. "It was a good memory," she said, "for a while. Until I found out that while I was making a clumsy attempt at pubescent flirting and thought my brother was securely station in front of the TV, he was actually, secretly, sneaking upstairs and marking off the second to last X on the map behind the poster in his closet. He'd found another 'treasure", but this was no toy. Later, we found this skeleton key among his finds, tucked away in the creepy-ass crawlspace beneath the stairs with the rest of the dug up 'treasures' he believed the ghost of David was leading him to. And for fuck's sake, it was in the hollowed out remains of a broken turtle shell..."

Rachel was fidgeting, tapping her index and pointer finger like another cigarette needed to appear between them, now.

"Hey," Donald kept his tone light. "I know this isn't easy. I really appreciate how open you've been. Let's talk about this in the way YOU'RE comfortable with. Why don't you go back to telling me about getting ready? For the dance?"

"I can do that. I'm fine." Rachel was back, tough and amused and a little broken. It was better than haunted. "We, um, we'd gone upstairs to change...

Tasha was meticulously painting the white high heels with the fake blood we'd bought at the thrift store.

"These may take a little bit to dry," she instructed

I was in the bathroom applying the blood on my face and arms while doing my best not to stain the sink or the counter. I knew Mom would throw a shit fit if the bathroom didn't look immaculate. As I placed the shoes on the open windowsill, hoping the cold autumn air would help the blood dry quicker, I noticed a bunch of cigarette butts strategically hidden in the crack. I emerged from the bathroom looking like the telekinetic prom queen herself.

"How do I look?" I shyly wondered.

Tasha smiled,

"Like a girl in dire need of a tampon."

I stuck my tongue out, then packed my sneakers away for after the dance.

“So, what's this about vitamins?" Tasha finally asked.

I peeked out my door to see if Charlie or anyone else would be in earshot of us.

"Janet and I think that our mother has been intentionally giving Janet the wrong pills and our brother pills he doesn't need," I confessed.

"When our parents were separated for a few years, she started giving my brother these pills she kept in a Flintstones container but were actually some kind of drug."

Tasha appeared confused.

"When were your parents separated?"

I was restless,

"They separated at the end of 1991. That summer, our dad tried to murder all of us with his car after a pool party."

Tasha's eyes grew big.

"Holy shit!" She squealed.

"Why would your mom want to get back together with him?" She asked.

I grabbed a cigarette I’d hid in the crack of the window and was now pacing while smoking.

"She gave up smoking and drinking cold turkey," I began.

"She was lonely, she didn't really date...save for this family friend who turned out to be a real fucking weirdo.

I think finally being a responsible parent and adult started to depress her.

Our parents have one of the most toxic relationships you could possibly imagine. When they're together, they just drink and fight, drink and fight, and ultimately Janet, Charlie and I pay the price. Everything must be within walking distance otherwise; we never go out. Unless, of course, you're Janet, who is way more resourceful than I'll ever be. They don't like to mingle with other parents and they sure as fuck don't want anyone to get in the way of their drinking time.

Before you? The only other person or people I hung out with were Charlie or Janet and her friends. I just thought it would be such a waste of time trying to socialize with other kids when I would never be able to do anything with them unless their parents included me. I also have such a crippling fear of bringing anyone over here to meet my parents."

Tasha started giggling.

"Wow," she gushed.

"So, am I like breaking your social hymen?"

"You REALLY do love vaginas, don't you?" Rachel retorted.

Tasha shrugged.

"What can I say? I'm all about the clams; I'm never for the hams."

She then noticed Charlie still dressed as a mini Kurt Cobain in his ripped jeans, converse sneakers and flannel shirt climbing up the stairs. She then turned to Rachel and joked,

"But, for this little guy, I think I'd make an exception."

She then wrapped her arm around him with her

blonde wig and tiara on. I held up a finger, ran for a Polaroid camera and motioned for them to get closer together. Tasha leaned into Charlie and stuck her tongue out toward his cheek while he made a silly face.

After the flash, a piece of photo paper emerged from the camera and I started shaking it.

"When are we leaving, Sissy?" Charlie moped.

"Oh!" Tasha jumped.

"That's my cue!"

She grabbed her wedding dress and ran into the bathroom to change... When the picture developed, I grabbed a black sharpie from the vanity, dated it and wrote "Kurt + Courtney '94" on the bottom white corner.

"Here, Charlie" I said and handed him the photo.

"Keep this somewhere safe. This is a memory and a girl you're going to want to hold onto. Trust me." I smiled.

We waited as Tasha barreled out of the bathroom with a tattered wedding dress with lipstick smeared across her face and began mouthing loud guitar sounds and strumming in the air. Miraculously, her platinum blonde wig and tiara remained intact despite some heavy head banging. In that moment, I felt myself falling in love with this goofy misfit who'd approached me at the library. I turned to see this look and smile on Charlie's face that I had never seen before that moment. Maybe it was excitement? Or happiness?

I couldn't quite tell. Honestly? I didn't care. Even if for just one night, me and Charlie could forget how messed up our little family was and Tasha could feel like a normal teenage girl, that was all that mattered. We three walked out the door and down the driveway onto the street when I abruptly stopped after seeing our dad's Hyundai pull in.

I began to approach it as Charlie and Tasha followed behind. Our father exited the car and slammed the door without speaking a word. He just marched up the steps and into the house where the sound of a beer cracking open permeated from the screen door.

I approached Mom who looked shaken over what was surely another fight over Janet, or maybe all three of us kids. She wiped the tears from her eyes then addressed me.

"Where are you taking your little brother looking that THAT?" She hissed.

"It's the night of the Halloween dance at the club." I mumbled.

"The one you told me I should take him to."

Mom began ransacking her purse frantically before retrieving a cigarette with her trembling hand and awkwardly attempting to light it for a few seconds. When she finally succeeded, she began to calm almost immediately.

"And who are you supposed to be?" She asked.

"Carrie White." I softly spoke.

I felt Tasha right up against me with one hand wrapped around Charlie's.

"Hi!" Tasha opened.

"I'm Tasha; I'm Rachel's friend from school."

Mom turned to me with an emotional but gleeful stare.

"You actually made a friend? That's wonderful!" She doted.

"Let me guess," she playfully spoke.

"Kurt Cobain and Courtney Love!"

Charlie began smiling and nodding.

"Yep!" He laughed.

I turned to Tasha and Charlie.

"You guys go ahead; I'll be right behind you."

Tasha nodded and looked down at Charlie, who was now leading her by the hand away from the house.

"Mom," I started.

Mom motioned for not to say anything.

"Make sure you kids have a good time. It's probably going to be a rough one when you get back." She warned.

Our father emerged from the kitchen with a beer in hand as he leaned over the balcony and stared me and Mom down. I waved at him, but he just quietly took another sip from his beer. I then nodded and walked after Tasha and Charlie. My arms were folded, and tears caused streams of mascara to run down my cheeks, mixing in with the fake blood that hadn't fully dried yet.

When I caught up to them, I was in a headspace but didn't want to create any visible signs of distress.

"Sissy," Charlie addressed.

"What's wrong with your eyes? Were you crying?"

Tasha's look of concern grew even stronger.

"Well, of course, Charlie!" I smiled.

"I have to get into character before we make it to the dance, don't I? Wouldn't you cry, too, if your classmates dumped pig's blood all over you after you spent so much time trying to look beautiful or handsome?"

Charlie nodded.

"I guess I understand."

The club was a fifteen-minute walk from the house. No one said very much during that time. Tasha and Charlie walked hand and hand; I could tell Charlie was nervous, but maybe not about the dance. He kept looking up at Tasha, shocked and moony-eyed. Meanwhile, I was preoccupied with Janet's whereabouts. I also couldn't understand a motive for our mother's actions regarding messing with Janet's medication and the revelation that she had been giving the right pills to Charlie. Then a deranged thought entered my head, but it was far too fucked up to even be remotely conceivable.

As we got closer to the building, the bass from the music inside grew more thunderous and the cacophony of teenage and children's voices made it more difficult to hear anything Tasha or Charlie could be saying. The outside of the building was completely decked out in Halloween decorations. Charlie's excitement appeared to be reaching its zenith as he started pulling Tasha more and more as we made our way toward the front door, which was opened by one of the counselors who was dressed like Lurch. He even waved a feather duster at the three of us as he closed the door behind us.

Inside, black and orange streamers were raining from the ceiling and there wasn't a corner or wall without cut-out of mummies or vampires or spider-webs and decal bloody handprints.

"I didn't make those ones," a voice cut through.

Rachel turned to see Janet, who was dressed in a Mighty Ducks' jersey with black streaks under her eyes, arm in arm with Ricky, who was dressed like Benny from *The Sandlot*. Janet was pointing at the bloody handprints on the wall and whispering in Ricky's ear. He shook his head and made a stern face at her while she laughed maniacally.

Her hospital wristband was still attached to her.

"What happened today?" I begged.

Janet just shook her head at me and kneeled to talk to

Charlie. When I looked at Ricky, he just shrugged and took a sip of punch from a Halloween themed Solo cup. I then felt a tap on my shoulder and turned to find Hesh and Dimes dressed as Kerri Manahan and Natasha Brown (the fellow skater who'd clubbed her). Hesh was wearing a brunette wig and wielding a paper towel roll wrapped in tin foil while Dimes had a blonde wig on and a medical wrap around his ankle.

Every time someone walked by him, he'd just scream out "WHHHHHHHHYYY" with both his hands extended very dramatically. I couldn't help myself; it was probably the best costume there.

"You didn't tell us you were coming," Hesh teased as he went in for a hug.

"And who is your friend? And WHY are HER and CHARLIE'S costumes better than OURS? WHHHYYYYYY?" He joked.

I grabbed Tasha's armed and pulled her over to introduce her to Hesh and Dimes.

"Tasha this is-" The boys both smirked.

"Tasha?" They both asked.

"How do you know the haunted house girls?" They again asked in unison.

Tasha folded her arms and made a diva-like face.

"I think the question is, why DOESN'T everyone know Charlie?"

She then pulled him in front of her and placed her hands on his little shoulders.

"Charlie's our boy!" Hesh announced as he and Dimes both fist bumped the boy, respectively.

"Your grandparents actually let you out?" Dimes asked.

Tasha shrugged and motioned for Charlie to join her over to the refreshments table.

Janet then maneuvered her way in between me and the boys.

"Scotty was looking for you," she grinned.

I rolled my eyes at my sister and sighed.

"Cool." I mouthed.

"I'll make sure to say hi."

Janet became very defensive.

"Why are you being such a bitch?" She scorned.

"He REALLY likes you, Rachel."

I again shrugged.

"He's a cool guy. But so, what if he likes me? I'm not really into that right now." I argued.

"Well, you got to be into something if you think you're going to tag along with us anymore." Janet warned.

"That's alright," I assured her.

"I have my own friend." I smiled.

Janet sneered in Tasha's direction.

"The lesbian? You know she only says that to get attention. “Janet remarked.

"She used to date Scotty until he dumped her sorry ass for being so weird. Is that the kind of girl you want to be associated with?"

I thought what I was feeling was defensive, but really it was more protective over my new friend.

"Beats the hell out of being associated with you." I answered.

I then pushed my sister away and walked over to Tasha and Charlie. I could feel Janet watching as Tasha and I teased with one another and joked with Charlie.

I motioned for us to enter the gymnasium where a

local DJ was playing mostly stuff, you'd hear on Top 40 radio. “Whoomp! (There it is)” echoed throughout the basketball court as Charlie danced around Tasha and me. I did my best to fight off all the insecurities Janet was constantly perpetuating in my head. What if she was right?

What if Tasha was just some socially awkward home school kid who just wanted the attention so she could upset her uptight grandparents? What if I let my guard down and let Tasha in only to be outted as gay myself? While I know I could be painfully naive often, I just couldn't believe that someone would do something that malicious. Tasha didn't seem as vindictive or manipulative as Janet. And what if Tasha was the one for me?

Dad barely had words with me as it was. He was way more focused on Janet. In fact, if the shoe were on the other foot, I would put money on the fact that an attempted suicide made by me would only, God forbid, get the attention of either Charlie or Tigger, the family cat. I even imagined laying in a pool of blood on the kitchen floor as Dad walked over my dead body to get into the refrigerator for another beer. Even though my body was still bobbing and weaving, Tasha could tell that something had upset me enough that I was merely just going through all the motions of fun without experiencing any.

The gymnasium grew more and more crowded as the music went on. My morale had plummeted since my interaction with Janet. Even though Charlie appeared to be having the time of his life, much to Tasha's elation, I know she hated seeing me so indifferent. She then placed Charlie's hand around my wrist.

"Stay with him for two seconds!" She shouted.

Charlie and I both looked puzzled as Tasha sauntered through the sweaty crowd of dancing youth in her heavy wedding gown meanwhile keeping her arms spinning in the air. Charlie looked on as I tried my hardest to keep any eye on Tasha but lost her whereabouts. Charlie tugged at my dress.

"What is it Charlie?" I shouted.

He continued yanking until I knelt on his level, something I had taught him to demand of people all the time. I thought it was rude for anyone to try to have a conversation over his head, metaphorically and literally. I looked down as he just stared up with this little face. I bent down and adjusted his wig.

"What is it, Boo-Boo?" I asked.

Charlie leaned in close to my ear so no one else could hear.

"Are you going to ask her for the last slow dance?"

I was shocked.

I backed away unintentionally, steamrolled over by his powers of observation.

"I mean," he joked,

"she is MY date. But I'd be willing to share her with you. Considering." He smiled.

As Reel 2 Reel's “I Like to Move it” faded out, the DJ addressed the packed auditorium of kids with way more energy for dancing than he probably anticipated.

"I don't know if ya'll met my friend Courtney yet," he bantered as Tasha mugged for everyone.

"But she just made the first request of the night, and she'd like to dedicate it to Carrie White."

I felt myself turn beat red as what felt like the entire auditorium shifted and began staring at me.

"When Courtney Love of all people asks you to play some New Kids on the Block," he continued,

"how could you possibly say no?"

He then spun "Step by Step" to the elation of teenage girls and the groans of teenage boys.

Tasha was impervious to the attention as she marched her way from the stage back down to us.

"Sorry, Hubby," she joked to Charlie.

"Had to help your sister catch her second wind!" She laughed.

"Here," she motioned.

She reached out for my bloody hands and we began swaying back and forth together before Tasha managed to spin me around like a ballerina and maneuvering Charlie right back in between us. I couldn't stop laughing as Tasha mouthed along with the words of the song while doing what she called "washing windows."

Right as "Hey, Yeah, I Wanna Shoop, Baby" echoed from the speakers, Janet approached us with Scotty and Sideshow Todd in tow. The latter were dressed as Bart Simpson and Sideshow Bob, respectively.

"Tasha?!" Todd announced as he leaned in for a bear hug.

"Dude!" She returned.

"Your hair is the greatest thing I've ever seen," she squealed as she started massaging her fingers through it.

"Is your dad still making you work his makeshift haunted house this year?" She asked.

He nodded with a local of stoned mirth.

"Although, since you haven't been around," he started,

"he's made me stand in as Frankenstein's bride. I think that's his way of punishing me for having hair like this."

Tasha held her hand over her mouth as she started laughing hysterically at the notion of this scrawny kid with the wild curly hair in all the bride make-up.

"Whose bride are you tonight in that dress?" He joked.

Charlie immediately stood in front of her.

"NO WAY!" Todd cackled.

"My dude!"

He held his hand down as Charlie slapped his on top of it.

"Hey, my man." He said to Charlie.

"You want to go on a candy haul with me and Scotty?"

Charlie nodded excitedly.

"What about you, grungy mamma?"

He turned to Tasha.

"You want to help your husband sneak a bounty of Butterfingers out of this joint?"

Tasha turned to me, and I knew she immediately picked up on the noticeable tension between Janet and me. She knelt with her back turned to Charlie and enticed him with a piggyback ride out of the gymnasium.

"Talk outside?" Janet asked.

I nodded and we stepped out a side door to the outside basketball courts.

"Look," Janet started.

"I realize that anytime something happens with me, you get stuck picking up all the emotional slack with Mom, Dad and Charlie. Which is why I don't blame you hating me so much. But, the more they focus their drunken wrath on me, the less they'll take out on the two of you." She argued.

I stopped dead in my tracks and let out a groan of ennui.

"THAT'S IT!" I screamed.

"For the first time, I'm actually happy, despite all the bullshit they put us through and that's what's driving you crazy!

That's why you can't stand her! That's why you keep trying to make me doubt myself and her. You can't stand it when people start to think for themselves! Or God forbid, feel something that you haven't told them to feel!"

Janet stood there with her arms folded and nostrils flaring.

"You want to hit me Janet? Go ahead. I'll provide the Cabbage Patch doll THIS time!" I asserted.

Janet was now nose to nose with me.

"Alright, Rachel." Janet acquiesced.

"Run around with your little lesbian girlfriend. Keep stealing Mom's cigarettes. For God's sake, rebel against something. You have every right to. Just keep one thing in mind; this town hated us before we even showed up. To make matters worse, our own parents hated us before we showed up.

Do you know how many feelings, urges and desires I've ignored and jeopardized for the fear of our father trying to take them away from me or punish me for having them in the first place? No matter who you really are, Mom and Dad will never accept you for it. Fact. This is a person who has nothing to lose and only herself to take care of, so there's no consequences for coming out of the closet. Me? I'm already a goner.

All that little boy will have after they finally break me down, is you. And you know what? I've never been prouder of you than I am right now. You're standing up to me. You've been standing up to Mom. You're giving our brother all the opportunities our own parents refuse to, and not only are you realizing how important it is to have a friend...you're learning something about yourself that would kill a normal person.

I know it's unfair, and I wouldn't hate you for breaking under the weight of the responsibility...the same way the two of you were a responsibility I wasn't cut out for. You are all Charlie has. You and I can't expect anyone inside there to understand that. Do you really think that if you make the move and show her that you want her that she's not going to want you to come out of the closet like her? Then what?

Mom keeps replacing my pills with pills that aren't containing my mental illness to the point where I get thrown into a psyche, or God forbid, jail? You come out with your cute little girlfriend there, and you know the first thing Dad will do? You're going to the same pray the gay away camp that Ricky's brother is rotting in. The more of a scene you make and the more attention you bring to yourself? The more attention is being brought to our parents, two reclusive alcoholics who would never break their endless cycle of inebriation and apathy if they didn't have bills to pay.

I don't care if you don't like Scotty. Obviously, you won't if you're not straight. But he likes you. It's a cover, Rachel. When you grow up like us? You start developing A LOT of those. Who is going to talk Charlie through this if they get what they want? Who is going to save that poor kid from the person who is going to grow up unable to save himself if he doesn't have one of us to walk him through it? It's your life Rachel. Do what you want with it.

We're already going home to a shit show tonight. Do

you want to add a homophobic beat down in addition to what Dad's probably already planning once we walk through that door? I know you don't want to hurt her, but she's not family. Survive now. Live when you get out of here." Janet cautioned.

She turned her back to me and walked back inside of the club.

I stood in silence and watched as a group of teenage boys and the object of her affection treat Charlie like a prince. Maybe Tasha will understand. That gesture though? The song request and trying to get Rachel out of her head...that has never happened before and probably never will again. Immediately, she started entertaining thoughts of how she could make up to Tasha one of the shittiest things she'd have to do to keep the cover Janet told her about.

As the night carried on, the two finalists in the costume contest were Hesh and Dimes for their hilarious take on poor sportsmanship and Charlie and Tasha for Kurt and Courtney. While it truly was a difficult decision, in the end? You couldn't ignore the cute seven-year-old and his much older girlfriend. They won a gift certificate to a local pizzeria and would get to choose the song that closed out the night. Tasha told Charlie that she would take the blame if he wanted to pick one of his favorite slow songs in the hopes that he'd get to dance with his little crush Destiny.

The funny thing? After almost two hours of being at this dance, and not once did he even attempt to approach that girl or make a move. He never left Tasha's side. It started to worry me that maybe her brother didn't understand that not only was he too young for her, but he was also the wrong gender. By the final hour, all the kids were back in the gymnasium as the music started to wind down to the pivotal last dance. The DJ addressed the crowd once more, announcing the end of the annual Boys and Girls Club Halloween dance with the song picked by the costume contest winners.

Charlie walked on stage and dedicated All 4 One's "I Swear," to the runners up Kerri Mannigan and Natasha Brown. The audience immediately broke out into laughter as Hesh and Dimes embraced each other as their respective rivals, and with Hesh's arms on Dimes' shoulders and Dimes' hands on Hesh's waist, they began swaying just before the initial "I Swear," filled the room to light bouncing off a disco ball at the center of the room. I knew what I had to do and started looking for Scotty.

When Charlie finally tracked me down, my waist had Scotty's arms wrapped around it, and I could see the hurt in Charlie's eyes. He'd planned this for me. Me and Tasha. And I'd ruined it.

I watched him survey the gym and catch a glimpse of both Tasha, who was sitting on the bleachers with the defeated wallflowers, and his little crush Destiny, her hair in braided pigtails, wearing traditional native garb from the tribal dress on her body right down to the handmade moccasins on her feet.

She was all alone. Waiting for someone to dance with her.

Tasha who was now holding her blonde wig in her hands. She dropped it on the floor and removed her long jet-black hair from its ponytail and massaged it with her fingers. And then I had to look away, as Charlie approached her with his hand extended to her. Later, when I could finally ask him about it, he told me what he'd said.

"Will you dance with me?" He asked.

Tasha smiled at him.

"What about your crush?"

Charlie smiled.

"I'm looking at her." He confidently answered.

VIII
BEAR HILLS, MASSACHUSETTS
APRIL 8TH, 1995-SEPTEMBER 30TH, 1995-

Following my inability to come out of the proverbial closet at that fateful Halloween dance, the tension between me and Tasha was palpable. However, Tasha's newfound affinity for my little brother afforded me another chance at redemption. As 1994 ended, I knew I would have to make up for humiliating Tasha and taking Janet's advice to repress who I truly was to keep the peace at home from our tyrant of a father. On New Year's Eve, we had been invited to a party at Scotty's house, since New Year's fell on a Saturday and his mother had left that previous Thursday to indulge herself during a weekend-long bender. Naturally, he threw such an event at the behest of the other boys as Scotty himself never trusted that a house full of kids wouldn't destroy his home.

However, we knew the possibility of cultivating a more desirable social reputation was something Scotty couldn't pass up on. It was the first night in YEARS that Charlie was the only Harris child left at home, as we'd had convinced our parents we were attending a sleep over at a mutual girlfriend's house. While Scotty's mother was vigilant of how much alcohol was available to her, Bobby (his older brother) had been sneaking booze liter by liter into a stash in the cluttered basement for years. It was enough to knock a few of the Sandlot dudes on their asses while giving me enough of a buzz that at the stroke of midnight, I kissed my soon to be girlfriend in front of everyone.

The moment was met with plenty of fanfare with the exception of Janet and Scotty, one of which felt betrayed out of an understanding to keep each one's respective cover while the other I knew had been working up the courage all night to kiss me himself. I didn't want to hurt him, but making up with Tasha was most important to me, After the kiss, I had whispered in Tasha's ear,

"1995 is going to be OUR year."

Janet would later quote that back to me as "Famous last words." For the most part? 1995 was a pretty exciting year. Charlie was still riding a newfound wave of popularity with his male peers for not only bringing an older girl to a dance, but one who had an affinity for other girls. It certainly captured their prepubescent imagination, enough to warrant some new friends for Charlie.

One of which was a stout kid named Terrence who was known for his affinity for cheese balls during sleepovers with Charlie, and for his Jim Carrey impressions. While Janct and I teased Terrence behind his back, we both agreed that the most natural fit for a scared of his own shadow milquetoast like Charlie was a kid who was as gregarious as he was insufferable at times with how remarkably desperate he was for the limelight. This was also how we first got our hands on a Ouija board. After Charlie had confided in us that he had played with the spiritual conduit, I immediately proposed to Tasha and Janet that we could possibly trick Terrence into bringing it over so we could finally contact the little boy who was allegedly buried in our home.

One year after the death of a pop culture icon, Terrence arrived at the Harris home with Ouija board and backpack in tow. After the two boys passed out on the pullout sofa in the living room following a night of binging on cheese balls and ice cream floats, Janet snuck upstairs and retrieved the board out from underneath the coffee table where Terrence was keeping his stuff. She returned to the family room where Tasha was lighting a handful of Mom's red taper Christmas candles which I'd retrieved from the unfinished side. The Sandlot dudes were there simply out of the sheer amusement of watching three girls attempt a line of communication with the dead.

"Milton Bradley really doesn't know what kind of goldmine they have on their hands," Ricky joked.

"I mean, screw Monopoly...who wants to own Boardwalk when I can talk to the dead?"

We three girls scoffed at him while his friends snickered.

"I'm not moving it; YOU'RE moving it," Sideshow Todd quipped, imitating the commercial.

"Will I be tall enough to slam dunk?" Dimes heckled back.

"You're never going to reach anyone with THAT thing," Scotty sneered.

Janet, Tasha, and I all looked up at him.

"My mom's board?" He continued.

"I've SEEN it. It's like...actual black magic."

"I've seen your mom's Ouija board," I answered.

"It looks JUST like this one." Scotty shook his head.

"No," he assured her.

"It's not.

She purchased it from this pagoda an old witch in Salem owned. It's the real deal. When she'd have enough vodkas in her, I'd ask her about it: where it came from, why she owned it. Cue all the laughter...she was trying to reach Elvis."

Scotty paused while a few of his friends and even the girls snickered under their breath.

"You might have heard of the seller." He teased.

"Her name is Angelica Bruno."

Tasha immediately stood up and looked at him.

"You never told me that's who your mom bought that creepy Ouija board from." She asserted.

"Who is Angelica Bruno?" I politely asked.

"She's this weird old lady," Ricky answered.

"She kind of resembles, well, you know Patty and Selma from the Simpsons? Like them, only like, an actual witch who walks with a cane. She has a television show on public access. If you turn on the Spanish channel after, like, eleven, she has this show that tapes some of her live appearances at like those Shriners' Auditoriums and stuff. You never heard about her on the local news?" He asked.

Janet and I shook our heads.

Ricky stood off the couch and over to the table where the girls and I were kneeling with the Ouija board. He sat in between me and Janet and reached for my wrists. I hesitated at first, until he made a face at me. He then massaged my wrists with his thumbs and worked his way up to my open palms and pressed his index and middle fingers down on them. He then rolled his eyes into the back of his head and began speaking in tongues.

"So," he answered.

"That is kind of her gimmick. She is famous for it.

She's like the Bob Ross of spiritual con-artists. Until this ONE time." He teased.

"What?" Janet begged.

"Two towns over," Ricky answered, "in Cypress, Massachusetts. There was that guy who nearly murdered ALL these people in a town movie theater. This police officer named Leonard had been watching her program one night with his girlfriend and she had the palms of this creepy looking guy in her hands. She started divulging this plan he'd had to murder all these people at the movie theater the next night in ridiculous detail. Rather than get offended or threaten to sue the station, he just sat there with this sick grin across his face. All these people who were planning to go see Batman freaked out after word of mouth got across town.

This guy Leonard, who I think was like a rookie at the time or something, managed to get a search warrant. When he showed up at the guy's apartment, the guy just opened fire on him and the back-up he showed up with. Leonard killed this guy; I think they said it was a point-blank shot in the head. When they started ransacking the apartment, they found a copy of the Anarchist's cookbook along with ALL these homemade bombs and shit like that. And the guns? Holy shit, the arsenal this dude had in his little bachelor pad was ridiculous. It REALLY fucked this woman up. She went from being a street vendor in Salem, to this like sky's the limit television personality and just walked away and vanished after that.

It was some seriously spooky shit." Ricky laughed.

"I don't really believe in all that stuff," Scotty inserted.

"But I've seen the kinds of people who show up in my living room late at night with my mom. And it's nothing to laugh at." He finished.

Tasha hit me,

"Did I not tell you that Angelica Bruno was the way to go?" She hissed.

I then looked at Scotty with a devious stare.

"What?" Scotty answered.

"NO!" He protested.

"NO! We are NOT bringing that thing into THIS fucking house. NO GOD DAMN WAY."

We stood to our feet while Ricky and the others did the same.

The rest of the kids waited outside as Scotty quietly shut the door to his porch behind him. The Ouija board was secured snugly under his right arm. He looked as though he was going to change his mind once he reached the bottom step; we watched the hesitation come over him and then abruptly disappear a multiple number of times.

"What are you waiting for, man?" Ricky whispered.

Scotty shot him a dirty look then continued toward the rest of the group.

"You REALLY are scared of that thing, huh?" I asked.

Scotty shook his head.

"It's not the board that scares me," he answered.

"It's how you're going to use it."

All the kids once again filed into the Harris family basement, this time replacing Terrence's toy Ouija board for an authentic one. As soon as they laid it flat on the coffee table, the wooded planchette began moving, seemingly all by itself, arbitrarily over the board.

"It doesn't like it here," Scotty claimed.

Everyone turned to him in disbelief.

"Someone please tell me that's battery operated,"

Dimes cried.

Tasha shook her head and reached for my hands.

"Place them on the planchette," she instructed.

The trepidation in my eyes told the story, but I nodded and placed the tips of my index and middle fingers on the planchette which caused it to stop moving.

"I once saw one of these at the mall," Hesh started.

"Instead of letters and numbers, it was all sex positions. Why couldn't we have played that one?" He joked.

"The girl to guy ratio isn't exactly in your favor buddy." Sideshow Todd teased.

"We're trying to reach the spirit of the boy who used to live here," I began.

"Can you help us contact him?"

The planchette motioned my hands over to the far left of the board, hovering over the word YES.

"Please let us know when he gets here," I pleaded.

The planchette started moving again, this time hovering over the letters H-E-R-E.

"You're here?" I called.

The planchette once again hovered over the word YES.

"What is your name?"

My hands began to scan over the letters D-A-V-I-D.

"Hi, David." I greeted.

"Can you help us?" I asked.

"My little brother-"

before I could finish, the board spelt out Charlie's name.

"That's right," I answered.

"His name is Charlie."

I turned to see everyone else's mouths wide open,

except for Tasha, who had her hands over her mouth. I then turned my attention back to the board.

"How do you know my brother's name?" I asked it.

The board then spelled out the word "DANGER."

Obviously, I was concerned.

"Is Charlie in danger, David?" I asked.

The planchette returned to YES.

Before I could ask another question, the board spelled out the word K-E-Y.

"What key?" Tasha asked.

I removed my fingers from the planchette for a few seconds while it spelled CRAWLSPACE out by itself.

"Where is there a crawlspace?" Ricky asked.

Janet and I exchanged a glance when we heard a clang against the concrete floor outside the playroom doors. We ran out of the room to investigate the sound and saw the padlock locking the boiler room shut was halfway across the room. Janet bent down to retrieve it and held it up to me. Then the door seemingly open by itself.

"Wait here," I instructed, and crept down the stairs as the others trickled from the playroom to see what was going on.

"Why is the room padlocked shut?" I heard Ricky ask.

I looked back to see Janet approaching the doorway to keep an eye on me and prevent the cat from getting out.

"Our parents, for one reason or another," she started, "refuse to fix our cat. So, when she's in heat, our father locks her down here, so she doesn't annoy our mother."

I listened to her as I descended and then as I made my way around in the darkness. “What’s taking so long?" Janet whispered through the crack in the door.

I was as quiet as I could be and cringed with every

clang and clatter I made as I ransacked through Dad's tools. Finally, my hands wrapped around a familiar shape and with the flick of my thumb, the darkness gave way.

"Found a flashlight!" I announced.

Ricky and Janet had remained by the doorway while Hesh, Dimes, and Sideshow Todd raided the refrigerator near the bathroom door. We'd left Tasha and Scotty vigilant over the board in case it continued spelling out instructions to the kids.

The awkward tension between them seemed to have dampened by the time the rest of us started to file into the room. I knew Tasha felt bad about 'stealing' me from him, especially since they'd known each other for so long. Later, she told me she just asked about his mom, and that he insisted there were no hard feelings since he and I hadn't been a serious couple. I trailed in behind everyone holding up the key that Charlie had hid with all the toys he'd dug up. When I knelt in front of the board, the planchette immediately pointed to YES on the board.

"What does it open?" I asked.

The board spelled out E-V-I-L.

"Evil?" I repeated.

But when I leaned in to ask a follow up question, the planchette started to move down the board where it read GOODBYE.

"You have to say goodbye back," Scotty insisted.

"Goodbye, David!" I hastily shouted.

"God forbid she's not courteous to a spirit, Scotty." Hesh joked.

"It's a rule," Scotty insisted.

"Anytime you're dealing with the spiritual world, there are these unspoken laws, if you will."

Janet and I studied the key for a while.

"What did it mean by evil?" Janet asked.

"It's part of the town lore," Tasha revealed.

"According to who you talk to, or what you've read, it's believed that once the Shaman was burned to death, his ashes were locked away and buried somewhere in Turtle Rock." She finished.

I turned to Janet

"That must be the final X!" I exclaimed.

"Charlie must know where the body is buried."

Janet nodded to herself,

"And if he unlocks the box," she began,

"he'll release the curse on the whole town."

I held the key so tightly it bit into my hand.

"We need to bury this somewhere Charlie will never think to look for it." I insisted.

"What is your brother deathly afraid of?" Ricky asked.

Janet and I looked at each other as if we both had the same great idea. Five minutes later, we all found ourselves outside a neighbors' home just a few blocks down the road.

"Your brother is scared of Mr. Lerner?"

I approached the chain link fence and hoisted my body over it and onto the other side.

"No," I answered.

"But he's deathly afraid of his Rottweiler."

I became conscious of every footstep as I navigated a foreign backyard in the dark.

I stopped when I spotted a stake in the ground with a chain attached to it. I used my hands to furiously dig as big of a hole as I could possibly make. Once I felt I had pulled up enough of the ground, I dropped the key in and covered the hole back with dirt. As I stood to my feet and turned, I spotted Mr. Lerner's dog watching me from behind a door where he'd punched the screen out, undoubtedly chasing a trespasser. I didn't think in that moment, just ran as fast as I could and sprinted back over the fence. When I landed on the butt of my denim jeans, I was face to face with the dog, who was salivating behind the fence with a profoundly ravenous appetite.

Tasha and Janet helped me back to my feet while the boys looked on,

"So..." Ricky started.

"Are we done with this?" He begged.

Tasha and Janet motioned their heads at me.

"Mom and Dad are going out next Saturday," I spoke to Janet.

"They're going out for drinks and line dancing with friends," I continued.

"What's your point?" Janet demanded,

"Anyone want to do a séance?" I asked.

Scotty appeared mortified.

"Do you have any idea how much bad energy you're bringing into your house?" He demanded.

"I can't believe I'm saying this," Ricky chimed in.

"But I think I agree with Scotty on this one. Maybe you should just leave well enough alone; I'm quite sure we have enough bullshit going on in our lives already." He insisted.

I turned to Janet, knowing that if anyone could galvanize interest in talking to David again, it would be her.

"Tasha," Janet started,

"Rachel has NEVER seen *The Amityville Horror*. Why don't you bring it over next Saturday? After we put Charlie to bed, we can watch horror movies and do a séance. If the little blonde boy talks to us? Cool. If not? Maybe we can figure out if Elvis really is Scotty's dad." She joked.

Scotty turned to Ricky and pleaded him with his eyes not to go along with it. Unfortunately, Ricky was the leader of their little group and NEVER said no to Janet.

"So, it'll be like a supernatural version of the Maury Povich show?" Ricky joked.

"I'm in!"

He turned to the others who were all nodding.

Scotty sulked quietly and when the following Saturday came, all the boys arrived on their bikes after seven while we girls set up the basement. We decided to move one of the dining tables from the unfinished side across from the staircase and next to the refrigerator. This way no one would have to kneel uncomfortably like last time.

Tasha came down the stairs to inform me and Janet that Charlie was sleeping soundly and to bring three candles down to place on the table. She noticed a stack of witchcraft books I'd taken out of the library.

"I see you've been studying," she teased.

I shot her a playful dirty look.

"I know enough," I replied.

The boys knocked on the basement door before entering the now dark and candle lit room.

"This isn't spooky at all," Sideshow Todd announced.

"It has to resemble the spirit world," Tasha answered.

"I'm with you," he joked.

"So, the spirit world has a washer and dryer? Nifty. Does the spirit world have any Mountain Dew?"

We rolled our eyes and Janet removed a can from the refrigerator and handed it to him.

"Hopefully, the afterlife is as accommodating as you ladies are." He joked as he cracked his soda open and pulled out a chair.

Ricky maneuvered around the table and gave Janet a peck on her cheek while she straightened the table runner. She did her best to hide her smile from the others, but I couldn't help but notice the lines in the corners of her mouth. My prognostication regarding 1995 seemed to still hold up. Scotty appeared out of the bathroom,

"Um, guys?" He started.

"I realize Rachel is the brains behind this operation, but I couldn't help but notice that none of the mirrors, windows or even the television screen are covered up."

Everyone stared at him like he was a leper.

"What's your point?" Janet snickered.

"Anytime my mom hosts these things," he continued.

"She typically goes on and on about making sure that there are zero possibilities for any spirit to enter our world through anything that could be manipulated into a gateway." He asserted.

"On a scale from one to banging the leaders of dad bands," Hesh joked,

"How cocked was your mom when she said this?"

The rest of the boys snickered.

"He's right," Tasha agreed.

"We don't know what we're possibly going to be dealing with. We don't want any room for error. Janet, Ricky...cover EVERYTHING. Rachel, make sure that door is locked so Charlie can't get down here." she instructed.

I immediately ran up the stairs and turned the lock on the basement door handle. I assumed Ricky and Janet, who were still flirting and kissing, would be able to follow instructions. After fifteen minutes of me studying my book, and the two lovebirds finishing their tasks, everyone sat around the table.

"We have to hold hands," I instructed.

"And we CAN NOT, for any reason, break the chain."

The rest of the kids complied while I shut my book and placed it in the middle of the table where the candles were burning. I fidgeted in my chair for a few moments before taking a deep breath.

"According to the book, all of us are supposed to chant the following in unison," I began,

"Spirits of the past, move among us. Be guided by this world and visit upon us." I dictated.

I looked around the circle at the rest of the kids, who seemed sheepish by the request. I made a face and began the chant again, this time with Tasha joining and eventually everyone else. We kept repeating it for several more minutes until the room was dead silent.

"Um," Todd awkwardly spoke.

"I don't think it's working." He joked.

Hesh started moving around like a snake and moving his head from side to side before speaking what was believed to be Klingon.

"What was that Klingon for?" Dimes laughed.

He repeated speaking this way before curling his lip and moving his hips and doing an Elvis impersonation with his voice.

"Uh, I'm asking the spirits if uh. Elvis is that young man's daddy-o." He laughed.

Scotty sighed, while the girls and I rolled our eyes and the boys snickered. Once again, the room was silent.

"Well," Ricky spoke.

"I think this was a bust."

Suddenly the candles blew themselves out and "You ain't nothing but a hound dog crying all the time..." filled the pitch-black room.

"OH, FUCK YOU GUYS!" Scotty yelled.

Janet began screaming bloody murder while crying,

"Where is that coming from?"

Suddenly all of them dropped their hands and began running in all different directions looking for a light switch.

Hesh and Dimes ran up the stairs and barreled through the door in a three stooges' fashion, Dimes taking down Hesh as he tripped over his heels. Scotty ran for the playroom with Ricky to find the lights, while Tasha tried to console Janet.

"WE WEREN'T SUPPOSED TO BREAK THE CIRCLE!" I shrieked.

In the other room, apparently Scotty and Ricky were both on all fours brushing their hands against the walls in search of a light switch. As Scotty massaged the gritty paint with his fingertips, he immediately felt a tight grip around his wrist which caused him to scream. Ricky eventually found the light switch, but the lights didn't appear no matter how many times he flipped the switch up and down.

Tasha immediately grabbed one of the candles out of the holder and began fidgeting with the lighter before getting some glow. We three girls then ran for the playroom where we noticed a naked man restraining Scotty to the floor. Scotty tried violently to release himself from the man's restraint, but he was completely overpowered. The man then opened his mouth so wide that it felt inhuman, his lips stretched from Scotty's nostrils down to his chin. Scotty was now trying to make sounds through his groaning and choking while his legs kicked violently. Tasha noticed a wooden baseball bat leaned outside the doors leading to the playroom and handed the candle off to me. She grabbed it and started swinging wildly before catching the man in temple of his head and knocking him off Scotty.

Ricky immediately tackled him to the ground and began violently pounding on the man's flesh before finally, he overpowered him and tossed him across the room. He then whimpered and slurped as he held his hands up in terror, the dim candlelight revealed a truly repugnant looking character.

"J-J-Janet," I stuttered.

"I think that's one of the Pipe People."

Janet immediately threw herself at the man and started digging her fake nails into the back of his ears, breaking skin and drawing a pool of blood. The man wrestled her off him before crawling out the basement door and galloping away like a dog. I ran over and knelt over my sister while Tasha and Ricky tended to Scotty, who was covered in what appeared to be an odious smelling bodily fluid. Hesh and Dimes came barreling through the basement door from the outside.

"Who or what the fuck was that?" They both yelped.

As the kids were tending to one another, I noticed that the sheet Janet had placed over the television wasn't secured properly. Before I could get up to adjust it, I noticed the silhouette that resembled a human figure crawling through it. It turned and stared at me with red eyes just before jumping up and disappearing through the ceiling. With my mouth agape and sweat pouring down my forehead, I just kept my eyes on the television, unable to make a sound or even move a muscle.

This is one of the parts I'm unsure about. All I know is what Charlie told me. I guess in the meanwhile, upstairs, the door to Charlie's room swung open seemingly on its own. The brass knob caught the corner of the wooden door frame, which woke Charlie out of a sound sleep. As he rubbed the exhaustion from his eyes, the silhouette of a person stood quietly at the foot of his bed. Charlie was about to scream when the shadowy figure revealed two red eyes which seemed to inflict a kind of paralysis on him. The man then held his fingers in the air and maneuvered them like he was playing a flute. The covers lifted from Charlie's body and he levitated from just a few feet above his bed and landed on the ground with his feet firm on the hardwood floor.

The man was still moving his fingers like he was playing a flute as Charlie in a catatonic state, followed behind him obediently. Unbeknownst to the rest of the children, Charlie had left the house and was being led down the street to Mr. Lerner's house. The shadowy figure gestured toward the fence as the chain broke free and the gate swung open. Charlie, still catatonic, walked over to where Rachel had buried the key and started digging his tiny fingers into the dirt before retrieving it. The shadowy figure backed away from the gate and was leading Charlie back down the street with Mr. Lerner's dog in pursuit. He was in a trance and the memories are hazy, but he remembers stopping in the street and turning to face the beast.

Meanwhile, back at the house, Tasha was in the

unfinished side with Ricky, searching for the electrical breakers. Tasha was right next to him with a lighter to help him navigate the box, and he started playing with every switch he saw until all the lights came back on. When they came back into the playroom, Janet was hysterical, staring down at the blood caked under her fake fingernails and down her fingers. I helped Scotty to his feet and rushed him into the bathroom where I attempted to wash all the thick, black fluid off his face. We were completely unaware that Charlie was now following behind the shadowy figure into the woods, going up to G.G. Rock. He thinks that the shadowy figure stopped and pointed even deeper into the woods and seemingly disappeared.

Charlie kept walking until he reached a rock with a turtle painted on it. Hundreds of crucifixes dangled from the branches of trees while there were signs planted everywhere reading DANGER! NO TRESPASSING! He finally reached a point where there was a chest resting on the edge of the cliff overlooking the pond below. He pulled the key from the pocket of his pajama pants and placed it into the lock. He then backed away from the box in which the key seemed to turn itself, unlocking it. A heavy wind passed through Charlie and pulled the box open, blowing a cloud of heavy ashes into the air along with the shape of a monster that extended its arms in the air and snarled at Charlie before being carried along with the wind.

Back at the house and in a moment of clarity, I realized that no one had checked on Charlie after the incident. I rubbed Scotty's back as he continued puking all the contents of his stomach into the toilet before I ran up the stairs as fast as I could. The door to the basement was already opened, which concerned me. I tripped and fell, crashing face first onto the hardwood floor upstairs. Despite having possibly knocked several teeth out and bleeding profusely, I crawled toward Charlie's door. I reached my hand up and turned the knob to find him sleeping soundly, completely unaware of the events that took place just a few moments earlier. I shut the door and rested against it, laughing to myself with a mouthful of coppery blood before sobbing and holding my head in my two hands.

Months would go by before anyone talked about the incident again. It wasn't until a Fourth of July cook out later that year that my Mom revealed something that troubled me deeply. Aunt Nicole was asking why our parents never come up to Maine to spend the weekend, to get away from the kids and have time to themselves. Her mother answered simply,

"Last time we even stepped out for a NIGHT," she started,

"We came home the next morning to find Rachel with broken teeth, Janet hysterical and Charlie filthy."

When Nicole asked what she meant by filthy, Dianne explained that Charlie must have gone to bed still covered in dirt. It was under his fingernails, on his face and even on the soles of his feet."

I even remember hearing stories about Lerner's dog being found with a broken neck outside of the fence the day after the storied séance. A lot of the other neighbors chocked it up to a hit and run, but this newfound evidence with Charlie, I couldn't help but think the worst possible case scenario. I then started thinking about how Charlie was now being given vitamins again, while Janet's mental health declined intensely. So much that Ricky broke up with her a few weeks after and we stopped seeing any of the guys around the house. The only constant was Tasha, who in her own subtle way would try to get me to talk about the events that unfolded that night.

After the barbeque, I went back into the house and sat on the couch in the living room, staring blankly at the television that wasn't on. After I sat in the serenity of silence for several minutes, my attention was immediately turned to Dad's police scanner resting on the mantle over the fireplace. The knobs were turning on their own, trying to find a specific channel; that's when I heard a dispatcher sending first responders to Scotty's address. As I listened in horror, Janet ran inside and pleaded with me to come back out as Ricky and the others had shown up to the cookout on their bikes. When I followed my sister down the stairs of the patio to the gate of our driveway, Ricky was hysterical while the other boys were trying to hide their tears.

"What happened?!" I cried.

Ricky composed himself long enough to blurt out,

"It's Scotty."

When we arrived on the scene, the cops were already putting up orange sawhorses to keep oncoming traffic from getting in. There were three news vans already parked outside of Scotty's house. I watched with disdain as the talking heads were prepping their hair and make-up to get camera ready. Tasha recognized one of the officers who was standing with his back to the house and his arms folded; it was the same officer who came to her house the night her mom tried to kill herself. She sheepishly approached him, expecting him to bark commands at her and eventually shoo her away.

As she walked toward him, he immediately looked at her and smiled.

"Hey, little darling." He greeted.

"You're not with the press, are you?" He joked.

She shook her head and tried to fight through the tears to ask him what was happening. The officer knelt on one knee and wiped the tears from her cheeks.

"Do you know the family who lives here?"

She nodded while streams of saline moistened her quivering bottom lip. He nodded solemnly and rubbed her shoulders to comfort her. He then leaned in and whispered in her ear. While the other kids were corroborating, I couldn't take her eyes off the scene. The officer stood back to his feet and pulled a card from his breast pocket and started scribbling something on the back of it.

He hugged her once more before handing off the card and sent her back to us. Ricky pushed past us and ran up to her.

"What did he say?"

Tasha placed the card in the pocket of her cut-off denim shorts and shrugged.

"He wasn't the first on the scene," she answered.

"He's just here to make sure the press doesn't cause any commotion."

Ricky gave her a suspicious look.

"Then what the hell did he write on that business card!" He demanded.

Tasha started to walk away when Ricky grabbed her arm and twisted her around.

"WHAT DID HE SAY!?" He screamed.

Tasha then pulled the card from her pocket and threw

it at Ricky before storming off.

Ricky bent down and unfolded the card. It read "Your life matters," and underneath was presumably the young officer's phone number. We watched Ricky chase after Tasha and grabbed her arm again. When she turned to face Ricky, she immediately threw a punch that Ricky dodged, and then wrapped his arms around her in an awkward hug. Tasha began sobbing. She told me later that as she leaned into Ricky's ear, she told him,

"He's one of the cops that specializes in family crisis cases," she cried.

Ricky then stared into her eyes as she started to mouth,

"I think he's gone."

Tasha and he just embraced one another.

We went from concerned to despondent when we witnessed EMTs exiting the home with someone under a white sheet on top of a gurney. The officer noticed the horror on our faces but couldn't console us as he started pushing all of the news crews away.

"No," Janet cried.

Everyone held hands much like we did the night of the séance, only this time we were all standing side by side instead of in a circle. Later on, that evening, we were all at G.G. Rock, still in disbelief over what we'd witnessed. The benefit and the curse of a small town is that gossip travels fast.

"Suicide," Todd spoke.

"It doesn't make sense."

The rest of us were quietly sobbing as Todd continued repeating that train of thought over and over.

"Yes, it does," I asserted.

The others were disturbed by my announcement.

"We have to get into that house," I pleaded.

The others scoffed

"Rachel," Ricky stood up.

"Look...I love you and your sister a lot. But I'm sorry, I'm not humoring any more of your haunted house girl babble bullshit. My best friend is fucking dead. He's just a kid. And he's dead." He cried.

"You want to know if there were handprints." Janet announced.

She turned to me as I sobbed and nodded at her quietly with my arms folded around my body, trying to console myself.

Hesh turned to us,

"Handprints?" He asked.

Ricky then shook his head violently.

"No," he muttered.

"NO! Janet you told me that YOU put those handprints on your brother's wall!" He screamed.

Janet then turned to me with a look of sadness on her face which caught Tasha's attention.

"The second time I saw Rachel," Tasha answered,

"She told me that when she went into her brother's room, she saw handprints too."

Janet stood up in front of me,

"AND YOU DIDN'T SAY ANYTHING?!" She aggressively asked.

Sideshow Todd and Hesh ran in between us.

Dimes doing his best Bill Murray version of Hunter S. Thompson's voice bluntly yelled out,

"WILL SOMEONE PLEASE TELL ME ABOUT THESE FUCKING HANDPRINTS?!"

Ricky couldn't help but laugh as the others seemed to smile and calm down. Janet still had her eyes staring through mine, however.

"What did you see?" Dimes interrupted.

Janet turned to Dimes, who looked uncharacteristically horrified by everything. She then sat back down on the rock and divulged the details of the night she tried to kill herself.

"The day we moved in," she started.

"All of these parents started talking to ours. Saying all this creepy shit about the house and the town. I went in what was soon to be my brother's room to move all my shit in there. I didn't want to live in the same room with HER again. When I went into the closet, I saw this writing on the wall; it was addressed to my brother and it looked like a map. Every single toy he dug out of our yard was found on one of the X's on the map. I tried to cover it up. I used to sneak into his room every night to make sure he didn't find it. One night when I went in there, something happened." She paused.

"What?" Tasha insisted.

Janet took a deep breath.

"When I pushed open his door, I could hear little kids crying and talking to me. One by one, these tiny bloody handprints started appearing all over his walls. As they covered every inch of paint, I turned to see my little brother sleeping under a giant X with an arrow pointing down at him. I looked down and I had a razor blade in my hand. A voice kept badgering me to DO IT ALREADY, LET US GO! They wanted me to slash his throat. Instead? I cut my wrists." She cried.

"I saw that too," I whimpered.

"The next morning, I went into the room and I saw their handprints and the X over his head. What if Scotty went home and saw something similar?" I begged.

"WE HAVE TO GET INTO THAT HOUSE!" I screamed.

The others looked amongst each other quietly, looking for an unspoken unanimous decision or an excuse to be depressed. The faces all pointed at Ricky who sighed before nodding in approval. The kids then rode their bikes back to Scotty's house, which was blocked off with police tape.

"What do we do if his mom is still inside?" Hesh wondered.

Dimes looked at Sideshow Todd who simply answered,

"Then we blame it on Elvis and ask her to read us Bible passages. Just get your ass in there already."

One by one we all circled around the house to the back yard where we dumped our bikes on the ground and scaled the side of the house leading to the window into Scotty's bedroom. When we all made it up to the roof outside of the window, Ricky, knowing that Scotty never locked it, jimmied it up as quietly as he could as each of us rolled into a pitch-black bedroom, terrified to make a sound.

"Did anyone think to bring a flashlight?" Dimes whispered.

Everyone turned to me. I removed a tiny black search light from my purse as we began scanning the walls or anything for handprints.

"Well," Todd spoke.

"I guess this theory is a bust."

The door to Scotty's room immediately swung open as his mother in her nightgown shuffled in with a bottle of vodka in one hand and a pistol in the other. She swung the arm with the vodka up and emptied the contents of the liquor down her throat until the bottle was empty, then swung the other hand wielding the gun up to the left temple of her head. The kids were doing their best not to scream or even breath when she reached for the light switch revealing all of them surrounded by a gurney with a white sheet in the middle of the room.

"Oh good," his mother drunkenly slurred,

"You're all here." She pulled the trigger and splashed blood all over the walls, the kids and the white sheet.

As her body slumped to the ground, Janet began shrieking while Tasha and I did our best to place our hands over her mouth. The boys noticed the blood that splattered them began trickling off their bodies and crawling up the walls of the bedroom. The blood started spelling out something in cursive on the off-white walls.

"YOU'RE ALL GOING TO DIE!"

The period under the exclamation was a child's handprint. The kids all recoiled in fear as the white sheet sat up and began laughing manically. One bloodied hand tugged and soiled the white cloth as it tossed it to the floor revealing a cadaverous Scotty.

"Am I still a joke to you?" He ominously chuckled.

The kids shook their heads vehemently and gasped.

"Your nightmares are just beginning," he laughed, gurgling on his own blood and violently slamming his head against the gurney before turning and staring right into my eyes.

"Your secret is going to ruin you," he growled before puking black vomit all over her.

"At what point," Todd screamed.

"Do we decide to leave? His mom killing herself. Dead best friend talking to us? Or the black vomit?"

The rest of us looked at one another in disbelief.

"BAIL, YOU FUCKING IDIOTS. BAIL!"

We immediately began rolling out the window without caution and letting our bodies fall to the ground hard. After we caught our breath from having the wind knocked out of us, we all jumped on our bikes and sped away from the scene of another horrific incident.

Scotty's mother was buried in a plot right next to his plot a couple of weeks later. We had decided at that point that perhaps we should all go our respective, separate ways to subdue what we had unleashed after our séance. I couldn't subdue my curiosity unfortunately, and at the behest of Tasha, we wound up at the library nearly every day after I got out of school to research where Veronica Bruno currently resided. After weeks of searching, Tasha had tracked her down to a nursing home two towns over. Knowing that we couldn't trust any adults to help us in our search, I saved any lunch money my parents gave me and stashed it away for a couple of weeks so Tasha, myself and Charlie could afford what would be an expensive cab ride to finally meet with the enigmatic medium.

On a Saturday in September, we arrived at the Glendale Rehabilitation and Nursing Center in North Glendale, Massachusetts. After convincing the woman at the front desk that we were long lost grandchildren, we secured our visitor passes and rode an elevator to the second floor where they kept all the dementia patients. When we approached Ms. Bruno's room, she was luckily the only occupant. When we sheepishly got to the open door, Ms. Bruno was nonchalantly reading a People magazine with Macaulay Culkin on the cover next to the headline "Brawl in the Family."

"Come in," a raspy, chain-smoking voice called to us.

"Before I'm incontinent." She joked.

Tasha and I shoved Charlie in first, who appeared horrified by the wizened witch. She immediately sat up and reached for her cane and motioned for him to come closer. He reluctantly complied but wasn't at ease until she reached over to a dish next to her and handed him a peppermint candy. We followed not long after and sat on her bed while she sat in a rocking chair.

"Boy, one thing I hadn't anticipated," she laughed,

"Was the god damn Internet. I should've seen that coming." She then reached for a pouch on her bedside table and appeared to be shuffling a deck of cards.

"I'm intentionally avoiding the obvious," She answered.

"I know you want me to hold your brother's hands, Rachel. But I already know...you aren't going to like what I tell you." She insisted.

"Can I get you girls anything?" She asked.

"Candy, muffins or a shot of whiskey?"

We both declined by shaking our heads.

"Alright," she coughed,

"Then I guess I can't stall any longer."

She reached for my hand and then flipped it over and scanned from my palm down to my wrist. She grazed her thumb over the wrist for a while,

"Destiny," she spoke.

"Destiny for you won't be a mistake. Reverence for this little gentleman sitting next to me," she vaguely answered.

Victoria sighed as she brushed the hair out of my eyes,

"But Destiny will emerge from tragedy for you, dear." She lamented.

She then turned her attention to Tasha, who was noticeably intimidated in the presence of a woman she had heard so many stories about her whole life. Victoria motioned for Tasha to reach out her hands to her. Tasha initially turned down the offer, but I turned to her and just nodded toward Victoria. Tasha very timidly handed Victoria her hands, which Victoria received with tremendous care and made a point to be as gentle as she could.

As this old woman's thumbs scanned the palms of her hands, I saw Tasha's face tighten in a surge of emotion...

"Sweetheart," Victoria began,

"You harbor too much pain for such a young woman. Most of which is borrowed.

As any good daughter would, your concern is reserved for your mother. It's going to take a long-time love, but you and your mother will be reunited. Unfortunately, the bond you two share will always be through the commonality of tragedy. And yes, you will be free. Free from prejudice, self-loathing and eventually fear. It will come at a price, but ultimately it will be worth it. To love openly, freely and without hesitation. That will be the key to your emancipation my sweet girl." She softly assured her.

"What about me?" Charlie interrupted.

Victoria turned her head to see a smiling little boy reading her People magazine. Victoria released her hands from Tasha's and turned to find Charlie with his palms waiting for a reading.

Victoria approached his palms with visible trepidation,

and as the tips of her fingers grazed his hands, she looked up to see the blue missing in his eyes. They were grey, almost foggy. We watched her struggle as the palms of his hands revealed ancient markings in the form of festering blisters. He pulled her in, and the old woman began to howl as Charlie's nose started bleeding profusely and Victoria's eyes matched the grey nothingness of Charlie's. We watched on in horror as Charlie's hands tightly wrapped themselves around Victoria's wrists and the woman fell into what appeared to be a deep hypnotic state. This lasted just a few minutes until Charlie released her, and Victoria fell back into her chair dizzy and exhausted.

Charlie stood in a catatonic state for several minutes before coming to and immediately asking,

"Can you read my palms?"

Tasha climbed off the bed and reached for several tissues to clean Charlie up. She led him into the bathroom and closed the door behind them while I tended to Victoria.

"Ms. Bruno!" I screamed.

"Are you okay?"

The old woman leaned into hug me and wrapped her wizened hands around mine. She then raised her head and pulled my ear toward her mouth and began whispering to me. Five minutes later, Tasha and Charlie emerged from the bathroom as I kissed Victoria on her brow and positioned her comfortably in her chair.

"We should go," I insisted.

Tasha nodded and we scurried out of the old woman's room and ran out of the building and back into the cab that I had instructed to wait in the parking lot.

"Sissy," Charlie cried,

"Is Ms. Bruno going to be okay?"

I tearfully nodded at him.

"She's a very old woman," I lied.

"She's very tired today. She just needs her rest. She told me that we can come back to visit her some other time and she will read your palms."

I then held my brother close and kissed the crown of his head while he smiled and nodded at me. When we made it back to Bear Hills, I sent Charlie back into the house and paid the cab fare while Tasha lingered in the driveway with her arms folded. I was vigilant of the backyard and motioned for us to sit over by the side of the house where we could talk privately. Once we were crouched down, Tasha was in a frenzy of curiosity.

"What the fuck happened back there?" She asked.

I then divulged everything Victoria had divulged to me. How Charlie, in a somnambulistic state, had exited the home and dug up the key and killed Mr. Lerner's dog the night of the séance. How he'd crossed over into Turtle Rock and unlocked the box and released the spirit of the dead Shaman onto the town.

"Oh, fuck..." Tasha cried.

I shook my head and began to cry.

"This is all my fault," I sobbed.

"I did this to him."

I curled into a ball and rocked back and forth as Tasha tried to calm me down. When Tasha held my face in her hands, mascara running down both cheeks, I revealed,

"It chose him."

Tasha was confused,

"What do you mean?" She cried,

"What chose him?"

"The house," I explained.

"The town, the curse, even the evil. It chose Charlie. Victoria said it had something to do with something that happened to him before we got here. Something he buried at our old house."

That's when I had a revelation.

"What is it?" Tasha asked.

"I remember," I gasped.

"Before we moved here. I remember hearing Charlie leave our house in the middle of the night. He went outside and dug a grave for the imaginary friend my mom convinced my brother had killed himself. It was after she called our father to come pick him up a few days before we were supposed to spend the weekend with him. Charlie was with our father all alone that whole night. When he came home?

He was just off; he was different. He wasn't the same imaginative, naive and sweet little Boo-Boo that everyone loved. He was defensive. Scared. Always tense and anxious. The next day, I dug up the hole he made through this broken fence in our grandparents' backyard. I dug up his blankie. I couldn't believe that he wanted to get rid of something that was so special to him. He always told me that he wanted to have a son someday so Blankie could be his best friend and so the two of them could stay best friends forever. I have it in our room. I was just horrified as to what happened that would make him willingly get rid of it." I finished.

"He isn't pure," Tasha spoke.

"What?" I demanded.

"Whatever happened the night he and your father were alone...it took something from him." She answered.

"Something so sacred and important to him that he felt

wounded, if not completely ruined. He had to give up his youth, his childish things, his..."

I stared right into Tasha's eyes,

"His innocence." I blurted out.

Tasha nodded.

"His innocence," Tasha continued,

"That's what protected him. Now, he's fair game. But, something about him must be toothsome to whatever needed him to open that box. Something in this house still needs him." She spoke.

I sat and tried to wrack my brain for an explanation.

"Something about home," I murmured.

"What?" Tasha questioned.

"Victoria," I continued,

"Kept saying something about Charlie being able to understand the concept of home. Having this ability and this power to vanquish evil if he can find 'home'."

Tasha was puzzled but offered,

"Do you think maybe," she started.

"The little boy that died here needs Charlie to help him crossover?"

I shook my head.

"This felt bigger," I asserted.

"Like, it isn't just one person. Like he's supposed to lead numerous bodies to this conceptual idea of 'home'."

We ruminated on this for hours. As night fell, I was in my pajamas watching my brother sleep soundly, completely unaware of what had really occurred between him and the medium. I awoke the next morning to our parents talking loudly in the kitchen.

As I shuffled my socked feet across the slippery hardwood floors that our mom must've recently cleaned and onto the cold linoleum of the kitchen, I rubbed the crust out of my eyes to recognize an image on the television screen.

"Victoria Bruno passed away last night," a TV anchor announced.

"At the age of 73, one of New England's most revered and recognized mediums has died."

I stood in front of the television, frozen.

"While the cause of death won't officially be released until the completion of an autopsy, the staff at her nursing home cited total cardiac and respiratory failure as the reason." The anchor continued.

"The Massachusetts native was certainly the subject of folk lore around the greater New England area, but it was her short-lived television career that made her world renowned-"

The anchor was cut off when Mom pointed a remote at the television and shut it off.

"Good!" Dad curtly dismissed.

"She was a fucking fruit, anyway."

He then turned back to the stove where he was scrambling eggs for breakfast.

"Rachel, sweetie," Mom spoke.

"Tasha is on the phone."

I turned my attention to my parents, who I could tell were annoyed by my behavior, and nodded.

"I'll get it in my room." I insisted.

I saw them exchanged suspicious looks with each other as I hurried back into my room to take Tasha's call. While I quietly spoke into the phone to figure out when Tasha and I could meet up, our mom was finally losing it. I don't know what she was doing upstairs. She was probably trying to eavesdrop of my phone call with Tasha. All I know is that the whole house heard her scream from Charlie's room. I burst out of my room just as Dad barreled past, screaming for me to turn my ass back around and shut my door. And terrified, I did, slamming it behind me. But then I heard the ever-familiar sound of a struggle, and I knew that whatever had kept my dad's hands to himself since we'd moved to Bear Hills had expired. When I finally got up the courage to leave my room, I found only my mom, flat on her back and face busted in, surrounded by the bottles of pills and Flintstone vitamins we knew she'd been screwing with. And I hated her for it, but still, seeing her like that brought back all the awful memories our parents had sworn we were leaving behind when we moved. I was horrified, frozen until my battered mother finally sat up, and I felt Charlie appear and disappear just as quickly from my side in the doorway. I registered the telltale sound of his feet against the steps,

"I'm going to Tasha's," I didn't stop to see if Mom had even heard me, just flung myself back into my room, out the window, and down to the lowest part of the roof. I swung down, and then ran around to the front where I knew I'd find Charlie, and dragged him with me.

Mom would tell the story later, on days where she rode the fine line between intoxicated and shit faced. She'd say that she was in the hall when she heard the door to Charlie's began to squeak as it swung open.

As she stared through the crack, she couldn't help but notice handprints all over his walls similar to the night Janet had attempted suicide. Her eyes widened as she tiptoed into Charlie's bedroom. As she scanned from one side of the room to the other, she stopped at the wall Charlie's bed was pushed against. She then looked up and saw an arrow that pointed to an X with "Die Charlie Die" written just above it. In a frightened gasp, she inadvertently fell back with all her body weight against the door, slamming it shut. As she turned to reach for the knob, the closet door swung open revealing the map we knew Janet had attempted to hide with that Power Rangers poster.

Mom would say that she reached behind her for the knob as a child's laughter permeated from inside the closet. Reaching her free arm out to open the closet door completely, she pivoted her body away from the door, barely registering the autonomous click of the lock as she walked into the closet to berate her son for scaring her. As she peaked in, an odious smell stung at her nostrils and she let down her guard to turn her head and sneeze, but as she turned back, the cadaver of a young child collapsed on top of her, sending her crashing onto the hardwood floor. As she shrieked and attempted to wrestle the body off her, its eyes opened, and a hand covered her mouth.

"No more vitamins mommy," it pleaded.

"They're hurting me. You're hurting me. Why do you want to hurt me?" It begged.

She shook her head and let out several muffled screams as the cadaver pulled out a Flintstones vitamin bottle with its free hand and dumped the contents on her chest. She kept trying to fight her way out from under the body as the pills began to crack open one by one with maggots seemingly hatching out of them. As she shook her head violently, the cadaver removed its hand from her mouth and squeezed her cheeks and lips together as it grabbed a handful of maggots.

"Mommy," it spoke.

"Now you can hurt, like I hurt."

He then shoved a handful of maggots into her mouth as she gagged and finally screeched so loud that her husband came crashing violently through the door knocking it from its hinges only to find his wife swatting and wrestling with nothing. He'd knelt over her and retrieved the vitamin bottle with several pills scattered next to her.

"So, you were hiding her meds," he ominously answered.

When Mom came to, she realized that the whole ordeal was seemingly just a violent hallucination. Bewildered, she looked up at her menacing husband.

"I should have burned down that house when I had the chance," he threatened.

He stood to his feet and looked over his shoulder to see if any of the children were present. He then turned back to his wife and pulled her by the collar of her shirt and sucker punched her so hard the scene was eerily reminiscent of the last time he broke her nose.

"Death do we part," he threatened.

"That might be sooner than later."

We sat on a swing set in the backyard of Tasha's grandparents' house as Tasha climbed out a second-floor window before shimmying down the side of the home and approaching us. She immediately hugged and rubbed the head of Charlie before embracing me as I hopped off the swing and lunged at her, seeking comfort.

"It's starting again," I cried into Tasha's ear.

Tasha raised my head to eye level,

"What is?" She begged.

Leaving Charlie to pump his legs on the swing set, Tasha and I found a spot on the corner of Tasha's street to talk and smoke cigarettes.

"He's worse than ever," I admitted.

"Last week, Charlie asked if Dad could teach him how to ride his bike. All the neighborhood kids ride religiously and Charlie can just barely keep up just sprinting beside them. They mock him by riding fast, knowing he can't keep the pace. Finally, he pulled his bike out from under the patio and asked Dad to teach him. He boarded the bike and our dad sent him off in a push of gravity while those same kids watched on, congregating on their bikes by G.G. Rock. The fanfare seemed to galvanize Charlie's courage but low and behold he came crashing off a curb and was thrown over the handlebars.

Rather than encourage my brother to dust himself off and get back up, Dad picked the bicycle up and hung it in the air before thrusting it back down on top of our brother, screaming profanities about him before turning his back and walking back to his beers while shouting words like "retard" and "asshole". He told our mother that night that Charlie made him look like a failure as a parent. Swearing up and down that Charlie can ride a bike and swim and that he's just doing it intentionally. Our mother's retort. She pulled all of us kids in Charlie's room and explained that our dad's temper predates to when our father would wet his bed, so our grandpa would dress him up like a girl and make him knock on every bunk on the naval base with a wig and dress and tell every seal that he'd wet his bed." I sobbed.

"Your mom is a victim who is using what little power

she has to victimize all of you," Tasha retorted.

I took another puff of my cigarette before emphatically telling another tale.

"Charlie also thinks he's having visions of the future," I warned.

"That same night, Charlie was having problems sleeping because of his stomachache. He kept circling the bathroom, which is right by their bedroom door. He swears that while the door was open, and their television was on as they slept soundly, it blew up and caused a fire strictly in their room. As he approached the room, he swore the door slammed and locked in front of him. Janet came home from being out with the guys to find our brother slumped over the door, pounding so hard to wake them up that his bloody handprints were all over it.

She then ran down and found the fire extinguisher and broke their door open to reassure Charlie that they were alive and fine. Our father promptly knocked her out and sent her tumbling back down the stairs after. She's in the hospital again. Because of HIM. Tasha, I don't know what to do. I think he's going to kill us. In fact? I'm sure of it." I cried.

IX

BEAR HILLS, MASSACHUSETTS
JUNE 6TH, 1996 - NOVEMBER 1ST, 1996

In 1996, I couldn't help but still dwell over the quagmires of the year that preceded it. Ever since we'd performed the séance in our basement things had become more and more unsettling for all parties involved. The lingering curse seemed to affect Mom the worst. One evening, she was startled out of a sound sleep after a nightmare that felt like she swore was a lucid vision of the blonde boy's death. As Mom explained it, she awoke in a cold sweat only to find a little boy standing by her bed side. In her groggy state, she didn't put too much thought into the situation as her maternal instincts kicked in. Reaching for her son's hand, she quietly instructed him to follow her back to his bedroom where she would tuck him back in.

As he held her hand firmly, the two shuffled out of the bedroom, doing their best not to cause a stir that would awaken our petulant and overworked father, who had successfully drank halfway through a thirty rack of light beer after working a double shift. While his snores seemed to be indicative of his heavy, inebriated rest, Mom had become weary around her husband due to his familiar violent demeanor. After the mother and son exited the room, she quietly lectured him on the importance of walking softly around his father, especially after he retired to the bedroom for the evening. The boy seemed to heed her words with an obedient and beatific smile from ear to ear. When they approached the door, Mrs. Harris turned the brass knob as quietly as she could, revealing a sight that still haunts her to this day"

Charlie nuzzled up with a plush Freddy Krueger I had bought for him, sleeping as soundly as our mother remembered when she's tucked him in the first time that night. It was painstaking, but Mom choked her fear down her throat as far as it could go while the boy whose hand she was holding pointed at the bed and simply spoke,

"Mommy."

As her memory serves, she then knelt before the specter of this child with both her hands firmly placed on his shoulders and emphatically begged him to leave this family alone upon correcting him about his title for her.

"I am NOT your mommy,"

she repeated over and over, like it was a newfound mantra of hers. When pressed on the events that followed, there was no definitive timeline or clarity to correlate with a timeline.

All I could remember is our mother turning into a lapsed Catholic, who must have exhumed a box back from her days as a CCD teacher at the family's church in Pine Banks in hopes of recovering several crucifixes and figurines of Jesus Christ. It seemed that every day that the kids came home from school, a new set of rosaries were fashioned over yet another doorknob while another miniature statue of the Martyr was keeping vigilant eye over the haunted family in a new corner of the house. Many of them were arbitrarily placed there presumably after Mom had consumed enough alcohol to wash away the aftertaste of such a profoundly disturbing experience. While Janet found our mother's frail psyche comical (and justifiably so) me and Charlie couldn't help but dwell over the impending implications it would have with her relationship with our cynic of a father.

One night, after realizing that I'd be the only child in the house as my two siblings were both invited to sleepovers over the respective friends' houses, I approached our mother, who was sitting all alone in near darkness save for several candles that were lit in the middle of the family's kitchen table. She had been nursing her infamous "blue cup" from the time she had woken up until the present. Her long, bony fingers fidgeted with a cigarette placed in the middle of an ashtray overflowing with tobacco-mitigating ruminations, while her eyes appeared disturbed and unfathomably distraught, be it from her thoughts or her alcohol consumption. She didn't break out of her funk, even after I pulled a chair next to her and waited to be addressed properly.

It was when I slid Mom's cigarette pack toward me under the palm of her sweaty hand and removed one to light it that Mom even turned her head from the cigarette her fingers were unable to grasp.

"What do you think you're doing," she slurred.

I exhaled a miasma of smoke and stared so piercingly into our mother's eyes I could see the vast abyss of perpetual sadness in them.

"Have you seen the little boy?" I asked.

Mom finally maneuvered the cigarette from where it was resting and managed to secure it in between her index and middle fingers only to realize it had burned down right to the filter.

"What, so you're going to tease me too?" She hissed.

She then angrily reached for the cigarette in my mouth and placed it in her own.

She took an emphatic drag as if the cigarette contained oxygen itself before sloppily answering,

"No. I made him go away. I made him crossover." She slurred some more.

"So why are you out here all alone? Knowing that there's no possible way you could put yourself to bed without assistance?" I scowled.

"I thought you said you were done with this lifestyle after you left Dad. So, what? You're back together and now it's like you picked up right where you left off?"

Mom stared daggers at me, her youngest daughter, and balled up her fists like she wanted to take a swing.

"Oh, you're going to hit me?" I antagonized.

"No, Mom. That's your husband's job."

I then removed myself from the table and slammed the chair back under it.

Mom stumbled to her two feet just enough to barely display a height difference between us, as if to remind me who was bigger. Unfortunately, the alcohol made it difficult for her to find her footing and she fell back down in her chair, kind of slouching over toward the table.

"So, once again...this is all MY fault?" She shouted at me.

I stopped dead in my tracks and turned to face my belligerent drunk of a mother.

"No, Mom," I answered.

"Actually, for once? I'll admit that it's mine.

That night that you and dad went out to get shitfaced

and line dance to that awful fucking Billy Ray Cyrus song you mistake for being music? I performed a séance, and I spoke with the little boy. Ever since that night? I have wanted nothing more than to slit my wrists open as penance for what came after. Scotty killed himself. Then his mom died. Charlie has been freaking out, and Dad keeps wailing on Janet. Then I realized that everything that has been happening to us for almost a year now? It's not because of a séance; it all started with you feeding Charlie those fucking pills you lied to everyone about.

It's like you wanted him to go fucking crazy, feeding him the pills that belonged to Janet. And not giving them to her was making her go fucking crazy! So, is that what you want? Are you trying to make us all go crazy and then kill each other? Would that make you fucking happy, you desperate and lowly excuse for a would-be fucking parent?!" I cried.

Mom once more tried to unsuccessfully stand to her feet to comport herself as a formidable foe.

"You want to know what I was giving your brother?" She arrogantly spoke.

She then raised her arms in the air and squealed,

"HAPPY-PILLS!"

just before she appeared to get dizzy and fell face first into the table and onto the floor.

"Yeah," I mocked.

"I don't think it's the house that's cursed anymore. I think it's the bullshit excuse for a fucking family you and Dad created."

I then turned my back to our wounded mother and ran down the stairs through the basement and out the door. I didn't return home that night. Instead, I found refuge at

G.G. Rock, where I crawled in between two rocks, and rocked back and forth, sobbing. The next morning, I climbed back into my bedroom through the unlocked window and entered the kitchen where our parents treated me like nothing had happened. Somehow Mom must've come to before her husband returned home from work, managed to NOT burn the house down with her candles and put herself to bed before she could cause further damage to herself.

That seemed to become a recurring weekend ritual with Mom. It forced us, her daughters, to make ourselves scarce around the family home, leaving Charlie the only child under the same roof as Mom and her husband when he eventually came home from work. However, Charlie had found a cozy haven in solitude and cable television. All of us were given cable boxes after we'd witnessed Dad nearly murder our mother during a heated argument about money. Unless it was for a meal, or to play with his friends, Charlie never left his room. This would become an issue for him at school as the only thing that truly enraptured Charlie were the movie monsters he watched every Saturday night, or the cartoons he saw on MTV.

When Charlie left his previous school to attend a new one as the town underwent a near decade long renovation of all their old buildings, he started fourth grade with a glorified sociopath of a teacher named Ms. V. Her methods were abrasive and boarded on abusive with her students. She had become popular for being the teacher to throw Nerf balls at incompetent and distracted students and standing on her head when her insubordinates drove her crazy. Charlie was different though; he was quiet and vulnerable and she prided herself on deliberately exploiting his misgivings about passing the two subjects he struggled with the most as a special education student, which also happened to be the two subjects she specialized in: mathematics and science.

Something about Charlie REALLY irked this woman. Enough so, he managed to amass an impressive number of unexcused absences his fourth-grade year which were chocked up to a newly developed stomach ailment he was beginning a long and painful relationship with. His little friends often corroborated his stories about her dressing him down in front of his peers (which consisted of two classrooms of children as she worked in collaboration with another teacher named Mr. Berg) and taking any chance she could humiliate him to the point of him having difficulty focusing on his work due to his anticipating the next time she would make a mockery of his stupidity or inability to socialize with his peers.

Charlie once confided in me that she bullied him so badly that he started having suicidal thoughts. I tried my best to make myself emotionally available to Charlie, but as fate would have it, both of our troubles were just getting started. Thursday, June 6th, 1996 would follow us to our very graves. Charlie came off the bus daunted after another tedious day of being humbled by Ms. V, while I was feeling the pressure of Tasha's impatience at my inability to come out of the proverbial closet and treat her publicly as an actual girlfriend. No matter how persistent my pleas regarding our father's belligerent intolerance for lifestyles that didn't fit in his white bread mental cul-de-sac mentality, I also simply wasn't ready for that profound public self-affirmation.

A seemingly innocuous conversation turned

contentious after Tasha took my inability to stand up to our tyrannical father as a giant turn-off.

"You know," Tasha hissed,

"You and your sister are always claiming to be so worried about who will take care of your brother, but how do you expect to take care of him when you can't even stand up for yourself?"

I knew Tasha's logic was bullet-proof, but much like my mother, my inability to reconcile with someone else's affirmation about me threw me into an irrational frenzy. I knew that I lacked conviction when it came to my own respective passions, but it was a different story when I wasn't providing the narrative. How could someone who allegedly loved me, condescend to me in such a manner?

"Well?!" Tasha demanded,

waking me from my seemingly dormant state of quiet introspection.

"It's easy to stand up for what you believe in," I sneered, "when your antagonists are demented geriatrics who you keep drugging!"

I paused for several minutes until I realized that Tasha's retort was a dial tone. I slammed the phone down before standing to my feet and climbing out my window, which was becoming an all too familiar conduit between my private hell and the one I shared with the rest of the world. I navigated the neighborhood with a brisk pace and with seemingly no predetermined destination that I was at least cognizant of at the time. My mind went completely blank, as if my brain was a computer that had overheated and powered itself down.

After several minutes of pacing through the neighboring streets, my lungs began to sting and drag my frail body down as they filled back up with panicked gasps that were desperate for relief. It felt like I had been sucked underwater and forced to thrash my way back to the surface for longer than my body could handle. Drowning. I always felt like I was drowning. When I finally felt liberated from this sensation that I had been choking on nothing, I realized that my frenzied mind had brought me to Ricky's house. Without hesitation, I approached the front door and rang the bell several times before resorting to frantic knocking on the door.

Ricky pulled the door open armed with a baseball bat.

"Rachel?" He asked.

"Are you okay? Why are you ringing my doorbell so much? I thought you were one those overzealous Jehovah's Witnesses." He joked.

"You'd pull a bat on a Jehovah's Witness?"

Ricky dropped the bat to the floor before stepping outside in his socked feet.

"Dimes never told you our Jehovah's Witness story?" He smiled.

He closed the door behind him and motioned toward the backyard. We took a seat on some outside furniture that his parents had bought to entertain guests during the annual summer block parties.

"We were at the North School baseball diamond," he regaled,

"when Dimes hit a grand slam right through one of the windows of that creepy church of theirs.

When we knocked on the door, we were pulled inside by the creepy men and women who were dressed like they belonged in a J.C. Penny catalog. Immediately, they started in on us, trying to convert us when all we wanted was our goddamn baseball back. Had they not heard the other guys yelling our names and looking for us, they probably would have kept us there as like sacrificial lambs or something." He joked.

I grumbled something resembling a chuckle but immediately returned to my morose state.

"What's going on?" He continued.

"I haven't talked to you or your sister in months and suddenly, here you are at my door."

I started to cry before curling up in a ball rocking back and forth.

"Tasha broke up with me," I sobbed.

Ricky's face was sympathetic with a hint of humor still lingering on his lips.

"So," he breathed. "You're single, then?"

I looked up at him with disdain.

"Sorry," he apologized.

"Are you sure? I mean, maybe she just needs some time to cool off."

I emphatically shook my head.

"I'll never be able to come out," I asserted.

"Come out?" Ricky questioned.

"You know," I breathed.

"Of the closet."

Ricky appeared frustrated and worried.

"Why not?" He asked.

"I mean, why can't you just own who the fuck you are? To hell with what all the other kids think." He gleamed.

I recoiled from the thought of such a thing.

"It's not the other kids," I cried.

"It's our father. I don't know if Janet ever gloated about this little factoid or not, but she was the only kid our dad wanted. My mom got really drunk once and admitted to me that he pretty much raped her in order to get her pregnant with Janet."

Ricky was curious,

"Then why do they fight so much?" He asked.

"When we lived out West, he worked at a painter. He was doing this job at a hospital out there and one of the wings caught fire. Had it not been extinguished in time, they surmised that half the damn hospital would've gone down in flames. They retrieved painting materials after it was put out, and our father was immediately brought up on charges and sent to a county prison. She never did say if he ever came clean about whether he set the hospital on fire intentionally or not.

I often wonder though, what if he did? When he and our mom were divorced, he left a message on our answering machine once, threatening to burn us alive in our grandparents two family house. I used to think of my dad as just being all bark and no bite. The way Mom reacted to that message? It was scary. It was as though, out of all his idle threats, THAT was the one to take seriously.

So, she scooped all three of us up in the middle of the night and we fled like a small group of refugees to her best friend's condo not far from here." I revealed.

Ricky was dumbfounded.

"Why the fuck did she move you all back in with him?" He shouted.

I shrugged.

"It's a long story," I answered.

Ricky reached for my wrist as I stood up, ready to walk away.

"How does THAT story end?" He begged.

"With us getting Charlie the fuck out of there," I insisted.

Ricky stood to face me.

"How do WE do that?" He demanded.

"We hide him somewhere and tell him to go color," I jested.

Ricky cocked his head as if he was profoundly caught off guard by my sudden wind of humor.

"Sorry," I answered,

"That's just something my mom yells when she's pushing him down a flight of stairs or into a locked room so she can get him out of harm's way."

Ricky reached for my hand. I looked over at him and then down at our hands clasped together.

"I won't let anyone hurt Charlie," he promised.

I wiped more tears from my eyes.

"And," he breathed.

"I'll talk to Tasha if you want me to. Anything to keep you from crying."

He then reached for my cheek and grazed his thumb across it as if smudging the tear through my pores.

"I'm tired of losing people," he choked.

"First Scotty, then my brother,"

I immediately interrupted him.

"Your brother?" I cried.

Ricky tried to fight off the tears; I watched as he tried to swallow that lemon-sized pain building in his throat before he could confide in anyone that his brother was no longer among the living. In fact, he hadn't been for months.

"He died at that camp my parents sent him to for

conversion therapy," he bluntly revealed.

"They found him hanging from his bunk bed. It was ruled a suicide and his body was cremated before a full-scale investigation was even underway. One of the pastors had called my parents and broke the news to them.

I found it really unsettling that neither of them shed a single tear when they found out. Frankly, I don't even think they expressed a second of grief before they started planning what to do with his body. Every question I had regarding a service was quickly averted to the point where they would get short with me if I didn't let up. Then, one day? They just showed up with this wooden box and insisted I say anything I had on my chest to it before they emptied the ashes into this beach near our summer cottage. It didn't feel like a good-bye, honestly.

I felt so rushed, and like I had to police any sentiments that I genuinely wanted to express. Then, they just took off. No invitation to join, just gone. It was like they couldn't get rid of him fast enough." He lamented.

"Why do you think they wanted everything over that quickly?" I inquired.

Ricky shrugged.

"There's a part of me that can't imagine what it must be like to lose a child. So, maybe that's justification for their irrationality? Then there's the conspiracy theorist in me that believes they were in cahoots with the pastor who oversaw the camp. Like, he was NEVER going to wake up one day and NOT be gay, you know?

Maybe they were pushed by the futility of what they were trying to accomplish and realized that people would figure out that it was glorified child abuse and bullshit; that it would make the church look bad. I honestly think the pastor murdered him, then hung him from his bunk to make it look like a suicide. Which is why my parents skipped the autopsy in favor of just having him turned into a pile of ashes so they could dispose of him before anyone became too suspicious. You probably think I'm crazy, don't you? There's no way adults could be that evil, right?"

I stopped in the middle of the street, just a few blocks away from my house. I then leaned into Ricky's ear.

"My mom convinced my little brother that his best imaginary friend killed himself," I revealed.

"He went mental, and my mom blamed his reaction on needing a father in the picture. That's how we actually wound up here together. When Janet found out that Mom was giving her the wrong meds to treat her bi-polar disorder so she could give the meds to Charlie, who isn't sick, she came to the conclusion that Mom was hoping one or both of them would go crazy and kill our father so she wouldn't have to."

When I pulled away, Ricky's face was flushed and ripe with horror.

"Wait, seriously?" I nodded and shrugged.

"Our mother doesn't know how to NOT be a victim. We think this might have been her way of trying to free herself from the abuser."

Ricky just held his face and shook his head.

"What the fuck is wrong with our parents?"

He started nervously laughing to himself which prompted me to do the same.

“You know,” he started, “between the Ouija board, the séance, Scotty wrestling with that naked pipe person think I heard you call it, and then his mother killing herself in front of us? None of that scares me the way my parents, or your parents scare me. Like, if this town is in fact cursed and all that boo-shit is real? It's not nearly as fucking scary as having to wake up in our families," he finished,

I paused for a few moments, letting the sentiment marinate a little bit...but strangely it made sense. If there was a devil, if there are ghosts, and if hell was Bear Hills? It didn't hold a candle to the fear of growing up behind the closed doors they felt imprisoned in.

Eventually, we walked side by side to my house where Ricky walked me to the stairs where we embraced one another, and he gave me a kiss on the cheek.

"I'll call you later," he promised.

I nodded and walked solemnly back into my house while Ricky watched on with sadness in his eyes.

As I walked past the kitchen and through the living room, Janet immediately darted from behind the curtains and backed me against a wall.

"What were you doing with Ricky? What, do you like boys now suddenly?" She accused.

I shoved Janet away, but she grabbed me from behind and pressed me once again against the wall.

"Why were you kissing?" She continued.

"Tasha and I got into a fight," I insisted.

"Ricky was just cheering me up."

I once again wrestled myself away from Janet and continued for our bedroom.

"If you're going to be a dyke," Janet screamed.

"Then be a fucking dyke. Otherwise you're just a whore who is just looking for attention."

I stopped dead in my tracks, then turned to Janet, who was smugly grinning at me with her arms folded and leg arched. This was the last memory I had before the events that unfolded. The story given to the police after Janet was removed from the home and placed in their custody, was following Janet's comment I apparently pounced on her and began unloading on her before Janet tossed me off and began manhandling me, which left me with two black eyes and a broken nose.

However, the damage inflicted didn't satisfy Janet, who then reached for a kitchen knife and began threatening to slit my throat. That's when our parents arrived from grocery shopping. Janet then threatened to murder all three of us. Then a chase ensued between father and daughter as he tried to disarm his teenage daughter. The pursuit had lasted for approximately ten to fifteen minutes when Charlie returned home from a friend's house and was immediately locked in the basement by Mom to get him out of harm's way. When the police arrived five minutes later, the Janet was disarmed and restrained by the officers who removed her from the home.

I was taken to the hospital by our father while Mom stayed behind to make sure Charlie would be cared for. And just like that? The Harris family imploded. Janet was placed in the psychiatric unit of Bear Hills Memorial Hospital for several weeks before being placed into a foster home three towns over. This left me and Charlie to our own devices while our parents dealt with frequent surprise visits from the department of child welfare, while my parents and I also attended weekly, nighttime meetings at another facility with Janet regarding how to curb and manage her anger.

All of this happened much to the ignorance of Charlie,

who was kept in the dark regarding the details of these clandestine Thursday evening meetings. He simply got used to the routine of being dropped off at our grandparents' house in Pine Banks and taping the television show *Friends* for our uncle. Eventually, he learned the true nature of these meetings after sneaking into our parents' bedroom and ransacking through their dresser, where he came across all the literature given to our parents by D.S.S. and whoever curates those meetings. Meanwhile, with Janet gone and our parents dealing with the aftermath, it essentially made me a surrogate mother to Charlie, who I took care of through the remainder of the summer.

Word of Janet's murder attempt and subsequent incarceration began to permeate all over the town. While it did nothing to affect our parents (although, even if it did chances are, they'd remain indifferent) it did no favors for Charlie or myself; we both suffered considerably on a social level. The neighborhood kids were instructed by their parents to involve themselves less and less with the Harris kids and were forbidden from ever stepping foot in their home. Save for the sporadic phone call from Ricky, Charlie and I talked to no one else the entire summer. I was used to social isolation, but it took a serious toll on Charlie even if it wasn't instantaneous. He spent the summer glued to the television, watching monster movies or playing video games when he wasn't building box forts with me.

When he did go outside? He would spend a lot of time alone at G.G. Rock playing by himself. I wish I'd known then what I do know: that the voices of children whispered to him, tempted him to cross the boundary to Turtle Rock.

Had the local children not ostracized him, I doubt he'd have gone anywhere near it, consciously anyway. He'd heard the rumors about it being haunted as much as any of us. But loneliness drove him to follow the voices, to find their source. To search for a friend.

I was back at home watching a movie in my bedroom while our father cooked on the grill and our mother did laundry. As Dad started piling burgers that bore a closer resemblance to hockey pucks on a plate to bring inside, Mom instructed me to go out in the neighborhood to find my brother and bring him home for dinner. My audible dismay had less to do with our mother's request and more to do with where I'd eventually find him. Since the séance, the only person who would even go near the woods next to our home (save for drunken teenagers late at night) was Charlie. For someone who was constantly picked on for being a helpless mommy's boy, Charlie was braver than anyone Rachel knew.

This too was a cause for concern. Charlie only exuded a sense of confidence when someone was building it in him. Like Frankie did. The only benefit to having an alcoholic for a mother was her inability to be a revisionist when she was inebriated. One of the Saturdays while our mom imbibed from the blue cup, I came out to the kitchen to make myself a snack when I found our mother sobbing in the dark holding one of Charlie's drawings. It was handed to her during one of Charlie's meetings at school. When she caught me out of the corner of her eye trying hard to make a clandestine snack, she called for me to sit on the couch with her.

"I don't want to sit with you like this," I sighed.

"You're too drunk to love. You're even too drunk to

pity."

This incensed Mom, who immediately snapped out of her drunken stupor and slapped one of the plates out of my hands, sending it crashing on the linoleum floor. She clenched her fingernails deep into the skin of my wrists, drawing tiny trickles of blood.

"Don't you EVER talk to me like you have a clue what it's like to be ME!" She howled.

We had crashed down to the floor on our knees when she slumped her body over my shoulder and whispered in my ear,

"Frankie died, twice," she revealed.

Whether it was the loss of her inhibitions, or simply harboring the weight of the sadness too long, Mom revealed one of the last skeletons she kept in her closet.

"Janet was the result of your father raping me. But Frankie? That was the result of me taking the power back and raping him."

She then motioned to her belly.

"He was in here. I felt it and I knew it. It was my little boy. And he killed him." She ominously sobbed.

Then the reason our mother left our father was finally revealed. While she was pregnant with Francis (a namesake of a late great uncle and war hero...despite how arguable that fact may be) they got into an altercation while Dad was drunk, and he punched his wife in the stomach.

The next morning, she miscarried. It has haunted our father to this day, that he essentially murdered who would've been his first boy. Charlie was conceived after the reconciliation that took place when the family traveled back to Massachusetts. Miraculously, Mom was pregnant, and it was a boy. This time, she was determined to come to term with her baby and give him the life that Frankie should have had. Being the superstitious type, Mom elected to devote herself to the church to potentially mitigate the warranted anger of a deceased child and the arrival of his successor. When Charlie began having visions of a friend named "Frankie", Mom knew immediately that this was no imaginary friend. It was her dead baby. There was something poetic about his immediate bond with the son that came through.

It proved that not only was Charlie her destiny, but Charlie also harbored unfathomable powers. To me, that revelation became even more unsettling when I realized what I'd done to my little brother by performing that séance. He was the conduit. Like our mother, I'd offered Charlie to them like chum in the water. Maybe it wasn't the Shaman who wanted revenge,

But the children he'd murdered. Charlie was their gateway back into the town and to all the parents they wanted to destroy. Why Charlie? When I trusted my instinct and found myself back at G.G. Rock, I could hear the sobbing as clear as day. It was Charlie, and something scared him.

It would be the last real conversation I'd have with my brother before the 'incident' took place. He had been curled up on one of the rocks outside of the path that brought people to the fork that led to the cursed mountain. When I confronted him, he was so pale he was damn near translucent. That's how I knew that something he saw resonated with him. I always made a point to get on his level when talking to him seriously.

"Are you hurt?" I cried.

Charlie turned to me stoically and reached for my hand, as I reached back, he placed two slugs into my palm and closed it.

"He wanted his headache to go away," Charlie cried.

"So, I made it go away."

I knew then that Charlie had seen Scotty.

"Who else did you talk to?" I demanded.

Charlie's body temperature dropped, and his skin felt like an ice box.

"The lambs," he mumbled.

"They want me to deliver Daddy to them," he shrugged.

I began shaking Charlie violently.

"Why?" I demanded.

"Why do they want Daddy?"

Charlie crawled out of his safe spot and rubbed his hand over my belly.

"Destiny," he ominously answered.

When Charlie finally seemed to calm down, I brought him home for dinner and devoted myself to making sure no one found out about Turtle Rock's intentions for our father, even if I wasn't so sure about them myself. Then I resorted to something I had decried with Tasha. I started drugging Charlie to get answers out of him without him being wise to it.

During the summer, I experimented with various cold medicines and cough syrups to manipulate my little brother into a similar catatonic state. One night, I offered to tuck Charlie in before drugging him. This turned out to be the most revealing evening of my experiment as I took a seat next to his bed while he tossed and turned in his sleep. When I reached out to comfort him, I felt his tiny fingers dig into my wrists as I faced the whites of his eyes rolling into the back of his head. As I froze in horror, the bloody handprints filled up the room and I could hear the cacophony of children screaming in my head.

"We're all lambs, Sissy," Charlie whispered.

"Daddy needs his lambs. Please don't cut our throats and burn us Daddy. We love you," he sang. His pre-pubescent falsetto then dropped to an evil baritone.

"Daddy doesn't love us. Daddy only wants to hurt us. Help us Sissy. Help us make the pain go away. We just want to go home. Sissy, can God even hear us?"

My mind was then compromised by sordid visions of the future. I recognized the white rubber of my converse sneakers lying languidly on the linoleum of the basement bathroom floor. My throat was burning with vomit and my nostrils were bleeding from the inability to produce bile. I felt dead, but somehow, I could still feel the coldness of the floor as my jeans were unbuttoned and peeled from my waist, like someone was removing skin.

I felt like I was dying and somehow as if I had been sacrificed to harbor new life at the same time. All I retained from the vision was a sense of genital mutilation and the worrisome look on the family cat's face. I was immediately released from Charlie's grip and realized that the crotch of my pajama bottoms was soaked in blood. I ran out of the room and into the bathroom, trying to subdue my sobs as I soaked my undergarments under the sink to camouflage the revelation of my possessed little brother's revelations of things to come. I resolved after that experience to simply let Charlie be, and to let things play out as the curse of the blonde boy would now dictate.

By the fall of 1996, Janet was once again reunited with

our family after one of her foster siblings attempted to poison their foster mother. Even though she was physically under the same roof, somehow, she felt even further away from the people she shared a home with. As a welcome home gesture, our parents allowed Janet to host a party in the basement for her new friends from the vocational school she was attending to become a beautician and the surrogate siblings from the home she had been living in. Still reeling from the heated break up with Tasha, I had a palette for decadence and had manipulated Janet's frail mental health into both allowing me to attend the party and letting me drink most of the alcohol provided by a friend she met at vocational school. I'd had enough of Janet's quasi-mental health issues, as I did with the handprints keeping her away from Charlie's room.

Charlie clicked off the tape player and removed his headphones. He started messaging the bridge of his nose with his index finger and thumb the way he did when he felt uncomfortable or awkward about a situation. In this case? It was underestimating just how lucid the memories will play themselves back in his head upon hearing Rachel and Donald's voices on these cassettes. Charlie always felt so guilty thinking about Rachel's passing, and how alone she must have felt in her final moments before she made the decision to take her own life.

He could not help but feel both resentful and relieved at Donald's inability to shut the fucking tape recorder off when Rachel excused herself to go to the bathroom. Maybe Charlie couldn't be there to tell her how much he loved her, but at least he felt like she wasn't completely alone anymore. As ridiculous as that would seem to other people who weren't Charlie and Rachel. It may have taken thirty years to be in that room with her, but Charlie got there.

Charlie began wistfully staring out the window of the train thinking back to that party Rachel talked about on the tape. She was right, If there was anyone in the house with "actual" mental health issues, it surely wasn't the girl putting her autistic former foster sister to run the basement doors like a bouncer at Studio 54. The main reason was to keep Charlie from interloping and potentially bringing their oblivious parents downstairs while the kids enjoyed the seemingly unsupervised gathering in an orgy of mind-altering substances. Unbeknownst to everyone else, Charlie had no interest in what his sisters were doing.

He locked his bedroom door shut and took a page out of Rachel's book by climbing out his bedroom window to avoid the need for an explanation as to where he was going. Really, it was to avoid Rachel at all costs as he intended to walk down to Tasha's grandparents' house and talk with her about Rachel's unusual behavior and his revelations about the lambs of Turtle Rock.

Tasha lived about fifteen minutes away from the Harris home. To any other young kid who had not spent the past three years chasing after neighborhood kids on their bikes so they couldn't ditch him, this might have seemed tedious. Charlie enjoyed escaping the bubble his mother cultivated for him. He knew that there had to be a world outside of the backyard, the neighborhood and even the fourth grade and he couldn't wait to explore it. The walk gave him time to reflect on some of the issues that were going on both at school and home that no one harbored a compulsion to ask him about. Charlie might have been young, but he was a precocious sort.

He knew that for a kid in the fourth grade, the paranoia he had about his safety from people he had been raised to regard as trusted confidantes and persons of authority who warranted his reverence, was odd. His parents, his teachers and even his friends were all the same no matter how good their reputations were on the surface. This is probably why Charlie gravitated to Tasha the way he did. While his age was a culpable party in how painfully naive, he could be at times, he did harbor a tremendously sharp intuition when it came to people. Something bad was going to happen that night to Rachel, and possibly even Janet if he didn't tell one trustworthy person about the things he would hear or see in both a waking state and in his nightmares. Every time he entertained these thoughts, his nostrils stung and chaffed as if he had breathed in too much smoke.

Something was going to burn, and he seemed to be the only who cared that his whole family was destined to burn with it if he didn't do something about it. When he arrived at Tasha's, the normally gregarious and rebellious teen looked like a scared and wounded animal as she swayed on the swing set in her backyard. She hung her head as if gravity were the noose around her neck and her body was too sore to even force her toes back on the ground. When Charlie was close enough, he was able to see two streams of mascara running down her cheeks and the crusted blood caked under her nostrils. When he reached his hand out for her, she immediately jumped up and fell on her bottom, frightened by even the motion of someone trying to touch her.

"It's me," he squeaked.

"Charlie."

One of her eyes peaked out of the hair that was covering her face and she immediately motioned her hands for Charlie to approach. The two just sat crouched in an earnest embrace as she rocked back and forth with the boy. She tried to muffle her sobs in the collar of his flannel shirt as he wondered,

"Did it get you, too?"

Tasha removed herself as she looked into his cold blue eyes for affirmation.

"The curse of this town," he ominously mentioned.

"It's coming for Rachel, TONIGHT!" He emphasized.

Tasha rubbed more tears from her eyes,

"It did, Charlie," she whimpered.

Tasha eventually divulged to Charlie that some girls from town had jumped her coming out of the library and mercilessly beat her for being a "Dyke". After the beating, she returned home to her two demented grandparents who would naturally react badly over her appearance, and that made it even more difficult for Tasha to bear the cross of her life. It was a scary time to be a child, or even a person. Regardless of the melting pot that was the splendid beauty of life, different was still punishable by beating or execution. Tasha's remorse over her temperament with Rachel only exacerbated her depression. All these kids with the common thread of fear, and yet there was no unifying force to lasso everyone's collective strength together.

Regardless of Charlie's unconditional love for Tasha, he knew that she wasn't strong enough to help him save Rachel that night. He helped her sneak into her grandparents' home and cleaned her up; he even exuded a rather impressive acumen for first-aid care as he made sure that all of Tasha's wounds were treated properly out of fear, they might be infected. Tasha gave Charlie his first kiss that night. As he walked back home, he kept touching his lips as if he wanted to preserve that only moment of actual love he'd ever felt up to this point. When he finally made it home, he couldn't help but observe a teenage boy approaching the basement with a heavy backpack. He trailed behind quietly to potentially get a glimpse at the contents in said backpack.

All he could hear were the clanking of bottles. While Charlie was reasonably naive about alcohol, he recognized the sound of bottles as significant after observing his father stagger out to the trash cans with what his mom famously called "Irish Luggage" in the form of green trash bags (although, they were actually black) undoubtedly harboring evidence of the consumption he and Charlie's mother indulged in the night before. When Charlie approached the door, he was immediately stopped by Janet's foster sister Melissa. He couldn't help but find the sight of her in her bib overalls, coke bottle eyeglasses and pig tails somewhat comical as she was well...slow. Charlie insisted on getting past the invisible velvet rope (so to speak), but Melissa wouldn't budge. So, he resorted to something that still haunts him to this day.

Because of Melissa's stunted cognitive development, her actual parents vehemently FORBADE her from ever viewing cartoons like *The Simpsons* or *Beavis and Butt-Head*. These were two shows that Charlie was exceptionally well-versed in as far as impressions went. With his shirt now over his head, he circled around the young woman chanting,

"Diarrhea, CHA-CHA-CHA!" and calling himself "The Great Cornholio" until the girl literally fell on her knees with her hands over her ears screaming to herself,

"I'm not allowed, I'm not allowed, I'm NOT allowed!"

Again, Charlie knew what he had done was downright evil, but he HAD to save his sissy. With the makeshift doorman suffering something of a psychotic episode he managed to slip into the room where Rachel was guzzling one red solo cup after another.

Before he even had the chance to lunge at her and knock the cup out of her hands, he felt pure muscle steamrolling him down onto the floor like sack of potatoes. When he looked up, some acne ridden and mustachioed teenager reached for his tiny body and threw it over his shoulders before power bombing him to the ground back outside, stopping a second to snicker at poor Melissa before he went back inside. Defeated, Charlie retreated to the front door and went up to his room for bed. He was too little to explore a second round with who was undoubtedly one of Janet's 'hired' muscles. If the Harris family's knives weren't sitting in an evidence locker somewhere in the Bear Hill Police Station, he might have entertained cutting that young man's throat for the sake of preventing what followed, the memory of which would manage to burrow itself deep into Charlie's psyche and resound in his head anytime he found himself alone in darkness.

Charlie dreaded listening to the rest of what he knew he was about to be said on this tape. How the party abruptly ended and Rachel how to be rushed to the emergency room to have her stomach pumped. No matter how old he got, the sound of her voice crying those two words still resonated in his head. He clicked the play button on.

"HAPPPPPY PILLLLLLLLS," Rachel cried out in what sounded like her best wicked witch impression.

“That’s actually how it sounded,” she laughed

“That’s not for dramatic effect.”

Donald smiled and nodded for her to continue.

“Charlie’s makes me feel like a fucking monster,” Rachel lamented

“I guess the sound of existential terror caused him to urinate in his bed. The struggle for Janet, Janet's friends, and our father to find out what had happened to me lasted for seven minutes but those seven minutes managed to feel like a lifetime to Charlie. Unbeknownst to Charlie, he was listening to the incoherent death rattles of a young woman succumbing to alcohol poisoning. While a cacophony of voices cried out,

"What did you take?!

Who did this to you?

Why were your pants unzipped?"

all competed for affirmations that weren't coming.

After seven minutes, our father couldn't help but appreciate the futility of reasoning with a teenager who’d consumed enough booze to constitute a suicide attempt. Of course, no one talked about it. Instead the goal became to rush me to the emergency room. Charlie knew this because he peeked out from the crack of his bedroom door after he’d frantically changed into a clean pair of briefs and watched as our father carried his daughter in a California Raisins comforter down the hall and out to his car. He made sure to hide out of our dad’s sight as he could be particularly cruel when it came to having "accidents".

Mom chocked it up to trauma that he suffered as a youngster himself.

Much like our father, Charlie would have accidents after profoundly stressful nights when the family ate dinner together. It wouldn't be uncommon for Janet to begin antagonizing our dad by tossing knives across the table at him or insulting mom.

In some ways, sadism is a learned thing. Our dad's brand of sadism was far more severe than his father's, and Charlie started to fear that he may develop his own more severe version for his kids, so much that Charlie would often attempt to slash his own wrists to rid himself of any monster's blood (as he began referring to the actual blood coursing in his veins) in an effort to kill the monster or prevent any potential progeny from carrying that DNA. Charlie thought a lot about having children since the time he was five. Deep down, he wanted to compensate for the family that he felt never wanted him. He treated the poignant ballads on contemporary radio as synchronicities of correlating introspection that at an unmentioned future date, he would get his do-over.

For now? He had to exist in the awful present. Around ten o'clock, which was WAY past his bedtime, Charlie snuck into the living room, peaking his head around the wall leading into the kitchen where he heard mom berating Janet and the only friend who lingered behind regarding their culpability in my seemingly near-death experience. She even accused Janet of being the one who poisoned her foster mother as an excuse to be released back into the Harris' custody. Following that troubling accusation, Janet accosted our mother (breaking her index and middle fingers) before leaving the house once more and taking her longest exile to date. Mom just slumped against the refrigerator sobbing in physical and emotional pain, according to Charlie.

Charlie told me that was when he went back to his room, knowing that he could offer our grown mother no real solace regarding the fate of both of her daughters. The following morning, I sat on the foot of his bed and tugged at his sheets to wake him up. God, thinking about it...the lack of color in my face, the odious aroma of vomit and feces that must have been coming off of me. It was like he couldn't tell if he was in the middle of a bad dream or if his sister had in fact managed to survive her ordeal from the previous night. When Charlie finally rose from his slumber, I immediately hugged him and handed him a cassette tape.

When Charlie accepted the tape, I snapped out of my near death induced stoicism momentarily to offer a vague explanation.

"Live Through This, Charlie."

He was enamored by the maniacal beauty queen on the cover with the word HOLE just above her crown. I very carefully stood to my feet and nodded at him before racing for the bathroom and slamming the door. Charlie was precocious enough to understand that what made this a gift was the explanation he'd find in it when he listened to it.

"If you live through this with me, I swear that I would die for you," resonated with Charlie not as a lyric to a song but as a promise from his sissy. While the lyrical revelation was touching, it was when our dad took Charlie out to find a costume for Halloween of that year that he became suspicious of the next obstacle the family would face.

The word "suicide" came up A LOT in Charlie's young life and he expected to find out that the incident with my alcohol poisoning was sure to be correlated with it. Instead, as Charlie approached the pitiful row of outdated latex masks from horror villains that were no longer relevant or the department store issued versions of monsters, our dad (best known for utilizing word economy) blurted out his reason for taking Charlie out.

"Janet isn't allowed back home again," he curtly shrugged.

His nonchalance about ostracizing his first born from her birth family didn't seem to bother our father all that much, at least that's how Charlie took it. He then knelt on Charlie's level (which Charlie found painfully condescending) and explained that the two of us may be in a little danger as Janet was not well and could be extremely vindictive.

Dad grabbed the department store Freddy mask from Charlie's hands and nodded at the clearance price of ten dollars before heading several paces ahead of his son to pay for it. Annoyed upon checkout, he threw it back at his little boy and the two enjoyed an awkwardly tense and silent car ride home from the Bear Hills shopping center. Once they were home, Our mother took her youngest child into his bedroom alone and attempted to talk to him like a tiny adult. She explained the severity of Janet's irresponsibility to Charlie regarding my drinking to the point of near death, and then went on to explain how much of a threat she could pose to us. While Janet was certainly selfish and completely wrapped up in her own life, Charlie couldn't imagine that she would ever do anything to intentionally harm her siblings. Then again, how many sane people casually throw knives at their parents from across the kitchen table to get attention?

On Halloween of1996, Charlie had a mask that made his head bigger than the rest of his small frame and an overzealous mother who wouldn't entertain the idea of Charlie getting to socialize with the other kids. After twenty minutes of trick or treating, mom and Charlie returned home. She ransacked his pillow case to diligently check every piece of candy for potential harm, while Charlie sat alone in a dark bedroom holding his mask in his hands as if he was realizing that trick or treating used to be much more fun when he still felt like a kid. He didn't feel like a little kid anymore; he felt like part of the collateral damage that comes with growing up in a broken home. He wasn't allowed to have imaginary friends, and yet real ones still eluded him.

He wasn't allowed to have one sibling, while the other one seemed to have a death wish that made her retreat further away from Charlie despite being one room over. He had a mother who treated him like a sympathetic bartender, and a father who absolutely resented him to the point of bodily harm to subdue any potential for a rival alpha male to suddenly manifest in him to overthrow dad. There was no refuge from the discomfort of not fitting in, or not being able to assimilate to any fragment of the world around him. It was also a difficult age because most of the other boys that Charlie did attempt to socialize with were obsessed with girls and touching themselves. Charlie felt too ugly for any girl to remotely pity him, and he and dad's unspoken "man talks" resulted in his discomfort if our father tried to kiss him goodnight or tell him that he loved him.

Whenever dad would try to kiss him, Charlie would squirm as if he was being given a shot in the arm. If he said he loved his son, Charlie would stoically answer,

"I know."

After a while, our dad must have realized Charlie stopped trying and he eventually followed suit. The damage was not only done; it was irreversible. To make matters even worse, Charlie couldn't relate to other boys. He was afraid of his body, especially when it came to his respective private parts.

Personal and emotional humiliation didn't just exist in Charlie's head; it was put out on display anytime Charlie walked into his fourth-grade class and became fodder for Ms. V. At ten years old, he already had the neuroses of a middle-aged adult. While he sniffled and did his best to keep the tears from soaking his cheeks, he struggled in the dark to find a pencil and piece of notebook paper to write a note. After twenty minutes of diligently committing his thoughts to a single piece of paper, he left his bedroom to see if his mother was done inspecting all his booty from that night's trick or treat haul. She handed him his pillowcase and left him to his own devices. Around eight thirty, he crawled into his bed and awaited his mother's nightly bedtime routine.

"Good night, sleep tight...don't let the bed bugs bite," she'd say.

"They won't," he smiled back.

"They wouldn't DARE!" She'd playfully snarled before adding, "Don't ya know!"

A nod to the mother of one of Charlie's favorite cartoon characters Bobby, from Bobby's World. Charlie had told me that he laid in his bed staring at the ceiling until he heard nothing but the silence of his two inebriated parents fast asleep. He immediately removed himself from his bed and went to his closet for a change of clothes, a flashlight and his pillowcase of candy. He carefully opened his bedroom window and turned to his desk where he grabbed his note and exited the home quietly with a flashlight and his candy on his person. In the middle of the night, he approached Tasha's house and dropped his bag of candy off under the swing set and tucked his note inside before running back home.

The following day, Charlie got off the bus and walked the ten minutes from his designated stop to our house, all he could think about was whether he got the Crunch bar to Reese's ratio just right for Tasha. As he approached the gate at the front of the house, there was a white plastic shopping bag hanging from it. He immediately recognized his name on an envelope attached to it. He opened the envelope which contained a cassette tape and letter addressed to him. The tape had a label that read,

"What love will sound like for you."

When he opened the note, he immediately saw the pink lip print on it. It read,

"Charlie, you have no idea how hard it is not to fall in love with you. One of these days, you're going to be happy. You deserve a life without monsters, ghosts and sadness. While you wait for your dream girl (and promise me when you do? Don't marry her unless it's on Halloween) just know that this is how you make me feel. Love, Tasha."

Charlie immediately ran up the steps to his house and into his bedroom where he put the cassette tape into his tape player. He then ransacked the shopping bag which contained several Twix and Milky Way bars. When he hit play, he immediately recognized the first notes of the song she put on his mix tape.

It was Janet Jackson's "When I Think of You".

A song he'd nonchalantly told Tasha reminded him of happiness. Charlie gorged on candy as he sat through two sides of Tasha's mix tape, which played every single song he ever told her reminded him of crushes he had on girls in his classes or simply good memories of his life. The tape finally ended with All 4 One's "I Swear", the song he'd had his slow dance with Tasha to.

I knocked on his door before pushing my way into his room and found a spot on his bed next to him. Charlie looked at me in fear as I listened to the song and started reading the letter addressed to him and seeing the chocolate stains on his face. I laughed and hugged him tighter than she ever had since he was born.

"Trust me," I joked.

"Getting over her isn't easy. Then again, maybe it's worse never getting over her at all. I wish that's a pain you wouldn't have to live with and a pain I'm so happy she gave to you." She cried.

Charlie handed Rachel a Milky Way as a truce.

"So," I said.

"I guess that makes BOTH of us hopeless romantics."

I remember placing my head on his shoulder as we both ate candy and listened to the song fade out and the tape deck click when the mix was finished. We were the last Harris children standing. We should have been inseparable. We should have lingered in that moment forever. Unfortunately, that's just how curses work. That's just when the evil begins to show up in life.

Take a tender and simple moment between two close

siblings, a bag of candy and a shared broken heart. As destiny would have it? Destiny wasn't far behind, and once she arrived, everything in the Harris home would go up in a burst of flames.

"I wrote her a note sissy," he smirked

"Oh yeah? What did it say?" I remembered asking

"He showed me the closest draft to what she eventually received but it read,"

"Dear Tasha, I wish I were gay too. Maybe then, you could love me the same way that I love you. Are you not allowed to trick or treat because you're gay? Or is it because you have no one to take you out? I would have liked to trick or treat with you. I went to every house I knew had all your favorite candy bars. I hope you're feeling better. Love, Charlie."

"He looked at me with so much pride in his eyes and then I had to say it,"

"Charlie," I cried.

"I'm pregnant."

X

The train had stopped momentarily to allow a few passengers to exit or enter accordingly. Charlie once again removed the headphones and placed them on the seat next to him. He was getting closer now, he knew this not because of the familiarity of the architecture outside of his window seat, rather the anxiety seemingly taking control of his whole body. He would equate it to how people must feel after being in a bad car wreck and driving by the spot where they almost died.

That was probably hyperbolic, but sadly it was reality to Charlie. When Rachel died, Charlie somehow managed to handle it in a way that scared everyone around him. Your sister committed suicide, how can that possibly be something you just get over? Admittedly, and very selfishly...the day he lost Rachel was the day she broke the news to him. He lost his big sister the day she became a mom, and while he was proud to be someone's uncle...he was still too young to not have his big sister.

Destiny Isla Harris was born Wednesday, July 23rd, 1997 sometime in between *Wheel of Fortune* and *Jeopardy Eastern Standard*. At least, that's how Charlie will always remember Rachel's tedious labor and how long he sat in the hospital waiting room expecting his first niece. He'd just managed to get out of the fourth grade and was dismayed to learn that Ms. V would be ravenous for more of his pride and ego in the fifth grade. He did his best not to care. He was anointed with one of the most prestigious honors his life would ever furnish him. He'd get to be an uncle. Granted, a young one but an uncle, nonetheless. Because Rachel still had no recollection of the actual act of conception (seeing as how she is a lesbian) the birth certificate for her first born was printed with a very humorous error.

Under birth father, it listed Mr. Harris. He joked upon her delivery and the revelation of this error by motioning to Rachel and saying,

"Well, I guess I'll take my baby now."

Yet, there was a look in Rachel's eyes that perhaps it wasn't as funny of a quip as all the relatives in her room made it out to be. In fact, while nursing her newborn daughter, she appeared even more defensive of the life cradled in her arms than at that outburst of awkward and inappropriate humor. It became an even more unsettling revelation to Charlie, who hadn't left his bedroom save for school or dinner since the news of his sister's teenage pregnancy became fodder for the rest of the neighborhood. There was talk about how the Harris' had raised two glorified harlots for daughters and now pitied Charlie was a damaged recluse of a son despite their lack of desire to allow their own children round out his otherwise messed up life.

With Janet completely out of the family and Rachel resting in the hospital, this could have afforded more opportunities for the Harris' to get to know their son and even attempt to open the coy child up regarding his desire to linger mostly in his bedroom while other kids ran around outside playing. Instead? They treated it like a profoundly overdue break from child rearing. Knowing this, Charlie started to develop an unnatural affinity for solitude at a young age and began sneaking out of the house even more to befriend the lambs of Turtle Rock.

Charlie's development seemed almost entirely indebted to specters and imagination, two things that offered him the only refuge available. That was until the homecoming of Rachel and Destiny. As a means of giving the baby more adequate space, their parents moved their bedroom furnishings into the basement and created a nursery for their first grandchild. Charlie felt his childhood ending with every snicker from one of his peers at the bus stop or another eye roll from a judgmental parent. To make matters worse, the only person who he could rely on was now preoccupied with her daughter. Understandably so, but ever since the delivery, Rachel was more guarded and less emotionally available for Charlie.

Out of his two sisters, Rachel was the only one who understood the diminutive introvert. After a few weeks of being thrown into premature adulthood, all Rachel knew how to do was exude contempt and paranoia. Mrs. Harris tried to allay Charlie's fears about her behavior by saying, "It's a phase all new mothers go through called 'postpartum depression,'" and while Charlie wasn't exactly at the peak of his intellectual maturity, the condition wasn't entirely foreign to him as Rachel began to remind him a lot of Kirstie Alley's character in *Look Who's Talking*. There was a scene where the character read about this condition in a baby book and scoffed at the mere idea of it, only to be blubbering over a television commercial in the next frame. Though, Rachel's tears never appeared as arbitrary or trivial as a new mom crying over a VISA commercial.

Rachel cried with her whole body, as if she felt physically mutilated. Charlie would sometimes hear her in the next room and would crack open the door to spy in on her. She would often be curled up in a ball with Destiny in her arms, crying like something had completely ruined her. It was like how she cried when Tasha broke up with her. Charlie tried to keep a brave face when he did go to school. No matter how many teachers or peers would try to make him feel badly about his sister's pregnancy and motherhood, he always managed to assert a positive outlook on it. That was until Ms. V humiliated him in front of two classrooms of children while Charlie read his weekly journal assignment aloud. Every week, the kids would take this cheap blue notebook home over the weekend and write about what activities they engaged in.

Most kids would write about day trips their families would take them on, or relatives they would visit for these elegant meals while basking in the warmth of so many generations of their pedigree in one dining room. Charlie's were almost always about his solitude in his bedroom watching monster movies or the stories he'd repeat from the lambs at Turtle Rock. This one week however, Rachel began to feel remorse for alienating Charlie from both she and Destiny. He was not only allowed to hold his baby niece, but she even walked him through the steps on how to successfully change a diaper. Unlike most kids, Charlie relished any opportunity to make himself a more productive uncle.

Unfortunately, his self-esteem was still fodder for Mrs. V. when he was at school. When she introduced the multiplication chart exercises, she would witness Charlie counting his fingers and quip

"Are you counting the number of potential fathers your niece has?"

Suddenly the math lesson went from Charlie learning his times tables to making sure his classmates knew the identity of Destiny's father was a mystery.

True to form, when Charlie gushed over his ability to change his baby niece's soiled diaper at what his sissy called "record speed," Ms. V immediately interrupted with,

"Class, just so you know, this is not how normal families start families. Kids your age have no business trying to play surrogate parents."

Of all the humiliations Charlie endured from Ms. V, this one hit a raw nerve with him. Charlie knew that he didn't have much to be proud of. He didn't come from an affluent neighborhood, unlike the other kids. There weren't goofy or embarrassing pictures of family vacations going down steep water slides in logs all the while making funny faces in his living room. The closest Charlie would ever get to that life, to a real family life, was that one dirty diaper. The first look of comfort from Destiny as Charlie put her in a clean diaper and held her in his arms, knowing that he did something for her no one ever did for him, was important to him.

He took care of Destiny; it was a selfless act for a kid his age, or so he originally thought. In that moment, addressing a class full of kids indoctrinated with their parents learned hatred of someone or something different...Charlie couldn't help but be taken to dark places. He stood at the podium before the class quietly for what felt like a lifetime but really was a matter of seconds before quietly walking to his desk in the back of the room. While other kids shared their stories about quality time with siblings or parents, Charlie tuned it all out and just took to doodling on a blank sheet of notebook paper. He had learned to hide his drawings form Ms. V as they were also fodder for her contempt for him.

Typically, Charlie stuck with drawing what he liked: horror movie villains, aliens, and futuristic dystopias. Somehow, Ms. V took this as a sign that Charlie was harboring homicidal tendencies and believed it would only be a matter of time before he took his deep-seeded sick fantasies of destruction out on the classroom. Later that afternoon, Charlie exited the school bus holding that blue journal in his hand. He walked in the door to find Destiny in her baby swing while his sister was in the other room folding laundry. He placed his backpack on the coffee table in the living room and crouched in front of her little cherub face. Quietly, he read his entry aloud to her, finding all the elation and pride that he was robbed of in class earlier that day.

He slowly peeled the pages out of his journal and folded them up. He then slid them into one of the pockets of his sister's diaper bag before kissing Destiny on the crown of her head and retreating to his bedroom. He sat alone in complete silence, just doodling away in a notebook that rested on his nightstand. A gentle knock at his door resounded before Rachel peeked her head in to check on him.

"How was school?"

Charlie turned his head over his left shoulder and shrugged and went back to his drawing. Rachel peeked her head around the corner to make sure Destiny was still breathing before entering the bedroom and standing just behind Charlie and looking over his shoulders.

From what she caught a glimpse of, there was a human being disemboweled by a terrifying manifestation of Charlie's imagination.

"That's a lot of blood, Charlie." She sheepishly observed.

"You know what? I think it'd be sweet if you could draw something for Destiny. Something cute, that would make her happy. Would you want to draw something for her, Charlie?" She diplomatically offered.

Charlie stopped coloring for a moment, then he slid the current picture he was working on under a pile of paper before turning to his sister with tears in his eyes.

"Oh, Charlie-" she sighed.

Just before Charlie could open his mouth, Destiny could be heard from the living room crying.

Rachel started to speak but Charlie interrupted her.

"She's probably hungry," he offered.

"You should check on her. I promise, I won't draw anything that will scare her."

Rachel gave Charlie a rueful smile before running out to her child. In that moment, neither one of them really needed to address the pint-sized elephant in the room. With Rachel being a mother, and Janet pretty much ex-communicated from the family, Charlie was on his own now.

That night, Charlie sat across from his father who was lecturing him after getting a phone call from Ms. V about his drawings and journal entries. He stared down at his plate, moving mashed potatoes from side to side with his silverware as his father addressed him with names like

"Retard" and "Low Life". Rachel sat quietly, not wanting her father's rage to be turned to her or her helpless infant. Mr. Harris was as aggressive as ever, namely because he didn't have to contend with a volatile Janet. His two younger children didn't have her tenacity, or her devil-may-care attitude when it came to squaring off with him. Mr. Harris appeared to relish the fact that now the only two kids he had to take care of were the ones who were the most subordinate to him.

Another Halloween came and went. This was the first year that Charlie opted not to go trick or treating. Instead, he sat in his bedroom and watched horror movies on cable television. Mr. and Mrs. Harris remained downstairs in their bedroom, and Rachel took care of Destiny in the living room. Charlie was quietly laying on his bed watching television when he heard something crack against his bedroom windows. The sound made him pop up and in fear as he turned to draw his blinds. Before he could register the sticky mess cascading down his window two more objects cracked against it once more. His bedroom windows had been egged. He turned toward the window next to that to get a good view, and saw all the kids in the neighborhood were dressed up in costumes and laughing maniacally as they toilet papered the outside of the Harris home and egged any windows they could.

Charlie's heart sank into his stomach. Rachel immediately barreled through his door holding Destiny in her arms, watching as her little brother was being taunted from outside his window. Whether it was her maternal instincts, or just the indignation of watching her little brother becoming more and more of an outcast, she plopped Destiny down in Charlie's lap before running out the front door and chasing the kids off the family's front lawn. One of the kids forgot to take their pillow case of candy with them and Rachel reached down and chased behind them pelting them with pieces of candy while they shouted disparaging words like "Whore" and "Slut" at her while they dashed into the night. When she walked back into the house, she still had the pillowcase of candy in her hand. She dropped it on Charlie's floor and reached for Destiny, visibly distraught by the children's comments about her.

Meanwhile thirty-year-old Charlie indignantly tried to get through Rachel's own account of that evening on the next cassette,

“I couldn't sleep at all that night. Long after I’d put Destiny down in her bassinet and both my parents and Charlie fell into deep rest, I remained in the family's living room in complete silence. My wearied mind couldn't seem to navigate its focus away from the names those children had called me earlier that night. It reminded me of how difficult growing up with a sister with a reputation like Janet's truly was. Her notoriously promiscuous behavior became profoundly cumbersome for me as I was often unfairly branded and dismissed regardless of my own sexual inexperience. I harbored a deep resentment toward Janet for casting such an uncomfortable shadow over me.

I also held Janet responsible for my rape. Janet was supposed to take care of me, protect me, or if nothing else at least prevent me from getting so drunk that one of her disgusting foster siblings couldn't take advantage of me. As I started piecing together fragments of that night, I became nauseated and managed to peel myself off the couch and scramble into the bathroom down the hall. For almost eight minutes, my head was inside the toilet regurgitating a thick black substance that resembled the charcoal that came out of me following my alcohol poisoning. With every gasp of air, I violently choked back, I panicked that I might potentially be asphyxiated by this repugnant bile.

Once the contents of my stomach were entirely emptied into the toilet, I placed my arms down on the seat and rested my head on them. Children's voices resounded inside the family's small bathroom. I was beginning to think I was going crazy until I realized that the window was cracked open. The voices must've been coming from G.G. Rock; it was Halloween after all, and it was a night famous for teenage kids stealing liquor from their parents and getting drunk in those woods. When I finally felt well enough to stand to my feet, I shut the window and checked on Destiny who was still sleeping soundly.

I reached for a baby monitor and walked down the hallway toward my bedroom when I found myself standing outside Charlie's door. Careful not to wake him, I slowly pushed Charlie's door open and peeked my head in to see if I could see him sleeping in his bed. To my horror, the bed was still fully made and the window right beside it was still open. I pushed myself into the room and with monitor in hand lunged for the window and climbed out of it, crashing onto the front lawn. As I rolled over on my back, my attention was taken to the toilet paper hanging from the branches of the tree overlooking Charlie's room.

I didn't know how, but in that moment, I knew where my brother was and what he was going to do. My muscles burned and ached, and the panic almost paralyzed me, but all I could think about was the night of séance when Charlie snuck out of the house unnoticed. Under the influence of the blonde boy, the lambs or even the shaman...I wasn't sure, Charlie was capable of doing awful things, like disembowel a dog that frightened him. What could he potentially do to a group of kids who routinely antagonized him and called his big sister a succession of unflattering names? Especially when they're so dangerously close to Turtle Rock.

I was never known for my exceptional athleticism, but one could've easily mistaken me for a track star the way I paced through the dark woods during those emotional moments, attempting to reach my brother before he reached those kids. A trail of discarded candy wrappers and empty beer cans acted like breadcrumbs, leading me right into the mouth of Hell. There were hundreds of crosses dangling from trees and Bible pages were strewn all over the ground. I couldn't even process the trepidation I felt staring at the town trying to quarantine its superstition with religious saint candles and various totems to their respective lords.

I started to approach the opening when awful screeching and sobbing sounds were broadcast out of the baby monitor. I glanced down to see the red light flickering up at me, and in that moment, I realized that I would forever be someone's mother before their sister. With my back turned to Turtle Rock, I started racing my way out of the woods and back home to take care of my baby girl. I re-entered our home the same way I had previously exited it. Once in my little brother's bedroom, I left everything as it was before I allowed my curiosity to get the best of me and took care of Destiny as if nothing had happened at all.

The following morning, I woke up in my bed with Destiny by my side with the sheets were dampened where she was resting.

I must have fallen asleep while feeding Destiny in the middle of the night. I sat up and placed several pillows around my baby before exiting the room. When I approached the living room, both of my parents were staring out the living room windows quietly.

"What's going on?" I asked.

Neither of my parents answered me. I shook my head and made my way into the kitchen to pour myself a cup of coffee. As I reached for a mug from the cabinet closest to the back door, I noticed a line of police cruisers parked all along the street and several neighbors congregating around together. It wasn't until I noticed the ambulance loading a body bag into the bus that I stormed outside of the house to start asking questions.

I approached our neighbor Fran, who was corroborating with one of the other neighborhood mothers but was immediately dismissed.

"I have nothing to say to you," she snarled.

I immediately was on the defensive.

"What happened?" I snapped.

"Don't have you a baby to raise, harlot?" Fran retorted.

I was almost taken by the insult until I asserted myself,

"Aren't you a grown woman?" I scorned.

"Keep building your walls and hiding your kids in protective bubbles. You can't keep life from happening."

I began to walk away before turning to our neighbor and snapping,

"By the way, your oldest daughter has Chlamydia. Yeah, I hear things too."

I then walked back up the stairs and into the house, slamming the door behind me and charged into Charlie's room.

"Charlie!" I screamed.

When I opened his door, he was not in his bed or near his desk. I pulled his closet door open to find clothing but no Charlie. I then stormed down the stairs and into the unfinished side where I ransacked his secret hiding spot. Still, nothing around. When I walked back up the stairs and out the front door, Charlie was positioned in the tree that faced his bedroom, watching as EMTs and police officers surveyed the woods next to the house and removed witness after witness. I scaled the tree and sat next to my brother who appeared annoyed.

"If you're wondering," he revealed.

"I did go up there to beat those kids up. But someone got to them before I did."

"Charlie, what did you do?!" I demanded.

"The lambs," he answered.

He then turned to me.

"Bryan Carmichael," he spoke.

"Does that name sound familiar to you?"

The gears in my head began turning as I was taken to memories of a male bully during my eighth-grade year of middle school. Bryan Carmichael used to taunt, tease and physically harm me in several of our classes. It was to the point where I was removed from Bear Hills Middle School and temporarily did a stint at Pine Banks Middle School.

"Why do you ask?" I demanded.

Charlie nodded toward the ambulance.

"That's who is in the body bag. I don't know much, but from what I was able to hear? He was burned alive last night, in the same fashion that Shaman was all those years ago.

I don't know what you woke up during that séance, but it's either protecting us or trying to kill us." he answered.

He started to shimmy his scrawny body down the tree, ignoring my bemusement.

"Where are you going?" I yelled.

"They want Dad," he answered.

"I don't know why, but I think all of this will end if I bring Dad up there."

I hopped down immediately and prevented my brother from entering the home.

"Why do you think that?" I demanded.

He coldly stared into my eyes.

"Because of Destiny," he curtly answered.

"You still don't know who her father is, do you?" He interrogated.

"They do."

He then reached for the doorknob when I jerked him arm behind his back and pulled him to the ground.

I held my body weight on top of him and cried over the shrieks of agony he released. I leaned into his ear.

"You can't do this." I warned.

"Not now. Wait until we leave here. Let me get her out of here."

When I-released Charlie, he was teary eyed and betrayed. I shook my head at him, and Charlie immediately ran as far as he could away from me. I watched on helplessly as my little brother physically and emotionally put a fair amount of distance between the two of us. What struck me in that moment was I no longer harbored the compulsion to chase after him anymore.

My parents had decided that for the first time in years they were going to host Thanksgiving at our home as opposed to visiting our maternal grandparents. Janet's birthday also happened to fall on the holiday that year and our parents had discussed potentially burying the hatchet with their eldest daughter and incorporating a modest birthday celebration into the family meal. The only problem was that neither parent knew where she had been living the past year or if she was even dating the same guy. Despite being a young mother, our parents were relying on me to reach out to several of Janet's friends to track her down. I would have protested, however, our father seemed exceptionally overzealous about the idea for some reason.

The only resource I could think of was Janet's former foster sister Melissa, who was a grocery bagger at the local market. The only issue with Melissa's schedule was that she typically worked nights so that she could attend high school, unlike me who'd dropped out before the conclusion of my freshman year. I didn't have my permit and the buses in town didn't run that late, but I also knew that my parents wouldn't agree to watch Destiny as it would cut into their drinking time. Charlie would've been a more viable option but following our confrontation at the beginning of the month, he would not acknowledge me or his niece. He also did not seem remotely interested in a family Thanksgiving.

I decided to bundle up the baby and brave the frigid New England air as I embarked on the twenty-minute walk to the market. With every sniffle from my runny nose, I became more concerned about whether Melissa was not only still employed by that grocery store but would indeed be working their tonight. Prior to Destiny's birth, I was very unsure of myself. However, the arrival of another life that I was directly in charge of keeping alive, safe and warm had only exacerbated my lack of trust in my intuition. Destiny was the kind of baby that never cried, which could be for better and for worse.

While many relatives were quick to refer to it as a blessing that the baby never seemed to fuss, I (being an absent-minded teenage girl at times) would go hours without thinking of changing Destiny's diaper only to find that my baby had been sitting in her own filth probably for hours. I would always wonder why Destiny would never cry when she soiled herself, then again...maybe she was as much of a people pleaser as I was. That is after all why I had taken my baby into the cold on foot at a time when most people would be eating dinner, just so I could try to get my parents' invitation to their daughter to come home for her birthday. That was when the indignation set in.

The more I thought about the lengths to which my parents would go to keep Janet a member of the family sickened me. Even though they'd also put just as much of an effort in ostracizing or excommunicating her, somehow, they'd always come to the conclusion that the family didn't work without their first born. I would never assert for a second that they'd ever go to such lengths for me or Charlie. Then there was the guilt over my relationship with my youngest brother. It wasn't like he was just a grade below me. He was still in elementary school. While it may not seem like it, four years is a long time to be stuck in a town like Bear Hills with parents like theirs.

As I approached the automatic sliding doors of the supermarket, I was immediately relieved by the first moment of heat upon my skin. I removed my hat and gloves and unbuttoned Destiny's coat to let her skin breathe a little. I navigated the store with the carriage, scanning each aisle for an eccentric looking bag girl. When I failed to spot her, I approached a young-looking clerk and asked if he may know if such a girl worked there.

"Excuse me," I pardoned.

The young man turned from the shelf he was stocking with a warm and pleasant demeanor.

"Rachel?"

I was confused.

"Do I..?" The boy smirked at her.

"It's Ryan," he responded.

"Ryan Powers? I was in home economics with you. Ms. Lacy told me she'd kick my ass if I ever touched an oven again because I almost set the classroom kitchen on fire?"

I held my hands over my face, chuckling.

"Oh my god," I laughed.

"I'm SO sorry, I wasn't a very sociable person in school. You must think I'm such a bitch."

Ryan shook his head and smiled at me.

"Is this?"

He motioned to the baby.

I nodded at him.

"She's beautiful, Rachel." He complimented.

"Thank you," I smiled.

"So, what do you do now?" He asked me.

I nervously laughed, to point out the obvious. Ryan immediately realized the absurdity of the question.

"I mean, are you being home schooled are you going for your GED?"

I shrugged.

"Right now, I'm trying to find this girl Melissa who I think works here," I answered.

"A little...eccentric. Big coke bottle glasses, braces, isn't allowed to watch *The Simpsons*?"

Ryan laughed and nodded at me.

"Yeah, she still works here. I think she's actually on her smoke break right now."

I squinted my eyes as if to reconcile with such a contradiction

"She can't watch cartoons where they say the word 'ass'," I laughed.

"But she can smoke cigarettes? 90s parenting, am I right?" I quipped.

Ryan chuckled with me for a few moments before we were left standing in front of each other in awkward silence.

"Well, thanks,"

I spoke before abruptly maneuvering the stroller around and walking away. Sure enough, when Destiny and I went outside, Melissa was standing by herself taking the occasional drag from a menthol cigarette.

"Melissa?" I asked.

Melissa sat up from the corner and looked at me like she was in the presence of a ghost.

"Hi, I'm, uh"

Melissa cut me off,

"You're Janet's other sister."

I paused for a second.

Actually, I'm her only-"

Before I finished my sentence, I remembered that because Melissa was on the autism spectrum, she probably didn't understand that even though she and Janet lived in the same foster home at one time, that didn't mean they were actual siblings.

"That's right," I instead answered.

"Speaking of which, my parents wanted me to try to track her down and see if she'd want to spend Thanksgiving and her birthday with us this year. You wouldn't happen to know where I could find her, do you?"

Melissa looked confused and frightened.

"You mean, you STILL live with HIM? After what he did to you?"

I had no idea what she as on about or how to answer...

"I could understand why you would still want to have your baby, but I never would've believed you'd let her grow up around him."

Immediately, I was defensive and incensed by where I thought Melissa was going with this.

"What are you talking about?" I demanded.

Melissa started backing away when I approached her.

"MELISSA!" I hissed.

"Janet didn't tell you?" Melissa cried.

"That's why she hasn't been around..."

I assumed that she was referring to the night I got alcohol poisoning.

"You realize that I was pretty much comatose that night?" I shrieked.

"You were in the bathroom for a REALLY long time." Melissa answered.

"Janet sent me out of the room to go get you, but your dad was already in there with you."

We just stared at each other in silence as if somehow now deciding to communicate telepathically and without saying it out loud. I have never been able to recall anything after those few minutes with Melissa; suffice to say I simply blacked everything out. I had no recollection of heading back home or how I even behaved around anyone following my revelation.

As each day approached and inevitably passed, I became more disgusted with myself. I felt violated in every way you could possibly imagine. And Janet knew?! Why didn't she say anything? When did Melissa divulge what she saw to Janet? Was it while it was happening? Why didn't Janet do anything?

Then there was Destiny. How could I ever look at this beautiful child and think of anything but how she came to be? It was difficult enough trying to navigate my sexuality as a girl attracted to other girls; this alone made me feel like a mongrel. It only became worse knowing that I had carried a baby that half belonged to my own parent. Of all the deplorable things my father has ever done, it turned out I couldn't even entertain the depths of how repugnant he was. Rape was a hard-enough concept to wrap my head around; throwing a dash of incest in there was simply adding icing to a cake that was entirely made from icing.

The problem with addressing it publicly was no different than coming out as a gay woman. I ran the risk of being persecuted by a man I had always feared, but now realized was clearly incapable of healthy human emotion. When our mother divorced him, the shame regarding why was enough to make him pull all those humiliating stunts in Pine Banks, like scribbling his then ex-wife's home number all over the place for weirdoes to harass her. As I sat and reflected over the sixteen years, I had been this man's daughter, all I was able to feel was the fear he had inflicted in his children and his wife. The parking garage incident, the answering machine threats and the countless spats with Janet...

As I began going back in time and over his catalog of sins, I began to understand why Charlie was so messed up. Not to sully my own trauma, but I couldn't imagine the pain of having something like this happen if I was a boy. I was lucky to have a brother like Charlie. Not only was he tolerant despite our father trying to indoctrinate so much of his own hatred and prejudice in him, but he was the absolute antithesis of our father. Charlie had a temper, sure. However, Charlie's temper would cause him to cry.

If Charlie became frustrated with a homework assignment or even a difficult video game, shades of his father would surface in the form of breaking inanimate objects in a fit of rage. Almost immediately after realizing the collateral damage his anger collected, he would fall to pieces, sometimes for days, over the fact that in that fleeting moment he was a mirror reflection of a man he detested. It's really sad to think about. From the perspective of a parent, could you ever live with yourself knowing that your child genuinely hates you? I don't mean, why they use the fear of them hating you as leverage to get what they want when they're being a brat. This isn't the same as being grounded and a child storming out of a room and screaming, 'I hate you' before slamming a bedroom door behind them.

This is someone regarding you as an abject nightmare, something that both haunts them and perpetuates their distrust in others to the point where they wish you ceased to exist from this very planet. Imagine you helped in the co-creation of life, something pure and innocent and when it develops and ages it looks at you not as a deity or miracle worker...but as if you're the devil himself. From the perspective of a child? Can you imagine a young child feeling anything but unconditional warmth and love for the person who helped create them? Biologically speaking, it's a marvel when this amalgamation of two lives who instinctively relies on these people for emotional and physical sustenance.... grows to detest you.

What kind of person do you have to be for a child to look at you and not associate you with happiness and love? Good memories of amazing family dinners, or those proud moments when you were there to see them achieve a milestone in their young life just to show you something beautiful in themselves? I had that connection immediately with Destiny, but because of my brother's relationship with our father and even my own relationship with our mother at times, I wondered if having kids would be no different from having parents. Even my relationship with my own sister made me question the reliability of unconditional love.

I also wasn't sure how to explain Janet's absence that coming Thanksgiving without it somehow going back to what happened that fateful night. Unlike my sister, I was a terrible liar. My parents would know as soon as I began spinning a yarn about why Janet wasn't coming that something was rotten in Denmark. I also knew that I wouldn't be able to get away with the simple explanation that I was unable to reach any number of Janet's friends. If you threw a rock, you were bound to hit someone who knew Janet or someone who considered themselves a dear friend of hers, even if the feeling wasn't exactly mutual.

I turned to the only person who I felt the most comfortable confiding in—Tasha. It had been a while since we'd properly talked, and while I had every right to feel that Tasha was being unfair regarding my opening up about my sexuality, I understood why Tasha took it so personally. When my baby and I arrived at her grandparents' house, I immediately thought about how to go about approaching a religious home when I had committed one of the most notorious of sins. Here I was, a sixteen-year-old girl with barely a ninth-grade education and a baby out of wedlock. Once again, I was started to have qualms about my ability to lie.

What if they ask me whose child that is? I wasn't concerned about Tasha's grandparents knowing as they were even more reclusive than my own parents. Not to mention, Tasha didn't attend public school. So, I would have to lie. As I stared down at the tiny cherub looking up at me, I couldn't help but feel a sense of conviction with Destiny. Everyone was making me feel like a criminal. Yet, I was the victim. Even worse? The child was the victim. Then I thought about how much easier it would've been for people to believe that my father did this to me if I had only come clean about my closeted sexuality in the first place.

Tasha had every right to be mad at me. I'd spent my whole life making excuses for why I couldn't own myself. Yes, this is my daughter, I thought. What's wrong with that? She's innocent. She is not a culpable party here. Not only are you hurting her with the slut stigma you're giving me, but considering she's the product of rape, you're not stigmatizing an actual victim. I went from afraid to outraged. I decided to approach the front door of the home with Destiny in my arms. I took several deep breaths before ringing the doorbell and awaiting another judgmental guillotine to come crashing down on me. A few more moments passed, and I rang the bell again.

While I stood at the front door, I started to hear voices coming from the backyard. I then placed Destiny back in the stroller and made my way to the backyard where Tasha and some guy emerged from his car. They were very touchy feely with one another as they approached me. Tasha was clearly smitten with this man who clearly wasn't a boy as he had a five o'clock shadow and his voice was much deeper than the boys our age. I was attempting to leave when Tasha noticed me,

"Rachel?" She cried out.

I stopped dead in my tracks, and slowly began to turn to face my ex.

I nodded casually as Tasha approached me for a hug before introducing me to her male counterpart.

"Rachel, this is Edgar, Edgar, this is Rachel."

The gentleman reached his hand out and I politely shook it to not draw even more attention to how awkward the situation had become for me.

"And who’s this?" Tasha playfully giggled.

"Um, this is Destiny," I stammered.

"My daughter."

Tasha's eyes grew as wide as saucers as she approached me for yet another embrace.

"Are you two?"

I motioned awkwardly at them both. Tasha smiled and rested her head on his chest.

"He's a janitor at the library. We met a couple months ago after my mom was released." She answered.

I could feel the look of disbelief on my face.

"They released her?"

While my amazement was evident, I hoped it didn't come across as insulting. Tasha then began playing with Destiny's lips.

"So, who's your new beau? And the lucky papa?" She laughed.

I just shook my head.

"It's a long story. And you know what? I must go. This was clearly a mistake."

I started to take off with the stroller as Tasha spoke softly to her new boyfriend and chased after me.

"RACHEL! WAIT!"

Tasha ran in front of the stroller so I couldn't get any further away.

"What's going on here?" She sighed.

"You clearly came here after all this time of us not talking for something important. So? What is it?"

I couldn't help but break down in a fit of tears.

"YOU are SUCH a BITCH!" I shrieked.

"You made me feel SO bad about not being able to own myself to the point where I became so suicidal after you dumped me that THIS happened!" I screamed as I motioned at the carriage.

"I tried to drink myself to death, to get over YOU! Next thing I know I woke up in a hospital, was told that I had nearly died, a few months later I was pregnant," I explained.

"There is NO beau. There was only rape. And after talking to one of Janet's ex foster siblings, I found out it was my dad. So not only am I the only real dyke here? I'm the only one with a fucking kid now. Authentic? You? Little Miss You-Owe-It-To-Yourself-And-Me-To-Come-Out-Already?

"Go to hell."

I hissed as I shoved Tasha out of the way and ran off with the stroller. That was the last conversation the two girls had with one another.

Charlie stopped the tape again and let out a deep breath. He thought back to his sister's funeral. He remembered Tasha lamenting over that when she spoke at the service a year later. Tasha had turned and walked back to her new life as someone who no longer wanted to get a rise out of people for fear that she'd wind up creating and subsequently destroying another Rachel. Little did she know what little time Rachel would have left.

Rachel never did have to lie about her ability or inability to contact Janet. One day? Janet just appeared. While she never moved back into the family home, she would occasionally make a cameo appearance in our lives. Thanksgiving and Janet's birthday were both observed as dad had hoped for. Janet would regale our doting parents in stories about her new waitressing job, her not long for this world quasi ex-gang banger of a boyfriend whom she now lived with and was eventually expecting to have a child with. Meanwhile, Rachel sunk further into depression while I got lost with the lambs of Turtle Rock and curse of Bear Hills. Quietly, we both envied Janet for being something that couldn't be if they spent their whole lives trying.

Charlie went back to the tape,

"Janet managed to convince herself of her own lies. How fantastic she was doing and how she was able to make it on her own after so many bad years. The truth was, not one of the three of us was going to survive what we came from. We may move far away from it, but it would stay with us forever. In December of 1997, the cracks in Charlie's foundation were finally beginning to show. While many could look back and get nostalgic about 1997 over the arrival of Leonardo DiCaprio as a budding new Hollywood hunk after the success of the film Titanic...Charlie would look back and see it through another point of view.

Charlie had always been a romantic; since the age of five when our parents first divorced, he had always expressed an interest in love and starting his own family. By the time he was a fifth grader, he began to take more of an interest in girls. There were some girls he would write draft after draft after draft of love letters for. Some he discreetly snuck into their backpacks just before lunch, and some he never delivered at all. However, he never revealed himself to be anyone's secret admirer as he was beginning to realize...he would never be as cute as Leo DiCaprio as one of his peers once astutely asserted. Charlie was used to rejection.

He had been unfairly rejected from a family he barely knew, a family of people who never had any interest in touching or expressing any kind of obligatory love for him. He had been rejected from his peers between Janet's reputation as a slut and Rachel's early motherhood. Now he was entering an even more painful stage in his young life. Now women were rejecting him as well. This was the age that Charlie decided that he would never leave Turtle Rock. It was the only place that made him feel welcomed and comfortable.

That's where he would go every day after school. Once he stepped off the bus, he would go visit his friends at Turtle Rock for hours. He even started opening to them about his issues with Ms. V, and how a crush of his made fun of his teeth that day at lunch after some food was stuck in his braces. There had even been a new trend in his classroom. All the girls started chanting "Not Leo DiCaprio" at him whenever they'd catch him looking at them. That was when the initial idea was germinated in his angry mind. He began drawing a comic book in which he would clip the actor's head out of popular entertainment or tabloid rags and gluing them over drawings of a body being mutilated in various fashions.

He called it "DiCaprio's Dead", drawing in the same font as his current favorite franchise horror film *Freddy's Dead: The Final Nightmare*. Initially it started as a joke but soon evolved into a form of catharsis for him. All the anger and humiliation he felt over his bodily imperfections found solace in the mutilation of someone who had everything that Charlie couldn't possibly fathom. The newfound notoriety also started to encourage Charlie to take his comic strip even further. After all, with an audience came the potential for friends or at least the illusion of friends.

The more the other boys in class encouraged him to draw these graphic comics, the less of a misfit he felt, even though Ms. V didn't shy away from any and every opportunity to humble the fifth grader by reminding him of his shortcomings both academically and emotionally. Any opportunity she could get to sully Charlie's self-esteem in front of his peers appeared to be something she relished. Undoubtedly, if the whispers about Charlie's new hobby ever made it from the back of the school bus to the classroom, it was surely become fodder for Ms. V's crusade to ruin his reputation. Charlie knew this, even the lambs at Turtle Rock knew this, but all advice they gave him went unheeded.

After so many years of feeling like he couldn't express himself or articulate the feelings of dread and unhappiness inside of him due to his parents' fear of him being taken from their home? Charlie welcomed any chance he could get to make an impression, even if it wasn't exactly a good one. Regardless of my parental responsibilities, I recognized this and would try to take the fleeting free moments I had and get inside of his troubled mind. One night, an opportunity arose when Charlie decided he wanted to watch movies out in the living room on the pull-out sofa. It became an important evening for us as it marked the end of my eleven-year old brother referring to me as "Sissy", a name that Charlie now believed made him come across as even more of a baby than the accusations from other relatives that his mother had turned him into a "momma's boy".

While Destiny slept soundly in her room, Charlie and I spent hours playing Mortal Kombat and watching some of Charlie's favorite horror movies. During that time, I would use casual conversation to gather information about Charlie's last year of elementary school.

"So, I'm no longer your sissy?" I asked.

Charlie had his eyes glued to the television and his fingers glued to the controller as the two went head to head in a bloody fight. Realizing that Charlie had no interest in engaging with me, I remarked,

"I guess I have to get used to this new Charlie sitting next to me."

After a considerable silence, Charlie ended the match with me by maneuvering his fingers frantically around the controller, prompting his character to decapitate me on screen.

"It just makes me sound like a pussy when I call you that," he balked.

"Everyone in this family wants me to be cute all the time. The cute little blonde-haired, blue-eyed kid that sort of looks like Macaulay Culkin and does the stupid *Home Alone* face. No one treats me like that anymore. No one treats me like I'm cute. Everyone just makes fun of the way I talk, how I dress or even how I get my haircut. Everyone thinks it's weird that Mom loves me, and that I want to be a father. I guess I just feel ugly and feminine all the time now." He lamented.

I wasn't used to this new abstract Charlie.

"Why do you feel ugly and feminine?" I asked.

Charlie elbowed me and motioned to the screen, which was prompting us to pick our characters for the next round.

"What does that even mean, Charlie? You feel feminine?" I continued.

Charlie was distracted for several moments then blurted out,

"Guys my age, we're not supposed to like...I don't know, we're not supposed to like Prince or be close to our mothers or sisters. We're supposed to beat people up and swear a whole lot and make girls think we're cool. I don't feel cool. I don't even feel like the other guys in my grade.

Since I was five, I always felt like I should've been a little girl. I was too sensitive and too skinny. Like, I have a girl's body and I don't really know how to be a guy." He casually complained.

I just remember my face wearing sadness wondering how I missed all these newfound insecurities developing in my little brother.

"Plus, between Dad and Ms. V?" He started.

"It's hard to feel like a real guy, you know. They both treat me like such a weirdo and because of that, everyone else treats me the same way. I just walk around all the time feeling like this weirdo that no one thinks is cute, and if they thought I was cute before, now all of those same qualities I still have are strange to them."

“I was just about to say something when he blurted out,”

"I guess that's what being gay feels like. Like there's nothing wrong with you but people manage to make you so uncomfortable in your own body that you just want to hide all the time."

This revelation made me tear up.

"That's EXACTLY how it feels," I whimpered.

Charlie nodded with his eyes still transfixed by the television screen.

"I figured," he answered.

"I guess we're just weirdoes," he chimed.

"We don't have to be," I insisted.

“I remember he just sighed just before his bottom lip started to tremor, like he was trying to hold back the tears and then he turned to me,”

"What if that's our fate?" He asked.

"If we make it out of this house, alive? What are the chances we'll make it out and be able to have better futures?"

Not long after that I went to bed and Charlie fell asleep on the pull-out couch.

“Is there any chance I could get some water?” Rachel asked,

"Of course, sweetie. We can actually take a little break," Donald answered

The tape began to trail off long enough for Charlie to come back to reality. At least he thought so. Having a past like his, Charlie was used to people awkwardly staring at him. In this case he couldn't help but notice a young girl leaning over the back of her seat on the train scrutinizing him. Charlie wanted to be polite, so he gave her a friendly wave and went back to the tape deck and cassettes.

He placed his headphones back on thinking that would be a subtle enough of a hint that perhaps the little girl will sit back in her seat are at the very least stare at one of the other passengers.

"One. More. Sacrifice." Hissed in his ears.

Charlie grew pale and rewound the tape, but no audible sound was coming out.

"One. More. Sacrifice." It repeated.

Charlie realized that the voice wasn't coming from the headphones but from the little girl who was still staring through him. Before he could rationalize what was happening, her nose began bleeding profusely moments before she fell back from her seat screaming. Charlie sat frozen as other passengers began running to her aide as the mother removed her from the floor and started tending to her nose. She held her hand up to the other passengers to assure them that her little girl was fine and appreciated their concern.

Charlie sat frozen as he watched the commotion begin to die down while the mother was handed a package of tissues by one of the other passengers on board. He was curious if anyone else on the train had heard what she had said to him, and why more people weren't crowding around him asking what the hell this little child said to this man before seizing and hemorrhaging from her nose. Before Charlie could question his sanity, he brought himself back to the tapes and tried to shake the jarring scene from his mind. Surely, it was one of many to come.

He hit play.

"I stared into the vanity mirror overlooking the bed where Destiny soundly slept.

I couldn't shake Charlie's voice from my head: namely his lament over a better future outside of this house. Everyone in the neighborhood chocked all the bad that developed in the home up to some ghost story or arbitrary superstition. I knew that it came down to more than that, but if I had to burn the house down...I would, just to prove a point. In that fleeting moment of irrationality, an idea finally manifested.

There was never going to be any way that our mother would believe my sexual assault, namely because our parents loved each other more than the kids they created. Decades ago, when Janet was born, Dad was imprisoned for allegedly trying to burn down a hospital he was contracted to do a painting job for. I had made peace with the fact that the only crime I could have my dad put away for would be something from his past. No matter how many people I screamed in the faces of, no one would ever believe that my baby was the product of incest. However, when our parents were separated, I remembered the answering machine tape that our mom was forced to use in court as evidence of Dad's sociopathic behavior.

He very drunkenly and nonchalantly mentioned how weak and old the foundation of the Pine Banks home was and how quickly it could catch fire. While it scared the shit out of all of us to hear our dad talking about this, the intimation became far more sinister when I remembered an altercation in which Dad tossed Mom to the floor just before blacking out in their bedroom. Mom had admitted that he did in fact start the fire and he had a history of arson. This, in addition to a myriad of other incidents, is why Mom was awarded full custody to begin with. He had a history of burning things; what if this house became another one of those things? It was unfathomable that I could consider such a diabolical thing, but in my moment of fear for my brother and my daughter, the only future I could conceive would exist only if this place burned to the ground.

I was awoken by the sound of my baby wrestling around in her crib. I quietly tip-toed into her nursery to get a peak. Destiny's brown eyes were staring into the void that was the silhouette of my presence. I carefully patted down the mat to see that her diaper had leaked through and onto the sheets. Without so much as whimper, Destiny patiently waited as I attempted to change her diaper in the pitch-black room. The tiniest of yawns escaped her heart-shaped lips as she reached up for my shoulder and rested her head, beginning to drift back asleep once I lifted her up.

"You're too good for this place,"

I whispered in Destiny's ear as I swayed back and forth with her before bringing her into my room, planting a kiss on her brow and placing her onto my bed. I created a fortress of pillows around her before making my way into the bathroom and blankly staring into the mirror. My reflection wasn't something I normally wanted to gaze at; I'd had an aversion to mirrors since I was a little girl.

Initially, the third Poltergeist movie was culpable for this, until I started going through puberty and began harboring a sincere resentment for our parents' genetic legacy.

After scrutinizing myself in the mirror for several minutes, I walked out into the living room to find Charlie sleeping in typical Charlie fashion: one leg stretched in the air, and the other leg still attempting to wrestle its way out of the blanket covering him. I smiled and casually walked into the kitchen to prepare a formula for Destiny where I saw the tower of empty beer cans overwhelming the trash can just beside their front door. While Charlie was certainly capable of preparing his own breakfast, I left a bowl and box of cereal out for him knowing fully well that our parents wouldn't be waking up until well after noon. I returned to the bedroom with the bottle and sat on the bed watching the sunrise while contemplating how much more of this life I could endure.

The countless threats from our mother to have Destiny taken away from me, the obvious sexual abuse that not only me, but also Charlie had endured at the hands of our sociopath of a father, made even worse by our mother's Stockholm syndrome with my Dad. It wasn't going to be enough to get Charlie and Destiny out of that house; I had to make sure that Roger would never ever get his hands on any of us ever again. Maybe it was postpartum, maybe it was post-traumatic stress, but within a matter of seconds I went back out into the living room to wake up my sleeping brother. In his groggy state, he tended to be very compliant and not ask too many questions.

"Charlie!" I shook,

"Charlie!"

Charlie's head began to rise as I whispered

"Can you go lay in my room with Destiny? I just have to run a quick errand."

He nodded and slowly rolled off the pull-out couch and shuffled his way into my bedroom and curled up next to his baby niece. I then put on a pair of slippers and made my way out to the backyard and into the shed underneath the home's patio. I tried to quietly maneuver around both my father's power tools and all the spider webs festooning the ceiling over the shed. As I approached the further part of the shed, I spotted two red gasoline containers right next to the propane tanks for our father's coveted grill.

I raced down a few blocks to the nearest gas station, and with only ten dollars in her pocket, filled both containers with gasoline. The walk back home was difficult as I wasn't famous for my muscularity nor for my reliability to not drop and spill things. However, I successfully made it back home where I hid the gas containers under a tarp in the shed. I then climbed back up the stairs, wiped off the soles of my slippers and sent Charlie back out to the couch so I could lay next to my daughter one last time. The only question was now, how would I manage to pull off the next part of my plan? And what was I going to do with Charlie and Destiny while I attempted to pull it off?

My eyelids became too heavy to hold up any longer and before I could finish the thought, the whole room faded to black. When I awoke Destiny was rolling to and from with her hands clasped and a smile on her face. I was smiling back at her when a loud clap could be heard just outside the door. I placed even more pillows around Destiny so I could quietly walk toward the door and pressed my ear against it.

“I’m late for work!” I heard Dad shout.

Before another handclap resonated in the hallways, I knew without seeing the backhand to our mother’s face. This was the type of confrontation between our parents that too many people had seen to pretend it never happened. I was unusually reserved; typically, during such events I’d spring into action and take the brunt of the last drop of our father’s anger...that was harder to do with Destiny in the picture. Unfortunately, this left Charlie next in line. I held the palm of my hand over my mouth as I heard the words,

“What are you going to do about it? You little pussy!”

before the next clap permeated from the living room and down the hall. This was the first instance of Roger unabashedly hitting Charlie in front of anyone. He always did so when and where no one could see.

Once the backdoor slammed and the sound of the Hyundai starting up and exiting the driveway allayed my senses, I immediately exited the room to find Mom on the ground sobbing with her right hand pressed against an already bruised cheek. I then turned down the hall to find Charlie stoically playing a video game with the signature red of a handprint against his face. When I knelt to address our mom

“I forgot to wake him up,”

That was all she could muster in her hysteria. In that moment, I became determined in my hatred of this woman who had no discernible maternal instincts whatsoever.

“You disgust me!”

I sneered at her before gathering Destiny in my arms, marching down the hall and grabbing my brother to exit the family’s home.

We wound up at a park right next to the police station. My brother and I were on swings as my foot rocked the carriage my daughter was sleeping in back and forth. I scrutinized Charlie, who was recoiled in fear, humiliation, and visible anger, and decided to finally confide in him what no one else could be willing to hear.

"Charlie?" I spoke,

"Do you know what rape is?"

Charlie's head rose and exposed his visible humiliation and sorrow, but still, he nodded.

"You know I'm gay, right?"

Again Charlie, with his head hung low again, nodded ever so casually.

"So how do I have a baby, right now?" I sarcastically sneered.

Charlie shrugged and mumbled under his breath.

"What are you saying?" he calmly asked.

"I thought it was one of Janet's friends," he cried. "You know, they probably took advantage of you when you were drunk.

I vehemently shook my head and blurted out,

"Dad."

"Dad?" Charlie sniffled

"Dad raped me that night," I sobbed.

Charlie immediately flung himself off the swing and gestured toward the police station next door.

"Rachel!" he cried out,

"We have to tell someone! We have to tell someone right now, while he's at work!"

Charlie began to motion again toward the police station where he was now marching, but I managed to stop him dead in his tracks.

"Charlie," I insisted.

"No one will ever believe us. No one likes us, remember? And you don't think that if we tried that, Dad wouldn't kill the three of us?"

I motioned to the stroller where Destiny was sleeping.

"Charlie, we have to be smarter than that."

Charlie appeared confused. To him, the most logical or rational way to deal with their sociopathic, rapist father would be to report him immediately. His past would hopefully be enough to convict him long enough that all three of them could move far away from him and never to be haunted by his abuse ever again.

"Charlie," I again insisted,

"Dad isn't someone who will simply go away. We can't trust anyone to do to him what we need to be done. He needs to go away forever."

"What should we do?" Charlie cried.

"I have a plan that'll make sure he never hurts any of us again. But I can't tell you. I just need you to hide for a while. I'm going to figure out the rest of the plan, but just wait until I figure it out, ok? And promise me. No cops. No Grandma and Grandpa. Just US."

Charlie hesitated but after seeing the intense welling of tears in my eyes, he complied.

"Aren't you going to change first?" He joked.

"You're still in your pajamas and slippers. And you wreak of gasoline."

I laughed before rubbing his head, kissing him on the cheek, and taking Destiny away from him.

"Wait!" He shouted.

I turned, almost annoyed.

"Where should I-I mean, if I hide, how will you know

where to find me?" He wondered.

"You only have three spots," I smiled.

"I'll know where to find you."

Charlie paused the tape. He remembered that day vividly...

That was the last time Charlie felt he was ever going to see his sister or niece alive, and despite her demands not to involve any kind of fallible authority figure, he couldn't help but stare at the payphone near the town hall. He waited for twenty-minutes, watching parents enter and leave the park with their young kids. One young father caught his attention over the others. His little boy was as rambunctious as Charlie remembered being at that age; however, this father was excited to watch his son scale the slides in the park and toss mulch around like it was confetti. Charlie's only memories of playing with his dad in the park often ended with his dad disappearing, much to Charlie's horror, forcing Charlie to assimilate into a group of kids with parental supervision so he wouldn't get kidnapped.

When his dad turned up, he always had the odious smell of hot yeast or a dead animal on him. This is how Charlie knew that his father had left Charlie in the playground so he could go to the nearest liquor store to pick up something to get him inebriated enough to care that he had a little one. There was no frame of reference Charlie could pull from regarding a normal childhood save for the family portraits of his friends and their families on amusement park vacations or milestones like a communion, or an aging relative celebrating a birthday past their 70s. The only things above the mantle in Charlie's home were beer can models fashioned like old pirate ships that some drunk with a hobby gave to his dad at their insipid moving company. Charlie felt uncomfortable around men, whether they were fathers or brothers or anyone who seemed like they could potentially dislike him. That was the precedent his father created for him; a little boy desperately looking for a man to cultivate him into something better...instead he was gifted with two delinquent sisters and a punching bag for a mother, all of whom answered to the belligerent abuser who would love nothing more than to burn the house down while they all slept.

In that moment, the smell of gasoline on Rachel made more sense....

XI
BEAR HILLS, MASSACHUSETTS. 2018

Charlie was snapped out of his headspace by the sound of the conductor alerting passengers of their final stop. It felt like the only good sleep Charlie had been privileged with for almost two decades. As he staggered to his feet, gathering all his belongings, he couldn't help but spot the specter outside the window awaiting his arrival. Janet, the only link between him and that horrific night, seemed impatient for him to exit the train. He was immediately aggravated by the cumbersome nature of her arrival to the station. He had no interest in engaging with anyone outside of the context of Ricky's funeral. Ricky's funeral was merely a catalyst for what he really came home to pursue, and it certainly had nothing to do with her.

When he finally exited the train, Janet made a point to approach him before he even had the chance to elude her company.

"Hey, little brother." She scoffed.

"Hi Janet," he answered coldly.

"Aren't you under house arrest? Violating probation? Or did you just skip out on jury duty? I'm forgetting why I really don't want you to be talking to me."

She sneered, but in a comical way, as if she understood the distance between them but was unwilling to let him be.

"What, no hug?" She joked.

Charlie gently pushed her away from him, and immediately put her on notice.

"I don't know why you're here...literally or figuratively.... unless you're simply trying to upset the diligent taxpayers, who keep you on the proverbial feeding tube you rely on. Regardless, I'm not here for you."

"Then why did you answer my call?"

"Because it was Tasha's number." He sneered back.

Janet became less humored by her brother's come backs. She liked him better before he could hold his own.

"You have nowhere to stay," she warned.

"I'll find a motel," he offered.

"I know you better than anyone, and you hate the idea of bed bugs...and let me assure you, any motel within walking distance from here? That's the only thing you'll find under the sheets with you tonight."

Charlie held up his index finger as if to flip her off by showing her his wedding band.

"I'll manage," he answered.

"Oh, so she's still with you then?" She venomously spoke.

"Figured after the career alcoholic you aspired to be, she would've murdered you and taken all your money by now."

Charlie's patience for his petulant sister diminished with every sight of her snaggle-toothed grin and the subsequent odious smell of her halitosis.

"I'd assume most men in this town would pick bed bugs over.... how much do you charge a night?"

Janet shed her somewhat friendly wit for a more

confrontational demeanor.

"You and Rachel did this to me," she growled.

Charlie, midway through the station, turned and finally addressed his sister in a demeanor which he wasn't proud of but had rehearsed his whole life.

"You know, it's a shame," he lamented.

"The night everything happened. The house would've burned down so much sooner had we had a little more kindling to light on fire. Unfortunately, that was the only time you weren't there to grace us with your presence."

As Charlie turned his back to Janet, she immediately began to fester so much that her fidgeting and snarls caught Charlie's attention. He turned his head to find a grotesque, cadaverous vision of his father staring back at him.

"You let them alllllllll alone Char.... LIEEEEEEE," he sang.

"But your blood courses with heroin and leprosy. All I have to do is touch him....and then he'll dance......"

Charlie's attention was then turned to the lifeless body of his baby boy attached to strings as this ghastly figure used him like a marionette.

"I'll make him dance and dance and DANCE.... because he's ours now Charlie, and I can make him do whatever I want!"

As Charlie charged toward the figure, he realized it was another figment of his warped imagination and in trying to stop himself, staggered before slipping off the ledge and onto the rail. When he came to, the announcement of another train's arrival made him scurry and scramble his way back to his feet and back up toward the station before he could be pulverized by an oncoming train. Shaken, he took a few seconds to collect himself before he spotted mutated Janet in the conductor's window, maniacally laughing and waving her languid, gangrene-covered arm.

As he sat on the concrete, terrified, he wondered how long it would take to grieve and say goodbye to an old friend, and if in doing so he could make all these visions stop. He knew Janet had been dead for a while. It was a heroin overdose: a particularly ugly kind of heroin overdose. He'd chosen not to return home to bury her. A Go Fund Me page gathered up a meager amount of resources to take care of that. She wasn't even buried; cremated.... though Charlie didn't have even the most remote idea of where the hell she would've wanted her body to go. He knew before coming home that he was an orphan, but the town had a certain way of making you feel guilty for taking pride in your orphanage. Unfortunately, the more you try to suppress your past, the more it festers inside of you...and while Charlie did have an adopted family, he knew the only person who really embraced him in that environment was Rachel's former social worker Donald.

Unfortunately, Donald's wife and kids didn't embrace Charlie the way that their husband and father did. Sometimes, the only reason Charlie could think that Donald cared so much about him was so he could learn more about what really happened that night in 1998. Eventually, there was an ugly divorce and Donald took Charlie with him. Donald's alcoholism became more evident and when Charlie was finally able to distance himself from all the toxic aspects of his past, he did so. Donald passed away a few years ago from esophageal cancer. The two were close, but there was always a nagging guilt that had if he'd never brought Charlie home, this man wouldn't have lost a life that could have been much more fulfilling and promising without the unhealthy obsession he had with Charlie's biological family. There was more guilt than resolution in Charlie's life, which in turn drove him to his own means of mitigating all these feelings of shame and guilt.

Even if Charlie could confront the specter lingering around him and threatening his future with Lorraine and Dylan, who's to say that Donald wouldn't manifest as some vengeful wraith coming for a restitution of flesh and soul for what happened to his perfect life before the Harris case completely consumed him. While Charlie ruminated over this, he was grateful that he was a light packer because the walk from the station to the nearest motel was long enough to make the callouses on his soles somewhat insufferable. When he reached the motel, it looked nothing like he remembered it. There was a time when the Bear Hills Motel was a hot spot for amateur porn filmmakers and acted as a makeshift shelter for battered women and their children. It made Charlie feel uncomfortable that they tore down the old flea bag and replaced with something that could easily be mistaken for luxury townhouses or condos.

It was late enough that Charlie could probably get away with calling it an early night so he could take an Uber to the funeral home for tomorrow's service, but not too late for him to walk to the nearest liquor store and stock up so he could get inebriated enough to sleep without missing his alarm in the morning. He had never been inside the old motel, but he could deduce that the interior design of this place was much less intimidating to someone looking for a cheap place to crash. In fact, he remembered going to grade school with a kid who lived in the motel with his mother at one point. A couple of mutual friends went over to play Super Nintendo with him, and at recess the following day, one of them even remarked that it looked like a place you would see in a porno.

There wasn't really a need to unpack his suitcase which (in addition to the tapes) only carried two outfits: dressier clothes for a funeral, what his mother would consider an after-school outfit (that's what he planned to wear to Turtle Rock) and something no one knew he possessed—his father's axe. Twenty years ago, Charlie discarded it in the place where he remembered seeing the pipe people. This was the same place where Donald found him, right across from the hospital that Rachel would become a patient in. There was this old colonial house that was as creepy as it was breathtaking. This must've been where "the pipe people" sought shelter. When he was instructed to hide, this was the only place Charlie could think to go as no one else would dare look there for him.

Instead, that's where he hid the axe. The same one he used to attack his father with, it felt poetic, seeing as how it was the same one, he'd pulled on his mother and sisters on numerous occasions. He completely forgot all about it until Donald passed away. When he was cleaning out the house, he found it under Donald's bed, though he could never rationalize a reason why Donald would even want it in his possession. Technically, it should have been considered evidence, much like all the kitchen knives that the police confiscated from the house when Janet tried to kill Rachel and their parents. His mother never got over that, and anytime steak was served, she'd break down in hysterical tears thinking about how they could never afford to replace them.

Taking into consideration possible cleaning staff, Charlie made sure to keep the axe hidden in his suitcase and under the bed just in case any destitute and poorly-treated housekeeper began ransacking personal possessions for anything they could pawn for gas or rent money. There was an internal debate Charlie had with himself for a good twenty minutes as to whether it was a good idea to drink, but with every glance of the clock, he realized that he should stock up before they closed and have a spirited debate with himself about it later. He wound up settling for a few nips of bourbon (like the ones they sell on airplanes) and a few tall boys of the only beer he could stomach. He sat quietly in his room nursing his drinks and trying his best not to get cold feet about paying his respects tomorrow to Ricky...but more specifically to the lambs who protected him that fateful night.

The older Charlie became, the more he wonders if he simply had a wildly active imagination, or if the spirits of all the dead children of Bear Hills did in fact protect him and Rachel the night their father was killed. He even wondered about the specter following him currently. He stared down at his beverage and wondered if maybe his drinking had reached the point of giving him delirium tremens. It felt too real to be a kind of psychosis, alcohol-induced or manic visions from being bi-polar. There was a long stretch after his son was born that Charlie didn't imbibe alcohol at all, and he faithfully took his mood stabilizers. It wasn't until he caught the first hint of paralyzing fear in his son's eyes that he realized something was haunting his new family.

That was the scariest thing about being a parent. Sure, the lack of sleep or the fear that his son might choke on his food or, God forbid, pop a foreign object in his mouth made Charlie a paranoid wreck.... but then there was the more elusive, intangible danger. Charlie was always desperate for companionship, in friendships and in love. His therapist had asserted that his incessant need for love and acceptance stemmed from all the macabre shit he'd endured as a young boy, but Charlie also knew that it came from his obsessive desire to start a family of his own. He lost everyone twenty years ago, and seemingly without warning. Even if Charlie hadn't beat Rachel to the punch by starting the fire, Roger was probably one or two more benders away from killing everyone who lived in that house.

While Charlie certainly felt culpable for expediting the process and being the only survivor from it (save for Janet, even though she died later), he knew deep down that his family was a grenade that had lost its pin long before Charlie had the courage to throw it. The house was less than a five-minute walk from the motel. It seemed weird that Charlie managed to walk right by it without so much as even noticing whether they used the land to build an even crappier property. Maybe it was the booze coursing through his veins, or morbid curiosity, but Charlie decided to take a walk just to entertain the recurring thought in his head of what stood where the horrors of his childhood were now buried. As he exited his motel room, he couldn't help but pick up on the smell of burning wood.

This was Charlie's favorite smell; it always reminded him of autumn and people warming themselves by their backyard fire pits. It also reminded him of the fireplace that they had in the home. Roger used to steal this paper that looked like the same kind that newspapers were printed on and he'd get one of those store-bought logs that you could burn. He'd then stuff these papers under the log, and it would create this illuminating and amazing blaze. Often, Charlie would just lay flat on the floor with his hands under his chin and just watch it burn. The smell made him nostalgic for Halloween and the old neighborhoods of Pine Banks.

Eventually, Roger invested in an axe so he could chop his own wood and save himself a great deal of money by not getting the expensive stuff at the local Caldor. That tool also proved to have an even more useful purpose: disciplining the kids and scaring his wife. As a boy, Charlie had never understood the reference, but months after purchasing that axe it became more and more common for people to joke that it wouldn't surprise anyone in town if Roger Harris turned out to be a real-life Jack Torrance. Charlie's father also wasn't stupid; the talk eventually made its way back to him and during one scuffle with their mom in which she locked herself in their bedroom, he chopped down the door and screamed,

"Heeeeeere's ROGER!"

Charlie would argue incessantly that he found Kubrick's films to be tedious and otherwise too large of an investment to make to appreciate them. In reality? He resented the film for inspiring one of the scariest moments in Charlie's life. Then again, it probably isn't too presumptuous to think that everyone perceives their own families like a waking horror movie at times. There's the dad who drinks too much, the mother who enables too much, and the siblings who you aren't quite convinced won't smother you in your sleep. At least, this was the reality of Charlie's life growing up. There was one memory that always reinstated that for him. Rachel and Janet never ever got along, Janet was the alpha bitch and Rachel was the fodder for all her cruelty.

One incident when they were younger, the two girls got into a fight over a shared Cabbage Patch doll. The fight escalated and during the tug of war, Janet managed to out brute Rachel and take ownership of the doll. Once it was in her hands? She tried to bludgeon Rachel with it, repeatedly beating her over the back of the head. Rachel often joked (being flexible with the word "joke") that if you rubbed your fingers against the back of her skull, you could still feel the imprint the nose of the doll made when she was being smashed with it. Once, when the girls got into an argument no doubt over something else VERY trivial, Janet instructed Rachel to sleep with one eye open. Given the Cabbage Patch incident, it scared Rachel enough that she bunked with Charlie later that night.

The two had an alarm clock radio in their room and during the Proclaimers "I'm Gonna Be (500 Miles)" Janet slid into the room with her stockinged feet and preceded to lip sync the entire song to Rachel in a very creepy way. After Janet exited the room in a fit of giggles, Rachel revealed to Charlie that she had wet the bed. Without giving Janet the benefit of making her sister lose bladder control, the two kids stripped the bed of his Jurassic Park bed sheets and buried them in the backyard. The next morning, their mother was baffled by the California Raisins on Charlie's bed but didn't feel the need to investigate the matter further. They had that kind of relationship; that's why Rachel took the fall for Charlie after he let their father fall to his death off Turtle Rock.

She was returning the favor of never letting her lose her dignity whenever Janet made her pee the bed when she was old enough not to. Neither child ever needed to exchange the appropriate gratitude for the other; it was part of the unspoken bond they shared as hostages to a family that got off on torturing them for being the only two with any sensitivity or ambition to one day escape when the opportunity presented itself. Charlie tried hard not to blame himself for Rachel's suicide in that facility; in a way, that's probably the largest contributor to why he never tried to reconnect with Destiny as an adult. It was his fault that Destiny didn't grow up with a mother. It was also one of a myriad of reasons Charlie wrote under a penname; he didn't want Destiny to find him having even a modicum of success as a writer and track him down to maim or kill his child as restitution for what he let her mom do. Being a father might have been the most selfish and dangerous act of carelessness in his entire life.

He didn't want his only son to have to pay for the mistakes of his past, nor did he want him to be held in the bondage by the curse of his last name. The smell of burning wood became more and more prominent the closer he got to the land where his childhood home once stood. As Charlie approached the property, he was mortified by the sight of an entire playground on fire. Before him was a teeter-totter with two children gleefully rising and falling while engulfed in flames and children spinning around on a medal sphere, undaunted by their roasting bodies, while the swing set just rocked back and forth with tiny, burning people. Charlie's mouth was agape while tears streamed from his eyes as he noticed a plaque which read "Where Childhoods Come to Die. Burn in HELL Harris Family". He couldn't move a muscle nor could he even exhume a scream of horror; he simply watched and the trauma of burning children brought him to his knees.

"Yo! Dude!" a voice called out.

Charlie immediately came to and realized that he was simply staring at an empty playground now referred to as "Harris Memorial Park".

"Hey man," another cried out. "Are you alright?"

Charlie was still unable to flinch much less acknowledge their sobering acknowledgements of his horrified face. When he was finally able, he simply nodded as the feeling returned to his fingers and his tall boy slipped form his hand, smashing to the concrete and spraying beer out of puncture holes in the can. He immediately turned and ran back to his motel. As he scrambled back inside, he fell to his knees, crawled quickly toward the toilet and began violently vomiting up a thick black tar. He began to choke and gasp on air as something violently made its way up his esophagus. He reached into his mouth and as he gagged, he started pulling out pieces of paper, which appeared to be divorce documents signed by his wife followed by a few pages of his recent manuscript. He rested his head on the toilet seat while out of the now teary and groggy eyes spotted a mirror which appeared to be bleeding.

He forced himself up and tried his best to wipe the blood from the mirror when he heard the door to his motel room shut violently. When he turned his attention to it, the ghastly specter of his father held his index finger to his lips before reaching under the bed and ransacking Charlie's suitcase and reaching for his axe.

"Sticks and stones will break your bones," he sang. "But Daddy's here to finally kill you."

The specter held up the axe and took a swing at Charlie, who desperately cried out and held his arms up to block the shot. It was bearing down on him when Charlie violently sat up in his bed. His attention was turned to his smartphone's blue blinking light. When he massaged his thumb print across the screen, he saw several missed calls and texts from his wife. The texts all contained photos of their son with desperate pleas from Lorraine as to whether her husband was still alive and okay. Charlie immediately jumped out of his bed and took his phone outside where he chain-smoked half a pack of cigarettes, sobbing at the sight of their child and trying to reconcile with the thought of his wife wondering if he was okay.

The reason he didn't think to call back or even reply to her messages? He wasn't sure if being okay was a reality for him. The world of Charlie Harris was one perpetual and unmitigated nightmare that made him feel guilty and ashamed that he had the gumption to invite another person into it, much less create another human to share the fear of this life with. If he was to write a book about fear, if he was to take away the façade of another person's name and with a newfound defiance say, 'this is me with all my baggage, fetishism, and torture.... this is absolutely me, now....' would she or Dylan still love him tomorrow?

He turned his mind to the funeral, to bury a friend who was merely a borrowed friend in a lot of ways. There came a point in Charlie's life when he felt ashamed of his sisters when he was old enough to feel shame. When they lived together before the fire, and through the controversy of death.... Charlie wanted sisters that were never his to begin with. The whole idea of family was an abstraction in retrospect. He would be the only living Harris to attend a funeral for Ricky, and he needed to do so with conviction despite how nauseating the social implications of that would become to him. When someone dies young, you tend to wonder why that is and then you're reminded of demons. Charlie got to the filter of his last cigarette, to the nicotine-stained fingertips of his index and ring finger before that revelation was enough.

The next day, he wore the Kohl's funeral fatigues that Lorraine helped him pick out and he braved the controversy of his reality. No matter how infamous the name was or how many people invested themselves in the morbid details of his past, somehow he managed to navigate his way through a sea of bereft individuals to kneel before a jaundiced individual whose family couldn't afford a Stan Winston make-up job for their son who'd succumbed to alcohol poisoning. Charlie could remember the face when it was alive, but the sound of Ricky's voice or even his subtle nuances were escaping those memories, and that's what drove him to tears. How is it that Charlie could still be haunted by a past he no longer recognized or remembered the sound of anymore?

"It's kind of inhumane, don't you think?" A voice resonated.

"It should've been a closed casket, out of sight and out of mind for the rest of us. But that's what his family wanted."

Charlie turned over his shoulder to see Tasha, or at least someone resembling Tasha, standing behind him.

"He asked about you every day," she insisted.

Charlie immediately stood up and embraced this pixie cut wearing woman in a dress blouse, dress slacks and ballet flats who was a far cry from her younger predecessor. She immediately squeezed him and pressed her lips against his neck and began to sob.

"I never thought I'd see you again," she cried.

Charlie rubbed her back and was doing his best to calm her hysteria when she blurted out,

"What REALLY happed that night? I need to know."

He released himself from her embrace and stared into the freckles of her eyes, looking for a shooting star.

"Why?" He begged.

"Because she is desperate to know why she's never met her uncle."

Charlie stopped keeping track of Destiny over the years, but Tasha is the last person he remembered her being left with. He just never expected Tasha to be responsible enough to care for her for so many years.

"Destiny?" He wondered aloud.

"You owe me a conversation," she asserted, then she embraced Charlie again.

"I know," he whispered into her ear.

Charlie spent the remainder of the service sitting as far back as he could, hoping that no one would recognize him or try to entertain a guess as to who he was. His somewhat haggard appearance would never tip people off that he was the last surviving Harris, but it also seemed to draw a lot more attention than he would be able to deflect if he stayed for the whole service. Tasha was seated in the second row next to a young girl who fit the description of his niece: blonde haired, skinny as a rail, and somewhat awkward in her demeanor.

Just from seeing the back of her head, in terms of her build...you could've convinced Charlie that it was in fact his deceased sister...well, the deceased one he cared about. Charlie removed his smartphone from his pocket and did his best to text a somewhat coherent message to the number that initially called him. He was hoping it wasn't a LAN line so that Tasha would know where to find him when in a matter of moments, he casually exited the funeral home. Ricky would've understood, or so he tried to convince himself. Just as Charlie slipped his cell phone back into his pocket and glanced up at the rows in front of him...all of them were empty.

It was just Charlie and the box containing his dead friend. Deep down, he knew that this was simply another delusion created by his manic brain, or perhaps another sleight of hand on behalf of his father. Charlie began to stand to his feet when he turned to find the casket empty. He furrowed his brow and became transfixed by the disappearance of Ricky's corpse. He started to back away quietly as to not draw any more attention to himself. Once he exited the viewing room, he quickly ran down the stairs toward the main entrance when he was greeted by Ricky's cadaver holding the door open for him.

"Welcome home, Chucky!"

it sneered as he hurried out the door and a few blocks away where he ducked into an alley to catch his breath.

Charlie was now sobbing and gasping for air. He didn't think he could take much more of this and started undoing his necktie and unbuttoning his collar to ease the sensation that he was being strangled. After fifteen minutes of gagging and sobbing, he eventually put as much distance between himself and Ricky as he could. He found a new, upscale bar in what used to be a rather uninspired town square. The only reason to bother taking your bike or walking to it with your friends was the pizza joint that everyone raved about (Charlie found it painfully mediocre), a tiny hole in the wall comic book shop (where Charlie spent most of his time amassing trading cards and pogs), and an ice cream parlor.

Unfortunately, all these things had been replaced by a Thai take-out place, pet groomer, and a now vacant Vape shop, respectively. The disappointment was enough to convince Charlie not to walk further and see that his favorite video store had inevitably closed and turned into something that would make him feel old and irrelevant. There was a used bookstore a few blocks away that he didn't recognize, so he decided to kill some time in there while he waited for Tasha to text him back. As he gazed in the window, he recognized all the usual suspects that tried to lure in potential buyers: books from the Harry Potter franchise, books from the Twilight franchise, and a vehemently anti-Donald Trump book beside a vehemently 'if you don't like Donald Trump , you're a libtard' book.

What particularly caught his eye was a book he'd only learned about during an episode of *Hard Copy* he'd watched not long after the events involving his family took place. A tell-all (but undoubtedly conspiracy theory) book about his very own family and their deaths. While the price of the now out of print book was somewhat steep ($40), his curiosity couldn't be mitigated, and he immediately entered the shop and asked the owner if he could purchase it. Ironically, as Charlie walked out with his generic white plastic "Thank you" bag, he noticed that the owner was quick to replace the gap left in the window with a copy of E.H. Ramsey's last best-seller.

"If you only knew," Charlie smiled under his breath as he made the long trek back to his motel room. Once he made it through the door to his room, he immediately began ripping off his dress clothes in favor of his grungier fatigues. He tossed the bag on the bed and decided to reach into the mini fridge near the bathroom for his nips and a can of Coke. He fixed himself a rather weak bourbon and coke before he sat back on the bed and thumbed through the hardcover which had clearly seen better days. For whatever reason, whether it was magazines or books, Charlie always liked to start from the back pages and flip his way back to the cover.

When he got to the front page, he couldn't help but notice some handwriting underneath the title which read,

"Stephanie,

These girls went to our high school! And I'm pretty sure my little brother knew the young boy. How crazy is that? Something COOL happened HERE!

Cyndi"

Charlie couldn't help but chuckle over the fact that while the events of 1998 had taken a severe emotional and intellectual toll on his life going forward, at least two high school aged girls thought it was cool. He immediately snapped the book shut and tossed it into the trash can before resting his forehead against the wall as more tears streamed down his cheeks. He didn't want this piece of trivial garbage to sully every bit of courage it had taken to make him ditch the stupid moniker and start being credited for writing the books he really labored over and harbored such a great deal of passion for. There was always going to be a catch to it, however.

Without even reading the book, he could surmise what someone would dare to publish about the family: the parents were two shut-in alcoholics who had no right to procreate, Janet was a trampy narcissist who everyone expected to die in the fashion that she did, Rachel was a sociopath and teenage whore, and the little boy probably would've grown up to shoot up a high school if he'd stayed. He'd heard it, read it, and had seen all the slanderous remarks before, and while Charlie certainly had no real attachment to most of his past...that was still his family. They were REAL people, and for so many years he struggled with the idea of 'real' given that his entire existence was based on so many falsehoods. It's cool that Bear Hills has this macabre piece of folk lore to emancipate it from the collective ennui of being otherwise painfully insipid...but why did his family's tragedy have to be the catalyst for that?

Then the qualms about his professional decision came flooding back into his mind. What if by coming out and admitting that he was Charlie Harris and that he was writing a book inspired by the events of his life, it didn't sell. What if people were so OVER hearing about this little, white trash, dysfunctional family who'd snuck into the suburbs and completely ruined its little town's reputation and they decided not only that it wasn't worth reading, but everything else he had published was now tainted as well? And then, what if the book is a literary smash and sells SO many copies and God forbid, even gets optioned into a major motion picture? Would he really want that? More specifically, would it simply get all that...not on the merit of his talent and work but because people felt it piggybacked on an otherwise lucrative scandal?

The fear of being considered a fraud, or a hack had haunted Charlie for as long as he could remember. It became exacerbated once he had a child, and wife. Despite Charlie's seemingly never-ending amount of emotional baggage, she had agreed to vow her life to him anyway. He couldn't help but think back to some of their more Lifetime Movie of the Week worthy battles, and how the two would just lose control and how he felt that his life was simply a burden on her and every single bit of him was going to contaminate her bright future. Dylan's existence made him panic because he went from his own tragic childhood to be a somewhat well-rounded human being despite his past. But the moment he first held Dylan in his arms and was now fashioning the title and responsibility of fatherhood, he became superstitious for the first time in his life.

The interloping insecurity of being cursed and subsequently passing the curse on to his child was now another motivator to seek oblivion. Maybe Charlie should embrace what potential death sentence awaited him at Turtle Rock and offer his soul and his body to the lingering specter of his family's past. Charlie had never stood a chance, but his little boy still did. He just didn't want to be a victim anymore; he may have been at one time, but he didn't come back home to solidify his victimization. He wanted to kill it, to burn it, to bury it, to expunge it once and for all. However, in this life (as it seemed) you were either a victim or a villain and Charlie couldn't relate to either.

He just wanted to enjoy his new life, his new career,

and for once? Feel the security of knowing that yesterday wasn't going to ruin tomorrow for him. After Charlie had ruminated a while, his phone began to vibrate on the nightstand next to the bed. He collected himself, assuming it might be a text from Lorraine with more pictures of their son, but when he checked it was a text from Tasha that simply read,

"J.J.'s Tavern. Come now."

He went into the bathroom to wash his face and to perform the breathing exercises his therapist had taught him. He then exited the motel with a large envelope and made the twenty-minute walk down to this little bar that sat on the border between Bear Hills and the town next to it. The entire walk, he rehearsed the entire conversation with Tasha in his head, as if he could have predicted both her questions and his answers.

Charlie only did this when he was nervous to meet someone, more so because he didn't want the last memory of him to be that of a sad, emotional vagabond who'd left this town as damaged as the author of that book about his family predicted. The obsessive rehearsal made him forget how daunting of a distance it was from his motel to the actual bar, so when he arrived on foot to the parking lot...he felt a sense of accomplishment that despite how out of shape he his body was, he wasn't paying for how much he seemingly pushed it. As he walked through the main door, he was greeted by a cacophony of voices all competing for as many ears as they could be heeded by. The clanging of glasses, waitresses yelling over the karaoke singers who were hoping to catch their big break in a Kelly Clarkson fashion, and poor lighting filled the establishment along with the odious stench of urine and cheap bathroom soap that adhered itself to the walls around you.

He stood for a few minutes surveying the area when he saw Tasha still dressed in her funeral clothes motioning for him to approach a booth in the very back. When he approached her, she stood up from the sticky cushions of the booth and embraced him even tighter than she had at the memorial service. When she let go, she took a few minutes to scrutinize every pore, every scar, and every inch of him from head to toe. She then motioned for him to sit and then began ransacking her large Coach purse for something. As Charlie removed his coat, he heard something slide on the table across to him. It was a copy of his last book.

"Destiny LOVES this!" She shouted.

"She said it's like *Fifty Shades of Grey*, only with a lonely guy and an android.

I asked her, "What's the difference?"

The two had an intense fit of laughter over that last remark. She then handed a pen to him

"Here!" She motioned.

"I was kind of hoping you could sign this for her."

Charlie was confused.

The author of this book wasn't Charlie Harris but E.H. Ramsey.

"Everyone knows you wrote it," Tasha answered.

She then turned to the author photo on the back flap of the book.

"You can grow that hair and beard as long as you want," she laughed.

"But I'll still recognize you in a line-up."

Charlie reached for the pen and scribbled his name on

the front page.

"She asks about you all the time."

Charlie looked like he was going to speak, and Tasha held her hand up to stop him.

"She understands. The whole town understands. Why would you want to be attached to what happened then? It shouldn't define you...which is why I guess I'm confused as to why you decided that you wanted to be you again."

She then motioned down at his left hand with the wedding band around his ring finger.

"You're married?" She smiled.

Charlie nodded.

"Tell me, did you wind up marrying your Courtney Love or did you grow up and settle for someone who actually loved you?"

Charlie smiled, pursed his lips and nodded.

"She's actually a nurse," he spoke.

"So, I'd say she's the antithesis of my type. She wanted to help people, not push them off the cliff."

Tasha smiled big at him.

A waitress approached their booth with a fresh drink for her, and Tasha motioned to the waitress and then him.

"Drink?!" Charlie nodded and just pointed at what she was drinking.

"But you HATE coconuts!" She teased.

"This thing basically tastes like a sexy Almond Joy!"

She then turned to the waitress,

"Get him a jack and coke!"

The waitress nodded and complied.

"You know," Charlie started,

"I probably shouldn't even be drinking. I had a thing with it for a while. Particularly that beverage. But I don't want to be rude."

Tasha held her hand under her chin and smiled.

"Sweetie?" She laughed,

"No one survives in this town without a couple of drinks. Just go home tomorrow a sober and better man; you of all people shouldn't feel guilty trying to cope with what this town and your family did to you. Hell, I drink because of it."

Charlie then motioned to the large envelope on his person. He slid it across the table and motioned at it.

"What is it?" Tasha shouted.

Charlie leaned in and whispered in her ear,

"It's exactly what you wanted. Answers."

The waitress returned with Charlie's drink, and while he nursed it Tasha removed a manuscript from the envelope and shook her head vehemently.

"No," she said.

"Not like that."

She slid the envelope back to Charlie and continued shaking her head.

"I don't want to learn from ANOTHER book what happened. I need to hear it from you."

Charlie let out a deep sigh and just looked around the room and shrugged at her.

She nodded and held her glass up to his and gestured for a toast.

"Drinks, first!"

Over the next forty-five minutes, Charlie went through his phone showing every solitary picture he had taken of Dylan from the time he was delivered until Charlie had boarded the train back home.

"What is it with your family?" She smiled.

"He looks like your clone! Seriously, blonde hair? Blue eyes? It's like you all come off an assembly line. You three were all like that too."

"So, I take it Destiny looks just like Rachel?"

Tasha immediately went quiet and continued scrolling through Charlie's pictures.

"Is that your wife?" Charlie nodded.

"What's her name?"

"Lorraine," he answered.

"She's beautiful." Tasha gushed.

"How did you two meet?"

Now Charlie was the one who appeared profoundly uncomfortable with continuing the conversation. Tasha waited impatiently for a good story. Charlie is a writer after all, so she just assumed it would rival that of *Wuthering Heights* or one of Shakespeare's plays.

"I was a patient," he curtly answered.

"She was doing her clinicals at the E.R. where I was moved. I, uh, I tried to kill myself. She was one of the students who was treating me. A few years prior to that, she had lost her mother to suicide, so I guess something just...I don't know, something must have compelled her to keep in touch. While all the signs were there of an obvious suicide attempt, I never confirmed what my true intentions were, so it was chocked up to an accident and I was discharged. Sometime down the road we happened to bump into each other at a coffee shop and got to talking. We exchanged info, and before I knew it, we were living together three months into dating."

He wasn't sure if it was the alcohol or if Tasha really had missed Charlie during his absence, but his affirmation appeared to strike a chord with her.

"I guess you can take the boy out of the town, but the town never stops haunting him." He joked.

"Are you...still?"

Tasha awkwardly began,

"You know?"

Charlie shook his head and laughed

"I was never a 'lacerate your wrists or hang yourself' kind of guy, I guess. I think I was always more into the incremental suicide, you know. Poison your body with inebriants for years, not listen to your shrink or your wife when they're trying to explain why you need to stop doing what you're doing to yourself..."

The tears continued streaming down Tasha's cheeks.

"And I brought you to a bar!" She cried.

Charlie reached his hands across the table for hers

"It's okay," Charlie reassured her.

"There are worse places you could've invited me."

"Have you gone back?" She sniffled,

"You know, since...."

Immediately Charlie's memories of watching a playground on fire shot through his mind.

"Once." He answered.

"It still smells like autumn all over the place."

She reached into her purse for her wallet and Charlie held his hand up at her and said,

"I got it,"

as he reached into his back pocket for his wallet and pulled out two crisp hundred-dollar bills.

"I like to over tip," he smiled.

Tasha was snuggled up in Charlie as they exited the bar.

"Can I call you an uber?" He gestured.

Tasha shook her head.

"I was hoping you could walk me home," she bluntly answered.

"I actually live in the apartments right next to where your home used to be."

As the two made the trek twenty minutes back toward the site of Charlie's old home, she continued pressing him about the events that had transpired twenty years ago. He didn't know if it was the nostalgia, or the booze...both were inebriating, so he started divulging tiny details.

"Rachel left me, in a park," he mumbled.

"She told me to hide, but for some reason I needed to go back home first...and that's when I heard their voices."

"Voices?" Tasha asked.

"I heard these voices when I returned home. I remember it like it was yesterday. I was in the backyard when the shed door just...opened. When I went inside, I saw two of my dad's gasoline containers and could just smell it everywhere. Earlier in the day, Rachel left me to babysit Destiny...when she came back, she just reeked of it. I don't know how, but I knew she had put those canisters there for a reason. The rest of the story is a little fuzzy to me...I just remember taking the two canisters into the unfinished side of the house where my dad used to lock up our cat...where the boiler was. And.... I just emptied both canisters in that room and made a little trickle of a trail outside the door."

"Why gasoline?" Tasha asked.

"She was going to frame our father...and burn our house down like he always threatened."

"What did YOU do?" Tasha begged.

"I called up my grandma," he started.

"Told her I was planning to trap a boogeyman and burn him alive."

"No..." Tasha cried.

The two stopped walking midway between the motel and the bar, and Charlie answered the question she kept asking.

"I left a trail of beer cans for him," Charlie divulged.

"When he came home drunk that night...there was nothing in the fridge. I told him that Mom was downstairs, and maybe she was keeping them cold for him. As soon as he saw the mess of beer cans leading into the room, I took his baseball bat to the back of him and padlocked him in the room. Earlier that week, I found a booklet of matches that Janet had left outside....and I lit them and tossed them to the ground and went back upstairs...thinking I finally killed OUR boogeyman."

Tasha couldn't believe what she was hearing and had a difficult time processing the whole story.

"What I didn't know?" He continued,

"His famous axe was locked in the boiler room with him. He chopped his way out of the room before he burned alive...he found our mom, and the two got in a back and forth fight over the axe. He knocked her unconscious with the butt of it before throwing her body down the stairs to burn alive. Brandishing that axe, he went looking for me just as our grandma left a message on the answering machine divulging everything, I had told her about killing our boogeyman."

Charlie started to gasp for air as he continued telling the story.

"He chased me up to Turtle Rock,"

"THAT'S WHEN WE SHOWED UP!" Tasha

interrupted.

Charlie nodded, and tried to wipe the tears as fast as they came.

"All I remember?" He finished.

"I was at Turtle Rock with my dad behind me as he cursed and threatened me. He eventually tracked me down and brandished his axe like he was going to finally correct the greatest wrong of his life. Rachel tackled him. The two got into a back and forth before he dropped his axe. I took the handle part to the back of his skull...he tumbled over the rock, and as he reached for my hand, desperately clinging for life? The boiler blew up back at our house...startling him, and he fell to his death."

Charlie then crouched down and began to sob as Tasha became stoic.

"Rachel told me to hide," he sobbed.

"So, I took his axe and I ran. Just before we left each other for good.... she told me she loved me, to wish her luck."

"And I had Destiny," Tasha mumbled.

The two stood for several minutes just staring at each other.

"I'm so sorry," he pleaded.

"I'm so sorry."

Tasha couldn't help but take pity on this little boy who was trapped in a man's body and immediately held onto him for dear life.

"It's okay," she reassured him.

He dug his fingernails into the back of her neck and shoulders.

"And now he wants my baby," he sobbed.

"Your baby?" She asked.

"He was going to hurt all of us. So, I killed him. And now he wants my baby."

Tasha propped Charlie up and firmly grabbed his face in her hands.

"Charlie, he's dead." She sobbed.

"He can't hurt you anymore. And I'm SO sorry that I didn't know."

Charlie cried in her arms for a while before finally composing himself and divulging all the events that brought him back home.

"He wants Dylan," he gasped.

"I have to stop him."

Tasha realized that she couldn't rationalize life and death with her friend anymore, and the two just walked in complete silence to the playground where his house once stood.

"Charlie," she pleaded.

"He's gone. He can't hurt you anymore. LOOK!"

She aggressively pointed Charlie's face toward the playground

"I'm tired of losing my friends, my past, and my life to superstition," she pleaded.

"This town isn't cursed. The decade we grew up in was. Our parents were manically depressed, alcoholic, drug users who never deserved us. THERE IS NO CURSE! THERE'S ONLY US!"

She then reached for his clammy and shaking hand and brought him to the swing set with her.

"Charlie, it's just US now." She pleaded.

"Go home, tomorrow. Go home...and put this place and its pain as far away from you as you can. Forget everything you think you feel, and please, please,

please...start over. For me?"

Charlie was slumped over on his swing, staring at his shoes

"I have to do one more thing," he threatened.

Tasha immediately shook her head at him

"No...no, Charlie. G.G. and Turtle Rock don't even exist anymore." She insisted. "LOOK!"

She motioned to the new housing developments.

"Just go home Charlie; go home and save yourself. For Dylan. There's nothing left here for you to face. I'm telling you...as someone who never moved on from it, it'll take you with it."

"What do you mean?" he asked.

"I had to convince myself," she started,

"That all my friends moved on. Went to college, met wives and husbands, settled down...started families, just so I could wake up every day. All my friends are dead. Heroin, Suicide, Murder...I lost everyone I loved."

Charlie reached for her hand.

"You didn't lose me," he smiled.

"If you go back there?" She sneered.

"Yes, I will. So will Lorraine, and so will Dylan. GO HOME, CHARLIE."

She then sat up from the swing and stood in front of him defiantly.

"Go home, Charlie. There's nothing left for you here."

She then walked across the playground and hopped the fence, the sound of keys jiggling in her pockets signaled to Charlie that he was once again all by himself with no resolution. Charlie swung on his lonely swing for twenty minutes longer before he heard a familiar voice calling to him again from the woods just outside the park.

"CHAR-LIEE!" It murmured.

Charlie assumed it was the alcohol in his veins and immediately sat up from the swing and walked back to his motel. Perhaps that explained his penchant for alcohol. His childhood only seemed to warrant the attention of strangers when he was so loaded that he had no choice but to rhapsodize for hours about how awful it was. With sobriety? You tend to understand how routinely shallow the question, "How are you?" truly is. Not when you're drinking.

When inebriated, an innocuous question such as "How are you?" becomes a waste basket full of crumpled up cacophonies or rhapsodies about how you're allowed to answer that question. Sober? You don't realize how condescending it is that such a question is, in the sense that it's supposed to be innocuous or almost rhetorical. You don't care how I am, so why the fuck did you ask me that? I'm an asshole for telling you. Well, then you're a bigger asshole for asking. THAT is how Charlie started to feel about this whole trip back home. It was literally the most expensive and emotionally manipulative 'how are you' he had ever been asked.

Every corner he walked down was another bad memory, another nefarious voice or another macabre scene. He had drunk his weight in amnesia just to wake up the next day hoping to not carry with him the cumbersome knowledge of his past. He supposed it was Tasha's assertive disposition for him to just go home and forget about it all that really perturbed him. However, he heeded the advice and staggered back to his lonely motel room in a place that used to host amateur pornographers and battered single mothers. And the plot of land that once hosted the haunted residence that ruined his family? The ashes were literally swept under a rug of political correctness and a playground was created to "honor" its former residents.

Then there was the alleged demolition of the very place that harbored all the curses of both a town and a family. As Charlie laid in his bed that night, he was both indignant and somewhat relieved. Maybe his drinking had become too much, and he had simply imagined the monster that goaded him to this half-assed homecoming. Real life was always way less interesting than imagination. Before he finally passed out, he started imagining what his next course of action would be now that he realized that all the monsters in his life were existential rather than tangible.

It was that moment where he didn't realize he fell asleep but couldn't trust the mechanics of his own body to decipher reality from a dream. The door of his motel room opened, and the gurgles of someone choking on their own blood permeated.

"Charlie! Charlie!" It demanded.

"They all forgot about me, Charlie. But I know you won't."

Charlie rolled over onto his side and attempted to fall back into a deep sleep when an odious stench punched through his nostrils and into his brain. When his eyes opened...there was that cadaverous vision of his father smiling through a mouthful of broken teeth. He then motioned to the television, which as soon as his finger addressed it, turned on to a breaking news report.

Charlie (still on his side) watched as the feeling of dread crawled up his spine like a family of ravenous spiders.

"We're coming to you live from Bear Hills, Massachusetts," the reported explained,

"Where the body of an unidentified woman in her forties has taken her own life."

Charlie's chest took in breaths that felt heavier and heavier as if he was inhaling cement with each gasp of air. "While we cannot release the name, there is no suspicion of foul play as this appears to be sadly...a suicide." Charlie's eyes teared up while the specter of his father began laughing harder and harder. Before the reporter could say another word, the television abruptly cut out and Charlie could now hear sirens growing louder and more accelerated as they raced down to where Tasha said she lived.

The specter then leaned into Charlie's ear,

"The body count will only grow the more you resist the urge to come back home to me." It warned.

"And baby Dylan is sound asleep in his crib as we speak..." it assured him.

Charlie immediately snapped awake in a cold sweat and with a weight still bearing hard down on his chest. He immediately rolled out of bed and reached into his suitcase for the axe, slipped back into his sneakers and faced the mirror one last time.

"What will he say," he spoke to his reflection, "If you go down without a fight."

He immediately reached down for his phone and typed "I love you" to his wife for the last time and pulled up a recent picture of Dylan and kissed it before he exited the room to face what he had spent twenty years avoiding. The warm air immediately crashed down on him like a violent wave and consumed him and even began coursing through his poison veins. As he walked out onto the street, which started out vacant...his veins began coughing out liquids from the last fifteen years; the warmth tickled his arms as his veins cried out in victory against all the poison he'd once pumped into them. Every step he took seemed to exorcise another demon of not just his past, but every past. Without even realizing, the ghosts of a town's history began manifesting out of nowhere and holding candles in a gesture of solidarity.

The cacophonies of voices grew louder the closer he came to that playground where his house once stood. Women, children, they all lit up the street that otherwise wouldn't be seen without their illuminating glow. So many forlorn and morose faces turned into ecstasy at the sight of Charlie passing them, brandishing that axe. Once he arrived at the playground and forced his way in, a group of delinquent youths stood up and acknowledged this lunatic with an axe.

"Hey man, we don't want any..."

One spoke.

His female companion immediately held him back as Charlie walked casually by him with his weapon. Charlie turned toward the two and winked. Before they could process the scene, Charlie hopped a fence and walked into the parking lot of the apartment that once led people to that infamous Turtle Rock. Before Charlie walked into the abyss that seemingly was not there, he turned to the couple again...he smiled at the young girl and nodded and walked into the darkness for the last time.

"What the fuck was that?" The boy scoffed.

The girl immediately shoved her boyfriend to the

ground.

"Destiny! Destiny, baby! Where are you going!?!?" he shouted as his young female companion hopped the fence and followed the stranger into the dark.

Charlie did not realize it, but the cumbersome weight of his life was also patiently waiting inside the body of another person close to him. She'd waited twenty years for him to find his way back into the darkness that spit the two of them out, and once this man...this fabled idea of her uncle, finally walked past her and acknowledged their bond, she was going to chase him through hell just so she could watch as he finally buried his ghosts.

Many years later when Dylan would ask Destiny how she and his father reconnected...she would always just smile politely and motion to a picture he'd found buried in his closet. It was the first picture taken of the two, and she would say...

"Your daddy and I killed monsters together so that you never had to."

Sometimes a fleeting memory of the way he held her as a baby would cross her mind, his goofy bowl cut, his braced buckteeth. Then, the memory of that night.

A tired man exhausted from running, realizing that there is no amount of distance a person can put between them and their past. It will always catch up to them.

While his hand trembled, he handed her the axe.

"You were never a mistake," he assured her. "You were always her destiny,"

"No," she corrected, "you were always mine."

She only remembered the weight of trying to swing an axe, while Charlie collapsed upon witnessing her beheading the imposing figure that postured before them.

That was when she realized the weight of his life had finally released him.

"I'm sorry you never knew your father," he coughed,

"I'm sorry you never had a childhood," she corrected.

Charlie stood to his feet, wrapped his arm around his niece and kissed her on the head. He then reached into his pocket for the key and handed it to her.

"Trust me," he laughed, "it's nothing to get nostalgic about."

Charlie then grabbed the axe from Destiny and tossed it into the woods.

"Let's find home."

ACKNOWLEDGEMENTS

This book would not have been possible without the endorsement of my wife Nina Brophy, a woman who literally demanded that the pages of my first unsuccessful manuscript be incorporated into the aisle we walked down at our wedding. When she saw ALL my rejections? She turned a devastating negative into a positive. Little did I know? That when we both walked down a paper trail of my words that one day, I would publish a book. She always told me that one day my words would come to fruition and for that unwavering support? I owe her a never let-me-go hug.

To the Atmosphere Press team who believed in me and worked with me diligently to make this dream a reality? Nick Courtright, who is responsible for me getting to see a labor of love finally come to fruition. Bryce Wilson, what can I say? I hope I was able to make you both proud and am humbled by your sage-like advice and inspiring demeanors as you helped me cultivate my craft. Bryce, the only person I ever met who felt as profoundly about the death as Ben Tramer as I did, I guess in another life we were destined to be kindred spirits. Kelleen Cullison, I cannot thank you enough for encouraging and supporting my work and helping me navigate the anxiety about being a first-time author and feeling that my work had any merit.

To my mother (Pamela Brophy) and my two sisters (Jennifer and Heather Brophy). There would not be a book without the stories we lived and the encouragement to share them. Then came the friends and supporters. Allison

Capuano who bought me a sportscoat after reading the first draft and telling me I was a writer. Kate Burnham, the woman who helped me to become the first one in my family to graduate high school, go to college, and keep writing. Melanie Faith, my poetry professor, my friend, my dearest confidante who gave me the courage to keep writing. Big Jim Murray, a DJ at WFNX, for telling me to leave radio and pursue my writing as he felt I would be more successful there. Rhonda Michaud, for encouraging me every day to stick with the writing and inspired the first poem I had ever published. Sean, who goaded my passion for horror and writing and always supported me, and God, so many more.

This book would not have happened without all the love, support, and encouragement from all of you. To everyone I knew, and everyone who worked in this little village.... this book is a thank you, a love letter, and my sincerest debt to your inspiration.

Finally, to the 90s? The culture was ambitious, the music was great, but for those of us walking amongst the anonymous middle-class nobodies? It was nothing to get nostalgic about.

ABOUT ATMOSPHERE PRESS

Atmosphere Press is an independent, full-service publisher for excellent books in all genres and for all audiences. Learn more about what we do at atmospherepress.com.

We encourage you to check out some of Atmosphere's latest releases, which are available at Amazon.com and via order from your local bookstore:

Olive, a novel by Barbara Braendlein
Itsuki, a novel by Zach MacDonald
A Surprising Measure of Subliminal Sadness, short stories by Sue Powers
Saint Lazarus Day, short stories by R. Conrad Speer
My Father's Eyes, a novel by Michael Osborne
The Lower Canyons, a novel by John Manuel
Shiftless, a novel by Anthony C. Murphy
The Escapist, a novel by Karahn Washington
Gerbert's Book, a novel by Bob Mustin
Tree One, a novel by Fred Caron
Connie Undone, a novel by Kristine Brown
A Cage Called Freedom, a novel by Paul P.S. Berg
Shining in Infinity, a novel by Charles McIntyre
Buildings Without Murders, a novel by Dan Gutstein

ABOUT THE AUTHOR

Eddie Brophy is a poet and author from Massachusetts where he lives with his wife and is a stay at home dad to his two sons. He holds his MA in English (my wife argues this despite the program being a poetry one, happy wife happy life) which he regrets less now as a result of this debut novel (we will debate this later based on how many people read this book). His poems have appeared in 'The Poet's Haven Digest: Darker Than Fiction' 'Rhythm of the Bones: Dark Marrow: Issue Two' 'The Penman Review' and 'Better Than Starbucks' His short story 'The B.K.R. Killer' can be read at Haunted MTL. You can read his previous publications and blog (This book also brought the revelation that he should probably start blogging, it's all about the platform!) at: https://eddiebrophywriter.weebly.com/

CPSIA information can be obtained
at www.ICGtesting.com
Printed in the USA
FSHW011658050521
81031FS